CAUGHT
in the
ACT

Jack —

A appreciate you
and your commitment
to the Lord!

Gayle Roper

Col. 3:17

AN AMHEARST MYSTERY

Book Two

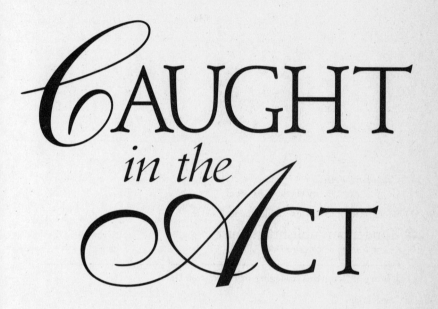

CAUGHT in the ACT

GAYLE ROPER

ZondervanPublishingHouse

Grand Rapids, Michigan

A Division of HarperCollinsPublishers

Caught in the Act
Copyright © 1998 by Gayle G. Roper

Requests for information should be addressed to:

ZondervanPublishingHouse
Grand Rapids, Michigan 49530

Library of Congress Cataloging-in-Publication Data

Roper, Gayle G.
    Caught in the act / Gayle Roper.
        p. cm. — (An Amhearst mystery : bk. 2)
    Sequel to: Caught in the middle.
    ISBN: 0-310-21909-4
    1. Women journalists—Fiction. I. Title. II. Series: Roper.
PS3568.O68C37 1998
813'.54-dc 21   98-23125
                                                      CIP

Interior design by Jody DeNeef

Printed in the United States of America

---

00 01 02 03 04 /❖ DC/ 10 9 8 7 6 5 4 3 2

For my sisters and brothers
at Calvary Fellowship Church,
especially those from the township building and the fire hall
"I thank my God upon every remembrance of you"

Acknowledgments

Special thanks for their time and expertise to Rick Albee, police officer, Chuck Gordinier, fireman and licensed EMT, and Harry Kraus, M.D. It's not everyone who will sit around and plot murder and mayhem with such cooperative enthusiasm. Thanks, guys. Any errors are mine.

Chapter One

I have to stop going places with Jolene Meister. Every time I go, catastrophe results.

"Merry, could you drop me off at my parents' after work?" she asked as we left *The News* office for lunch. She waited while I pushed open the front door and held it for her. "My father brought me in this morning."

It sounded a reasonable request to me. I'd only have to go out of my way a couple of blocks.

"Sure. No problem," I said. "I don't have anything I have to do until eight when I'm supposed to take a picture of the committee for the Amhearst Annual Christmas Food Project." Or AAC-FOP, as Mac, our editor, irreverently called it.

And that easily and innocently I precipitated my involvement in murder.

Again.

Jolene and I walked to Ferretti's, the best eating our small town had to offer. The winter wind on this dingy December Tuesday bit through my new red coat, and I suspected my nose was turning almost as rosy as my wool blend. The two scars on my nose that I'd gotten in a bike accident when I was eight years old would be turning a contrasting blue.

Ah, well, I thought. *If I smile, I can have a patriotic face: red nose, white teeth, and blue scars.*

Gene Autry was serenading downtown Amhearst about Rudolph the Rednosed Reindeer over a tinny public address system set up by Santa's little house. How come a cowboy had made millions off a deer's red nose, I wondered, and all I got from mine was a color scheme?

We were seated by Ferretti's hostess, a brassy blonde named Astrid whom Jolene knew.

"How do you know Astrid?" I asked. It never ceased to amaze me how everyone in Amhearst knew everyone else. As a recent arrival I found it both cozy and unnerving.

"I went to school with her younger sister Elsa. She's a real dingbat."

"Who? Astrid or Elsa?"

Jolene thought for a minute. "Both."

Knowing Jolene as I did, that probably meant that both women were very nice and rather intelligent.

"Does anyone ever move away from Amhearst?" I asked as our waitress, an older lady whose name tag said Sally, came to take our order.

"Sure," Jolene said. "Sally's daughter Caroline moved to California to be in the movies, right?" She looked at Sally.

"Yeah," Sally said. "But she came home last month and I think she's staying. Astrid's sister Elsa got her a job as receptionist at Bushay's. Elsa's Mr. Bushay's administrative assistant." Didn't sound like dingbat territory to me, but it sure sounded like Amhearst. "So, what'll you have?"

I ordered an Amhearst version of Caesar salad (there were bacon bits and red cabbage in it and not an anchovy in sight) and Jolene ordered a huge plate of eggplant parmigiana.

Sally disappeared with her order pad and I looked at Jolene.

"And how do you know Sally?"

"She and my mom were in the PTA together."

"And you know Caroline, the would-be movie star?"

"Sure. She was three years ahead of me in school."

"See?" I said. "Weird."

Jolene shrugged. "Small town." She pressed her hands to her cheeks. "Do I look flushed to you?"

"Like you're getting sick, you mean?"

She nodded. Jolene was a hypochondriac.

I looked at her big brown hair and bangs, her bright brown eyes, her flawless skin. "It's just reaction from walking in the cold. You look great to me." In an overblown sort of way.

Soon Sally arrived with our lunches and I looked from my salad to Jolene's spicy, cheesy, greasy dish. "How can you eat that and not gain weight? It's swimming in oil. It's not fair."

"Fair?" she said, leveling a forkful of dripping eggplant at me. "Fair? Is it fair that you have two gorgeous men chasing you? Huh?" She snorted, a noise that sounded decidedly odd coming from her delicate nose. "Don't give me fair, Merrileigh Kramer. I'm not listening."

I grinned at her like an idiot. I'd never in my life had one man chasing me with any real enthusiasm, and suddenly I had two. It made me feel nervous. It made me feel powerful. It made me giggle.

It also made me check over my shoulder constantly because Jack was in town and Curt didn't know it yet. I hadn't quite figured out how to break the news to my new boyfriend that my old boyfriend, suddenly ardent, had come a-courting. And what was worse yet, Jack didn't even know that a warm, delightful, and charming man named Curt Carlyle existed.

My brother's favorite nickname for me wasn't Marshmallow Merry for nothing. No spine. No guts. No idea how to keep this wonderfully ego-boosting situation from turning into a roast-the-marshmallow pyre.

"So you're saying that Jack just showed up at your door on Sunday?" Jolene said as she buttered a piece of Italian bread with real butter.

I crunched a particularly large chunk of Romaine and nodded. "You go with a guy for six years and he refuses to make a commitment," I began.

"Six years?" Jolene's voice squeaked with disbelief.

I held up a hand. "Don't ask. Just accept my word that he's charming and I was stupid. Anyway, I'd hardly heard a word from him since I moved to Amhearst in September, and boom! There he was. Although I guess it really wasn't boom, now that I think about it. Four months is hardly boom."

"Merry Christmas, my Merry," he'd yelled when I'd opened my door Sunday afternoon. He pushed a giant silk poinsettia into my hands, smiling broadly at my confusion. Then he grabbed me and hugged me tightly, crushing the poinsettia painfully between us. Obviously he thought he'd brought me a wonderful gift, and he wasn't thinking of the flower.

"What are you doing here?" I'd demanded, ever gracious.

"Is that any way to greet your sweetheart come this great distance just to be near you?"

I stared at him openmouthed. Just four months ago I'd have swooned with delight if he'd deigned to call me his sweetheart. Now all I felt was an incipient case of heartburn.

"I've moved to Amhearst," he said, taking off his coat without an invitation to do so. "At least for a while."

I think he thought I was paralyzed with delight, not horror, as I tried to imagine him fitting into my new life, a new life I'd found when I fled my old in despair over him.

He threw his coat across the back of the chair my cat Whiskers was sleeping in. A sleeve flopped down and slapped Whiskers in the face. He sat up with a sleepy scowl and decided right then and there he didn't like Jack. When Jack saw the cat, I could tell that the feeling was mutual.

Bad sign.

"You've moved to Amhearst?" I said, disbelief heavy in my voice. "Why?"

"To be near you, sweetheart." His eyes went soft and dark.

"But—" I sputtered. "Your job. You didn't quit your job!" Jack was a CPA with a large firm back home in Pittsburgh.

"Of course I didn't. I'm on long-term assignment here now. I'm doing an audit on Bushay Environmental which, as you probably know being a local reporter and all, is right here in Amhearst." He stated this information like he was the one who had personally laid each brick in Bushay's building and bought each sanitation vehicle with his own funds.

"Big deal," I told him. "Your company sends you here and I'm supposed to believe that means your undying affection for me?"

"They didn't *send* me," he said earnestly. "I campaigned for this job."

He reached for my hand, and I suddenly saw him as a giant vacuum cleaner, ready to suck me up and spit me back into the past. The image terrified me. I dodged him, leaned over, and filled both arms with Whiskers, who immediately began to purr and prod my chin with his head.

Jack either didn't understand my move or made believe he didn't. He kept on talking as if he always reached out and found nothing to hold on to, as if it didn't matter in the least to him that I preferred a cat to his hug.

"Amhearst isn't exactly a desirable location," he informed me as he leaned against the chair. "It's out here in the western edge of Chester County miles away from anything of real interest."

I scowled at him like he'd personally insulted me. I'd come to like Amhearst, and part of its charm was its rural setting. And Philadelphia was only an hour away, for heaven's sake. That's not exactly the end of the earth.

As usual he missed my reaction. I used to wonder if his lack of response to how I felt was a power play designed to get his own way or if he was just too dense to see what was in front of him. As I watched him in my living room, I decided he was just dense. That idea made me sad.

"I asked to be sent here instead of to Atlantic City," he said. "Now *that* was a plum assignment, but I wanted here." He reached over Whiskers and touched my cheek. "And all for you."

I looked at him doubtfully. Atlantic City in December didn't sound all that great to me. Atlantic City in July didn't even sound too great. I'd been there several times as a kid, and I couldn't imagine that the casinos had done anything to make the depressing, worn seaside atmosphere any more acceptable.

Jack continued to recount his version of his campaign for the Bushay job, trying to convince me of his ardor. "'You've got to send me to Amhearst,' I told Mr. Proctor. 'I want the Bushay job even though it means weeks away from home to complete it.'" He smiled impishly. "Obviously I didn't tell him about you."

I couldn't help but smile back as Whiskers jumped out of my arms. "Obviously."

"But *I* knew you were my reason," he said as he reached for me again.

I dodged his grasp this time by grabbing my coat from the clothes tree in the corner and throwing it over my shoulders. He might have made me smile, but after a four months' silence, I certainly wasn't going to fall into his arms just because he wanted me to. No, sirree, Bob.

"Well, I may have been your reason for coming here," I said. "But I'm not sure I'm your girl anymore."

And I walked out. I had absolutely no place to go, but I knew I'd never have such a wonderful exit line again. And six years of no commitment was a long, long time, no matter how you looked at it.

Jolene, beautiful Jolene, eyed me with something like admiration as she swallowed a mouthful of eggplant.

"So where'd you go?" she asked.

"To *The News*. Where else?"

"Was he there when you got home?"

"I didn't get home until 10:30, and Jack can't stand waiting for five minutes, let alone five hours."

"Five hours?"

I knew I'd made a mistake as soon as she spoke. I should have just said no, he didn't hang around.

"So what did you do for five hours?"

Suddenly I felt embarrassed because I knew what her response to my answer would be. I tried to think of an alternative answer that wasn't a lie, but I couldn't. I cleared my throat. "I had a date."

"What?" she shrieked, just like I knew she would. She started to laugh so hard I thought she'd choke on her eggplant. Everyone for tables around turned to stare, and I smiled weakly at them. Jolene didn't even notice. She was too busy wiping away tears of hilarity, and I couldn't help noticing that they did nothing to mar the beauty of her marvelously made-up eyes. Three cheers for waterproof.

When she finally caught her breath, she said, "This guy moves all the way from Pittsburgh for you and you go out with someone else?"

I nodded. Put that way, I had to admit I sounded terribly tacky.

"Merry, my estimation of you has jumped off the charts. You are a wild woman after all."

I stared at her. My mind tried to comprehend me as a wild woman, but the idea was as impossible for me to grasp as a soap bubble from a wand was for a child.

"You're so lucky," she said. "I haven't had anyone chasing me in years." Her lovely brown eyes looked forlorn beneath her brown bangs.

"Of course not," I said. "You've been married."

She shrugged carelessly—which said volumes about her view of marriage. "But I'm not married now."

"True and false. You're not divorced either. Maybe you and Arnie will get back together yet."

Again the careless shrug. Poor Arnie. I hoped he wasn't pining for her somewhere because it looked like he'd waste away to nothing before Jolene paid him any attention.

Jolene mopped up the last of her eggplant with the last of her bread. "So what did Curt say when he heard Jack was here?"

I concentrated on corralling the last of my salad. "He doesn't know yet," I mumbled.

"What?" Jolene started to laugh uproariously again.

I looked at her sourly. Clowns in the center ring don't give the laughs I did. And I don't charge admission.

"I haven't told him," I said with what dignity I could muster. "I'll tell him next time I see him."

"Don't give me that," said Jolene, smile a mile wide. "You're afraid to tell him."

I stuck my chin in the air and gave my version of Jolene's snort. I certainly wasn't going to admit she was right.

"One thing I want to know," Jolene said, making one of her patented changes of topic. "How can someone who looks so much like a football player be an artist?"

"You mean Curt?" I smiled, picturing Curt's dark curly hair and glasses and shoulders so broad he could block an entire movie screen at thirty paces. "I don't know." I tried to sound casual, but it was hard.

"I think I'm falling in love with you," Curt had told me just recently.

After I'd caught my breath, I'd said, "You can't be. We hardly know each other. Love takes time to grow." I knew that because my mother had told me so all my life.

Still, when he looked at me a certain way, my knees buckled, I had trouble breathing, and my heart *barrumped* in time with the Minute Waltz.

"Things between Curt and me are fragile," I said to Jolene, trying to explain. "New. Too new. I don't know how to tell him."

I must have looked as disconsolate as I felt because Jolene patted my hand. "It'll work out. Don't worry." She pushed her arms into the sleeves of her coat and grinned at me. "Just you keep me informed, you hear?"

We wrapped ourselves in our winter coats, scarves, and hats and took our checks to the cashier by the door. Jolene picked up a toothpick from the little plastic holder by the cash register and started poking, right there in the restaurant in full view of people. My mother would have a coronary if I indulged in such unladylike behavior. Somehow on Jolene it just looked cute.

Suddenly she pulled her toothpick out of her mouth and looked at me speculatively. "You didn't tell Curt about Jack. Did you tell Jack about Curt?"

I made a big deal of buying one of those little foil-wrapped mints.

She snickered. "I want to be around when they meet," she announced. "I'd never have believed it of you, but you're better than any movie I ever saw."

Blushing, I pushed open the door, hoping the frosty air would cool my flushed face.

"Wait a minute," Jolene said, tapping my arm. "I have to visit the ladies' room."

I shrugged and trailed along, admiring her black leather and faux fur coat and black boots. The lady had style if not class.

I followed her into the cozy, well-lit ladies' room and looked at myself in the huge mirror over the sink. My short, thick, overly curly black hair tended to take off with a life of its own, and today was no different. I ran my fingers through it, trying to calm it down while I waited for Jolene. I was no more successful in mastering it than I was in avoiding the Christmas arrangement and candle sitting on the countertop. I gave up on my hair, stared at the Christmas decorations, and sighed.

I was facing this Christmas holiday with some excitement (two men) but also with much misgiving. For the first time ever, I wouldn't be at home with my family for our warm and wonderful celebration. No fat Christmas tree with Grandma Kramer's direct-from-the-Holy-Lands angel gracing the top bough. No hot mulled cider that Dad tried to foist on anyone who entered our home. No marvelous turkey smells and no Aunt Sissy's famous pumpkin pie.

Every time I thought about my holiday solitude, my heart sighed and I suffered mild depression. As a result I hadn't done much decorating in my own little apartment on the first floor of an old carriage house. I had a wreath on the door but I hadn't gotten myself a tree or put electric candles in my windows like everyone else in Amhearst did. Of course I now had a silk poinsettia sitting on an end table.

It was my job that prevented a trip to Pittsburgh and home. I had only Christmas Day off, if being on call means "off."

"Someone has to be available in case a big story breaks," said Mac, my editor at *The News*. Then he grinned. "I guess you've drawn the short straw, Merry." He didn't even feel sorry for passing sentence on me.

I kept telling myself that I didn't mind. I was a career woman. I was pressing on with my new life. I was independent. But I didn't believe myself.

I thought of Jolene. She had her family right here in town. She would have a warm, cozy Christmas with hugs and presents and all that stuff. She wouldn't sit alone all day, staring at her cat. That would be me.

But, I reminded myself before I started weeping on the spot, I was the one with two men!

Not that I needed two or wanted two. One would certainly be more than enough since monogamy was my preferred lifestyle. I just had to decide which one. Most of the time I thought I knew what I wanted, but then I'd get scared and back off. Waffling Wanda was the alter ego of Marshmallow Merry.

"Hey!" Jolene said as she came out of a stall. "You're smiling to yourself. Which one are you thinking about?"

Before I had to answer, a paroxysm of sneezes gripped me and I began counting as I convulsed. Eight. Not bad. Eleven was my all-time highest. They had happened as I was driving on the Route 30 bypass, my eyes squeezing shut at each sneeze. I thought myself lucky to still be alive.

"Whew!" I said when I could breathe again. I swung my purse strap back onto my shoulder and slammed the bag itself into the blonde woman walking out of the other stall.

"Oh, I'm sorry!" I turned contritely.

She smiled at me, her gray eyes crinkling at the corners. "Don't worry about it. It's o—"

Her voice faded to nothing and her face lost its pleasant smile. She stared past me with a sudden look of great distaste on her face. I blinked and turned to see what she was looking at, and there stood Jolene. Her face had also lost all its charm and warmth as she stared back.

"Well, well," said Jolene, venom dripping. "Look who's here."

"Hello, Jo," the woman said in a tight, tense voice. "How are you? And how's Arnie?"

"We're both fine." Jolene matched icy politeness for icy politeness. I could get frostbite from the frigid atmosphere between these two.

"Tell him I said hello," said the woman.

"Like he cares," said Jolene. The words were spat like little pellets flying from a straw to land stinging blows on the back of an unsuspecting neck.

The woman flinched, then sighed in disgust. "It is always such a great pleasure to meet you, Jo. You have such a friendly and endearing manner about you. Always have."

Jolene bristled at the sarcasm. "Watch it, Airy. I don't like being in the same room with you any more than you like being in the same room with me."

My eyes widened. I am Polly Peacemaker. I hate confrontation and conflict, and if I'm caught in it, I never know what to do. But it appeared I was the only one uncomfortable here. These two women were obviously sluggers.

"Believe me," Airy said, "if I'd known you were going to be here, I'd have avoided Ferretti's at all costs."

Jolene, face haughty, sniffed. "My coworker and I were having a business lunch."

We were? I looked at Jolene with interest. Could have fooled me.

She smiled coldly and drew herself to her full height. "She's a newspaperwoman too."

I might be a newspaperwoman if someone generously defined my reporter/gofer position at *The News*, but Jolene was basically a secretary. I blinked at her healthy misrepresentation of her job, but I knew this wasn't the time to make a case for truth in advertising.

The woman sneered. "Don't give me that snotty attitude about your job, Jolene. I know what you do."

Jolene glared. "You just think you're so smart."

I looked at Jolene, strangely disappointed in the trite comment. Certainly she could do better than that worn-out old line.

"Tell me," Airy asked in a voice that dripped acid. "Which of us graduated valedictorian? Um? It *certainly* wasn't you."

I stared at the woman. At twenty-five years old or so, she was still bringing up high school? What was next? Elementary school jealousies?

"Like test grades show intelligence," Jolene scoffed with a wonderful disregard for the entire educational system. "I'd rather have my social smarts than your boring IQ any day, Airy."

"You *used* to be nice, Jolene." Airy nodded slightly as if agreeing with herself. "Up until about third grade. It's been downhill ever since."

Yikes, I thought. *Elementary school.*

"You never did get over not winning Most Popular at Oak Street Elementary School, did you?" Jolene sneered. "You've been jealous of me ever since."

"Oh, pu-lease! I'd kill myself before I ever became like you."

A woman pushed the ladies' room door open and froze, caught by the nastiness of the voices. She locked eyes with me for the briefest of seconds, then withdrew, condemnation in every line of her body.

Not me, I wanted to tell her. *I'm not fighting. I'm an innocent bystander. I know better. I have class.*

Jolene and Airy hadn't even noticed her. They were too busy pouring out a lifetime of vituperation.

Suddenly Jolene turned sly, an unpleasant smile crossing her face. "By the way, Airy, how's Sean?"

All color drained from Airy's face. "Don't you even mention his name," she hissed. "Don't you even *think* about him."

Jolene just smiled. If I'd been Airy, I'd have been tempted to sock her one for her arrogance.

"How do you like his new mustache?" Jolene asked innocently. "I think it makes him look quite debonair, don't you?"

"His new mus—How do you know?" Airy was so angry—and scared?—that she was sputtering.

"Come on, Airy." Jolene used her hands like a bully might taunt a smaller boy to take a swing, like someone might tell a driver how far forward he can pull his car. "Spit it out. I know you can do it."

Airy shut her great gray eyes and took a deep breath to calm herself. When she opened her eyes, she raised her chin and said in an urgent, passionate voice, "Sean is off-limits to you, witch. Don't you ever, *ever* come near him."

"You mean I shouldn't have had lunch with him yesterday?" Jolene put a hand over her mouth in mock distress. "Oops."

Airy looked as if she had turned to stone. She didn't even appear to breathe for too long a time. Jolene did everything but smack her lips at the reaction she had gotten.

I looked heavenward, sort of hoping the Lord would understand my unspoken supplication for peace and intervene. All I wanted was to get out of here, but I was trapped in the corner farthest from the door.

"Come on," I said, putting a hand on Jolene's sleeve. "It's time to go."

She didn't even hear me. Her whole attention was riveted on the increasingly distressed Airy.

"Did I say something that upset you, Airy?" Jolene asked. Her smile was decidedly unpleasant. "I'm sorry. After all, we're such old friends."

Airy swallowed and ran her tongue over her lips. "You leave Sean alone or I'll—I'll—" Desperation made Airy's voice quiver.

Jolene's lip curled in contempt. "Why don't you just settle for Arnie? You and he would make a great pair. The leftovers."

I hissed at the nastiness of the comment almost as loudly as Airy.

Suddenly a finger with a long vermilion nail was waving under Jolene's nose.

"Don't push me, Jo. I mean what I say about Sean. Leave him alone! You can't have him!"

"Nice nails," Jolene said as she tapped Airy's with her own perfectly manicured finger. "Phony, of course. Like you. Or—" She smiled nastily. "Or like you and Sean." And she turned away.

Airy reached out and grabbed Jolene's arm and spun her around. Jolene looked surprised in spite of herself.

"I mean it, Jo. *Stay away from Sean.* You may have taken Arnie away from me, but not Sean. Not Sean! He's mine."

Jolene raised an eyebrow and looked down her perfect nose. "Only if you can keep him, sweetie." She shook Airy's hand from her arm like she was flicking garbage off a plate and strode out of the room.

I was left staring at my toes, feeling most uncomfortable in the emotional backwash. What did one say to the loser in a catfight? It was one of life's little lessons that Mom, usually so good at preparing me, had neglected.

I heard a soft sigh and glanced up. Airy looked so sad.

"I'm sorry," I said, even though I had nothing to do with any of it.

Airy nodded and smiled weakly. "You'd think I'd have learned to deal with her by now, wouldn't you? I mean, I've known her since I was four years old. Princess Jo."

She pulled a packet of tissues from her purse, lifted the tab, and extracted one. She wiped ineffectively at her nose.

"Are you all right?" I asked.

She stuffed the used tissue back in her purse. "Merry Christmas," she said and walked out without looking back.

When I left the ladies' room, I looked to see if Airy was still in the restaurant. She wasn't but Jolene was, standing straight and beautiful and haughty. She was staring after Airy, and the look on her face was vintage.

It was a silent walk back to *The News*.

Chapter Two

Merry, come here!" Mac Carnuccio sat at his desk by the big window and cocked a hand at me.

I hung my red coat on the flimsy hangers by the door and hurried toward him. As I passed Jolene, she made believe she didn't see me which was fine with me. I honestly didn't know what to say to her after her performance at Ferretti's.

She probably wouldn't take well to, "You shouldn't talk to people like that, Jolene." Nor would she care for one of Mom's favorite Bible verses: "Do not let any unwholesome talk come out of your mouths, but only what is helpful for building others up according to their needs, that it may benefit those who listen."

Instead I concentrated on Mac, king of our little world, as, scowling, he rummaged through one of the piles of papers littering his desk. He did not find the treasure he sought.

Mac's style was exactly the opposite of our previous editor, the erratic stacks of paper being but one evidence. How he was going to work out as editor of *The News* remained to be seen, but in the short two weeks that he'd held the position, he'd put out a paper as good as or better than our former editor's paper. At least I thought so, should anyone bother to ask me.

And he clearly loved being in charge, taking a kid's pleasure in the subtle perks of power, especially the enormous desk by the window.

"I love sitting here," he'd told me last week as he leaned back in his new ergonomically correct executive chair, a personal purchase gotten on sale at Staples, the mega office supply store. "I feel like I own all of Amhearst."

I'd turned from the handsome dark-haired man and looked out on Main Street. It was an impressive sight with Jansen's Jewelry, Martha's Fine Tailoring, and Bob's Book Bin and Coffee Shoppe directly across the street, the buildings all freshly pointed, painted, and fixed up courtesy of a grant gotten by the local small business co-op. Next to Bob's the gold letters in the window of Grassley, Jordan, and McGilpin, Attorneys at Law, reflected in the watery winter light even though Trudy McGilpin no longer practiced law there.

"Monarch of all you survey, eh?" I'd said.

And Mac had smiled broadly at an iridescent gray pigeon taking its afternoon constitutional on the other side of his window. Then his face sobered.

"I'm not really editor, you know." He glanced at me. "The rag's up for sale, and who knows who will buy it and what will happen then. But"—and he grinned—"for now I'm acting editor. Me. Mac Carnuccio."

"A dream of yours?" I asked.

"Always," he said. "Ever since I saw Cary Grant in *His Girl Friday*, I wanted to be a suave, fast-talking editor."

Now this suave, fast-talking editor was waving to me, his Rosalind Russell.

I hurried between the dilapidated desks that made up the newsroom, zigging and zagging as necessary to avoid being eaten by the spectacularly healthy plants that Jolene insisted on growing here. The huge grape ivy that sat on the soda machine always reminded me of *Little Shop of Horrors*, and I made certain never to get a paper cut and bleed in its presence lest it eat me.

It had been joined on the soda machine by a gigantic red poinsettia, one of several that sat about the newsroom in case we forgot that Christmas was a mere week away. The double row of African violets luxuriating on the great windowsill of the picture window were blooming pink and purple and variegated in spite of the time of year, and Jolene's Christmas cactus with multiple blooms in a teeth-jarring shade of fuchsia hung nearly to the floor.

Mac's policy was the same as our former editor's: ignore the greenery and maybe it will die.

"Have I got an assignment for you, Beautiful. You'll love it!" Mac said as I stood before his cluttered desk.

"Okay," I said skeptically. Whenever Mac told me I'd love something, I got nervous. We were so different that most things he thought were great, I thought were vulgar, profane, and/or without redeeming social value.

"And if you don't love it," he said, "the penalty is dinner with me. Alone. At my place."

"I can tell already that I'm going to like this assignment a lot," I said. "A big lot." I smiled to let him know I knew he was joking about the dinner, though I wasn't certain he was. He asked me out with great regularity and I refused with equal regularity. I never could decide whether the invitations were a product of his Mac-the-Lecher joke mode or whether he was serious. The last thing I wanted or needed was an office romance with a guy like Mac.

"I already gave you the Longwood at Christmas assignment, right?"

I nodded. Longwood Gardens was a local wonder that I was to do a piece on for the December 26 issue. It was a safe piece that I could write ahead, an informative filler that wouldn't change, unless, of course, the conservatory decided to burn down or something.

"Good." He nodded. "Don't forget."

I scowled at him. Like I'd forget an assignment.

He ignored my scowl. "You know about His House?" he asked.

"Whose house?" I answered.

"*His* House."

I looked at him blankly.

"You know. Like in God."

"God's house? Like in church?"

"What's church got to do with anything?" Mac looked as confused as I felt.

"Church is God's house," I explained.

"Oh, yeah," said Mac. "I guess it is. But I'm not talking about church. I'm talking about His House."

We were back where we started.

"His House," Mac explained, "is a place for girls in trouble."

"Ah," I said. "In trouble with the law? With pregnancies? With their parents?"

"Probably all the above, but mostly with pregnancies," he said. "I want a story on some of those girls. I want a tearjerker for the season, you know? I want to wring the readers' hearts."

I nodded. I could do that.

He swept on. "I want your story to be so compelling that our readers will admire these girls, no, will *love* these girls for their courage to carry their babies instead of terminating their pregnancies. I want heartbreaking stories of desperation and blossoming maternal love, of perseverance in the face of abandonment by families and, most terribly, by the babies' fathers." He rose from his seat, carried away by his own rhetoric. "I want the readers to cry!"

I stared at him in astonishment. Where had all that emotion come from?

He grinned sheepishly as he noticed not only me but Edie Whatley, the family page editor, staring at him.

"Lapsed Italian-Catholic guilt," he explained as he sank into his new chair. "I'm conflicted over abortion. I'm conflicted over the Church. And Christmas always makes it all worse. I mean, what if Mary had aborted Jesus? Did you ever think of that?"

"Mac!"

"And then there's all the other seasonal questions. Should I go to midnight Mass on Christmas Eve? It sort of makes me feel good to go, you know? But isn't that hypocritical if I never go any other time? And shouldn't you go to church to talk to God, not to get a warm seasonal buzz? But it'd make my mother happy. The question is: would it make God happy? And why would he want to see me after the way I've acted the rest of the year? If there is a God. And if he wants to see people."

I couldn't help laughing at his expression, but I realized he was asking some very serious questions.

"Come to church with me on Christmas Eve," I said. "Would a Protestant service count with your mom?" I leaned over and whispered conspiratorially, "I have it on good authority that it counts with God. Not that yours doesn't too."

"Is that a date?" he asked with great eagerness.

"Absolutely not." Again I didn't know how to take the dating reference. "It's an invitation to spend time with God. He does like to see people."

"So you Protestants say. And no, Faith Community Church wouldn't count with my mom."

I shrugged. "If you change your mind, let me know. You could sit with me."

His eyes lit up.

"I wouldn't want you to feel awkward in strange surroundings," I said primly.

"Too kind," he said sarcastically.

There was a moment of silence while he fumbled through another stack of papers. He grunted with satisfaction as he pulled a slip of paper free. He handed it to me.

I read *Dawn Trauber, Director, His House*, followed by a phone number.

"Call her," he instructed.

I nodded. "Thanks. I agree with you. I think this will be a great story."

"It better be, Schweetheart," he said in his best Humphrey Bogart. "I may not go to Mass, but consider me the Little Drummer Boy bringing my gift of the story to the manger. You're the drum I'm beating on, pa-rum-pa-pum-pum."

I went to the file cabinet along the wall, slid the gigantic jade plant—now festooned with a equally gigantic red bow and white twinkle lights—to the rear of the cabinet, and dived into the H drawer. Certainly the clipping service had something for me on His House. I pulled the information out.

I carried the file back to my desk by way of the soda machine. As I walked past, I let down my guard and tossed my head. Just that quickly I was attacked by the great grape ivy. Its tentacles reached out and wrapped themselves about my curls, twisting and twining themselves until I was imprisoned against the dollar change slot.

My file fluttered to the floor. I gurgled in outrage and began struggling with the vines. I didn't want to be too rough because I was more afraid of Jolene, the mad gardener, than I was of the plant, but I didn't want to be dinner for a carnivorous organism either. So I pulled and twisted and twisted and pulled. No sooner did I get one curl free than another fell prey to the shoots.

I could just see the headlines: "Reporter Strangled: Coworkers Ignore Pleas for Help." Or "Woman Vined to Death. 'But it seemed such a nice plant,' friends say." Or "No Merry for Christmas: Woman Eaten Alive."

No matter what I did, the plant kept hold of me, slapping me in the face and blinding me with its leaves. As I struggled, a tendril reached down the back of my collar and wound itself around my neck. I felt it begin to choke me.

"No!" I cried and began to lash out wildly. I felt my feet slip on some downed leaves just as Jolene and Mac reached me. I grabbed for them to keep from slamming into the floor, but they calmly sidestepped and grabbed the falling grape ivy instead. I hit the floor with a great thud that rattled my teeth, but all I heard was, "Thank goodness! We caught it just in time." That was Mac.

"Merry! How could you? What were you thinking? You might have harmed it." That was Jolene.

As I sat there with my skirt around my ears and my hip announcing its fury at my inconsiderate treatment, Mac and Jolene patiently unwound the vines from my hair and with a great show of concern put the plant back in its place on the soda machine.

"Poor thing," Jolene murmured as she patted the villainous tendrils of green. She wasn't talking about me.

I pulled myself to my feet and limped back to my desk. Then I saw my file splashed across the floor and limped back over to collect it, keeping a wary eye on the plant.

"Merry," Jolene said in a clipped voice, "how could you be so careless?"

I turned to defend myself, only to see Mac standing behind her laughing so hard he couldn't talk. He just kept pointing to his shirt collar.

With as much dignity as I could manage, I felt my own neckline. A viney tentacle resting there immediately twined itself about my finger.

I pulled the scrap of green from me and threw it on the floor. "It's like a starfish and regenerates itself," I cried. "Watch out or it'll take over the newsroom!" I wanted to stomp on the creeper but knew it would be seen as overkill. So, nose in the air, I limped haughtily back to my desk.

In a minute a laughing Mac stood beside me, offering a peace Coke. The absurdity of the whole thing struck me about the time I took my first swallow. Mac had to swat me on the back several times to prevent me from choking.

"You made my day, Merry," Mac said as he walked away. "You made my day."

In the work situation, all I ever wanted to be was a consummate professional. Well, professionals are people who please their bosses, aren't they? I perked up a bit.

Finally I got to the His House file which wasn't exactly fat, but it did contain several news articles, many of them about local church women's groups who had showers and in-gatherings to benefit the House. There were several pictures of smiling women sitting behind stacks of hand-knit baby sweaters and blankets while boxes of diapers rose like block towers beside them. There were three articles about the House itself with pictures of the huge, old Victorian home just east of town and of the folks who staffed it.

I looked carefully at the picture of the director, Dawn Trauber, a thirty-something woman who reminded me of Jane Pauley. Same nice face. Same warm smile.

According to the article that chronicled her coming to His House, Dawn had wonderful credentials. She had a degree in social work from Philadelphia College of Bible and an MSW from Temple University in Philadelphia. She had worked for several years as a caseworker in the county foster care program and also served as a houseparent at a children's home near Lancaster. According to the article, she had now been in Amhearst four years.

There was nothing in the file about any of the girls who stayed there.

As I thought about it, I wasn't surprised. If I had to stay in a facility like His House, I didn't think I'd want my story and picture splashed all over the local paper. Obviously I couldn't keep my situation a secret. I might not even want to. But to let a bunch of strangers in on it was another whole issue.

Well, Lord, I thought, *you're going to have to help me find a way to do this story. I don't think it's going to be easy.*

I called His House and asked to speak with Dawn Trauber. When she came on the line, I explained who I was.

"I'd like to come out to His House and do a holiday story about some of your girls. You know. Coping with extraordinary circumstances at a time of year that's often difficult in the best of situations."

"Well," Dawn said, drawing the word out. I could hear the reluctance. "Certainly you can speak with me and certainly you can find out all you want about how we operate. As far as talking to the girls themselves, though, I don't think it's a good idea. They deserve their privacy."

"What if one or two are willing to speak with me?"

"We'll see. Come out and let me meet you. I need to assess whether I can trust you. Some media types want a story regardless of who they hurt."

Not me, I wanted to protest. Sure, I want a good story, but I have my limits. Instead we made an appointment for the next morning, and I hung up uncertain whether this drum was going to rum-pa-pum-pum.

Suddenly Jolene, swathed in leather and faux fur, stood at the side of my desk. I looked at my watch. Exactly 5:00.

"Ready?" she asked. She smiled sweetly if somewhat vaguely at me, the very picture of a lovely, somewhat ditzy woman without a care in the world. In other words, she had returned to the woman I worked with each day. Gone was any shred of the mad gardener who let me fall while she saved the plant or the shrew who had so masterfully dissected Airy at lunch.

Airy. What kind of a name was that? What was it short for? Arianna? Ariadne? Arabelle? Certainly not Aristotle.

"What's Airy's real name?" I asked as I tucked all the clippings into the His House file and slipped it back into its place in the H drawer. "And how does she spell it?"

"Airy?" Jolene asked as she checked her hair in the mirror she carried in her huge handbag. She sounded as if she'd never heard of anyone by that name.

"You know," I prompted, "the woman we met in the ladies' room." Though come to think of it, I hadn't met her. No one had been in an introducing mood.

"Oh." Jolene nodded in remembrance as she dropped the mirror back into her bag. "Valeria."

"Valeria?"

Jolene nodded. "Valeria Lucas Bennett. Sounds high society, doesn't it?" And she laughed sarcastically.

I shrugged my red coat on and we left *The News* by the back door. Jolene talked as we crossed the parking lot behind *The News* building.

"When she first moved here when we were little, she was Val. I started calling her Valentine's Day when we were in first grade. *Valentine's Day, go away. Don't come near for another year.*" Jolene sang the rhyme. "She decided she didn't like Val anymore. I suggested Larry from Va*leria*. She said that was a boy's name. She finally picked Airy. I think she meant A-r-i but I changed it. I told her she should be A-i-r-y, like a breeze floating wherever she wanted to go. *Airy, Airy, quite contrary, How does your garden grow? With weeds and seeds scratching your knees and ugly prickers all in a row.*"

Jolene must have been a great friend. I shuddered for poor Airy as I unlocked my car doors. We climbed in and I cranked the heater as high as it would go.

"Airy and I were best friends," said Jolene as she loosened her scarf. "We were always next to each other all through school. Lucas and Luray—that's our maiden names. By the way," she said as I turned toward her parents' home, "I need to stop off at my house for a minute."

"Oh." I thought of her very upscale condominium in the new development on the old Greeley farm south of town, fifteen minutes from here. How like her to neglect to mention this little detail until now.

"I don't mean the condo," she said, reading my mind, a trick of hers I found very disconcerting. "I mean my house. I need to see Arnie, and he's there."

"You have a house and a condo?"

She nodded and looked at me as if to say, "Doesn't everyone?"

"How long will this take?" I asked, knowing that I couldn't refuse no matter how much I wanted to or how long it would take. After all, she was already sitting in my car.

"Not long. No more than fifteen minutes."

"To get there or to talk with Arnie?"

"Yes."

Sighing softly I joined the line at the traffic light, weary folks limping home for the night. I told myself I wasn't being taken advantage of, that I was happy for the opportunity to help Jolene. I liked going miles out of my way. After all, I had nothing better to do, unless you counted eating dinner, relaxing a minute before running out again, or petting Whiskers.

Fifteen minutes later when we pulled up before a gorgeous, gigantic *mansion*—I couldn't think of any other word for the glorious vision in front of me—I decided that maybe helping had merit after all.

"This is your house?" I managed to sputter after staring open-mouthed in astonishment. I looked at Jolene with her cloying lily of the valley perfume and big hair. Thoughtfully I glanced at her coat. Maybe that wasn't faux fur after all.

"Yeah, it's mine," she said carelessly as she climbed out of the car.

Light streamed in wide ivory ribbons from Palladian windows and picture windows, bow windows and plain old regular windows, casting a golden glow on perfect shrubbery and a winding brick driveway and front walk. Through one large window a Christmas tree trimmed in little white lights twinkled from its place next to a sofa bigger than my entire apartment. A chandelier that looked like it would fit in well at the White House shone through the great window over the double front door.

"Look at all those lights," Jolene said in disgust.

"They're wonderful," I said, mesmerized.

She gave her unladylike snort. "All I see is dollar bills. But Arnie loves lights. When he was a kid, they didn't have any money. I mean none. His mother would only let them have one light on at a time, and that was a sixty watt. Now he puts on every light in the blasted house, all a hundred watt. You need sunglasses at midnight! 'I can afford it,' he yells. 'Don't you turn a single switch off!'"

I grabbed my camera from the backseat. At least I wouldn't have to worry about using a flash.

"Has the paper ever done a feature on this place?" I asked. I could see it as the first in a series of Great Homes of Chester County, some new like this, some historic, some remodeled barns like the one over on Route 322. Maybe the first Wednesday of every month or something. I'd have to talk to Edie Whatley, the home page editor. This was more her territory than mine, but I'd love to do such a series.

"Did you sell your condo?" I asked as I scrambled out of the car after her.

She shook her head.

"But you live here."

She shook her head again. "I live at the condo."

"But—" I stopped halfway up the walk and stared at the magnificence of it all. I counted eight windows facing the front on the second floor, not including the Palladian one over the door. I couldn't even begin to imagine how big the bedrooms were that had all those windows. "Why live there when you have this?"

"Because Arnie goes with this."

I'd never met Arnie, but how bad could the man be if he could provide all this electricity?

"Why did you two break up, Jolene?" I asked as I gazed at the brass carriage lamps on either side of the front door. If a guest ever clonked his head on a corner of either of them, solid things that they were, the blood would flow freely. But at least there'd be ample light for treating the wound and mopping up afterwards.

"Irreconcilable differences," she said.

"Yeah? What about?" I leaned to the left and peered into the dining room. The great china cabinet against the far wall was magnificent. I wished I could see the contents more clearly, but like a mirror the glass front reflected the wall sconces—more brass—and the crystal chandelier over the mile-long cherry table. So I stared at the silver tea service on the sideboard instead. Like Jolene ever served tea.

Suddenly I could hear my mom, loud and clear.

Merrileigh Kramer! What are you doing, asking such personal questions about the demise of Jolene's marriage? How rude can you get? Apologize right this instant!

It's the opulence, Mom. It threw me.

It's greed, Merry. And poor manners—which you never learned from me.

I reached to Jolene and placed a hand on her arm. "I'm sorry," I said. "I had no right to ask what went wrong. That's your private concern."

"I don't care," she said. "Everyone asks. Even my parents." She turned and opened the door.

I blinked. *Even* her parents? If I ever separated from a husband, should I ever actually get one, my parents would be first in line asking why. And I'd better have a good reason too.

I followed Jolene inside, my heels click-clicking on the parquet floor of the entry foyer. Ahead of us, rising to the second floor in a great curving sweep, was a staircase worthy of Scarlett and Rhett. It had a broad banister that called out for someone to sit astride it and slide from top to bottom.

Don't worry, Mom. I'll be good.

But it would be fun!

The foyer walls were papered with a yellow and cream floral sateen fabric with thin navy stripes running through the pattern. I reached out a finger and it bounced on the batting beneath the fabric. This was real class.

Jolene ignored the beauty of it all and kept talking. Of course she'd seen it all before.

"Arnie and me had differences over *everything*." She waved at the foyer chandelier. "Electricity. Me working. Eating dinner at my parents." I knew Jolene ate there every night. "Where to go on vacations. What wallpaper to pick. Can you believe he hated this?" She pointed at the fabric.

Arnie was obviously a philistine.

"Then we couldn't decide whether to buy a weekend place down the shore or up the mountains. And he couldn't decide on fidelity."

I was so busy photographing the yellow living room with its pale yellow carpeting and its accent wall of navy paper patterned with white daisies that I almost missed Jolene's last comment.

I lowered my camera and looked at her with compassion and sympathy, but she was stalking across the foyer toward the back of the house, apparently uninterested in my commiseration.

"Arnie!" she bellowed. "Where are you? I haven't got all day. Dinner's waiting and you aren't invited."

I followed her, my head swiveling as I walked, trying to take it all in. Suddenly I stopped before a painting of a Chester County stone farmhouse surrounded by snow-laden evergreens. I checked the bottom right corner, though I already knew what I'd see. Curtis Carlyle. GTG.

"Jolene, you've got an original Carlyle! You've got one of Curt's pictures! How come you never told me?"

She stopped and turned to look at the picture. She shrugged. "I forgot. But I've got a question for you. What's that GTG thing in the corner after his name? It is GTG, isn't it?"

I nodded. "He puts that on all his work. It stands for Glory to God."

She looked at me without comprehension, then at the picture.

"It means that he's thanking God for the talent and opportunity to paint," I explained.

"Oh," she said. She looked at the picture once more, shrugged again, and continued her trek across the vast expanses of foyer.

I looked at the picture again too and smiled. What a great guy he was. I stretched out my hand and traced the GTG. What a wonderful, great guy.

I turned back to Jolene just as she entered the kitchen at the far end of the foyer. In profile, I thought, she was as beautiful as she was full on. She went with the lovely house. She really did. I raised my camera, flicked the switch to continuous exposure, and pressed.

As the lens click-clicked, she stopped abruptly, frozen. I heard a quick intake of breath and saw a flash of tightening jaw through the viewfinder. Then she let out an unearthly shriek.

"Arnie!" She ran into the kitchen, out of my sight for a moment. "No! No! Arnie!"

The hairs on my arms rose at her tone, and I ran into the kitchen myself. I froze for an instant too.

On the floor by the stove lay Arnie, staring upwards, blood puddling beneath and beside him on the yellow tiles. Jolene knelt in the blood, shaking him, calling him, trying to rouse him.

She would never succeed.

Chapter Three

Several things raced through my mind at the same time.

Arnie was dead, very dead.

He didn't die naturally.

Jolene cared for him more than she realized, judging by her tears.

She was destroying crime scene evidence.

She was ruining her leather and fur coat.

Arnie had been a very handsome man.

He would never need all his lights on ever again.

With that final, sad thought, I set my camera on the table, ran to Jolene, and caught her by the shoulders.

"Jo, come on away from him," I said softly. "The police won't want us to touch him or move him." I could see smeared blood where she had dragged Arnie as she tried to lift him into her arms. Her hands were red from where she'd pulled at him.

"Merry, we've got to help him!" Her brown eyes shimmered with tears and pain. "CPR! Do you know CPR?"

I knelt beside her and hugged her. I could feel the sticky blood beneath my knees. "Jo, it won't help. He's dead."

"No, he's not," she said, pulling away from me. She reached for him again. "He's still warm."

I pulled her hands back. "Jolene, look at me," I ordered. Amazingly she did. "He's dead," I repeated softly. "Someone has killed him. We don't want to move him or do anything that would cover up evidence."

She stared at me. "Someone killed him?"

We turned together and looked at Arnie. He lay staring blindly at the ceiling, gravity pulling his eyelids back into his skull. His shirtsleeves were rolled up to the elbows and one pant leg was crumpled about his calf. There was a round hole in the left lower chest area of his tan button-down shirt, not far below his heart. I knew there was a corresponding hole beneath the shirt where the bullet had pierced his body. Blood had poured from the wound, soaking his shirt and the upper left area of his brown slacks, though it wasn't flowing anymore. Arnie's heart no longer pumped.

I didn't want to think about the tremendous internal damage and the exit wound beneath him from which blood must have rushed in a torrent. It was hard to comprehend that the great pool of it covering the yellow tiles had recently flowed through his veins as surely as mine swept through my body.

"Come away, Jo," I said as I stood and pulled her up with me. "We need to call the police."

I led her to the kitchen table and chairs, pushed her into a chair, and grabbed the phone. I dialed 911 and asked for help, which a confident-sounding voice assured me was only minutes away.

"Jo," I said as I hung up in spite of the fact that the voice wanted me to stay on the line. "Is there someone else we should call?"

She looked at me blankly. "Like who?"

Many days I wondered about Jo's mental acuity but tonight I knew the slowness was shock. "Like Arnie's parents. Brothers and sisters. Pastor. Your parents."

Jolene nodded. "Oh, yeah. Well, no." Each word sounded like its own little sentence. "He didn't have a family. His mom's dead and his dad disappeared when he was four. There are no brothers and sisters. And there's certainly no pastor. Arnie hated organized religion. Too phony and interested in making money."

She made a distressed face and sighed in pain. "I'll have to tell my parents face-to-face. It's not telephone news, you know? My dad will be so upset. He thought Arnie was a great guy. The son he never had. He especially liked giving Arnie Christmas because Arnie never had much of one before we married." She shook her head. "Poor Dad."

I looked at the man on the floor. Poor Arnie was more like it.

Since Jolene had no calls to make, I quickly dialed *The News*, connecting with Mac's desk.

"Mac, I'm at Jolene and Arnie Meister's house. Jolene and I came in and found Arnie shot to death."

"Poor kid!" he said, and I wasn't certain whether he meant Jolene or Arnie. "Let me talk to her."

I gave Jolene the phone and listened to her murmur into it. Suddenly she held it out to me. "He wants you."

"You know what you've got to do, right?" Mac said in my ear.

"Yeah, I know." A story by deadline tomorrow. *The News* is an afternoon paper of twelve to sixteen pages, and our deadline for news is nine, editing ten, and it's ready for delivery by noon.

I hung up and led Jo to the foyer.

"Give me your coat," I said and helped her slip out of it. "We don't want to get any more blood through the house than we need to."

I took mine off too and we dropped them in a pile on the parquet floor. Then we went into the living room where we sat awkwardly next to the beautiful Christmas tree on the sofa bigger than my apartment. But there was blood on our shoes and clothes as well as our hands, and we marred the pale yellow carpet and the huge sofa. Jolene never noticed.

She stood up almost as soon as we sat down. "I can't leave him there alone on the kitchen floor," she said, tears wet on her cheeks. She started unsteadily toward the kitchen. "I can't."

I nodded and followed her. "We'll sit at the table."

"I want to hold his hand."

I didn't know what to say. I remembered that when my Grandmom Richards died, my mom had sat by the bed for some time, holding her hand and smoothing back her hair.

"Just adjusting to the final good-bye, Merrileigh," Mom had said with a sad smile as she'd straightened the collar on Grandmom's nightgown.

But this was a violent death, a homicide. I remembered Sergeant William Poole of the Amhearst police saying, "The first rule of any investigation is never touch anything at a crime scene! Never, never, never! It contaminates the evidence and makes convictions hard, should we find the perpetrator."

"I think we can't touch him," I said as I led Jolene to a kitchen chair with a yellow plaid seat cushion.

She sank into the chair and laid her head on her arms on the table. I looked at her sadly, wishing I could ease her sorrow and knowing I couldn't. I patted her on the shoulder a few times.

Then I turned to the room. I put my hands behind me and began to make a slow circle of the kitchen, looking at everything and anything. Who knew what would be important for my story? Or for the solution of the crime?

"Jolene," I said hesitantly. "I've got to take pictures." Even as I asked, it seemed so intrusive to go flash, flash here and flash, flash there, especially since I knew the victims.

She raised her head. "For the paper?"

"Yes," I said. "But also to reconstruct the scene and look for possible clues."

"Don't put Arnie in the paper," she said. "Not like that."

"Don't worry. I won't. These pictures are just for me."

She gave me a watery, wavery smile. "You've got the detective bug."

"Sort of," I confessed, blushing at the actual verbalizing of that thought. How pretentious of me. How unfeeling. "But I won't take any pictures if you don't want me to."

"The cops are going to photograph him, aren't they?"

I nodded.

"Then you might as well too. Just don't put Arnie like that in the paper."

"I'll tell Mac," I promised.

I picked up my camera and began circling the room. As I walked, I talked, as much for myself as to keep Jo from falling prey to greater shock.

"How'd you meet Arnie?" I asked as I snapped the refrigerator and the couple of notes that were held to it by magnets shaped like fruit. One note from a scratch pad said: *Jolene—5:30.* The other, an 8 x 10 printout on a certificate template read: *$50,000.00!*

Jolene raised her head from her study of Arnie. "We met the first day of kindergarten. He was this shrimpy little kid with big glasses and a bigger mouth. He liked to boss everyone around. I hated him."

I glanced at Arnie. "He's no shrimp now."

Jolene shook her head. "But he was all through high school. The littlest guy around. Mr. Brainiac. He and Airy were quite the pair. Two dweebs. They deserved each other."

I thought of the beautiful Airy Bennett. "Dweebs? Airy? Arnie?"

Jolene sniffed. "I just hung out with Airy because I felt sorry for her. And people were just nice to Arnie because he'd tell you all the answers or write your paper for you or whatever—for a price. He loved that kind of stuff. But Airy wouldn't even let you copy her homework. 'It's cheating, Jo.'" Jolene's voice took on a hard edge. "She was the most self-righteous thing!"

I'd never let anyone copy my homework either, but I thought I wouldn't tell Jolene.

In the sink I noticed two glasses with dark liquid dregs. I leaned over and sniffed. Iced tea. I tried to see if there was telltale lipstick on one of the glasses, hard to do since I couldn't pick them up. *Cherchez la femme* and all that stuff. If Jolene hadn't been keeping Arnie company anymore, maybe someone else had.

I sighed. She (if there was a she and not just a collection of glasses beginning in the sink) either wore that lipstick that never came off or she wore none. Or she'd wiped the glass clean of any evidence. Interesting thought, that. I wondered if the police would be able to raise prints. I made a mental note to ask and took a picture.

"Did Arnie like iced tea?" I asked. "There are a couple of glasses here with tea in them."

"Yeah," she said, turning to look at the sink. "He drank it all year long. And it couldn't be instant stuff either. It had to be real. And not the bottled stuff. I mean real, like boil the water, put in the tea bag." She sighed. "I was going to give him a Mr. Tea or whatever you call it for Christmas. So he could make his own stupid tea. I already have it wrapped." She looked at me and her face crumpled. She wailed, "What do I do with that package now?"

I had no answer, but I don't think she expected one. She hugged herself and went back to staring at Arnie.

I noticed a wastebasket tucked in the corner by a cabinet. I walked over and peered in. I saw crumpled paper towels with a blue hearts and flowers pattern on them, a clear plastic wrapper from some package, an empty half-gallon Tropicana orange-tangerine juice container, and the box and refuse from a Lean Cuisine dinner. No clues as far as I could see, but I took a picture anyway.

"If Arnie was such a brainiac dweeb," I said as I took a picture of the bullet lodged in the cabinet directly behind where Arnie must have been standing when he was shot, "how did you two ever get together? And how did he get to look like this?"

I glanced again at the man lying on the floor. He must be six feet tall, his arms bulged with muscles, and there were no glasses in sight.

"After high school he went away to college," Jolene said. "His mom was so proud. He'd earned all these scholarships and stuff. I didn't see him for about three years. Then I went to a New Year's Eve party and there he was. I couldn't believe it! 'You can't be Arnie Meister,' I said. But of course he was. 'I'm just a late bloomer,' he always said, smiling like he was proud of it. A growth spurt and contact lenses took care of lots of his problems. And he pumped iron all the time. There's all kinds of weight equipment in the room down the hall." She got up and wandered in that direction. "He and my dad ..."

"Um, maybe we'd better stay here," I said, reaching out to take her arm. "We don't want to destroy clues."

She stopped at the kitchen door and looked at me vaguely. She returned to her chair and her staring at Arnie. "He was gorgeous, wasn't he? I fell for him big time."

"And he fell for you?" I prompted as I took a seat beside her. I pushed her gloves and scarf away from the table's edge.

Jolene smiled at some memory. "It took a couple of months. After all, he'd gone with Airy for years. I had to convince him to drop her."

I looked at Jolene. "Arnie had been going with Airy?"

"Since seventh grade," Jolene said.

"And you cut her out?"

"Yeah." Jolene unconsciously sat straighter. "I cut her out. It was easy."

I nodded as I leaned back in my chair and crossed my legs. Yes, Jolene was a wonderful friend, and the ladies' room animosity made more sense.

"Would you say Airy was a late bloomer too?" I asked.

"She's still waiting to bloom," Jolene said with more than a trace of the nastiness I'd seen earlier. I also recognized a case of wishful thinking. Airy had definitely blossomed.

The ringing of the doorbell caused us both to jump.

"I'll get it," I said. I stuffed my camera in my purse and went to let the police in. Two uniformed officers stood on the doorstep. I led them to the kitchen where they took one look and phoned home. In a few more minutes, my friend Sergeant Poole of the Amhearst police arrived. A crime scene team from the state police followed quickly, as did the coroner.

In no time Jolene and I found ourselves back on the huge couch again, our scarves and gloves tumbled in the pile on the floor in the hall.

"What will I do about the blood on my coat?" Jolene asked, staring across the room at the collection of garments, fixing on a problem that had comprehensible ramifications. The busyness of the men in the kitchen and their purpose were too much to think about, and they left her bewildered and overwhelmed. "I love that coat. Arnie got it for me last year, before our troubles."

"Don't worry about it. I'll take it to the cleaners for you when I take mine," I said.

She looked grateful and slumped back on the sofa. The brightly lit room was an oasis of quiet amid the activity taking place in the rest of the house. We sat there silently and waited as we had been asked by Sergeant Poole.

Finally both Jolene and I were interviewed though neither of us had much to say. Well, I hadn't much to say. Jo had a life's worth to talk about. Of course they separated us for the questions.

When it was my turn, I sat stiffly in one of the cherry diningroom chairs. I hoped I didn't appear guilty of anything because I wasn't.

I just get a guilty complex around extreme authority. I remember the time I lied to my mother about where I got the candy bar ("Ana's daddy bought it for me.") and the time I covered for Carrie, telling her mother she'd spent the evening at the library with me ("Please, Merry! If my father finds out I was with Paul, I'm dead! Dead!"). Or I remember the time I got a ticket for going 45 in a 25-mile-per-hour stretch back home.

So I sat straight and still, stoically waiting my grilling. At least I now knew what was in the china cabinet on the far wall since I sat facing it. One shelf was Royal Doulton figurines, their colorful images a contrast to the shelf of sleek, sophisticated Lladro porcelains. The top shelf was full of collector's pieces of blue Wedgwood with rings of white flowers encircling them.

Where had the money and the good taste for those things come from?

I smiled at Sergeant Poole and said in what I hoped was a natural voice, "What can I do for you, William? I'd like to do anything I can to help."

We went through my name and address and occupation, though he knew them from our previous dealings. He didn't seem to be overjoyed to be dealing with a reporter, even one he knew. I think he thought he'd lost his ability to investigate out of the public's eye.

He was right. My fingers were itching to get back to my computer and write up a story for tomorrow's edition, and I needed to take a couple of pictures of the cops at work.

"How did Mrs. Meister get the blood on her hands and her coat?" William asked me suddenly.

"She knelt beside Arnie when she first found him. She tried to pick him up and hold him. She didn't realize he was dead."

"Um." He said and waited. I waited too because I didn't have anything else to say. He knew me well enough to realize that if I had been trying to protect Jolene or if I had anything further to say, I would have blurted it when he waited. That authority reaction thing again.

Finally he asked, "What do you know about the victim?"

"Very little. I'd never met him. In fact, I'd never even seen him until I saw him in the kitchen."

"Not a great way to make an acquaintance." And he smiled sympathetically.

I smiled back and relaxed a bit.

"Why did you come here today?" he asked.

"Jolene—Mrs. Meister—was supposed to meet her husband here."

"*Meet* him here?"

"Yeah." I was puzzled by his emphasis on the word.

"Doesn't she live here?"

"No. They were divorcing and she lives in her own condominium."

His eyebrow rose. "Acrimonious divorce?"

"Not that I know of," I said, knowing exactly what he was looking for. The spouse is always the first suspect.

"Would you know if things were nasty between them? Are you and Mrs. Meister good friends?"

"Work friends, that's all."

He nodded. I could see my influence as a character witness shrinking like a blown-up balloon without a knot in the end.

"Why were they meeting?" he asked.

I shook my head. "I have no idea. She didn't tell me. She just asked for a lift."

"She doesn't have a car?"

"Her father drove her in to work today."

"She lives with her parents?"

I shook my head. "I told you. She owns a condo. Maybe she'd spent the night with them or something because it was icy." But it hadn't been icy last evening, I thought. Things froze during the night. Had her father driven out to her place to get her and then drive her into town? Whose idea would that have been? Was she overdependent or he overprotective?

"Was Mrs. Meister surprised when she found her husband?"

"Very," I said, picturing her response. "I think she was devastated." I paused, then asked a question I wanted answered. "How long do you think he's been dead?"

He raised his eyebrows, then said politely, "I'm not giving half-baked opinions to the press, Merry. We'll wait for the coroner's report."

"Don't get so testy, William. This isn't for publication," I hastened to assure him. "This is for me. I want to know how close you think we came to walking in on a murderer. I mean, nothing appears to have been touched or stolen. Is that because we arrived and scared someone off? Is there a very mad person out there who might not like us anymore?"

He studied me for a minute. "Okay, off the record. I don't think you scared anyone away. I think he's been dead for maybe three hours."

"Why do you think that?"

"You sure you want to know?"

I nodded, hoping I wouldn't regret this.

"Several reasons," Sergeant Poole said. "The white, waxy condition of his skin, the flatness of the eyes indicating loss of fluid, and the lividity."

I nodded. I'd noticed the purple-blue on the back of his arms and on the underside of the exposed calf where the blood had gathered in response to the pull of gravity.

"And," he finished, "rigor appears to have begun in the smaller muscles."

"But he's still warm to the touch."

"The body cools slowly, a degree or two an hour."

"Dust to dust doesn't take long, does it?" I asked rhetorically.

Sergeant Poole grunted noncommittally and returned to his agenda with a bang. "Where were you all afternoon, Merry?"

"Me?" I think my voice squeaked, I was so surprised.

The sergeant nodded.

"At work," I said. "Lots of people saw me. I spent the afternoon reading up on His House."

"Whose house? This house?"

I shook my head. "His House. With a capital H. Like in God's House."

"You were researching churches? For a Christmas article maybe?"

"No," I said patiently. "His House, that place east of Amhearst."

"Oh, yeah. The home for pregnant kids."

I nodded. "Why do you want to know what I was doing? You don't think I had anything to do with Arnie's death, do you?"

William Poole smiled slightly. He had an interesting lopsided smile which sat pleasantly on his furrowed face. "Not really, but I have to ask. It's what I get paid for. Now what about Mrs. Meister? Where was she all afternoon?"

"At work, too," I said.

"Do me a favor," he asked congenially. "Write down the times you had any conversation or contact with Mrs. Meister during the afternoon. One of my men will stop by for the list tomorrow."

I nodded. "I'll have it ready." I'd be more than happy to provide Jolene's alibi.

"Do you know you have blood on your hands, Merry?"

I looked at my hands and shivered. The blood was dried around my nails. "I got it when I pulled Jolene away from the body," I said. "I know I have some on my shoes and on my coat from when I knelt beside her. Even my knees."

Shortly after that, I was dismissed. Both Jolene and I were in the living room waiting for permission to leave when an officer came to us.

"We're going to remove the body now," he said. "I wanted to warn you because I don't know if you want to see him carried out in a body bag. I'd like to give you the opportunity to leave the room."

I glanced at Jolene who looked horrified.

"A body bag," she whispered. "Oh no!"

I heard the wheels of the gurney roll across the parquet. I grabbed Jolene, turned her from the door, and held her as they wheeled Arnie from his brightly lit home for the final time. I felt my eyes fill with tears, and I didn't even know the man. I couldn't imagine how Jo felt. Her shoulders were shaking.

When Jolene and I were finally given permission to leave, I glanced at my watch. It was 8:30. We'd been at the house for about three hours. I was already a half hour late for the photos of the AAC-FOP committee, and I had to take Jolene home yet. I shrugged. Hopefully the committee had lots of last-minute plans to make and would still be there by the time I managed to make it.

We drove back to Amhearst in silence. I didn't know what was running through Jolene's mind, but I was thinking about one second you're alive, and the next you can be dead. One minute your brain is zipping electrical impulses all over your body, the next it's flat line. One minute your blood is racing through your veins, and the next it's a pool all over the yellow tiled floor.

A mystery, if ever there was one. What did you think about this phenomenon if you didn't believe that absent from the body was present with the Lord?

We drove through downtown Amhearst, past the cluster of brightly decorated stores open until nine in a mostly vain attempt to attract the Christmas business back from the malls. As we passed *The News*, I asked, "Jolene, where exactly do your parents live?"

Shortly we pulled up before half of a double house on Houston Street in the older, less prosperous part of town. The light by the front door showed a porch covered with bright green indoor/outdoor carpeting and lined with black wrought iron railings. In spite of it being December, two white molded plastic chairs sat on either side of a small white plastic table in the center of the porch. On the table was an arrangement of plastic greens and an angel whose head turned from side to side. A wreath of plastic greens with a mashed plaid bow hung between the storm door and the inside door.

I couldn't imagine anything more unlike the mansion we'd just left.

Jolene turned to me and grabbed my arm. "Come in with me, Merry. I can't face my parents alone. They loved Arnie. They really did."

The last thing I wanted to do was help break the news of the tragedy, but I opened my car door and climbed out. We started up the steps as the door of the other half of the double opened. A man in a camel topcoat came rushing out only to stop short when he saw us.

"Jolene," he said and sort of reached for her.

I was aware of the curtains parting on the front window of the other half of the double.

"Reilly." Jolene acknowledged, nodding at the man. She kept walking up the stairs, making it obvious that she wasn't stopping for conversation.

Reilly watched her with a hungry expression, but when Jolene kept moving, he went down the steps to a car at the curb.

"Who's he?" I asked as we reached the porch.

"Reilly Samson. He lives next door, or rather he did growing up. He has his own place now. He works with Arnie."

"And her?" I indicated the gap between the curtains next door.

"Old Mrs. Samson, the world's nosiest neighbor," Jolene muttered. "Reilly's grandmother. Wait until she hears about Arnie!"

"Did she like him too?" I asked as I smiled and nodded at Mrs. Samson. The curtain promptly fell back in place.

"Hated him."

"Why?" I asked, somewhat startled. Up until now it sounded like everyone loved Arnie or at least the adult Arnie. He had become a prince among men.

"Who knows why?" Jolene said in a voice that clearly indicated she wasn't interested in talking about it. "She's just a bitter old lady who hates everyone."

"Even Reilly?"

"Sometimes I think so."

"Even you?" I couldn't resist asking.

"Especially me," Jolene said.

"Really? Why?"

"Because I got rich." With that, she opened the front door.

The house was a typical East Coast double with two stories plus basement and attic. The rooms ran in a front-to-back pattern of living room, dining room, kitchen, and back porch on the first level with a large staircase in the front hall running to the second floor where a center hall opened into three large bedrooms and a bath. The third-floor attic where the roof pulled the walls in would be a single huge room. A postage stamp of a backyard finished the property.

As soon as we came through the front door, an older man and woman rushed into the hall, swooping down on us and burying us in solicitude and questions about Jolene's tardiness. I was surprised because I hadn't realized that Jolene's grandparents lived here too.

"Come in, come in," the man kept saying to me, beaming as he tried to take my coat. A slight Southern accent colored his voice. "I'm so glad Jolene brought a friend home with her!"

"Are you all right, Jolene Marie? You know how I worry when you're late," the woman said, scanning Jo's face and hugging her shoulders. "You don't look well, dear. Maybe we need to make it warmer for you? We can turn up the kerosene heater. Or maybe you just want to come into the kitchen. I saved your dinner. There's plenty for your friend, too. Are you certain you're all right?" And she pulled Jolene to her bosom again.

Jolene pulled away from the smothering arms and said, "Mom, that's enough! Dad, make her stop."

Mom? Dad? Not Grandmom and Grandpop?

"Easy, Eloise," Jo's dad said, patting the woman on the shoulder. "We need to meet Jolene's friend."

Suddenly I was being stared at by two curious elderly gnomes, one with vague blue eyes, one with sharp brown ones.

"This is Merry Kramer, Merry as in Christmas. We work together," Jo said unenthusiastically.

"Merry," said Jolene's mother, smiling sweetly at me. "What a lovely name, especially this time of year. Were you born in December, dear? I just bet you were."

"June," I said.

"Oh," said Jolene's mother, looking confused. "I thought she said Merry."

I must have looked equally confused because Jolene's father said, "The month of June, my dear. Not the name."

The woman smiled sweetly. "Oh, of course. Silly me."

She looked older than my Grandmom Kramer by several years, though I knew she couldn't be. Grandmom Kramer was seventy-nine and there's no way she could have a daughter as young as Jolene. Of course the appearance of age could have been caused by this woman's determinedly gray hair and the too-tight permanent, the unbecoming glasses and the lined face. Grandmom Kramer was a great fan of Loving Care and Cover Girl, and she single-handedly kept her health food store manager in designer duds. I even suspected plastic surgery and liposuction, but I'd never mentioned it to my parents, who would be shocked at the very idea.

As I smiled my sweetest at Jolene's mother and father, I searched my mind for Jolene's maiden name. Carlsbad. Mammoth. Jewel. It had something to do with caves or caverns. Ah! Luray!

"Mr. and Mrs. Luray, how nice to meet you." I shook their hands prettily. My mother would have been proud.

"Right this way, girls," Mrs. Luray said. "The food's waiting."

Mr. Luray was still attempting to wrestle me for my coat, and my stomach was growling at the wondrous aromas that filled the air. No wonder Jolene came home for dinner every night. "I can't stay." AAC-FOP was waiting. "I'm sorry."

"I wish you would," said Mr. Luray, fingers wrapped around my coat collar as he tried to drag it off my shoulders. He was bald, homely, wore thick glasses, and had muscles on muscles. It was obvious he and Arnie had bonded over weights. "Jolene doesn't bring friends home much."

"Dad," said Jolene sharply. "Let Merry alone, for heaven's sake!"

Mr. Luray nodded pleasantly. "Okay. If you say so." His hands fell from my collar.

Mrs. Luray peered first at Jolene, then at me. "You do look pale, Jolene Marie. You do. So do you, Merry, but then maybe you're always pale. I wouldn't know, would I?" She smiled vaguely at me, patting my hand. "But are you sure you girls are all right? Have you had a disagreement or something? I know that when I have a fight with Mrs. Samson, Dad can always tell because I look so pale." She smiled at me again. "Not that we have that many fights, you know. But that's how it shows when we do. Or maybe," and her smile faltered, "maybe you had a fight with Arnie, dear? You didn't have another fight with him, did you, Jolene Marie? I can't stand it when you two fight." She looked like she might cry.

"Now, Mother," said Mr. Luray. "Don't get yourself so worked up. Your heart will start fluttering."

Jolene looked at me in helpless frustration.

"Do you take heart medicine, Mrs. Luray?" I asked.

"Aren't you sweet to be concerned," she said. "Yes. I keep it handy all the time in case I need it."

"Where is it?"

"In the kitchen on the windowsill over the sink. And upstairs both in the bathroom and on my night table."

"Mr. Luray," I said with an authority it would be hard to question, "I think it would be a good idea if you got your wife's medicine."

Mr. Luray looked at me with narrowed eyes, saw something in my face, and headed for the kitchen and the windowsill.

"Bring a big plastic bag back with you, Dad," Jolene called. A muffled assent drifted to us.

"What?" Mrs. Luray seemed confused, which I began to suspect was a normal situation. "What's wrong? Jolene Marie, why do I need my medicine? Oh, I knew it! You and Arnie did fight! You didn't hit him, did you, dear? Tell me you didn't hit him! Or throw something at him. It's so unladylike."

"Mom!" Jolene shouted fiercely. "Shut up!"

Mrs. Luray and I both stared at Jolene, I in startled disbelief at her tone of voice, her mother in obedience. "Yes, dear," she said sweetly.

Oh boy. Mrs. Luray needed a few lessons from Grandmom Kramer in developing a backbone.

Jolene shook her head, her mass of brown curls quivering with a violence to match her words. "Can't you ever shut up? I can't stand you when you run on like that!"

"I'm sorry, dear. I didn't mean to upset you, but then I can see that you're already upset, aren't you? Why, dear? Tell Mommy. You'll feel better if you tell me. Don't worry. I can take it. Just tell me. You did fight with Arnie, didn't you?"

Jolene put her hands to her face in frustration.

Mr. Luray walked back into the room, a pill bottle clutched in his right hand and the plastic bag in his left. Jolene took the bag and handed it to me. She folded her coat and as I held the bag open, stuffed it in. "My scarf and gloves are still in the car."

I nodded, pulling the ties to shut the bag. "I'll get them."

"What's she doing with your coat, Jolene Marie?" Mrs. Luray asked, her expression concerned. "That's a special coat. That's the one Arnie gave you. What's she going to do with it?"

"It's dirty, Mom," Jolene said through gritted teeth. "She's taking it to the dry cleaners for me."

Mrs. Luray's face lit with joy. "Why, how sweet, June," she said to me.

I opened my mouth to say, "Merry," but refrained. She wasn't listening to me anyway.

"Daddy," said Mrs. Luray, her high voice tinged with sorrow. "Jolene Marie and Arnie had a fight. She's just going to tell us about it. Isn't it too sad?"

"What's wrong, Jo?" Mr. Luray said. His manner was stark and aware.

"Yes, dear," fluttered Mrs. Luray. "Tell us."

Jolene cast a fleeting, highly annoyed glance at me though I knew it wasn't me she was annoyed at. She took a deep breath, then looked steely eyed at her parents. "Arnie's dead," she said baldly. "He was shot."

Mrs. Luray gasped once, twice, three times, clutched her chest, and sank to the floor.

Chapter Four

I stared at the frail woman lying on the floor, my heart palpitating as if I were about to have my own coronary. "Should we do CPR? Should I call 911? Do you stick that medicine under her tongue or something?"

Jolene and her father looked at each other, then shook their heads in unison.

"Don't worry," Jolene said. She stood over her mother without moving. "She'll be okay."

"Jolene!" I fell to my knees beside the unconscious woman. "What if she dies right here on the floor?"

"She won't," Jolene said wearily. "She never does."

I stared at Jolene, then at her father, aghast. They both continued to ignore Mrs. Luray in favor of a conversation about Arnie.

"Is he really dead?" Mr. Luray asked.

Jolene nodded.

"Shot?"

She nodded again.

He hugged himself and a tear slid down his wrinkled cheek. "Oh, Jolene! Why? Who?"

"I have no idea, Daddy." Jolene went to her father and wrapped her arms around him. She held him and rocked him gently back and forth like a mother might comfort a hurting child. His shoulders shook and his breath came raggedly. The man was heartbroken.

I was moved by his grief and her compassion, but I kept looking at Mrs. Luray, lying there on the floor. I reached past the kerosene heater to the red and green floral sofa, pulled a fuchsia and kelly green afghan off the back, and tucked it around the woman. At least now I knew where Jolene got her vibrant sense of color.

I pushed Jolene and her father from my mind and concentrated on finding Mrs. Luray's pulse just like they taught us back in Girl Scouts, taking care not to use my thumb. I didn't want to feel my heart's cadence when I was searching for hers.

I expected to find a thready, thin, and erratic rhythm. I blinked. Her pulse was so strong you'd have thought a tympanist was in there whopping out the "wonderful, counselor, the mighty God, the everlasting Father, Prince of Peace" section of last week's performance of *The Messiah* at the Community Center.

"She's fine," I blurted.

Jolene released her father and they both looked down at me.

"Always," Mr. Luray said. He sniffed and swallowed. "Come on, Jo. We'd better get her on the sofa before she comes around. She'll be upset if she finds herself on the floor."

Jolene nodded. She and her father bent in unison and lifted Mrs. Luray, afghan and all, and laid her gently on the sofa. Jolene stuck a fluffy kelly green pillow under her mother's head. They'd obviously done this many times before. Flabbergasted as I was, I continued to kneel over her vacated place like an idiot.

"I'm sorry if you were scared," Mr. Luray said as he held out a hand and helped me to my feet. His muscles were definitely the real thing. "It's just Eloise's way of dealing with things she doesn't want to think about. If you pass out, you block them, at least for a time." He looked at her affectionately. "She's very delicate, very sensitive, you know."

I looked at Mrs. Luray. I wasn't certain delicate and sensitive were the words I'd have used.

She began to stir. "What happened? Where am I? Alvin?"

Mr. Luray sat on the edge of the sofa and opened the pill bottle. He slid a flat, white disk into his hand. "Shh, Eloise. It's okay. I'm right here," he said. "Here's a pill. Put it under your tongue and you'll be fine in no time."

She opened her mouth obediently.

Jolene leaned toward me. "It's a Tums," she whispered.

I stared at Mrs. Luray. Grandmom Kramer looked better all the time, liposuction or no. "Does this happen often?"

She shrugged. "Depends on how you define often. She was passing out several times a day when Arnie and I first separated. Now she can talk about it without any trouble. You saw that."

"Oh!" said Mrs. Luray suddenly and in great distress.

I spun around, expecting her to go down again as she recalled the terrible news about Arnie.

"Smell that!" she said. "Jolene, your dinner's burning!" She struggled to her feet and moved quickly to the kitchen. "I'll save it!"

Jolene watched her mother leave the room, then went to her father. She patted his shoulder. "Are you all right, Dad?"

He smiled sadly. "Not really." He put his arm around her waist and they leaned into each other, sorrow etched on both faces.

I collected Jolene's coat and let myself out as Eloise Luray called, "Everything's all right, Jolene Marie. I saved your dinner for you."

The clock in the bank tower read 9:15 as I drove past. Bone-weary, I wanted to go home and climb into a hot tub and soak away the traumas of the day, to gather Whiskers into my lap and hug his soothing silkiness close, to drink a decaf diet Coke and eat a fistful of Oreos. I sighed at that lovely dream and added a MacDonald's cheeseburger and fries to the menu. Then, replete, I wanted to pull my pillow over my head and sleep and sleep, provided I didn't dream of Arnie.

Instead, dutiful employee that I am, I drove to the Community Center.

Would the AAC-FOP committee still be meeting even though I was over an hour late? Yes, they would and they were. I raced into the meeting room, hoping the blood on my coat didn't show and that no one noticed my fingernails and knees. I hadn't had time or opportunity to do anything about cleaning myself up. At least the blood on my shoes was long dried or worn off.

I found the committee huddled around a table, faces focused in concentration, papers strewn in organized chaos. A barrel-chested man with a mane of white hair and a slight limp was prowling the floor, talking and gesticulating, but I hardly noticed him.

All I could see was Curt. He looked so strong and sane and normal. All I wanted was his embrace to wash away the past few hours.

When he saw me, he lost his previously polite, I-wish-I-were-somewhere-else expression and smiled broadly. He even gave a little wave. I wiggled my fingers in return.

"We can do it, folks!" the white-haired man was saying, and I pulled my attention reluctantly from Curt. The man's words were laced with a heavy Southern accent that was pleasant on my ear. "I know we can do it. We can feed not only the needy of Amhearst but of the surrounding communities too. This year we'll have the best collection of goods ever. Why, we're almost past last year's total, and we have another week to go. And the local grocers have yet to make their contributions. With the coverage *The News* is going to give us, the Amhearst Annual Christmas Food Project will make history!"

He was so good at pep talks that even I, weary as I was, felt a slight urge to cheer with the other wildly clapping people around the table. Instead I concentrated on dragging my camera out of my purse.

"And here, I presume, is our photographer now!" The white-haired man swept his hand toward me and everyone turned.

I smiled weakly and sort of bobbed my head in apology for being so late.

"Come on, everyone," the man said. "It's free PR time. Let's get ourselves set for our picture." And he began giving orders. "George, you sit there and, Milly, you sit beside him. I want people to see that we have men and women, black and white, involved in this wonderful project. Allison, you stand here by me, and Curt, stand right there in the middle. You're our celebrity and honorary chairman, and we want to take advantage of that. Elena, you and Julio stand on the other side of Curt."

I didn't move, overwhelmed by the white-haired man. I might be the photographer here, but he was clearly the one in charge. I bet he was in charge everywhere he went, whoever he was. I had to admit that he had gathered as politically correct a group of people as I'd ever seen in my short time in Amhearst.

I felt Curt's eyes on me and became unexpectedly shy. I studied my camera intently, adjusting this and manipulating that. My problem was that I could never quite figure out how to react to him in public.

When I went with Jack, he ignored me most of the time, sort of expecting I'd follow along, which like an idiot I did, so public response wasn't an issue. Now I worried about Curt. I couldn't rush to his side because we weren't really going together or anything—though I suspected that was more my fault than his. I also couldn't ignore him. Basic manners aside, I didn't want to. I mean, maybe someday we would be going together. I hope. I think. Maybe.

So I stood there flat-footed and thought about how gorgeous he looked and how worn I must look and how shallow I was not to be thinking of the tragedy of Arnie. It wasn't an evening to bring out my best.

Curt ignored his orders to go stand in the middle and walked over to me. "Hello, Merry."

I looked at him and sudden tears sprang to my eyes. "Hi." It came out as a whisper. I realized for the first time how close I was to losing control. Murder and fainting women had that effect on me.

Curt took my arm, concern leaping to his face. "Are you all right?"

"Barely."

He began to lead me to a chair. "Sit down."

I pulled my arm free and shook my head. "If I sit, I'll start to cry and ruin my professional image. If I have one left after my lateness."

He started to protest but I cut in. "I'll tell you all about it later." I saw over Curt's shoulder that the white-haired man was bearing down on us. "And you'd better go stand in the middle before you're dragged there."

He moved to stand between Allison and Elena, and the white-haired man came up to me.

"Hello, there, darlin'," he said, smiling with great charm. "I'm Harry Allen Bushay."

He said Bushay with the accent on the first syllable, sort of like Jolene said Luray. I looked at him with interest. Was this the

Bushay of Bushay Environmental where Jack was working on his audit?

"How do you do, Mr. Bushay." I extended my hand and Harry Allen Bushay took it and shook it and held it a minute or two too long. He leaned close.

"Just call me Harry Allen, darlin'."

"Thank you," I said noncommittally.

With a cozy, just-between-you-and-me grin, Harry Allen turned and took his seat at the end of the front row next to Milly. I snapped several pictures, hoping that everyone looked decent in at least one of them. I had pulled out my spiral tablet to get everyone's name when Harry Allen handed me a sheet of paper.

"Here are our names," he said helpfully. "They are in order and all spelled correctly."

"Thank you," I said as I flipped my tablet closed. "How thoughtful of you."

"I'm a thoughtful kind of guy," Harry Allen said. "Darlin'."

I smiled weakly. The last thing I felt like dealing with tonight was a flirt with white hair, no matter how premature the white or how charming the manner.

I needn't have worried. Harry Allen turned and with a clap of his hands called the AAC-FOP meeting back to order. "Only fifteen more minutes, people. Only fifteen more minutes."

Everyone took their places at the table except Curt.

"I don't have to stay," he said as he walked up to me and helped me into my coat. "I'm only the honorary chairman."

I made believe that his concerned glance hadn't brought tears to my eyes once again. "It must be tough being a celebrity," I teased as I blinked like mad. "Why, I even saw an original Carlyle hanging in a mansion tonight."

He grinned. "I hope you were properly impressed."

We walked out of the meeting room and into the front hall, shoulders rubbing companionably. I still had trouble comprehending that this man said he was falling in love with me. Me!

Why me, I kept asking myself, with all the beautiful women there were around? I was slim enough and not too tall, but I had a too-curly permanent, a striped nose, and a prickly side to my nature that had been asserting itself with a vengeance since I'd moved to Amhearst. I kept waiting for him to realize his mistake, change his mind, and fall for someone like, say, Airy, someone beautiful and lovely and all those other wondrous, feminine things. Why, I bite my nails, for heaven's sake!

Curt stopped in the hall and checked over his shoulder. When he was certain we were alone, he put his arm about my shoulders and turned me to face him. "What's wrong, Merry?"

This time tears did fall. "Oh, Curt," I sobbed, burying my face in his chest. "We found him shot, and then she tried to move him and the police questioned us and her mom fainted and they ignored her and—"

"Whoa," he said, patting me gently on the back. It made me want to burp. "Just cry and then tell me. Both at once doesn't work too well."

Of course, as soon as he told me I could cry, the tears dried up. It was sort of like a toothache disappearing as soon as you entered the dentist's office. I stayed huddled against him a few minutes longer, listening to and enjoying the strong, comforting rhythm of his heart.

"Poor Arnie," I said as I stepped reluctantly back.

"Arnie?"

"Meister, Jolene's ex or almost ex. Though now I guess he'll never get to full ex status, will he?" Somehow that seemed very sad. Not that ex status was a good thing, but never to achieve it or anything else ever again, *that* was sad.

"If I follow you correctly, you're saying that Jolene's husband has been shot?" Curt said.

I lifted shaking hands and brushed my hair out of my eyes. "Killed. Murdered. We found him."

He looked at me with such concern that the tears sprang to my eyes again. This man could do extraordinary things to me.

Suddenly the phone on the receptionist's desk in the darkened office to our right began to ring. I jumped at the noise, then looked at Curt.

"Should we answer it?" I asked.

He shook his head.

"But maybe it's for someone here." I took a step toward the office.

He put a hand on my arm. "The answering machine will get it. That's what it's for."

Sure enough, the machine kicked in after the second ring.

"If anyone can hear this," a voice boomed loudly, "and Harry Allen Bushay is still there, please get him to the phone! It's very important! It's an emergency! This is the police."

Curt and I looked at each other. Then I lunged for the phone and he took off for the meeting room.

"We're getting Mr. Bushay," I told the person on the other end. "He'll be right here."

"Thank you," said a familiar voice.

"William, is that you?" I asked.

"Who's this?" he countered suspiciously.

"Merrileigh Kramer."

There was a short pause. Then William asked, "What are you doing at the Community Center with Mr. Bushay?"

"Taking his picture, Sergeant."

"What?"

"For the paper. He chairs the Amhearst Annual Christmas Food Project, and my assignment is to take a committee picture. I'm just fortunate they were still here because I was very late." I minded my manners; I didn't say it was his fault.

"Interesting that you have been with two people closely associated with Mr. Meister this evening, isn't it, Merry?"

Harry Allen was associated with Arnie? How? "Coincidence, Sergeant," I said.

"So you say," he answered, but I could hear a smile in his voice.

Before I had time to respond, Harry Allen came hurrying down the hall, his limp exaggerated by his fast gait. Worry and apprehension were written all over his face. He grabbed the phone from me.

"Yes?" he barked. "What is it?"

Whatever William Poole said, it seemed to alleviate Harry Allen's fear. His shoulders eased and his brow cleared, at least for the moment. Then, abruptly, he jerked upright.

"What? You can't be serious!"

As Harry Allen listened some more, I looked at Curt. Should we leave or should we wait and see if he needed assistance of any kind—though the idea of Harry Allen Bushay needing assistance seemed ludicrous to me.

"Yes," he finally said. "I'll come right away. No, I do not wish to wait until tomorrow. I want to get it over with. I'll be there in a few minutes."

He hung up the phone and stood still a minute, lost in thought, appearing almost disoriented.

"Can we do anything for you, Harry Allen?" Curt asked. "Can we help in any way?"

He looked up. "Yes," he said. "You can tell the committee that the meeting's over for tonight."

Curt nodded.

"Oh, never mind," Harry Allen said in disgust. "I'll do it. I have to go back in anyway to get my coat. I have to go to the police station."

I looked at him with great interest. "Arnie Meister?" I asked.

He focused all his intensity on me. "How did you know that call was about Arnie Meister?"

"I talked to Sergeant Poole tonight at Arnie's house. I was with Arnie's wife when she found his body."

One bushy eyebrow rose. "Bad?" he asked.

I nodded, tearing up yet again. Curt put his arm around me and patted my shoulder comfortingly.

Harry Allen snorted, half in distress, half in disbelief. "Arnie Meister's dead. Murdered. Absolutely unbelievable. Wait till they find out that he and I had a big fight yesterday. I mean a *big* fight. And wait until they try to get me to tell them what it was about." He looked at us, his lips clamped together. "I'm not talking to anyone."

Chapter Five

Curt and I sat in a booth in a quiet corner of McDonald's. I stared unenthusiastically at the cheeseburger in front of me. The very thought of it had made my mouth water. Until now.

"Come on, Merry," Curt urged. "You've got to eat. You'll feel better if you get some food in you."

I pulled a french fry out of the red cardboard holder and nibbled. It took a lot of effort to swallow.

"I've lost my saliva," I said, trying to generate some by swishing my tongue around in my mouth. "Everything's sticking in my throat."

"Take a drink."

I obediently sipped, and the moisture helped the dryness in my mouth. Maybe the Coke's bubbles would settle my stomach.

"There was so much blood, Curt. It's hard not to keep seeing it." I shivered as I looked at the little pile of catsup he had squeezed next to his fries.

He took my hands in his. "It's okay, Merry. You'll be okay. Just give yourself time. In the meantime, you've got to eat. Come on. Eat." He took my cheeseburger and put it in my hands. "Bite. Chew." He watched as I took a nibble. Satisfied, he took a huge bite of his Big Mac.

The door behind me flew open and the draft wrapped itself mercilessly around my feet. I shivered and glanced over my shoulder. Anything to stop staring at the cheeseburger. I was surprised to see Airy Bennett and a strange man walking toward the ordering line, but not half as surprised—and distressed—as I was to see my old

Pittsburgh flame and current Amhearst pursuer, Jack Hamilton, trailing them.

Ack! I thought as I turned back to my cheeseburger with something akin to panic churning my already teeming stomach. Just the perfect ending to a perfect day. Jack and Curt and me, a jolly threesome at McDonald's. Rub-a-dub-dub, three men in a tub. I could feel an ulcer developing as I sat there.

I knew there were girls somewhere who knew how to handle potentially touchy moments like this, but I surely wasn't one of them. I shrank as low in my seat as I could, holding my breath.

But Jack didn't see us. He was too busy talking to his companions. He paused in his story only long enough to order his meal and follow Airy and the man to a table across the room. Risk diminished.

But not alleviated. He might glance around the restaurant at some point and see me. Surely even self-absorbed Jack got curious about the people around him, didn't he? I sat stiffly, waiting for his cry of recognition, dreading what I knew must be my ultimate humiliation. When my heated imagination began to conjure scenarios worse than any possible reality, I forced myself to peer oh-so-casually in Jack's direction.

Whew! He was facing away from me. Maybe the dreaded Jack-Curt confrontation wasn't going to take place this evening after all.

The relief made me hungry, and I began eating my cheeseburger.

"What does it say about the condition of your eating habits if you can feel strength flowing through your body as the result of one of these?" I asked, extending my burger toward Curt.

"Not much, I'm afraid." He looked up. "And hold on, here comes someone to our table."

My appetite dried up again.

"It is you, isn't it?" asked Airy Bennett as she stopped beside our table. She looked anxiously at me. "You're the woman who was with Jolene Meister earlier today, aren't you? I recognize the red coat."

Airy, not Jack! And thankfully she couldn't see the bloody hem tucked under the table. I'd been able to wash my hands and knees in the ladies' room, but there was nothing I could do about the coat for now. "Yes, I am," I said with a relieved smile.

"Well," she said, "I've got to apologize. I am very embarrassed by the way I acted."

I waved my hand in a dismissive gesture. "Don't worry. It's okay."

"No, it's not," Airy said. "Though it's kind of you to say so." She smiled, and I thought she was probably a nice person when away from Jolene. At least she didn't deny her complicity in the fight.

She continued. "Jolene has brought out the worst in me for years. I'm always dumb enough to get sucked in, no matter how many times I promise myself that it will be different the next time I see her. I think I'm doing really well, and then I see her again and *boom!* I explode." She sighed. "Maybe someday I'll grow up." She said it without much hope.

"Don't worry about it," I repeated. "As far as the traumas of the day go, it's at the bottom of the list, believe me."

Since she didn't know about the traumas at the top of the list, Airy thought I was just being polite. "Believe it or not," she said, "it's not like me to be so nasty."

I nodded; I could believe her easily. Standing here with her coffee in her hand, she looked like a regular person, reasonably polite and intelligent. Besides, I knew Jolene.

"When I told Sean about how I made a fool of myself, he couldn't believe it." She glanced back toward Jack and the other man. "That's Sean," she said. "The blond guy."

Sean looked up at that moment and smiled widely at Airy. I noticed the mustache Jolene had referred to. It wasn't very obvious at this distance, his being blond and all, but it looked nice as far as I could tell. He saw me looking at him and dipped his head in acknowledgment. Jack started to turn to see who Sean was looking at, and I spun around so fast I made myself dizzy.

"By the way, I'm Airy Bennett," she said, holding out her hand. "We never did get introduced this afternoon." And she grinned ruefully.

"Merrileigh Kramer," I said. "And this is Curt Carlyle."

Airy looked again at Curt. "Of course," she said, and I grinned proudly at him. Big-time artist. Name recognition. "Mr. Carlyle. I thought you looked familiar. You teach phys ed and coach—what? Soccer or something?"

So much for being a famous artist. I was disappointed, though he didn't seem to mind.

"I coach soccer and tennis," he said, "but I don't teach anymore."

"I was a senior the first year you taught." Airy grinned. "We girls were all so impressed to have a single male teacher who was good-looking and all. I bet they miss you now."

"I doubt it," Curt said with his charming smile.

Airy suddenly waved her arm toward Sean. "Come here, honey," she called. "I'd like you to meet some people."

"No, no!" I all but shouted. "Don't bother him." I wondered if I could slide under the table before Jack saw me, but Curt and Airy'd probably notice. As it was, they were staring at me because of my outburst. I smiled weakly.

The blond man walked to our table, soda cup in his hand. Introductions were once again made.

"So you like to eat late, elegant dinners just like we do," Sean said, raising his cardboard cup.

"Class all the way," agreed Curt.

We all smiled and wondered what to say next. Into the little silence my social bomb detonated.

"Merry? Merry! Is that you, sweetheart?" Jack had approached when I wasn't looking. "What are you doing here?" He slid into the seat beside me and kissed me on the cheek. His breath smelled like french fries. He looked absolutely delighted to see me.

I sat turned to stone. I wanted to look at Curt and see his reaction, but I couldn't make myself lift my eyes from the stupid cheeseburger.

"This is the girl I was telling you about," he said to Airy and Sean, no doubt beaming as he took one of my fries and dunked it in Curt's catsup. "She's the reason I took the job at Bushay. Isn't she wonderful?"

Help me, Lord! Help me get out of this mess! I'll never shirk from saying what needs to be said again. I promise! Just please don't let it get any worse!

Jack looked at me. "Sean here works at Bushay. He's their comptroller, and he's helping me get acclimated as I begin the audit."

I found I could look at Sean, and I smiled weakly. "That's nice."

"I'm Jack Hamilton," Jack said, stretching his arm across the table to shake hands with Curt. "Merry's boyfriend."

Oh, Lord, I asked that it wouldn't get worse!

I still couldn't look at Curt who no doubt was wondering how he could have fallen for someone cowardly enough to keep Jack's presence a secret. Or maybe—and I almost gasped audibly at the thought—maybe he thought I was trying to be coy and play him against Jack!

"Her boyfriend?" Curt said. "Really?" I shivered as I heard the acid in his voice.

"Really," Jack said happily, complacently. "She's my best girl, my only girl." With a proprietary air, he slid his arm across my shoulders.

I jerked as the weight of his arm fell on me. When I did, my left elbow snapped forward, bumping hard into my Coke. It toppled, the lid popped off, and the dark liquid ran unerringly and with great speed across the table and into Curt's lap.

I groaned and squeezed my eyes shut.

Curt sputtered as the cold Coke drenched him. He jumped to his feet as much as he could in the booth and grabbed for a cluster of napkins. He built a paper dam to hold back the surging flood, but it breached the dam at the sides and made new caramel-colored spatters on his khakis.

Such was the state of my nerves that I started to giggle. I slapped a hand over my mouth, horrified at myself, but I couldn't stop.

"I'm sorry," I said or tried to say. I think I got as far as *I* before the giggles got me again. I may not be good at a lot, but at making a fool of myself, I'm first-rate.

"Are you okay, old man?" Jack asked Curt with a complete lack of genuine interest. If I wanted to think bad thoughts, I'd think Jack was enjoying the whole mess.

"Here." It was Airy thrusting a handful of napkins at Curt. She slapped others down on the soda on the table, sopping it up. She at least had been practical and run to the condiment stand where she'd grabbed as many napkins as were available.

"We need a cleanup over here," Sean called to a girl behind the counter. She nodded and disappeared into the back, never to return.

"Thanks," Curt said as he took the proffered napkins from Airy and brushed at his soaked pants. He tried to slide out of the booth without getting splattered any more and ended up sitting on a couple of ice cubes that had flown straight and true to where they could do the most damage.

"You'd better go home and get changed," said Jack blandly. "We wouldn't want you to catch a cold or anything. I'll take care of Merry."

He sounded so proprietary that I almost gagged. That's what happens, I told myself, when you neglect to tell someone that things have moved beyond his knowledge of the situation.

Curt looked at me and I looked sadly back. I had stopped giggling, but now all I wanted to do was cry. What must he think of me? Idiot? Fool? Keeper of dark secrets? He probably hated me for not being open with him.

Well, no, I caught myself. Not hate. That was too nasty a word for Curt. Maybe he just disliked me, thought I had deceived him, had duped him, had played him false, had hoodwinked him, had defrauded him, had taken him for a ride.

I took a deep breath. When I started reeling off synonyms, I was in way over my emotional head.

Too much for one day, Lord. Way too much.

"Merry, are you all right?" Curt asked quietly as he stood beside the booth.

I saw that he understood how confused, distressed, and embarrassed I felt. Maybe he even understood what a rotten person I was sometimes. Tears began to slide down my cheeks. I didn't deserve someone as nice as him to fall for me. I deserved someone insensitive and unfeeling like Jack. Not that I wanted him, but I deserved him.

Airy looked at me in surprise. "It's okay, Merry," she said kindly. "His slacks will clean."

Jack looked at me and stiffened when he saw the tears. "Geez, Louise, Merry. What's the big deal? It's only spilled soda."

"She's had a very bad night," Curt explained. "I need to get her home."

Everybody looked at me and all I could do was nod and sniff. I smiled a wobbly smile in Curt's direction and grabbed my scarf and purse. Not only did I need to get out of here before I made a greater fool of myself, I had to get Curt away before he mentioned the cause for my bad night. It appeared that Airy didn't yet know that Arnie was dead, and I didn't want to be there when she found out. Curt, of course, didn't realize the danger.

Poor Curt. It was hard to be a principal player in a story when you didn't know all the plotlines.

Airy looked at me and made concerned noises in her throat. She reached into her purse and pulled out her tissue packet and handed it to me. I took it with shaking hands and decided she definitely was nice.

"I'll be okay," I managed shakily. "Curt's right. I just need to get home."

Jack sat like a lump, blocking my exit. I nudged him pointedly. He looked at me and smiled. He didn't move.

"We all have bad days, Merry," he said with what he considered to be sympathy. "You just can't let it get to you."

"This was a bit more than your average bad day," Curt said as he reached over and wiped a tear from my cheek.

My heart swelled with delight. He was defending me in spite of what a dodo I'd been! How sweet!

"Let me out, Jack," I said. "Now."

Jack buckled under the gaze of the entire group and began to slide to the edge of the bench. I pushed him along as hard as I could. When I got free, I would just grab Curt's arm and pull him out of the place before he talked too much.

I heard Curt take a deep breath and saw Airy, Sean, and Jack look in his direction. Jack even stopped sliding to listen.

No, Lord! Please, no!

I socked Jack in the shoulder. "Move!" I hissed desperately but to no avail.

Curt the Kind, Defender of Distressed Damsels, said the inevitable. "Merry and a coworker found the coworker's husband murdered this evening."

Everybody blinked in surprise and turned to me. I smiled weakly and watched Airy for her reaction.

She saw me looking at her and began to draw back. I could see her taking "coworker" and running with it. "Who?" she asked with real fear.

"I'm sorry, Airy," I said sadly. "Arnie's dead."

"Arnie." It was a whisper. She staggered and her face lost its color. Sean grabbed her arm and lowered her to the chair across the aisle from us.

Curt looked at her, consternation on his face. "I'm sorry," he said. "I didn't know...."

I gave Jack a final shove and freed myself from the booth.

"They were old friends from school," I said, squeezing Curt's hand. "You couldn't have known." I knelt in front of Airy.

"Where? When? How?" she mumbled, her eyes bright with tears. "Who? Who would do a terrible thing like that to poor Arnie?"

"He was shot at his house sometime late this afternoon," I said. "Jolene and I found him lying on the kitchen floor." That warm, yellow room appeared in my mind, Arnie lying in the middle of the yellow tiles, and I felt sick all over again. "I have no idea who's responsible."

Airy shook her head at the enormity of it all. "I can't believe it! Why would anyone do that? Arnie was such a great guy." She looked at Sean, her great, gray eyes shimmering with tears.

Sean had his arm around Airy's shoulder. In a tight voice, he asked me, "You mean Arnie Meister, right?"

I nodded.

"Is that the guy from Bushay?" Jack asked Sean. "The guy I met yesterday?"

"Yeah," said Sean, shoulders slumping. "The guy in marketing. Airy's known him for years. They actually went together for several years before she met me." And he patted her shoulder awkwardly but tenderly.

"Wow," said Jack, shaking his head in amazement. "I never knew anyone who got murdered before."

We all chose to ignore his comment.

"I'm sorry, Airy," I said, taking her hands in mine. They were ice. She nodded dumbly.

Sean left her side, went to their table, and got her coat. He came back, pulled her to her feet, and helped her into the coat. He reached into her pockets and pulled out her gloves. She stuck her hands in them without being aware of what she did.

"Come on," Sean said to her as he pulled her hair over her collar. "We're going home." He handed Airy her purse.

She blinked, looked at the purse in her gloved hands, then reached for her neck. "My scarf," she said.

"Is it in your sleeve?" Sean asked.

She shook her head.

Curt moved to their table and checked the seats and the floor. He shook his head, too.

"It must be in the car, honey," Sean said. He pulled her collar up and kissed her. "Come on."

He took her elbow and led her outside. As soon as the door swung shut, Curt touched my arm and indicated the other door. I nodded and we turned to go.

"Merry, wait," Jack called as he ran to the table and grabbed his coat.

"Another time, Hamilton," Curt said as he let the door fall shut on Jack's protests.

I got into my car and drove home with Curt following in his car. I turned down the lane that led to the converted carriage house where I had an apartment and pulled into the little parking area. We walked down the sidewalk to my first-floor apartment, passing the great lilac tree, creaking in the cold.

Curt took my key from me, inserted it in the lock, and opened the door for me.

"Thanks," I said. "I'm sorry."

He looked down at me, his eyebrow arched above his glasses, his lips in a wry smile. He shook his head. "You are amazing."

"In a good sense like, 'Wow, you're amazing!' or in a bad sense as in, 'Ack, you're amazing'?"

"Both," he said.

I nodded. "I was afraid of that."

"But we'll talk about it another time. Right now you just need to get in there and get to bed."

"After I write my story."

That was the first time he noticed that I had my laptop slung over my shoulder.

"Merry!" he protested, ever my protector. "You've been through enough for one evening!"

I put my hand over his mouth. "Curt, we've had this discussion before. I have a job I love and I'm going to do it, even when it's difficult." I stared at him.

He just looked at me and shook his head. "Amazing." Then he bent to kiss me good night, his arms wrapping tightly about me. I hung on, drawing strength from his strength. His love and understanding scared me because they seemed too good to be true, but there was no doubt about it: He was a great hugger and kisser.

He finally pulled back and said huskily, "Good night, Merry."

He walked back to his car whistling *Merrily we roll along, roll along, roll along.*

He liked to whistle it, he said, because I was the only person he knew who had her own song.

I was smiling as I shut the door behind me. I was still smiling as I walked to answer the ringing phone.

"And just who was that big oaf kissing you on your front doorstep?" an angry voice demanded.

Chapter Six

Where are you, Jack?" I demanded after sputtering with anger for what felt like forever.

"Look out your window, sweetheart, and I'll wave to you."

The joys of cell phones. Anyone can call you from anywhere at anytime, even your own parking lot.

"You're spying on me!" I charged. "You followed me home!"

"Somebody's got to take care of you, baby, because you're sure not picking your company very well."

I pulled the phone from my ear and stared at it in disbelief. The nerve of the man!

"Who I come home with is my business, not yours," I hissed.

"Since when, sweetheart? What you do has been my business for more than six years."

I found myself shaking my head furiously. "No," I said. "Not anymore. And don't ever speak to me in that tone of voice again! And get out of my parking lot!" I put the receiver firmly back in its cradle.

"Whiskers, can you believe that?" I demanded.

Since Whiskers hadn't heard Jack's comments, he didn't answer, but he jumped onto the table beside the phone and reached for my arm. He wanted a good scratching. It had been a long, lonely day.

When the phone rang again, we both looked at it, but neither of us answered. I didn't need to be insulted again and neither did the cat. When the ringing persisted, I lifted the receiver, heard, "Merry!" in Jack's most critical tone, and replaced it in the cradle without saying a word.

I gathered Whiskers in my arms and, lugging him and my laptop, went to the bedroom. I put the cat on the bed and got into my warmest pajamas. I listened to the phone ring four more times, silenced each time only when I lifted the receiver and set it back down to break the connection. Then the doorbell rang, but I refused to answer. In no time, the phone rang again. I broke the connection, then reached behind the bedside table and unplugged the wire from the jack.

"Come on, baby," I said to him. "Let me give you some treats."

I padded to the kitchen, the cat following, purring loudly enough to wake the elderly retiree who lived in the other downstairs apartment in our four-unit converted carriage house. I pulled the jack out of the kitchen phone too, hoping nothing really important happened overnight because I certainly wasn't going to know about it if it did.

"It's my fault, Whiskers." I stared bleakly at the kitchen cabinet. "I never told him how different things were now." Whiskers ignored me, totally preoccupied with vacuuming up the treats I tossed down for him. "But I didn't really know he was even a consideration until Sunday. I hadn't heard a word for several months, then there was one phone call a couple of weeks ago, then nothing again. How was I supposed to know he'd decided what he decided?"

I put the cat treats away on the high shelf that Whiskers couldn't climb to and paused as a thought crystalized that made me furious all over again.

"And why would he think that I'd just be sitting around mooning over him anyway? Why would he think that when he said jump, I'd ask how high?" I glared at the cat who was now grooming himself with total disinterest in my monologue. "Because I was stupid enough to live that way for six years! That's why!"

I stalked back to the bedroom and climbed into bed. I stacked the pillows behind me and started writing. The adrenaline from my anger at both Jack and myself fueled me. An hour later I e-mailed two fifteen-inch stories on Arnie's murder to the paper, one straight news, the other a human interest piece. In the latter besides lots of stuff I knew from Jolene I included the innocuous statement Harry Allen Bushay had given me about Arnie's death.

"Arnold Meister was a reliable and able employee," Harry Allen had said for attribution as he and Curt and I left the Community Center earlier in the evening. "Bushay Environmental will certainly miss his contributions to our workforce."

Somehow the words hadn't sounded complimentary but critical when spoken, but they read nicely. I found the lack of any character qualities in the statement fascinating even though I had no idea what that absence meant, if anything.

Tomorrow morning I needed to call Harry Allen and probe. Tomorrow I'd also process my film and see what I had. Tonight, though, I was shot. Wasted. Wrung out. Drained. Fatigued. Bone weary.

Still I picked up my Bible from my nightstand and read for a bit. I was reading the Christmas story from Matthew's gospel this week. Then I planned to do the same in Luke. Since this was going to be a very untraditional Christmas for me, I decided the comfort of the familiar story might help me feel less abandoned. Certainly Mary and Joseph had found themselves alone in more unique circumstances than I could even imagine. If they could do it, so could I. Of course, God was directly involved in their story; it is, after all, his story too.

But I was a Christian. That meant he was involved in my story too. "I will never leave you nor forsake you," he had said.

Lord, you know how alone I'm feeling. You know that everything that's ever been Christmas to me—except you, of course—is in Pittsburgh. Mom, Dad, Sam, Grandmom Kramer, Aunt Sissy, and Uncle Arch. What am I supposed to do on Christmas this year? Watch Whiskers open his rubber mouse?

Maybe you could encourage Maddie and Doug to ask me over? What are best friends for if not to make Christmas less lonely? Or maybe Curt would ask me over or out to dinner or something? I've been praying about this for a couple of weeks now, and so far nothing's happened. I don't mean to complain, Lord. I really don't. Well, maybe I do, just a bit. But please, Lord, don't let me be alone.

Suddenly Arnie swept across my mind. Poor Arnie. No more Christmas worries for him. And poor Jolene and Mr. and Mrs. Luray.

Okay, Lord. So my situation isn't as bad as lots of people's. But that doesn't mean it's good either, you know.

I sighed so loudly that Whiskers raised his head and blinked at me.

"Sorry, baby," I said. I scratched behind his ears as he purred sleepily. Then I lay down. I was certain I wouldn't sleep. I was too keyed up about Christmas and about Arnie and about Jack and Curt. But I was also exhausted. To my surprise my alarm wakened me Wednesday morning before I even realized I had slept.

As soon as I thought the dry cleaners would be open, I slipped out of the newsroom and dropped off the plastic bag, my coat, scarf, and gloves now stashed inside with Jolene's things.

"How's next Friday for pickup?" the woman behind the counter asked.

I blinked. "Next Friday? But the sign in the window says you have twenty-four-hour service."

"That's only if you ask."

"I'm asking," I said. "We need these things back. That's my new coat in there." Like she actually cared.

The lady hummed "Silent Night" as she wrote out the slips. I checked them when she handed them to me and almost swallowed my tongue.

"These prices are unbelievable," I protested, pointing to them just like she hadn't seen them recently.

She shrugged. "Yeah, I know. Twenty-four-hour service is expensive. And that coat's leather and fur."

"Fake fur," I said.

"Real fur," she said. "And blood's hard to get out. Were you guys in an accident or something?" She looked me over, searching for injuries.

I didn't want to discuss Arnie with her, so I said, "Sort of."

I was still reeling from the price as I drove back to *The News*, but I figured Jolene could handle the costs since she was, as she had said, rich.

Which brought an ugly thought to my mind. If Arnie had had enough money for all that electricity and the glorious house to shine it in, who inherited that money? Jolene? Surely that wasn't why she declared she was rich, was it? Talk about a motive that screamed, "Look at me!"

And where had that money come from to begin with? I distinctly remembered Jo telling me that Arnie's family had no money and that he went to college on scholarships. Though a job in "marketing" undoubtedly paid better than anything his mother had ever seen, it didn't pay on the scale I'd witnessed.

At least it didn't pay legally.

Immediately my mind began spinning. Bushay Environmental. I'd heard about corruption in the waste management business almost all my life. Was Harry Allen Bushay dumping illegally? There were vast tracts of open land, thousands of rushing streams, and huge stands of deciduous and evergreen forests in sparsely populated central Pennsylvania. Of potential secret dumping sites there was no end. Was Arnie facilitating or organizing such activity? Was that how he got his money? Was activity like that possible with the tight laws we now had on the books?

There were a couple of even more scary questions if any of this were true. Did Jolene know where Arnie got his money? Did she care?

Was I going crazy, groping, stretching, reaching beyond the possible or probable? Or was I on the trail of a big story?

Only time and some deep digging would tell. When I got back to the office, I immediately made a phone call.

"Bushay Environmental, Caroline speaking," said a lilting voice. It must be Caroline, recently returned from Hollywood, if I remembered correctly. Bless little Amhearst. "How may I help you?"

"Hi, Caroline," I said. "Welcome back!" I tried to sound enthusiastic and friendly, not at all like a reporter.

"Thanks," she said. "It's good to be back."

"You don't miss the bright lights?"

Caroline laughed. "Well, sort of. But I decided I liked eating regularly better than being blinded by bright lights."

I laughed too and decided Caroline was probably going to be all right back here at home. "Look, I'm calling for some information about any publications I might read to learn more about the waste management business," I said.

"Well." She was polite but hesitant. She was, after all, still fairly new to the job. "I know we get a publication called *Waste News* around here. It's an industry newsletter."

"Great," I said, jotting the title down. "Just what I needed to know. Thanks." Then, as if it were an afterthought, I asked, "Could you connect me with Elsa?"

I hoped she didn't say "Elsa who?" because I didn't think Elsa-the-sister-of-the-hostess-at-Ferretti's would be a satisfactory answer.

"Sure. Just a minute. If I disconnect you, call back, okay? I'm still learning this phone system."

I wasn't disconnected and in a minute I was talking with Elsa.

"Hi, Elsa. I saw Astrid the other day." I wanted to establish some kind of contact before she realized she hadn't the vaguest idea who she was talking to.

"Ah. You must have eaten at Ferretti's."

"I did," I agreed. "Great food."

"Well, she and Dom pour their whole lives into that place. I keep telling her she works too hard, but does she listen?"

"You know what sisters are like," I said sympathetically. "But I didn't call to talk about Astrid. I really called about Arnie Meister."

She let out a sigh. "I tell you," she said, her voice heavy, "I can't believe it. I really can't. I went to school with Arnie, you know."

"I know," I said. "That's why I called you. Are they planning anything for him at work? Like a memorial? And could an outsider like me come?"

"I don't know what we're going to do yet," she said. "It's too soon. But I'm sure the family's going to plan something, don't you think?"

"What family?" I asked bluntly.

Elsa sighed again. "Tell me about it. It's so sad! I never understood why Jolene would leave Arnie. I mean, rich, handsome, and nice. What more could a girl want? Of course I never understood why he married her to begin with. Not after sweet Airy all those years!"

"I bet everyone at work liked him, didn't they?"

"Oh, yeah. What's not to like?"

"Even Mr. Bushay?"

"Mr. Bushay likes everybody," she said, though I thought maybe I detected a bit of hesitation.

"Oh, I guess I misunderstood. I thought Arnie and Mr. Bushay were having some problems. Maybe I just heard wrong."

"What do you mean?" She was suddenly cautious.

"I heard they had a fight just the other day. I mean, wasn't that a shocker?" I tried to sound properly scandalized. "Here are these two great people, and suddenly they're fighting!"

"I know," she agreed, clearly still upset by the memory. She hesitated again, but I could tell she wanted to say more. I waited. "I heard their voices through the door, you know?"

"You heard the whole thing?" I didn't have to pretend to be stunned. I was.

"Well, yes and no. I heard their voices roaring at each other the whole time, but the words were muffled by that big door of his."

"So you couldn't understand any of it?"

She hesitated. I waited, holding my breath. Finally she said, "If I didn't know better, I'd say they were arguing about the Communists."

"The Communists? But who argues about the Communists these days?" And what could they possibly have to do with waste management and illegal dumping?

"I know. It doesn't make any sense, does it? But I think I heard Commies this and Communists that."

"Amazing, Elsa. And weird." Disappointing was what it really was. Here I'd thought I was onto some good information. "Well, let me know if you're doing anything for Arnie. And may I speak to Mr. Bushay, please? He's such a hard guy to get hold of, you know."

"Oh, not really." She almost giggled. "It's not golf season."

"But where was he yesterday afternoon? Answer me that."

"Well, he did take a really long lunch, but he was here from three on. You must have called early in the afternoon."

"Where does he go for these long lunches, Elsa? Ferretti's isn't exactly high-roller territory."

She actually laughed. "He hates Ferretti's, though of course I'd never tell Astrid. She'd want me to quit out of loyalty to her and Dom. I think it was the red cabbage in the Caesar salad that finally got to him. He always goes to the Country Club."

"Even in the off season?"

"Sure. They've got a great cook."

I smiled to myself. I could easily check this lead out. I made my voice brisk and businesslike again. "Well, he's in now, isn't he?"

"Oh. Yes." She had forgotten that I hadn't called to speak with her. "Of course. Who may I say is calling?"

"Merry Kramer."

There was a pause during which she must have realized she didn't know any Merry Kramer. Then I heard the silence of being on hold. Finally Harry Allen's voice boomed in my ear. "Merry Kramer! What a wonderful pleasure!" He made it sound as if my call had made his day. "And when will the article and picture about the Amhearst Annual Food Project be in *The News*? Do you need some more information?"

"Actually, sir, I'm—"

"Sir?" I could hear the pretended horror in his voice. "Sir? My dear Merry. You make me sound like an old man! It's Harry Allen to you."

"Thank you," I mumbled. "Ah, Harry Allen, I wanted to ask you—"

"Are you all ready for Christmas, Merry? Do you have your shopping done? Will you be spending the holiday with your family?"

"I'm afraid I won't be able to get home this year," I said. "Christmas will be somewhat solitary." Somewhat? Totally!

"Yes," he said, his voice several decibels softer with sympathy. "I know what you mean. My wife and I are separated, and Christmas is always a lonely time." He sighed. Then abruptly he said, "I must go, Merry. A very important call has just come in. Any questions about the food project can be handled by my secretary. Thank you for calling." And he was gone.

I put the phone back in its cradle thoughtfully. Harry Allen Bushay wasn't a stupid man. He knew exactly what I wanted to talk about. He just didn't want to talk about it with me.

Communists, Elsa had said. Was there such a thing as selling waste management secrets to—who? Who were the Communists these days? Anyone besides Fidel Castro? So assumption number one had to be that Elsa had misunderstood. Whatever they had argued about, it wasn't political.

Had Harry Allen caught Arnie in some illegality? Did he hope to protect his company's reputation by keeping such actions by one of his employees quiet? If he wanted it kept quiet, he certainly wouldn't murder the guy and attract all that attention, would he?

Or was he protecting himself? Maybe it was the other way around and Arnie had caught Harry Allen out and Harry Allen felt he had no option but to kill his accuser.

And just where was Harry Allen early yesterday afternoon? At the Country Club eating lunch for three hours? My list of things to learn was growing by the minute.

I turned to my computer and went to the Internet. When it asked me for an address, I typed in Waste News as two words. Nothing. I tried it as one word, two caps. Zip. All caps. Zip. No caps. Bingo. I was in a website for *Waste News.*

I quickly skimmed the news briefs and found several that dealt with shenanigans by carters and haulers. Men in New York and Chicago were being tried for everything from extortion, racketeering, and price fixing to illegal dumping. The briefs neglected to say how they had been found out.

I clicked on a New Products and Technology site and learned more than I wanted about new balers, new pumps, new composting systems, and new truck cleaning systems. Considering what they hauled in those trucks, the latter seemed very practical and pertinent to me.

I linked to the web page of the Solid Waste Association of America and learned about WASTECON, the big annual convention. I linked to Region 3—Delaware, District of Columbia,

Maryland, Pennsylvania, Virginia, and West Virginia—and found EPA regulations and news.

Noting links to several other organizations and publications, I signed off for the moment. I could find out some basic industry information without too much difficulty, but could I find out anything about Bushay Environmental or Harry Allen Bushay specifically?

For the next little bit I scrambled like crazy trying to get both Jolene's work and mine done. She, of course, had not come into the newsroom today. I realized quite quickly that I'd underrated Jolene's contribution to *The News*. Her dumb blonde act covered a very organized mind, and she did a lot more than make the newsroom resemble the Philadelphia Flower Show. As the day wore on, I began to feel more and more like the proverbial sluggard to Jolene's ant. She had lists for everything, even her watering schedule. She had all her correspondence up-to-date, all the filing done, and I realized with a shock that she was our excellent clipping service.

"Go to the ant, thou sluggard," I muttered in King James. "Consider her ways and be wise."

When I got a minute, I sat down and worked on the list of all the times I'd seen Jolene in *The News* office yesterday afternoon, just as Sergeant Poole had requested. I'd fax my list as soon as I finished. Being Jolene's alibi was the least I could do for her, and the quicker I could do it, the easier her life would be. To my surprise, the list was very short.

I'd seen her return to the newsroom after lunch.

I'd seen her when she saved the life of the grape ivy.

I'd seen her when she wanted to leave at five.

For the almost four hours in between I hadn't consciously noticed her—which of course meant absolutely nothing, right? At least I certainly hoped so. I decided I wouldn't fax my non-list after all. I'd wait until someone showed up to collect it. Why prejudice the authorities against my friend any earlier than needed?

I'd processed my pictures from the murder scene first thing in the morning, and I laid them out on my desk again. I was as drawn to the shots of Jolene as a voyeur to an uncurtained bedroom window. I had inadvertently created as compelling a record of her innocence as I could imagine. Her shock and distress were evident. Certainly when Sergeant Poole saw the copies I'd messengered to him, he'd realize her innocence. The traditional suspect, the spouse, would fade from the list of possible perps, and her unaccounted afternoon would be immaterial.

When I found myself studying Jo's eye makeup in one of the pix and wondering how she applied it so neatly, I realized I had wandered far from my purpose. I scooped her photos into a pile and turned them facedown. It was time to study the other pictures without the emotional distraction of these.

I turned to the kitchen shots I'd snapped while Jolene and I waited for the police. They seemed utterly innocuous to me. No matter how I studied them, I always ended up with the same things: trash, dirty glasses, a bullet in the cabinet, and notes on the refrigerator.

I studied the trash. I'd read enough mysteries to know that collections of things always held hidden clues, but I certainly couldn't figure out what they might be. Orange juice containers were orange juice containers. Frozen dinner wrappers were frozen dinner wrappers. Clear plastic was clear plastic, and if it had packaged something significant, I sure couldn't tell what it was.

And the drinking glasses. It was the same thing. Dirty glasses were dirty glasses. There was no poison in the dregs as far as I knew, and even if there was, it was immaterial. Arnie had been shot. If there were fingerprints on the surfaces, I couldn't identify them. That was a police matter, and I could only hope they'd be kind enough to share what they found with me. I made a note to check.

I studied the picture of the bullet in the cabinet. I knew the police would be able to find out a lot of information about the bullet, but unless someone found the gun that the bullet came from, the value of that information was limited.

I was intrigued, though, by the certificate that read $50,000. What did it mean? Salary? His, hers, or theirs? The amount owed on the mortgage? Considering that house, the figure was more likely the amount owed each month. Or maybe it was the amount paid or demanded for an illegal dumping activity? Now that was something everyone posted on their fridge. So what did it mean? And how could I ever find out?

When I finally had time to talk to Mac after lunch, we didn't discuss my questions about the murder. I wasn't willing to reveal my detectival inclinations just yet lest his ribald and caustic humor have a field day at my expense. I needed to do more work, to have something besides questions, before I suggested anything to him.

"Nice articles on the murder," he said as he poured water from his coffee mug onto the African violets. I decided it wouldn't be prudent to tell him that you shouldn't pour water on their leaves. The plants would probably survive their improper watering, but I might not live through his rebuttal.

He saw me smirking at his housekeeping and snarled, "One word to anyone about this and their keeping gets written into your job description."

I held up my hands and bit the inside of my mouth so not a trace of a smile showed. "Would I ever mock you?"

"Any day you thought you could get away with it. Now, anything about who killed Arnie?"

I shook my head. "I've been on the phone several times with Sergeant Poole. They're waiting for autopsy reports, for interviews, stuff like that. I thought I'd go out to His House while we wait. I'll interview Dawn Trauber and see how that story develops."

He nodded. "She's really pretty," he said, his voice strangely wistful. "A class act."

I looked at him. When he teased me and asked me out, there was never that longing note in his voice. I thought of Dawn's picture with her warm smile, her kind eyes. "I didn't realize you knew her," I said.

"I don't. Not really. I've just met her at civic events or at brief interviews. Stuff like that. Nothing substantive. She probably doesn't even remember me."

I nodded and started to turn away.

"Think she'd go out with me?"

I blinked and stared at Mac. Where had that come from? He saw my stare and immediately regretted his comment. I realized it would be wise for me to see a joke where one hadn't been intended.

I leaned over and said conspiratorially, "I bet she'd go to church with you."

He looked as startled as I had a minute ago, then saw by my face that I was trying to be funny. "You don't know what you're talking about," he huffed.

"You're right," I agreed, "but I bet I'm right." This time I walked to my desk.

"Merry," Mac called as I walked out the door in my old navy coat. "Pa-rum-pa-pum-pum."

I nodded. "Pa-rum-pa-pum-pum."

Welcome to His House," Dawn Trauber said a short time later. Her smile was wide, her brown eyes alight with goodwill. She stood back for me to walk into the large front hall of the great Victorian that housed the ministry she managed.

I looked around with undisguised interest. The rooms on either side of the front hall, painted a warm cream with mossy green carpeting laid wall to wall, were used as office space. I could see a woman busy at a computer, a man reading reports, and a woman in a glass-enclosed area talking earnestly with a girl.

"Betty here works full-time in the office and her husband Ken is our maintenance guy. They have an apartment over the garage and live on site." Betty glanced up from her computer and smiled.

Dawn indicated the woman in the glass cubicle with the girl. "Julie is our counselor. She has an apartment on the third floor. Roger here is a lawyer and board member who comes in at least weekly to be certain we're in compliance with the law in any area we might touch on state or federal regulations."

Julie, behind her soundproof glass and deep in conversation, was unaware of my presence, but Roger looked up and smiled.

Small poinsettias sat on Betty's desk and a table in the hallway. A large artificial tree sparkled in the great room that stretched across the middle of the house. Someone had plastered the bulletin board over the hall table with a mix of Christmas cards and pictures of babies in cute and overly-cute Christmas outfits. Gold tinsel outlined the collection and paper chains sprinkled with glitter hung everywhere imaginable.

"There's a lot of Christmas glitz here," Dawn said. "The girls love decorations, and their idea of beauty is often—" She shook her head in mock horror. "But they're fifteen, sixteen, and seventeen," she said in explanation.

As we walked into the great room, I could see what she meant even more clearly. While the carpeting was the same mossy green and the sofas and chairs were muted cream, forest, and crimson plaids and stripes, the decorations were another story. The tree held the gaudiest of baubles, and on the top bough perched an immense angel in a violent violet robe and sparkly golden wings. String after string of twinkle lights blinked off and on in oddly unsyncopated patterns.

"Very cheery," I said, trying to put a positive spin on what looked a decorator's nightmare.

Dawn grinned. "Yeah. They're working to keep their Christmas spirits in spite of their situations."

I nodded. I understood the fragility of seasonal emotions. Last night when I'd answered the phone to hear Jack's outraged voice, I'd lost my Christmas spirit, at least temporarily. And whenever I thought of Pittsburgh, well ...

The unknowing object of Mac's interest sat across from me on a hunter sofa piped in crimson. She looked friendly and charming and very competent. Maybe there was more to Mac than I thought if he was attracted to someone like Dawn. Maybe he wasn't suffering just a Christmas guilt trip but a compelling need to analyze his life. Maybe he was examining his priorities and finding them empty. Maybe he wanted to change. Maybe he felt the need for God and was searching.

Maybe I was reading too much into one short comment.

Behind Dawn the tree lights blinked madly, enough to give anyone with brain wave difficulties a major seizure and me a splitting headache.

"Can you stand the blinking?" Dawn asked with sympathy. "I can unplug it." And she got up and did so. She was wearing jeans and a bright red sweater with a Frosty the Snowman on her right shoulder. She saw me looking at it. "Lonni gave it to me," she said. "I've got to wear it."

"How old's Lonni?" I asked.

"Seventeen. She's one of the older ones. At the other end of the spectrum there's Karyn with a Y. She's thirteen. The boy's fourteen."

"Thirteen!" I knew babies were having babies, but thirteen!

"Her mother brings her in each day for counseling. Julie's talking with her now."

"Do you counsel many girls who don't live here?"

Dawn nodded. "We have an extensive outpatient counseling program, though no one else is Karyn's age, thank goodness! She's such a sweet girl, young for her age. She brings a different stuffed animal with her every day." Her eyes got a sad, faraway look. "She didn't even know what was happening to her."

At that moment a bright-eyed, well-groomed, healthy child appeared in the doorway, her pregnancy far advanced, a Pooh Bear cradled in her arm.

"Hey, Karyn," Dawn said, rising, the sad look banished. "How are you feeling today?"

"I'm getting kicked to death, Miss Trauber."

Dawn laughed. "I just bet you are. It won't be long now."

"Mom and I have our bags packed," Karyn said. "Maybe I'll have a Christmas baby, just like Mary." Her face shone at the idea.

"Maybe," Dawn said.

"Then every year everyone will think of my baby when they sing about Jesus." She hugged Pooh. "Wouldn't that be great?" Her face grew pensive. "But he'll always get cheated on birthday gifts, won't he? That'll be really sad. But—" The smile reappeared. "—it'll be worth it to share Jesus' birthday."

Dear God, I asked, *how can such innocence and naiveté be having a baby?*

The front door opened and a woman came in.

"Hey, Mom," said Karyn. "Let me get my coat." She put Pooh down and grabbed a Land's End Squall from the clothes tree in the corner. It zipped over her amplitude, and I realized it was probably her father's coat, borrowed for the duration. She gathered Pooh and walked smiling to the door. Her mother, haggard and in obvious emotional pain, followed.

"Her mother says that every time she looks at Karyn, it's a knife in the heart," Dawn said.

I looked at the closed door. "I can't even imagine."

Suddenly the door flew open and several girls in various stages of pregnancy fell in. Instantly the air was crackling with energy.

"Hey, Miss Trauber," called a tall, skinny girl with a ponytail and a tummy of magnificent proportions.

"Hey, Pam. How are you feeling today?"

"Let me tell you, sitting in school is getting harder and harder every day! I want this baby to come now! I got to be able to breathe again, you know?"

The other girls all laughed with understanding as they thundered toward the stairs and their rooms above. One of the girls grabbed *The News* on her way past. The sports pages were on top, and I thought Larry Schimmer, our sports guy, would be glad to know he'd been read.

"Was that Karyn leaving?" Pam asked, pausing with one foot on the stairs.

Dawn nodded.

"Poor kid," said Pam. "We pray for her all the time."

The other girls nodded agreement.

"It's bad enough for us," said the girl with the paper. "But she's a baby!"

And they were gone.

Dawn smiled as she resumed her seat beside me. "You can see why I'm very hesitant to have the girls themselves featured in the paper. Legal issues aside since they're all underage, they don't need the publicity. Nor do their parents."

I thought of Karyn's mother and had to agree.

"We have eight girls currently in residence," Dawn said, "and half of them are here with the full support of their parents. The others are having great problems with family. All but one are having trouble of one kind or another with the babies' fathers or his family. They've come to us at various points in their pregnancies, and we keep them through delivery and, if they give their babies up for adoption, for a month or more after they deliver."

I looked at her in surprise. "Even those who are getting along well with their families?"

Dawn nodded. "We keep them beyond delivery to help them through the grieving process. Giving up a baby is like a death, you know. Everyone else tells them to forget what happened, to put it behind them, to get on with their lives. They mean to be kind, but they aren't. Emotional chasms take considerable time to climb out of. We let the girls cry and talk about their babies. We listen to their dreams and prayers for the little one they gave up, their worries about the people who have taken him or her. We look at the newborn pictures over and over and over because they need someone to do that with them."

I didn't tell Dawn, but I'd tended to be one of the get-over-it people. Not that many people I knew gave up their babies. Most of them kept them and began the complicated dance of survival that goes with single motherhood, educational needs, jobs, social stagnation, and loneliness. Still adoption had always fascinated me. "Do many of your girls give their babies up for adoption?"

"A lot more than the national average," Dawn said.

Pressure, I immediately thought. *Oh, I hope they don't put pressure on these girls.*

Dawn understood my unspoken thought. "We're careful to put no pressure on these girls. We present to them all the options with their difficulties and benefits. To adopt or keep is one of the most difficult and far-reaching decisions of these girls' lives. They have to reach whatever conclusion they make themselves."

I knew from my research that about ninety-five percent of the unmarried girls who had babies kept their children. "Why are your numbers different from the general norm?" I asked.

"Two reasons, I think," Dawn said.

But I didn't learn those reasons. A scream caused us both to turn abruptly toward the steps. The girl who had retrieved *The News* sat there, her hand pressed over her mouth, a look of horror on her face. I thought she had gone upstairs with the rest.

"Lonni!" Dawn ran to her. "What's wrong? Where do you hurt?"

Lonni looked at Dawn, shook her head, and hand still pressed to her lips, raced outside, *The News* scattering across the floor in her wake. Dawn raced after her.

I watched them go and thought that it wasn't a physical problem that had made Lonni cry out. No one in the throes of pain could run so agilely and quickly. So something else had distressed her.

I gathered the paper thoughtfully and folded it into a neat pile. Had something in here caused that flight? I figured that the one person I couldn't hold accountable was Larry Schimmer, the sports guy. Lonni should have been well finished with that section, even if she'd read it thoroughly which she probably hadn't. And no one would react to the latest win or loss of the Amhearst Avengers so radically.

On the sheet facing me was a headline that read *Youth Held in Hit and Run.* Another said *Underage Drunk Driver Goes to Trial in Deaths.* Did she know these boys? Was one of them her baby's father? Was that what set her off?

As I pondered that interesting and appalling idea, another scream cut the air. This one came from upstairs. Immediately voices called and feet ran and an excited young face peered over the railing from upstairs.

"Miss Trauber! Miss Trauber! It's Pam! Her water just broke! I think she's in labor!"

My heart stopped momentarily. Then I rushed to the door where Dawn had disappeared. I looked madly to the right and left and saw Dawn and Lonni huddled under a bare beech tree in the back-yard. They were deep in conversation, and I hesitated. What if I was interrupting some major discussion?

Then another scream sounded from upstairs and my decision was made.

"Dawn," I yelled. "Dawn! Pam's in labor!"

Dawn and Lonni looked at me, at each other, and ran for the house. On the step, Dawn paused.

"Lonni, we'll talk again. We're not finished."

Lonni said nothing, but she looked angry and balky.

Suddenly the whole complement of girls rushed down the stairs, Pam in their middle. One held her hand, another had her suitcase, and a third had a big red Bible. I felt like I should boil water or tear sheets or something.

Pam looked both shocked and elated. "This is it, Miss Trauber," she whispered, holding her belly.

Dawn grinned and grabbed Pam in a bear hug. "Dear Jesus, be with Pam! Take care of her and this wonderful baby. Give them safety. Give Pam joy."

As the girls all but shouted "Amen!" Pam groaned again with pain.

"Blow!" yelled Lonni. "Come on, Pam. Out your mouth! Wush, wush, wush!"

"She doesn't want to breathe," said one of the girls with a scared half-smile. "She wants drugs."

Everyone laughed as Pam nodded vigorously.

"Car's ready." It was Julie, the counselor. "Here's your bag, Dawn. You guys have a wonderful time. We'll be fine until you get back."

Dawn helped Pam into the backseat and a reclining position. She noticed me as she climbed behind the wheel.

"I don't know how long this will take," she called. "I'll contact you in a day or so, okay?"

I nodded. As we all waved good-bye, Lonni yelled, "Call us, okay? Call us as soon as anything happens!"

We walked inside with a mix of contained excitement and anti-climax. There was still a lot to happen, but we were no longer directly involved.

I asked Julie, "Will Dawn stay the whole time?"

Julie nodded. "She's Pam's coach. She's there for as long as it takes."

"That's nice," I said.

Julie looked at me with a raised eyebrow. "No, it's not. It's necessary. Pam has no one else."

"No one?" I thought of the tall, outgoing girl.

"No one. Her father she never knew. And her mother left town three weeks ago for parts unknown. Her brother's in jail. She absolutely *needs* Dawn and me and the other girls." She gestured at the others as all but Lonni straggled back upstairs. She stood in the corner hugging *The News*.

I nodded at Julie, realizing that I couldn't begin to imagine the magnitude of Pam's need, but beginning to get a small understanding of what His House was all about.

Pa-rum-pa-pum-pum, Lord.

"Besides that," said Julie, "a first pregnancy is a first pregnancy and a first baby is a first baby. It should always be treated as the miracle it is, regardless of the situation. Dawn's there to hold Pam's hand and count the time lapse between contractions and give her a drink whenever she needs it. She'll encourage her when she wants to give up. She'll push her hair from her forehead and mop her sweat and hug her and get giddy when the baby finally comes. And she'll weep with her when she kisses her baby good-bye." Julie looked at me to see if I understood. "Dawn'll give Pam positive, godly memories of an otherwise terrible, terrible time."

I walked slowly to the door, thinking of what Julie had said. And I'd thought Karyn naive.

I was so lost in thought that I jumped when Lonni said in my ear, "Excuse me. Did I hear you say you were looking for a girl to interview?"

I looked at her and nodded.

"Well, I'd like to give an interview," she said, her voice hard enough to cut glass. "I've got lots to say."

I smiled. "That would be wonderful. When do you want to talk?"

"Now?" she said. "I want to tell you all about the person who has made my life a living hell."

I looked at the girl with concern. It seemed obvious that whether she had information for my story or not, she needed to talk. Dawn had left with Pam, so I was now to be her listener.

"Come on," I said, heading for the sofa where I'd recently sat with Dawn. She followed me and flopped awkwardly down. As I watched her try to find a comfortable place to put her arms, I guessed her to be about six months pregnant.

"You know," she said, "you think there's someone you can really trust, and then all of a sudden you find out how wrong you were!" She fell silent, but her whole countenance screamed rage.

"A guy?" I asked. Given her situation, it didn't seem a huge risk.

"Oh, yeah." She stretched her hand out toward me, looking oddly vulnerable for someone so angry. "I can't believe how he turned on me!"

As I opened my mouth to say, "Tell me," five girls came running down the stairs and flopped in the various chairs and sofas about the room. One grabbed the TV remote and what I imagined to be the first of several programs that ran for the rest of the evening flashed onto the screen.

"We were talking!" Lonni yelled.

The girls looked at her and shrugged. "So who's stopping you?" one asked.

I looked at Lonni and patted her hand. "We can talk later."

She scowled furiously at me, but I knew she wasn't angry at me. The rest of the world maybe, and some guy in particular, but not me. "Saturday," she said. "I'll meet you at Ferretti's. Then no one will interrupt us." And she stalked upstairs to brood.

Chapter Seven

One of the first things I did when I got to work Thursday morning was call Sergeant Poole to see what was new on the Arnie Meister murder.

"Ah, Merry. Such a delight to hear your voice so early in the morning," he said. He was so good at PR that I almost believed him.

"Has the autopsy report come back yet?" I asked.

"As a matter of fact I have it on my desk in front of me as we speak."

"And?" I prompted when he stopped speaking.

"Patience, patience. I'm opening the folder, not stonewalling you. Here we go. Arnold James Meister, age twenty-seven, was shot with a .38 caliber handgun, probably a Smith and Wesson. That finding is consistent with the bullet recovered from a cabinet in the Meister kitchen. The bullet has been sent to the state police lab for further analysis. The shot entered Mr. Meister's lower left chest, traveled on a slightly upward angle, emerging just below his left shoulder blade. There was great internal trauma in spite of the through-and-through wound, but the cause of death was basically exsanguination and shock. We're just lucky that the bullet didn't distort inside the body. At least we've got some information from ballistics."

"Tell me more about the gun. What's it like?"

"If it's an S&W .38 Special like we think, it's double action. That means it's a gun that doesn't need cocking and has no safety. You pull the trigger and that's it. It's a good gun for quick action, but you have no room for error with it."

"Thanks. And do you know who used this gun yet?" I asked, typing as we talked.

"The investigation is moving apace. We are doing everything in our power to bring to justice the person responsible for this most heinous crime."

"That's it, William? No suspects? No motives?"

"That's all I've got to say, Merry." He was so polite I wanted to scream.

"What about fingerprints on the glasses in the sink?"

"The FBI has them and will run them through AFIS." AFIS—Automated Fingerprint Identification System—is a great aid in law enforcement with its millions of prints on file for comparison. But it only works if there's an exemplar fingerprint to match the questioned print against. "We don't know anything yet. But don't hold your breath on this."

"What," I hastened to ask before he hung up on me, "did Harry Allen Bushay and Arnie Meister fight about the day before Arnie died?"

There was a short silence. "I'll call you when we have anything to add to what I've already said." And he was gone.

I shrugged and pulled out my pictures from the scene. I hadn't really expected an answer to that last question, just hoped.

I took the pictures to Mac, and much as he wanted an interesting picture of the murder scene for today's paper, I had none that were usable. They were all too static, totally unacceptable. He had to settle for a picture of Sergeant Poole and the coroner talking together. He was also less than happy with "the investigation is moving apace."

"Apace? Apace? He actually said 'moving apace'?" He leaned back in his new executive's chair and scowled at me like it was my fault the sergeant used archaic words. "He actually said 'heinous crime'?"

"Mac," I said, ignoring his pique. I checked over my shoulder to be certain no one was close enough to hear me. "You don't think Jolene had anything to do with this, do you?"

He looked at me, absolutely flabbergasted. "Jolene, the Queen of Confusion? The Mistress of Melodrama? The High Priestess of Hypochondria?"

If that were me talking, all that alliteration would have meant real concern about Jolene, but I think all it meant in Mac was overkill. "I don't really think she did it either," I said. "I just don't know where she was Tuesday afternoon."

"Don't worry," he said. "She was out running errands for me."

"She was?"

"She was," Mac repeated. "I've talked to the police several times, and they've got a copy of my list of errands. I can only assume they're checking with the stores and such for verification."

I don't know whether he could read my face or whether he was just feeling openhanded. Either way, Mac said, "Here." And he handed me a piece of paper. "Check them yourself if it'll make you feel better. But don't bother to check Staples. I have the receipt and the office supplies. Or the MAC machine. She gave me the receipt and the cash she withdrew for me. Or the grocery store. I got the orange juice and bread I asked for. Or the drugstore. I got the prescription and the athlete's foot stuff. Or Bob's Books. She brought me the books and did so without telling me what she thought of my reading habits, which is more than I can say for Bob. Or the Hallmark store. She brought me the Christmas cards. But you can check the other places."

"You sent her on private errands on company time? I am shocked."

He looked at me, not quite certain whether I was teasing or not. Neither was I.

"When I'm editor for real, I'll be more careful," he assured me.

Right.

I glanced at the list he'd handed me. Hennessey's Pharmacy. Bob's Books. Staples. A MAC machine. Grocery store. Hannah's Hallmark Center. "There are no other places left to check," I said. "You have proof she was at every one."

"Sort of puts a hole in your Jolene as murderer theory, doesn't it."

"Um." I thought for a minute. "Ah-hah! But when was she there?"

"What?"

"When? When did you send her on the errands? When did she come back?"

He looked at me and shook his head. "You're hopeless. Are you sure you weren't Nancy Drew in a previous life?"

"I never had a previous life. This is my one and only. Now come on. When did she leave?"

"Well, you and she made that ghastly public spectacle of yourselves in the ladies' room at Ferretti's."

"How'd you hear about that?"

"I have my sources."

"Astrid," I said. Mac ate there all the time. "And it wasn't me. Just she."

Mac looked skeptical but said nothing. "Then she came in and went to her desk. Then you came in and we talked about His House. Then the plant attacked you. Then I sent her out. Must have been about 1:30-ish."

I nodded. "Good. Good. Now when did she come back?"

Mac thought. "About 4:45. At least that's when she gave me the things."

"It took her more than three hours? But everything except Staples is right here in Amhearst. And Staples is only fifteen minutes away by the bypass."

"So she got stuck in traffic."

We looked at each other, speculation dancing in the air between us.

"Do you have the receipts?" I asked. "They'll have the time on them. At least Staples and the MAC machine will. And probably the grocery store."

Mac spun around and pulled out a file drawer. He rifled papers for a minute, then pulled out a Staples receipt. I leaned across his desk to read over his shoulder. In the upper right-hand section of the receipt, just below the name, address, and phone number of the store was the date, 12/18. Immediately following was 02:38 P.M.

"How about your withdrawal slip for the MAC machine?" I asked.

He stuffed the Staples receipt back in the drawer and fished out his wallet. A little storm of white MAC receipts fluttered to the desk.

"You have entered them in your checkbook, haven't you?" I couldn't resist asking.

He ignored me as he searched for the pertinent one. "Here." He spread it on his desk for us to read. Right at the top of the receipt was a row that read "Date, Time, Location." Under Date was 12/18 and under Time was 02:05.

"She stopped to get your money on the way to Staples," I said. "How about the grocery receipt?"

He shook his head. "Long gone. Just like the orange juice. Do you realize I'm going to have to buy my own on my way home?"

I ignored what might have been a plea for me to shop for him. It'd do him good to suffer the trauma of the grocery checkout lines like the rest of us. It might help make him a man of character.

"I'll check the times she visited the other places," I said, "just to be sure. But, Mac, I can't believe she really did it. Look." And I laid the pictures of Jolene on his desk.

They drew him like they did me. Imperious, impatient beauty giving way to disbelief and absolute horror.

He shook his head, momentarily at a loss for words. Finally he said, "After the cops see these pictures, they'll never doubt her innocence, that's for sure. Or else," and his habitual cynicism surfaced, accompanied by a sardonic smile, "I've got Meryl Streep's long-lost sister working for me."

Feeling something akin to desperation, I said, "That's the trouble with murder. It makes everyone suspect everyone!"

Mac tsk-tsked like an old maid aunt. "Merry, Merry, do you mean you suspect me?"

I frowned at him. "I've got another question for you. A totally different area. What, if anything, do you think Arnie's job had to do with his death?"

"What?"

"Bushay Environmental. Illegal dumping. The mob."

I waited for his mocking laugh. Instead he surprised me by saying, "Who knows? Why don't you find out if there's a connection? Wouldn't it be something if Harry Allen Bushay, outstanding, upstanding citizen, was bent?"

I didn't tell him I'd already begun my preliminary digging. Instead I nodded and changed the subject. "Have you ever been to His House?" I asked.

"Whose house? Harry Allen's?" he asked, his eyes back on his flickering computer screen.

"Mac," I said in exasperation.

He looked back at me, frowning. Then, "Oh, that house. No, I've never been there."

"It's marvelous," I said. "Impressive. Interesting. I met a sixteen-year-old named Pam who Dawn had to rush to the hospital to have her baby while I was there!" I still smiled at the memory of the excitement. "And a thirteen-year-old who's due at any minute."

"A thirteen-year-old?" Mac looked horrified.

I nodded. "Cutest little thing you ever saw."

"Didn't anyone ever take time to tell her the facts of life?" Mac said.

I shook my head. "I don't know. It's just very, very sad."

We were quiet a minute, thinking about Karyn. Then I said, "Your Dawn is a neat lady. I liked her a lot. We didn't get a chance to talk too much because Pam chose that moment to go into labor, but we're going to get together another time."

"She's not my Dawn." I thought I heard some regret in his voice. "And how'd you make out in terms of interviews with the girls?"

"It's a touchy situation," I said. "Dawn doesn't like the idea much, and if you'd seen the mother of the thirteen-year-old, you'd know why." I pulled a couple of Whiskers' hairs off my slacks before I continued somewhat hesitantly. "One of the girls did offer to talk with me."

"Yes!" Mac was clearly pleased. "Was she a good interview?"

"I haven't seen her yet. We're scheduled to have lunch Saturday. She's meeting me at Ferretti's."

"Wow! Working on your day off! I'm impressed."

"Enough to give me a raise?"

He gave me a look. "I haven't even gotten a raise yet, and I'm the new editor, for Pete's sake. Take your place in line."

"Do I hear disgruntled?" I asked.

He shook his head. "Just a man who hates living in professional limbo."

"You could always quit."

"Right. And you could become editor."

We looked at each other and laughed. Both ideas were preposterous.

"Mac," I said slowly. "About this interview with Lonni. Something doesn't feel right to me."

Mac misunderstood. "Well, she approached you, didn't she? You didn't pressure her or anything."

I shook my head. "That's not what I mean." But I didn't know how to articulate what I did mean. It was too nebulous, amorphous, indistinct, unclear, cloudy, vague, without form. But my mental litany of synonyms told me how unsettled I was.

Mac waited to learn what I meant, but I just shook my head. "Let me do the interview and then maybe I'll know what's bothering me."

Mac nodded. "And talk to the mother of the thirteen-year-old."

"What?"

"You can't or won't talk to the kid, so talk to the mother. Talk to the father. I suppose it's too much to ask, but you could talk to the baby's father. Any of those sources ought to give you some great quotes."

I walked back to my desk berating myself for not having thought of the mother angle myself. "At least three points of view," an old journalist back in Pittsburgh had told me when I began as a journalist. "The best pieces have three points of view."

I had been willing to settle for only two: Dawn and the girls. But the parent angle was a great angle, a touchstone angle since so many parents feared finding themselves in just that position.

As soon as I got back to my desk, I called His House and asked for Dawn. While I waited for Betty to get her, I called up the His House file on my terminal, ready to add to my notes.

"Any news on Pam?" I asked when Dawn came on the line.

"Baby boy, born at 12:01 A.M. Pam and the baby are doing well. I'm wiped out. This coaching is hard work! Too little sleep."

"Does the baby have a name?"

"David. Pam says"—Dawn's voice thickened with emotion—"she says she hopes and prays he'll become a man after God's own heart like the original David."

I found myself swallowing hard too. "So what happens next?"

"She has two days to enjoy David before she comes back here and he goes to his new family."

"Don't they take the baby right after he's born and the mother never sees him again?" I'd read my quota of gothic novels and heard more than enough adoption horror stories on TV talk shows.

"No, they don't grab the babies and run these days. Pam will get to feed David and change him and talk to him and cuddle him and do all those other wonderful mommy things."

"For two days." What a dreadfully short piece of both his life and hers.

"For the duration of her hospital stay, which in Pennsylvania happens to be mandated to be at least forty-eight hours."

"And she'll still be able to say good-bye after having him that long?" I was floored.

"Not easily. Not easily. But she's got to make this decision from strength, not weakness. And she's got to have memories to help stem the flood of regrets that will crop up later. This caring for the baby in the hospital isn't just a His House policy. It's in keeping with the latest sociological findings as well as being about as humane as a closed adoption can be."

"A closed adoption?"

"The birth mother and the adoptive parents don't know any identifying information about each other. There are also open adoptions where the birth mom gets to choose the adoptive parents, sometimes even meets them, sometimes visits in their home after the adoption to keep contact with the baby. We let our girls decide what format they want to follow."

"And Pam chose a closed adoption?"

"Yep. She said she didn't want to know where David went because she wants his new parents to be free from the beginning not to worry about her. She says God can put him in a better home than she ever could anyway."

"Wow." I was impressed. "What other things do you do with the girls to make the separation easier?"

"We suggest they send something with the baby, something that shows they loved the child."

"Like what?"

"Like a letter or something made expressly for the baby. It's important for both the mother and the child. She knows she has a chance to convey her love and the child knows he was loved, not abandoned."

"Can you tell me what Pam has done?"

"She knit a sweater. She'd never knit before in her life, and Pam's definitely not the domestic type, but she persisted through countless dropped stitches and rip outs. She ended up with a little yellow sweater she's so proud of. And she's written David a note. Again, she's not a great student, but it'd make your heart break if you read it. She loves that little boy fiercely."

I had some friends who had had babies and kept them, mainly because they couldn't stand the idea of giving them up.

"I didn't get an abortion," one of my friends said when she was five months pregnant, "because I believe those incredibly tiny feet and those tiny hands and that little beating heart belong to a real baby. But I'll keep the baby because they're *my* baby's feet and hands and heart. No one else will get to care for her. Only me."

I knew she was stating the feelings of most girls and young women who are pregnant outside marriage and who choose not to terminate their pregnancies.

"If Pam loves David so much," I asked, "then how can she let him go?"

"That's why she can let him go," said Dawn softly. "We try to teach our girls to make choices for their babies based on the same kind of love God showed when he sent Jesus. God made his choices based on our need, not his. Pam needs to choose based on David's needs, not hers."

"But there's so much heartbreak in giving up a child!"

"That there is," Dawn agreed. "There's heartbreak all over an unwed pregnancy, no matter what you do. But remember, Pam has no one to help her, and I mean that literally. Her family's nonexistent. She's only finished ninth grade, so she has no education, no training, no skills, no job prospects. If she keeps David, what does she do? Flip burgers all her life? Who can raise a family on that kind of money? Go on welfare? Okay, say she does go on welfare for a time so that she can go back to school. Who keeps the baby while she goes to school? The baby's father? He disappeared even before he knew Pam was pregnant. Day care? Day care costs money. A friend? All her friends are either in school or not trustworthy. And there's the issue of a dad. Pam says her baby deserves a dad. Not a father, mind you. He's got that, just like all the rest of us. A dad."

Abruptly Dawn stopped. I waited.

"I'm sorry," she finally said. "I tend to climb on a soapbox."

"Don't apologize. I need this information for my article."

"Thanks," she said. "Now I've got to go. Karyn's here. She and I are talking the realities of life again today."

"She wants to keep her baby?"

"She does."

"Her mother?"

"She's torn. This is her first grandchild, but this is also her daughter who is barely past childhood herself. What's best for the baby? What's best for Karyn? And can they possibly be the same? Terrible choices no matter how you look at it."

"I'd like to interview Karyn's mom," I said. "Can you give me her name and number so I can contact her?"

After a short, considering silence, Dawn said, "Why don't I ask if she's interested, and if she is, she'll call you."

That wasn't the way I'd prefer, but I also knew it was all I was going to get out of Dawn.

"Okay," I said. "And when can you and I get together?"

Dawn thought a minute. "I have to go into Amhearst on Saturday to take Lonni. She's already asked me about three times. I could meet you while I wait for her to accomplish her secret project."

"Ah, I'm afraid I'm her secret project," I said. "She and I are having lunch together."

"Oh." There was a definite unhappy tone to the single syllable.

"She approached me, Dawn. I didn't go to her."

"It's okay," Dawn said. "If she wants to speak to you, it's her choice. I'll have to trust you to handle her honestly and kindly."

I had to laugh. "You're good," I said. "Concrete instructions about my expected behavior disguised as confidence in my character."

Dawn laughed back. "You're on to me. It doesn't work any better with the girls. How about if we meet for something to eat Sunday after church? You go to Faith Community, don't you?"

"How do you know that?"

"I've seen you playing in the bell choir."

"Small world," I said and hung up after setting a meeting place. I had just hit *close* on my His House file when the phone rang.

"Hi, Merry." It was Curt.

As always my stomach fluttered more than a bit when I heard his voice. At the same time my heart contracted with caution. Sometimes I felt like I was driving myself into schizophrenia over this man. Well, not over the man. He was wonderful. Over how I *felt* about the man. Or how I dared allow myself to feel.

"Curt," I said. I blinked as I heard myself. My voice was soft and almost sexy, quite a feat coming from someone I consider about as sexy as cold spaghetti. I became brisk to counter my inadvertent slip. "What can I do for you?"

"Are we still going to Longwood Gardens this afternoon?" he asked.

"Absolutely," I said. "I've got to do a feature on it. Something nice and changeless and holiday-ish so it can go in the paper the day after Christmas and I won't have to work Christmas Day."

I knew from my research that Longwood in its present form had been developed in the early part of the twentieth century by Pierre duPont of the world famous family and chemical company. What were originally private gardens had been opened to the public, and Pierre duPont had endowed the Gardens to this end. I also knew that the name duPont had recently had the onus of belonging to John, jailed for killing Olympic wrestler Dave Schultz while a horrified Mrs. Schultz watched.

"And you're sure you want me tagging along?" Curt said. "After all, I asked myself along when I heard you were going."

"Somehow going to a place like Longwood doesn't sound all that much fun alone," I said, trying to avoid saying how much I was looking forward to going with him.

"You sure you wouldn't rather go with Jack?"

Did he sort of spit out the word Jack, an eminently spit-able word now that I thought about it? Smiling at his (maybe) little show of jealousy, I said, "I can't go with him. He's at work."

"Umph," Curt grunted, and I had to smile even more.

"I'll expect you about 12:30," I said. "We'll get lunch in the cafeteria at Longwood like we planned. We just have to be back by 7:30 for the final bell choir practice before Christmas."

When I walked out to the parking lot at 12:30, I felt sort of tingly with anticipation. A whole afternoon with Curt, and not a chance of Jack showing up to mar the mood.

Easy, girl, I told myself as I climbed into Curt's passenger seat. *This is strictly a business endeavor. You're researching a story. This is not a date. There are no romantic overtones.*

Right, I thought as I buckled myself in. Besides, he's probably waiting to hear all about Jack and why I hadn't mentioned the little fact of his presence and what did I think I was doing, trying to play both ends against the middle and was I just stringing him along for the fun of it and did I plan to dump him now that Jack was here and what was so great about Jack anyway and ...

I sighed.

"What's wrong?" Curt asked as we drove south on Route 82 through open, rolling fields that were beautiful even in the starkness of winter.

"I'm a mess."

"Oh." Curt nodded with understanding.

"You don't have to agree," I said tartly.

"I don't," he said.

"Well, you just nodded like you did."

"Only trying to be amenable."

"Which is more than you can say for me, right?"

He glanced at me as I huddled against my door. "I'm not touching that comment for anything in the world."

I stared out the front window and berated myself. Why was I being sharp with him? It was Jack I was mad at. Or me. But not him. Definitely not handsome, huggable him. I sighed again.

"What's wrong this time?" he asked.

"I'm a mess. I am. I'm a mess."

He reached over and ran the back of his fingers softly over my cheek. "You look pretty neat to me."

I caught his hand and held it to my face. "I didn't ask him to come here, you know," I said with something like desperation. "He just showed up." I was afraid he wouldn't believe me.

"I know."

"You do?"

"You couldn't be that devious if you tried."

"I bet I could. If I tried."

"Do you want to be devious?"

"Well, no."

"Then why are you being defensive? I think I just paid you a compliment."

"That was a compliment?"

He nodded. "I happen to think it's good to be open and honest instead of devious."

I thought about that for a moment and smiled. "Thanks."

"Do you have to sit against the far door?" he asked.

"Well, no."

"Then move over to the middle," he said, patting the seat beside him.

I grinned as I unsnapped my seat belt. "Just don't have an accident in the next couple of minutes," I said as I slid over and dug out the center belt. We drove the rest of the way with our shoulders touching companionably.

Longwood Gardens in Kennett Square, Pennsylvania, was bigger and more wonderful than I expected. Of course I wasn't sure what I expected, but I knew it wasn't this magnificent place. Chemicals and murder were far from my mind as Curt and I strolled along the walkway from the visitor's center to the conservatory.

"Wait until dark," Curt said. "It's a fairyland with thousands of lights. These days when I think of Christmas, I think of Longwood."

"Not Jesus?" I teased.

"Of course I think of Jesus," he said. "There wouldn't be Christmas without him. I mean as far as celebration is concerned. The lights and the beauty."

"I think of home, and I get teary," I said. "I can't believe I'm going to be alone." And I got teary. Curt squeezed my shoulders with understanding, and we walked in silence for a few minutes.

On the pavement outside the conservatory was a great Christmas tree adorned with seedpods and pinecones and all manner of bird food. I pulled out my camera and took a shot or two. A pair of twins about five years old were eyeing the tree.

"What do you think of this?" I asked them.

"Where's the tinsel?" the boy asked.

"And the lights?" asked his sister.

"It's got fat on it," the boy said, pointing to lumps of suet.

"I want lights," repeated his sister.

I didn't bother asking for their names. I didn't think their quotes went with the tone of the article I had to produce.

"Come on," said Curt, laughing at the kids. "Time for lunch." He grabbed my hand and led me away from the conservatory and across a walking bridge to The Terrace restaurant, which offered sit-down dining or a cafeteria.

"The restaurant looks great," I said as I read the menu. "But we're in a time bind. We'd better go cafeteria."

We took our places in line and were presently overwhelmed by all the choices and specialty areas. At least I was. I hate cafeterias. There's too much available and it all looks good and I always pick more than I need and I never know where to find the butter or the beverages and then I never know where to sit and I stand there like an idiot with my loaded tray in my hands and the junior high lunchroom flashes in front of me like a slow-motion nightmare.

Then when I finally sit down, whoever I'm with has a meal I like better than the one I've got and I never even saw their stuff! I just know the staff saw me coming and hid all the best food until I was past.

But that was then, I told myself. This was now. I was the new Amhearst Merry, confident, secure, pressing on to a new life. I took a deep breath, put my fears behind me, and grabbed a tray. I wandered among the different food areas with what I hoped was a sophisticated insouciance. I took that soup, this salad, that sandwich. Finally I got everything I needed including a very tall Coke. Unfortunately they didn't have any Oreos to go with it, not even any pulverized ones to put on soft ice cream. I settled for a piece of lemon meringue pie.

Now all I had to do was find Curt so we could pay for all this stuff and find seats. Then maybe I could relax and enjoy my food.

I spun around to look for Curt and found to our mutual regret that he had found me. He was immediately behind me, laden tray with its tall ice water and hot coffee in hand. My tray crashed into his as I spun, and we watched in horror as his tray skidded over mine and upended my Coke which crashed into his coffee which took out his ice water.

The resultant tidal wave, ice floating on its breaking swell, swamped his lunch—a hot beef dish that looked much tastier than my tuna fish sandwich. I knew they hid the best stuff!—and rushed over the little lip of the tray onto his front. It cascaded down his open tan suede jacket, his yellow sweater, and his jeans to form a sickly brown pool around his feet.

I froze, mortified. All I could do was stare at the floor and the ice cubes skittering madly in all directions. I thought sadly about the character and humility I must be developing as I stood there in the ebbing flood. I thought about poor Curt, forced to develop some character too, as if his weren't wonderful enough already. And I wondered which was more painful coursing down your leg, ice-cold water and Coke or steaming hot coffee.

I thought that if I was ever going to faint, this would be a good time.

I could barely hear Curt's gasp, gurgle, sigh that rose from deep within him because of all the commotion that suddenly broke loose.

"Clean up by desserts," yelled a woman.

"Watchit, watchit," shouted a man. "Slippery!"

"Wow! That was great!" It was one of the twins, the boy.

"Better than lights," agreed his sister. "Do it again."

"Gimmee that, lady." A young man brusquely took my tray. "You, too, mister. And get outta the way so Hector can do the floor."

I stepped aside for Hector and his mop and bucket. "I'm so sorry," I said, finally making myself look at Curt. "Twice in two days!"

He shook his head. "Don't worry about it," he said with a certain resigned tone. "It was just one of those things. Why don't you take a seat while I go to the men's room and try to clean up a bit. Then," he sighed, "we'll start all over again."

"You're a very nice man," I said to his back as he stalked off. "A very nice man."

I didn't think he'd hear me, but he must have. He paused and glanced over his shoulder with a smile.

Eventually we purchased our lunch and I inflicted no more calamities upon us. As we ate, we managed to talk intelligently in spite of my obvious limitations. I even laughed at a few lame jokes Curt told to cheer me up. I downed my Coke in little gulps because my beef stew—I decided he had found a tastier dish than I and opted for his on my second chance—tasted dry in spite of the gravy drenching it. When Curt said, "Um, good," I realized it wasn't the kitchen's fault but mine that the stew tasted so wooden. Embarrassment deadens your taste buds.

Finally, when it was time to leave and I knew I could put it off no longer, I clasped my hands in my lap and looked him straight in the eye. There was something I needed to know.

Curt watched me muster my courage, and I could almost hear his mental *uh-oh*. He braced himself.

"Why do you like me?" I asked urgently.

He blinked and I waited while he carefully shrugged his arms into his jacket. Then he carefully stacked all the meal's debris from both our trays onto his. "If you were anyone else, I'd say you were fishing for compliments." He slid his tray over my empty one. "But as I said earlier, you can't be devious."

"I could be. If I wanted."

"Merry, I'm not impugning your intelligence here. I'm complimenting your character. And the answer to your question is that sometimes I wonder why myself."

We looked at each other, measuring the stability of this fledgling relationship. Then suddenly, for no reason that I could see beyond the fact that there was a relationship at all, we started to laugh.

"That's one reason," he said as he stood. "You make me laugh. And every time I'm with you, it's an adventure. And I mean that in the nicest way." He draped his arm over my shoulder as we walked outside.

It was time for me to get to work. We met with a staff gardener who explained how the conservatory displays were designed and mounted. An arborist told us how the lights were draped on the outside trees over a three-month schedule and then carefully removed over a one-month span. A Longwood spokesperson told us about the problems of squirrels chewing through wires and power outages from overloaded systems.

But no matter what anyone told me, I was unprepared for the glorious displays we saw. In the conservatory orangery marvelous banks of scarlet poinsettias edged squares of the most perfect lawn I'd ever seen. The rich scarlet was broken by clusters of creamy white narcissus and pink candelabra primrose. Giant hanging baskets of crimson poinsettias hung suspended over the lawns, and creeping fig wound itself up the grand pillars that supported the great glass roof.

At the far end of the conservatory the music room was decorated in antiques, the piéce de résistance a large and wonderful music box that played Christmas carols in the distinctive, plinky sound reminiscent of harpsichords and chimes.

In the east conservatory, bunnies fashioned from sea lavender skated on a small pond and people filed into the ballroom to hear a concert on the largest residence organ in the world. We sat next to the wall that hid the pipes, and as the organist played, I could see the fabric that formed the wall tremble under the sound waves.

When the concert finished, I reached to Curt to tell him how wonderful it had been. My hand brushed his thigh, stopped, and rested there a minute.

"Curt! Your jeans! They're still soaking wet!"

"Um," he responded. "Don't worry. They'll dry."

And he didn't even add "eventually."

By the time we emerged from the conservatory, it was both dark and cold with a nasty little wind blowing. I pulled on my gloves and wrapped my scarf about my neck, wishing for my new, warmer coat. Curt zipped his jacket and pulled up his collar. I pulled off a glove and stuck out my hand to check his collar. It was dry, thank goodness. No chapped chin awaited.

Then I looked around and gasped. The grounds, lovely by day, had been transformed. "You're right! It's a fairyland."

Giant evergreens were outlined with cones of lights running in straight lines from point to ground. Others had lights shining randomly from their needles much like trees at home. Deciduous trees from slight dogwoods to broad, towering beeches had lights wrapped about their branches, reaching in rainbow hues into the dark sky.

"The trees look like they're strung with Skittles," I said.

"Not M&Ms or Reese's Pieces?" Curt asked.

I shook my head. "Skittles."

We wandered toward the entrance slowly, hand in hand, enjoying the wonder and beauty of more than 400,000 lights. Snow started to fall, a light powder, touching everything with magic.

We came to the open-air theater where dancing fountains played under colored spotlights in time to music. We walked to the far side and stood waiting in the snow for the few minutes until the next performance began.

Suddenly music burst into the air and the fountains erupted, now splashing softly, now soaring majestically. The spotlights turned the surging water red and green and blue and white in time with the music. A gust of wind swept across the grass where we stood and I shivered. As "O Tannenbaum" began, Curt reached out and pulled me against him.

"I'll warm you up," he said into my hair.

Smiling, I leaned my cheek on his jacket. I straightened immediately. It was wet.

I looked up at him at the same time he glanced down. He knew why I had moved so quickly and he smiled. I shifted slightly and found a dry spot to lean on. Poor man. If he didn't get pneumonia, it would be a miracle.

As I turned back toward the dancing waters, the lights flashed a brilliant white, illuminating the audience as my eyes swept past. And stopped. And stared.

Standing at the other end of the grassy area were a man and a woman. Actually there were many men and women and lots of children, but one particular couple caught my eye. She was leaning back against him and he had his arms wrapped around her. They were the picture of a couple in love taking advantage of the opportunity to be close and keep warm. He leaned down and kissed the top of her head. She turned to say something and the reflection of the white lights bouncing off the fountains illuminated her face.

"Curt," I said in a strangled voice. "It's Jolene."

Chapter Eight

As soon as I spoke, the world turned black and silent. After a disorienting second, I realized nothing sinister or symbolic had occurred. Rather, the water show had abruptly ended.

Curt looked at me and through the smattering of applause from the crowd said, "What?"

"Jolene!" I hissed. "Look over there! It's Jolene with some man!"

Curt looked where I pointed, but there was no Jolene. At least there was no Jolene visible. The crowd was streaming out between the evergreens that marked the edge of the theater, and all we could see was a collection of bundled-up backs.

That's what we get for being nice and considerate and coming all the way to the far side when we got here! We should have hogged a spot by the door. Then we'd have seen her—and him!

"Come on!" I grabbed Curt's hand and pulled.

"Easy, girl," he said, but he didn't protest as he let me lead him toward the entrance.

"Easy, my foot! She'll get away!"

"Like she's an escaped convict or something?" he asked as we got caught in the press. I wished I had the courage to yell fire or stick my elbows out like an NBA player driving for the basket.

"But she's with some guy." I was as impatient with him as I was with the people in front of me. None of them had any sense of urgency.

"So?"

I spun around to face Curt. "So? So? So she's a new widow! She should be home mourning!"

"Merry," Curt said with some exasperation. "Think, for Pete's sake. She'd hardly be in deep mourning. She's been separated from Arnie for how long?"

I sputtered. "But you should have seen her. She was positively distraught when we found him. She cried and cried."

"Well, you were distraught, too, as I recall. And I seem to remember you shed a few tears of your own."

"It wasn't the same thing."

"How do you know? Anyone gets upset when they find someone they've loved dead, especially by suspicious means."

I heard the pain in his voice and remembered his sister Joan. Curt had had to deal with her death under unusual circumstances, and it came quite soon after his parents' deaths in an auto accident. "Well, yeah, but ..."

"Why," Curt continued blandly, "I bet I'd even feel funny if I found Jack dead." Again he sort of spit the name.

"Curt! What a terrible thing to say!" But I giggled when I thought of Curt's emotional response to something bad happening to Jack.

He nodded. "But I make my point. Finding anyone dead is distressing, and if you find someone you once loved, it's horrendous. But it doesn't guarantee deep mourning. As for the guy you saw her with, Merry, maybe it wasn't only Arnie who had a fidelity deficiency."

I stopped and stared at him. What was he insinuating?

I hadn't been aware of him herding me toward the entrance to the visitor's center, but I'd been a cooperative ewe to his border collie. Now he stood there politely with the door held wide while I stared at him. I snapped my mouth shut and walked slowly and pensively through the door.

"You've got five minutes before we have to leave if you want to make bell practice at anywhere near the proper time," he said. "You can go to the ladies' room or the gift shop."

"But not both?"

He grinned. "That depends on how much of a woman you are."

And with that ambiguous remark, he began to study the paintings offered in the gift shop.

I did both and took fifteen minutes instead of five.

"It was the long line at the cashier," I explained to the bell choir as I rushed to my place along the row of padded tables.

When I had flown into the room, dragging my coat off as I ran and tossing it toward a chair, they'd all been standing by their bells, staring at my empty spot and my waiting C sharp, C, B, and B flat bells. I pulled on my gardening gloves and looked at Ned Winslow, the director. "I'm sorry."

He nodded. "I'm just glad you showed. I was trying to figure out how I'd play your part and direct at the same time."

Ned was Minister of Music at Faith Community as well as a music teacher in the elementary schools in the Amhearst Area School District.

"You could have done it," I assured him.

He grunted noncommittally. "All right, people, bells up."

I loved bell choir, absolutely loved it. I am a marginal musician, and every week it took every ounce of my limited skill to perform adequately. I rarely concentrated on anything as hard as I concentrated on those four bells and the four notes that demanded their ringing. That evening I did quite well for the most part. When I did foul up, which was only once, as usual I did it royally.

It was when we were doing a final run-through with the vocal choir for the big Christmas Sunday morning number. I had a run of all four notes which meant I had to put bells down and pick bells up, to reach across and under and in general be more clever than I'm usually capable of being musically. When we practiced with just the bell choir, I did fine. Ned even complimented me for counting correctly and getting my bells up and down so agilely.

Maybe it went to my head. I don't know. All I know is that I got off count by two full measures, something a real musician could never understand but something that comes easily and naturally to someone like me. As a result I arrived at my notes way before anyone else in the whole room.

With fierce concentration and the resultant regrettable tunnel vision (and hearing), I rang my C sharp with just the correct flick of my right wrist. I quickly put that bell down on the padded table while I played C with my left hand. I reached left with my right and grabbed the B and rang it while I reached right with my left and put the C down and reached back left and grabbed the B flat. I felt so clever and ambidextrous. I was a musician, I was.

I was ringing the B flat with satisfaction and pride when I finally heard the cacophony I had created. I also heard Ned yelling, "No, no, no!"

I put my bells down and clasped my gloved hands behind my back. I smiled weakly at Ned. I knew I couldn't fool him, but maybe no one else would realize who the idiot was.

Foolish hope.

"Yes, Merry!" cheered my best friend Maddie Reeder, pumping her hands in the air. Maddie stood next to me on the right, playing D and E. The rest of the bell choir all clapped and grinned at me. I know they say it means you're a part of the group when they tease you, but ...

Fortunately Curt, who had dropped me off because there was no time to get my car from *The News* lot, wasn't there to see me be so wonderful.

"All right," Ned said with an unbelieving shake of the head. I wasn't certain whether he couldn't believe me or the rousing support of my fellow choir members. "Let's try again. Take it from the top, people."

I did fine this time, and I think I would have done so even if Ned hadn't so kindly helped me along with, "One, two, three, four, one, ready, Merry, play, *now*, two, three, four!"

I knew I'd have moments of cold terror between tonight and Sunday morning over the possibility of the same mistake happening in the middle of the Christmas worship service. I'd also have no nails left by Sunday. It was a good thing I hadn't asked anybody for a ring for a Christmas present. My hands would be too ugly to wear one.

"Maddie," I said as she drove me to my car, "pray for me that I don't ruin Sunday. I know I'm going to do it again!"

"No, you won't," she assured me, patting me on the back like I was a frightened kid. She was a high school teacher and knew about frightened kids. "You've made your mistake. Now you'll do it just right." But the assurances rang hollow because Maddie's almost as bad a musician as I am, and she suffers from nerves and inability as much as I do.

"So what's new on the news front?" she asked.

"I went to Longwood today to do research for an article."

"Not too tough an assignment," she said. "I absolutely love it there at Christmas. Of course, I love it there any time of the year. Was this your first visit?"

I nodded. "It was absolutely wonderful, even if I did manage to spill half my lunch all over Curt."

"You didn't!"

"And last night I spilled my Coke all over him."

"You're not trying to get rid of him, are you? Because if you are, let me tell you that you're crazy!"

"I'm afraid he's going to try to get rid of me after the way I've given him such a dry-cleaning bill! He was wearing a tan suede jacket."

"Ah, that jacket." Maddie nodded. "Maybe he will dump you. Joan gave it to him the last Christmas she was alive."

I looked at Maddie in distress.

"But I'm only teasing. I don't think you need to worry," she said hastily. "I've seen him look at you. Believe me, he likes what he sees."

I cleared my throat. "Jack's in town."

She turned to stare at me. "*The* Jack? Pittsburgh Jack? The one you moved here to escape?"

I nodded.

"What's he doing here?"

"He's doing an audit on Bushay Environmental, so he'll be here for several weeks, maybe even months. He *says* he's here for me."

"I hear a definite hesitancy there. You don't believe him?"

"I think I'm afraid I do."

"Ah, the difference a few months makes!" Maddie grinned at me. "If he'd showed back in September when you first came here, you'd have run right back home with him."

"I know. And I think the big change in me sort of scares me. For six years I thought I knew what I wanted. Now I don't want the same thing at all. Why not?" I looked at Maddie as if she could give me the answers. "How did I change so much in such a short time? And then there's Curt. He scares me, too. For lots of reasons. For one, he wants to fix things for me, sort of protect me from myself."

"He has a savior complex," Maddie said. "He developed it trying to help Joan with her problems."

"And since it didn't work there, he's trying it again with me?"

She nodded. "It's because he cares."

"I know that. That's what makes it so frustrating. He's wonderful and kind, but I'm learning that I'd rather fix things myself, even if I make a mess of them. At least it's *my* mess."

"But he's working at learning how to be supportive without strangling you, you know. He told me so."

I stared at her, her long hair falling in a brown velvet cascade down her back. "You talk about me with him?" Was I pleased or horrified?

"Only once, I think," she hastened to tell me. "And I brought it up. Curt's too contained to gossip, especially about you. I was just suggesting how he could have a better chance to win your heart."

"Maddie! You mustn't do that!"

She shrugged like it was no big deal.

"Maddie! Please! No more! Promise me!"

"What? You don't need or want help?" She was totally unrepentant.

"I need help all right, but it's with my inability to make a decision. Look at me. I shilly-shally. All the time. Look at Curt. He's so confident and secure—and he's not got much to hang on to. Life's been hard for him in lots of ways. Joan's gone. His parents are gone. He's basically alone."

"He's a strong Christian, Merry. He's learned what it means to trust in God, probably because there is no one else, at least no family. He does have a few friends to support him though."

I nodded. "I know. He's got you and Doug and that's great. I don't know where he'd be otherwise. But he's single with no relatives, you know? How come he's so assured and I'm so waver-y? How come I've got the strong family base and I'm the one who's always waffling and fearful?" The last was almost a wail.

Maddie shot me a piercing glance. "Are you asking rhetorically or should I give my opinion?"

"I want your opinion. I think."

"You love your work, don't you?"

"*The News*?" I nodded, wondering what in the world that had to do with anything. "It's wonderful."

"You even loved it when you were working at the other paper in Pittsburgh, didn't you?"

"I'm good at it. It's always different and challenging and never boring. I feel like I'm making a real contribution."

"How about when you first started?"

"When I worked summers as an intern in Pittsburgh, I was scared to death. I knew I'd never make it. But I didn't have any choice. I had to hang in there because the internship was a requirement for my journalism degree."

"So in time you learned you could do it and do it well?"

"Yeah."

"When you moved to Amhearst, how did you feel at first?"

"I hated it. I was scared all the time, scared I'd fail, scared I'd make a fool of myself, scared I couldn't manage on my own without Jack or my family."

"How about now?"

"I know I'll make it. I've learned to press on. I've found a church I love, friends I love, even a doctor I love. And I did it all on my own. My family is wonderful and I'll miss them like crazy on Christmas, but I'll make it without them. And I don't even want Jack around anymore. He's a distraction, a thorn in my flesh."

"Again it's taken time to learn these things about yourself, just like it took time to learn you're a good reporter."

"In other words, I'm a slow learner?"

Maddie shrugged. "I don't think I'd say it that way, but that's sort of what I mean."

"Great. I need a special ed class. And at my age."

Maddie paused for a stop sign. "Taking your time about things isn't necessarily bad. It'll probably save you from making lots of bad mistakes. Fools rush in, angel."

"I almost made the mistake of marrying Jack. I was a very slow learner there. Six years. And I only escaped because he's slower than I am!"

"But you learned."

"I think God took care of me because I was just too plain dumb to take care of myself."

"That too. And think about this: moving here to Amhearst has let you learn a lot of things about yourself, right? All those years you went with Jack, you submerged your personality to be what you thought he wanted you to be. Now you're learning what God wants you to be, made you to be. You're learning to make choices from strength, your own God-given strength."

We drove a couple of blocks in silence as I chewed on her words. Finally I said, "I feel sort of sorry for Jack."

"You do?"

I nodded. "He's not really that bad a guy. He's just got a commitment problem. Or he did. Poor guy. He came here thinking I felt the same way about him I'd always felt. Now he finds out I don't."

"You've told him then? Good."

I thought back over Jack's and my conversations. Had I ever told him? "I haven't spelled things out clearly. He probably just thinks I'm mad."

"Not good," Maddie said. She reached over and squeezed my hand. "You can tell him and still be kind. I know you can."

I grinned at her. "You're good," I said. "You make me almost believe that."

She grinned. "It comes from talking to high schoolers all the time. The girls are always telling me their troubles, and I'm always giving my opinions and advice. One of the main things I always say—aside from, 'Trust in God' any time I think it's appropriate—is, 'Be certain you choose from strength.' You chose about Jack for years from habit and desperation."

When I started to protest, she shushed me. "Yes, you did, and you know it. Distance and Curt have allowed you to see more clearly, and now you're choosing about Jack with wisdom and perspective."

"Is that what it is? Sometimes it feels like animosity."

"You're resenting those six years. You've got to let them go. After all, if you hadn't waited all that time, you'd never have become desperate enough to come here and you'd never have met Curt."

"And you," I said, smiling at my friend.

She smiled back and nodded. "Take your time over choices about Curt. You aren't under any time constraints there. No pressure except from yourself. Just enjoy him and see where God leads you. And make any choices from strength."

I nodded. She seemed to me to be speaking the truth in love if ever I'd heard someone do so.

"But let me tell you as your dear friend," she said with a grin, "if you let Curt get away, you're nuts!"

"Oh, I'm so glad there's no pressure here," I said, thinking that I just might agree with her. Probably did. Most likely.

At least I now understood why I couldn't make choices about him yet, not even about so fine a thing as loving him. There was too much fear, too many memories of six long, painful years with another who said, "I think I love you, but let's wait a while before we make any commitments. We'll talk again in six months."

As we pulled into *The News* parking lot, the car radio began playing "There's No Place Like Home for the Holidays." I sighed, homesickness washing over me.

"What are you doing for Christmas Day?" I asked.

"We're going to my parents' for Christmas morning, and then we'll go to Doug's for Christmas dinner."

"Sounds wonderful," I said wistfully. "I'm going to miss my family big time. I've never been away from them for the holidays before."

"It's not going to be wonderful," Maddie said in a tight voice as she stopped beside my car. She flipped the gearshift into park. "It's one of the hardest days of the year for me. The only one harder is Mother's Day."

I looked at her. "I thought you liked your families."

Maddie nodded. "We love them. All of them. They're great people."

"Are they all tall?" I thought of Doug Reeder who, at six and a half feet, strode with his head in the stratosphere. "And skinny like Doug, too?"

"The Reeders are all lean and lanky—they like *lean* better than *skinny*—even the sisters, who like *slim*. And everybody but Doug married tall." Maddie was a little over five feet and comfortably rounded. "I always come home from a Reeder gathering with a crink in my neck. Fortunately my family is more reasonable about height."

"Well, if you like everybody and can live with the crinky neck (which I'm assuming you can after eight years of marriage), what's the problem?"

Maddie was quiet for so long that I knew I had stepped into a very sensitive area. I reached out to her. "Hey, I'm sorry. I shouldn't have asked. You don't need to tell me anything here."

"It's okay," she said, turning to me. I could see tears glisten on her cheeks in the parking lot lights. "It's no great secret." She sniffed. "And I know I'm much too sensitive. Doug always tells me I'm overreacting. I know he's right, but—whew!" She sniffed again.

I dug in my purse and pulled out what was left of Airy's little pack of Kleenex from the other night at McDonald's. I pulled on the little tab to open it and offered her a tissue. Her hand was shaking when she took one. She blew her nose and dabbed at her cheeks. The tears continued.

"It's the kids, all those dear little kids," she said, pain in every word. "All the nieces and nephews. Everyone's got at least one but us. Even the younger brothers and sisters all have kids. And they're so precious and so cute and so huggable and I want one so badly I could die!"

"Oh, Maddie!" I bit down my surprise. She always looked so much the competent professional that I'd assumed she and Doug had chosen not to have kids or not to have them yet. Talk about looking on the outward appearance. I hugged her and she held on tightly for a minute before pulling back. She resumed the mopping-up procedures.

"I had no idea," I said. In many ways it was the fact that Maddie and Doug had no children that made my friendship with her so natural and easy. If she and I wanted to do something, we could. No mothering responsibilities held her back. I tended to forget that Maddie was thirty-one to my twenty-six because age was basically a nonissue in our friendship. But she had been married for eight years.

"All I've ever wanted was to be a mom," she said. "I know it isn't chic or stylish to be so elemental, but that's been my heart's desire ever since I can remember. I always did well in school, not so I could have a career but because I liked learning stuff. I do well as a teacher because I like teaching stuff. But I want to be a mom!"

"Isn't it still early in the game for getting too upset?" I asked hesitantly. Thirty-one hardly heralded the hour of midnight on her biological clock.

"In one way, yeah, but—" She took a deep shaky breath. "We've been trying for six years without success. We've been to doctors and specialists and clinics and hospitals. You name it; we've been there. Other teachers go to graduate school in the summer. I enroll in fertility programs. And nothing!" It was a cry from the heart, desolate and full of sorrow. "There's no concrete reason we can't have a baby—but we can't. 'Relax,' they all say, all the sisters and sisters-in-law who have conceived so easily. Or—and this one really makes me feel good—'God must have something special planned for you.' Sure he does. Sterility."

Oh, God, I was busy praying as she talked. *What do I say here? I haven't the vaguest idea. I don't understand how she feels. I've never felt like she has. I've never thought much one way or the other about having children. I guess I just always figured it would happen eventually, but I don't feel any yearning that way. Toward marriage, yes. Toward kids, no. I'm still too busy loving being a reporter and wondering about my man—a situation, by the way, where I'd be more than happy for your help and wisdom so I can choose from strength!*

"Do you want to come to my house for Christmas instead?" I asked. "No kids there. You could teach me how to make a turkey. Then I might have the nerve to ask Curt to come."

Maddie gave a hiccuppy laugh. "Thanks, Merry. You have such a kind heart. But I want to be with our families. I really do. I just have to accept that pain comes with the love. I just hope no one announces another pregnancy!"

I patted her hand. "It'll be all right," I said. "You'll see." Now there was a useful comment.

She shrugged. "I just have to watch that I don't get resentful about the joy they all take in their pregnancies and babies. They should be happy about them. They should laugh and brag a bit and be filled with satisfaction. After all, that's the way it's supposed to be."

"I'm going to pray for you," I said. "I'm going to pray for you every day between now and Christmas that you enjoy the day, that you enjoy your family. And I'm going to pray that you have a baby real soon."

"As they say," said Maddie as she sniffed one last time and stuffed damp Kleenex in her coat pocket, "from your mouth to God's ear."

I gave my friend a final hug, said, "I'll see you Saturday," and climbed into my car. Maddie backed out and drove away, but I sat for a few minutes, thinking. I tried to imagine what it was like to be Maddie and yearn for a baby so desperately. Then I tried to imagine what it was like to be Pam or Karyn and be having a baby so easily and inconveniently. I failed completely on both accounts.

God, I have enough trouble being me on days like today, let alone figuring out what or how someone else thinks. Just help me be a good friend.

As I pulled out of *The News* lot, I decided that all this thinking and heavy conversation had made me hungry. I needed a hoagie from John's. Dr. Merry's prescription for dealing with emotional trauma, whether mine or someone else's, was food, especially a mouthwatering sandwich that excluded only the kitchen sink. Besides, that disastrous lunch at Longwood had been eaten a long time ago.

I drove one exit west of town on the bypass to the strip mall where John's Pizza/Pasta was located. My salivary glands worked well as I stood waiting for the sandwich to be made. There was something about the smell of onions and garlic and salami and other wonderful spicy Italian fragrances that always piqued my taste buds. I carried my tightly wrapped treasure to the car and delighted as the fragrance filled its interior.

I was traveling through the wooded area between the mall and the bypass entrance when my eye was caught by bright beads of reflected light on the left side of the road. I looked just in time to see a deer and her sparkling eyes disappear into the thicket at the road's edge.

My breath caught in my throat at the beauty of her leap, and I was thankful she was safe and whole and well off the road. I saw deer carcasses lying on the shoulders of the roads all the time. I knew that literally thousands of deer were killed by cars every year in Chester County. I'd seen red stains on the Route 30 bypass from more than one deer who'd bought the farm, and I'd heard countless stories from people about their run-ins or near misses.

In fact I'd even pitched a story to Mac about an interview with one of the county game wardens, whose job was collecting the carcasses when and if he had the spare time from his other duties. As I understood it, there was even a special dump where he disposed of the bodies.

The little animals like opossums, raccoons, and rabbits that were run over got eaten as carrion by the crows and turkey vultures, but the deer needed carting off. The preferred carter was the one who had struck the animal, but for numerous reasons, it didn't happen that way a lot. Hence the roadside litter. Mac hadn't bought the idea of the interview for some reason.

"Deer are just a way of life around here," he said. "There's no story there. One ran into the side of my car a couple of weeks ago and broke its neck. Barely dented the car. I was standing there staring at the body when a guy pulled up behind me. 'Want the carcass?' he asked. 'It's the last thing I want,' I said. 'I'm just trying to figure out what to do with it.' 'I'll take it,' the guy said. 'I love venison.' I helped the guy stuff the body in his trunk, and we both drove off whistling."

"See? The game warden will make a great story."

"Nah, but the guy who took the deer might. Did I ever tell you about the time a deer jumped right over my car? I mean, right over it as I drove out near the country club. Cleared the hood with a foot to spare. Never stopped. And there was the time ..."

I walked away about then.

Now, breathing a prayer of thanks that the deer I sighted was already across the road and safe in the woods, I glanced back to the highway and there she was, a second deer, directly in front of me, blinded by my headlights. I'd forgotten the adage that where there is one deer, there are usually more.

She looked at me, startled rather than afraid, her ears and tail at attention. I didn't even have time to slam on my brakes.

Chapter Nine

It happened in slow motion even though I hit her at full speed. She smashed my headlights and the fragments of glass flew up over the hood, peppering the windshield, making me flinch. She flew up over the grill too, her huge body and frail legs landing with a terrible thud on the hood. I was sure she was going to come through the windshield and land in my lap. I just knew it. I imagined the hoofs kicking and slashing and the blood and guts. My guts.

Instead she kept sliding and sliding to the right across the slick hood until she fell off and disappeared into the darkness.

The car continued straight down the road for a few moments before I was capable of movement. Then I stamped on the brakes and pulled to the side of the road. I was shaking all over. I got out and leaned against the car and made myself take deep breaths.

When I knew I wouldn't keel over, I forced myself to walk on my wobbly legs to the front of the car and inspect the damage. I had no glass across the front of the car. Headlights, turning signals—all were gone.

I looked back up the road toward the accident site. I expected to see the deer lying in the road, but I couldn't see anything in the dark. I made myself walk back to where I thought I'd struck her. I couldn't let her lie in the street in agony if she wasn't dead.

Not that I knew what I'd do if I found her thrashing and moaning. Except be sick. I'd probably do that. I swallowed bile at the very thought of having to deal with an injured animal. Thank goodness I hadn't already eaten John's hoagie.

I knew I was there when my feet crunched on broken glass. But there was no deer in the road. I walked along the shoulder and even glanced down an embankment, but I neither saw nor heard an animal.

From deep in the woods a hoot owl shouted, "Whoo, whoo, whoo."

Suddenly I was uncomfortably aware of the darkness and the silence all around me. I walked quickly back to my car, glancing over my shoulder repeatedly. All I saw were wisps of my own frosted breath.

I put my key in the ignition, turned it, and to my surprise, the engine caught immediately. I had been certain the deer had damaged it too badly to work, and I just knew I was facing a long, scary walk to help. With relief I put the car in gear and because I had no headlights, drove myself slowly and cautiously home.

The first thing I did when I got home was call the state police and report my accident.

"I know the fact that she ran away doesn't mean she's okay," I said.

"Don't worry about it," the officer told me. "We'll take it from here."

Feeling very relieved and even slightly hungry again, I told Whiskers all about my trauma. He was not the least impressed. He was, however, very impressed with my hoagie. When I sat down in front of the TV to eat it with some chips, a decaf diet Coke, and a couple of Oreos for dessert, he sat on the back of my overstuffed chair and stared with single-minded concentration at the sandwich. He looked like a black and white, furry vulture.

"Not for you, baby," I said.

He answered by stalking out onto the arm of the chair and all but drooling in my plate. When I requested he retreat to the floor and used force to back up my request, he stalked away angrily, tail straight up in the air.

Well, I guess I'm sleeping alone tonight.

But the boy relented when he realized how much cozier it was resting against my side on a soft mattress than sleeping on the floor.

The next morning, Friday, only four days to Christmas, I called Mr. Hamish, the car rental man.

All I had to say was, "Mr. Hamish, this is Merrileigh Kramer."

"Miss Kramer! I have been waiting for your call."

"You have?" How did he know about my deer?

"Sure. I read in *The News* about you being involved in another murder. I knew it was just a matter of time." He was very taken with what he called my "exploits." "What happened this time? They shoot out all your tires? Your windshield? They run you off the road? They force you into an embankment? They cut all your hoses so you couldn't follow them and get the goods?"

Poor Mr. Hamish. He obviously watched way too much TV, and he was about to be disappointed big time. "I hit a deer."

"Ah," he said. "And the deer foiled your chance to get the crooks. What a shame. Really bad timing, huh. Then come on down. I'll have a rental ready."

"Thanks. I appreciate your quick help."

"Charge it to *The News* like before?"

"Not this time. I did this damage all by myself."

"Too bad. But I'll do the best I can for you. Where you taking your car for repairs?"

"Taggart's."

"Good choice. They'll fix the damage in no time. After the insurance guy sees it, of course. Just be sure not to claim the accident under your auto collision insurance. Claim it on your comprehensive."

"What?"

"It's a Chester County thing. There are so many deer getting hit around here that the companies pay up under comprehensive. They know you can't avoid the accidents. Them deer practically beg to get hit. It's a better deal for you. Collision's $500 deductible. Comprehensive's $50. And I got just the car for you."

If I dropped my damaged car off at Taggart's first, I'd need a ride to Mr. Hamish's. Since Mr. Hamish was pretty much a one-man operation, I knew he couldn't come and get me. I didn't feel right asking Jolene given the circumstances, and Maddie would be going to school. That left Jack or Curt. No contest.

"Why do you need to get your car fixed?" Curt asked when I explained that I needed a ride. "What happened, Merry? You're all right, aren't you?" I could hear the stress in his voice and it pleased me. He really cared.

"I'm fine," I said. "And I think the deer is too. At least I didn't kill her. She disappeared into the woods."

"Well, claim the accident on your comprehensive, not collision. And you're sure you're all right? I mean really sure?"

"I'm fine," I repeated.

"You're hard on my heart in more ways than one, lady," he said. "You get yourself into so-many scrapes!"

My spine stiffened. "Are you saying I'm careless or incapable or something?" My voice was frosty.

"Adventurous is the kindest way to say it," he replied. "And a tad defensive."

"I am not!"

"Hah!" he said and hung up.

Mr. Taggart promised quick repairs on my car, and I don't think it was just because Curt stood towering over both of us, looking unhappily at the imprint of the deer on my hood and the banged up front. Mr. Taggart was that wonderful thing, an honest mechanic.

When I climbed into Curt's car, he drove me quietly and capably to Mr. Hamish's. In fact he was so quiet he was withdrawn. The emotional distance he put between us made me nervous, and I started to bite my nails. Absently he reached over and pulled my hand from my mouth and held it. He might as well have been holding a dummy's hand. He wasn't present in the car, a great departure from his usual demeanor.

"What's the matter?" I asked uncertainly. For once I couldn't think of anything I'd done wrong.

He pulled into Mr. Hamish's, ignoring my question. "I'll give you a call tonight to see how the rental works out and to hear what Mr. Taggart says." And he reached across me and opened my door for me.

"Uh-uh," I said, slamming it shut. "I'm not getting out until you tell me what's wrong."

He looked at me and smiled, but he still wasn't present. "Go on. I'll talk to you tonight."

I sat with my arms folded, staring at him.

"You're going to be late for work," he said.

"So I'm late. I have an excuse. My car had to go to the shop. Now what's wrong?"

He stared at the steering wheel, his hands gripping it at ten and two.

"Curt, talk to me. What have I done wrong?"

He looked at me, surprised. "You haven't done anything wrong."

"Then what's the problem?"

He looked back at the steering wheel. His knuckles were white where they gripped it. He shook his head. "I need to think. I'll tell you when I know."

"When you know what?" I asked.

He shook his head again. "Go on," he said, leaning over and pecking me on the cheek. "You need to get to work. So do I."

I watched forlornly as he drove away. My world felt more than a little rocky with his strange withdrawal. There was no denying that I felt hurt that he couldn't discuss whatever was bothering him with me. Unless it was me.

On that happy thought, I made the necessary arrangements with Mr. Hamish, and I eventually pulled into *The News* lot in a brand-new white Sable. Mr. Hamish had done himself proud. Mac was climbing out of his red Miata as I climbed out of my rental.

"Where did that come from?" he asked, coffee and donut bag in hand.

"Mr. Hamish. I hit a deer last night."

"Claim it on your comprehensive, not your collision," he said. "Believe me, I know."

I called my insurance agent and started the claims process. He promised to go to Mr. Taggart's that very afternoon to check on the damage and issue a check.

"You'll use my comprehensive, not my collision, right?" I said.

"You're a smart girl," he said. "Especially for being new to the county."

After the day's paper went to press, I putzed around the newsroom doing things like answering my mail and reading about waste management on the Internet. I learned all about the Clean Water Act and the Clean Air Act established during Nixon's presidency. During Carter's administration came the Resource Conservation and Recovery Act which set time frames and methods of implementing the previous laws by establishing things like the Super Fund. Within the massive Code of Federal Regulations, anything pertaining to waste management was found in CFR 49.

When my mind was swimming with codes and penalties and uncertainty about how it all applied to Bushay Environmental and Arnie, I decided a trip to the dry cleaners would be just the thing to clear my mind. It would be a bonus if they actually had our coats cleaned. I took Mac's list of Jolene's Tuesday afternoon errands with me when I went.

Our coats were each packaged in its own plastic bag. All the other things—scarves, gloves—were sealed in a single small plastic bag. I pulled my red coat out of its bag before I left the store and looked it over carefully. They'd done a good job, and I put it on with pleasure. I hung my old coat on the hanger and slid the protective plastic down over it. I traded my old scarf for the new red paisley that matched my coat, its silky side against the collar, its warm wool side against my neck. My gloves had cleaned up well too, and I pulled them on. I laid everything on the backseat, taking care to spread the coats neatly so they wouldn't wrinkle.

My first stop on my investigative journeys was to Hennessey's, the drugstore down the street from the paper. I went to the back of the store to the prescription area. I stood patiently at the Place Order Here sign for several minutes before anyone noticed me. After I cleared my throat loudly for the third time, one of the three who had their heads together over some papers and who were doing a lot of pointing and head shaking, looked up.

"Be right there," she called.

In a couple more minutes she came to my area of the counter and asked, "Can I help you?" She was about my age and had dimples like I always wanted when I was a kid.

"I hope so. My boss, Mac Carnuccio at *The News*, was supposed to get a prescription from here on Tuesday—"

"He didn't get the wrong thing, did he? Oh, gosh, we didn't make a mistake, did we?" She glanced furtively at the two who still had their heads together.

"No, no," I hastened to assure her. "It's just that things have been a bit confused at the office recently because Mac's secretary—"

"Oh, yeah! Poor Jolene! Not that her and Arnie were together anymore or anything, but, I mean, murder!" The dimpled lady looked properly shocked.

"You know Jolene?"

"And Arnie, too," she said. "We graduated together. You never think someone you know will get murdered, do you?" She looked at me wide-eyed.

I looked back, thinking that everybody in Amhearst knew everybody else in Amhearst—except me. I knew hardly anyone.

The young woman whose tag said she was Lisa sighed. "Well, Jo was in here Tuesday for Mac's prescription. I remember because we talked for a couple of minutes." And Lisa shook her head in wonder. "She's just as snooty as ever. In fact, I was surprised she remembered me. I was never what you call popular." I thought I wouldn't mention her name tag and Jolene's ability to read. "Of course, Arnie wasn't popular either. Boy, that wedding was a surprise. I was sure she'd marry—"

"Lisa, stop talking and stick to business," called an angry voice that made Lisa flinch. "We still haven't figured out this mess you made. If there's no order being placed, get back here. You've wasted more than enough time."

Lisa stared at me unhappily. "If I didn't need the money for Christmas," she whispered, "I'd quit."

"One more quick question," I said. "Do you remember when Jolene came in?"

"Tuesday."

"Right. But what time Tuesday?"

"Just after I got back from my lunch break, about 1:30."

"Lisa!"

"I got to go." She turned.

I nodded and started to turn.

"Oh," Lisa added quickly, "tell Jolene I'm real sorry about Arnie. Even stuck-up people probably feel sad, don't they?"

My second stop was at Bob's Book Bin across the street from *The News*.

"Sure, Jolene was in here the other day," Bob told me after he put Bill Myers's *Threshold* aside. Bob went to Faith Community and stocked several Christian books along with his general market titles. "She was picking up an order for Mac. Don't tell him I said so, but the man has no taste in reading whatsoever."

"You can be confident I'll keep your opinion to myself," I assured him. "Can you remember what time Jo was in here?"

Bob frowned. "That was Tuesday and I was reading a Dick Francis. I finished it before three, Tuesday being a slow day. She got me just before the big race where the hero figures everything out. Must have been about 1:30–1:45. Somewhere in there."

Hannah's Hallmark was in the minimall east of Amhearst with the Giant food store, Fashion Bug, and Payless Shoes. Hannah's was crawling with people buying last-minute holiday cards and wrapping paper. With a sinking feeling I took my place in line so I could talk to the cashier. No one would remember Jolene with all the people rushing about these aisles.

I held a couple of small, colorful gift bags that I didn't need because I'd already sent my Christmas gifts to Pittsburgh long ago. I would buy them so the cashier wouldn't be upset at me for taking her time. While I waited impatiently, I marveled at the lady in front of me. She had her arms full of rolls of gift wrap and ribbon, pre-made bows and gift bags. Her bill came to $120. How much did her gifts themselves cost if the outsides cost $120?

Finally it was my turn, and I handed the cashier my two little bags, feeling quite the piker. Her hair was disarranged and her lipstick long gone.

"Has it been this crowded all week?" I asked.

"All month," she said, her voice harried. "It's been a madhouse all month!"

"I'm so sorry."

"No, no," she said, suddenly smiling broadly. "It's wonderful!"

"I take it you're Hannah," I said.

"Bingo. And that'll be $7.96."

"A friend of mine was in here on Tuesday buying Christmas cards. Jolene Meister. I don't suppose you remember?"

She just looked at me.

"They were for her boss, Mac Carnuccio, editor of *The News.*"

She shrugged. "That'll be $7.96," she repeated.

Sighing, I paid and carried my purchases to the car. So I didn't have the times Jolene visited the grocery store or Hannah's, but all the other times were early afternoon. Hennessey's—1:30. Bob's—1:45. MAC—2:05. Staples—2:38. I was willing to bet that Giant was the grocery store she visited when she stopped here at Hannah's. Even if she stopped here after Staples, by my calculations that left at least an hour and a half—from 3:15 to 4:45—unaccounted for. If she stopped at Giant and Hannah's on the way to Staples, it was even longer.

So where was Jolene in the late afternoon? What was she doing? She definitely had time to go to the house. But did she?

The last thing I did before returning to work was drive to the country club out by the reservoir outside Coatesville. The attractive white clubhouse fronted on the water, and the windows of both the formal dining room and the 19th Hole offered a charming vista of Canada geese skimming across the water or standing on one leg on the rime about the edges.

I looked into the 19th Hole and smiled at an attractive waitress.

"Want a seat?" she asked.

I shook my head. Standing in a private club without a membership made me feel like an underage drinker waiting to be carded.

"No thanks." I smiled pleasantly. "I was wondering if Harry Allen Bushay left his briefcase here earlier in the week? I think it was Tuesday."

She thought for a minute. "I don't know," she said. "But why don't you ask him?" She pointed across the room. "He's right over there."

Harry Allen chose that moment to look up from his menu. When he saw me, he smiled broadly, his pearly teeth nearly as white as his shock of hair.

I smiled weakly back and waved. I don't think I ran from the place, but it may merely be an issue of semantics.

I returned to the newsroom, planning to tell Mac my findings about Jolene and neglecting to mention Harry Allen, but he was away from his desk. I went to mine with that feeling of knowing something very interesting and having no one to share it with. I'd barely sat down before the phone rang.

"Merry, you've got to help me."

"Jolene?"

"Of course Jolene. Who else?"

I could think of lots of possibilities like Mom or Dad, my brother Sam, Curt, Jack, even Harry Allen Bushay for that matter, but I didn't name them.

"What can I do for you?" I said instead.

"I need to go out to my condo, but I don't want to drive out there alone. I'm a bit gun-shy about walking into places these days."

I could understand that. I wasn't too excited about it myself. I glanced at my watch. 3:30.

"Let me check with Mac. Are you at your mom and dad's?"

"Yeah, I've been staying here. I don't want to be alone."

I thought of the guy who had held her close and kissed the top of her head last night. That didn't seem too alone to me.

"And if you're good," she said, "Mom'll feed you."

"That sounds wonderful," I said, recalling the tantalizing fragrances of the other night. "Tonight I'll actually be able to eat. And I've got your coat and stuff. Wait until you see the price!"

Mac was preoccupied when I finally tracked him down, but he waved me off to Jolene's. "She needs you more than I do."

"Mac, you're a softie under your wise-guy front," I teased.

"Don't start that rumor, whatever you do," he said. "I have a reputation to uphold."

As I walked out of the newsroom, he called after me, "Pa-rum-pa-pum-pum."

I nodded. "Don't worry. I've got two interviews coming up, the kid Lonni tomorrow and Dawn on Sunday. I'll be ready by Monday."

Jolene was dressed in jeans and a plaid flannel shirt of her father's, and she had her hair pulled back in a ponytail. I'd never seen her in casual clothes before, and she was even more beautiful than when she was all gussied up. Real hair instead of big hair made her seem fragile, and I couldn't imagine why someone who looked like she did would hide all that beauty under the layers of makeup she usually affected. In her case, it was not an improvement but a veil shrouding skin and eyes to die for.

Her mother waved good-bye to us as we left. "Bye-bye, Jolene, dear. Good-bye, June."

I waved and smiled sweetly at Mrs. Luray, then looked directly at the split in the curtains next door and waved to it. The slit disappeared fast.

"Jo, has the lady next door always been so nosy?"

"Mrs. Samson? Yep. She's got no life of her own, so she lives through other people."

"What happened to Mr. Samson?"

"He was killed in Korea."

"As in the war? But that's over forty years ago."

"She's been a widow ever since. Could never find another man stupid enough to marry her."

"But she had kids, right? So she wasn't completely alone. Wasn't that guy the other night her grandson?"

"That's Reilly. His father is Mrs. Samson's son, and there's a daughter, but she was smart enough to move to Wyoming."

"Why do you dislike Mrs. Samson so?"

"Because she's nasty and pushes her nose where it doesn't belong. And she hates me."

"Your mom seems to like her."

"And you consider that a character reference, June?"

We pulled into Jolene's cul de sac, and she directed me to a beautiful gray stone-fronted condominium with shining white doors and shutters, a fascinating and varied roofline, and perfectly groomed shrubs. Light-sensitive electric candles shone in every window as they did in most of the windows on the street. A gorgeous wreath of greens, ribbons, silk poinsettias, pinecones, and a brass English hunting horn hung on the front door.

"Oh, Jolene," I said as I climbed out of the car. "It's lovely."

She grunted. "You're so easy," she said and led the way up the walk.

We were almost at the front door when the door to the neighboring unit opened and a white-haired lady of comfortable girth and a good-natured smile walked out. She led a Scottie dog on a leash. The animal gave a shout of joy when he saw Jolene. He threaded his way between the woman's feet and sat directly in front of Jolene, looking adoringly at her. Even sitting, his hind quarters twitched with excitement.

"Well, Jolene, honey," the woman said, her smile broadening. "I'm so glad to see you! And so's MacDuff. Aren't you, sweetie?"

MacDuff wagged his stubby tail harder. He continued to stare lovingly at Jolene, who continued to ignore him.

"Mrs. Forester," Jolene said with a noticeable lack of enthusiasm. "How nice to see you." She finally glanced down at the little black dog. "MacDuff."

MacDuff went nuts, whining, wiggling, wetting the pavement.

"Hi, MacDuff," I said, kneeling and holding out my hand. He didn't even glance at me. His eyes never left Jolene.

"Oops, excuse me a minute," Jolene said, apropos of nothing. "I left something in the car. Be right back." And she almost ran back down the walk. MacDuff tried to follow, but his lead brought him up short after five steps. He sat and stared soulfully.

"That girl," said Mrs. Forester with a strange mixture of approval and disapproval. "She's something. And don't think MacDuff is the only male who moons over her. Oh, no. Her husband may have just been killed, but she doesn't let that stop her, she doesn't." She glanced right and left like she was checking to see if we could be overheard. We couldn't, except by MacDuff, and I didn't think he counted.

"I don't like to gossip," she began. Yeah, right. Tell me another one. "But last night he was here again. Spent the night. They think nobody notices if he leaves at dawn. Naive, don't you think? Of them, I mean. Not me. They're not considering old people's bladders at all."

"What?" was all I could think to say.

She grinned her contagious smile and with a wave of her hand, she was gone, MacDuff waddling beside her.

I walked thoughtfully to the front door and stood waiting for Jolene. So someone was here with her last night. Not that I was surprised. Logic said it was the guy from Longwood. The question was: Who was he? Not Airy's Sean. Oh, please! Surely not him.

Jolene came up the walk with her leather and fur coat slung over her arm. She had her freshly cleaned gloves and scarf in her hand. "Almost forgot them. What are you standing here for? Go on in where it's warm."

"I'm waiting for you to unlock the door."

"Oh. Silly me," she said and tried the knob once, twice, a third time. "It's locked."

I looked at her strangely. "Of course it's locked. You've been out."

I held her fancy coat while she fished in her bag for her keys. She unlocked the door, and we walked into the entry. And stopped abruptly.

"Oh, Jolene!" My hand went to my mouth as I stood, appalled.

The potted plant that sat on the table in the entry hall was spilled on the floor, dirt making an ugly scar across scattered newspapers. The drawer in the front of the table was ajar and its contents hung out or lay on the floor. The mail from the past couple of days was strewn across the thick, white carpet. The coat closet was open and a number of coats lay in colorful puddles on the white floor, their pockets turned inside out, their arms bent at weird angles. Long scarves, short scarves, plaid scarves, plain scarves, leather gloves, knit gloves and mittens, berets, Indiana Jones hats, and ski caps festooned the entry like large chunks of confetti.

"Merry!" Jolene screamed, finally finding her voice. "I've been robbed!"

Chapter Ten

She rushed into the living room with me right behind her. Her sofa and chair cushions were askew or on the floor, silk flowers lay on their sides, magazines were strewn across more white carpet. Volumes of leather-bound classics sat in neat piles on the floor rather than on their shelves on either side of the fireplace. I was too busy taking in all the chaos to wonder at Jolene and leather-bound classics. That came later.

In the kitchen, drawers and cabinets were open, and sugar was spilled across the countertop. Pots and pans sat about on the floor, some upended, some with their lids neatly on.

"Don't touch anything!" I said as I stepped over a Crock-Pot and dialed 911. Not that Jolene was touching things. She seemed frozen in place, unable to believe what had happened.

When I hung up, she looked at me, eyes huge with distress. "Who would do this? And why? Do you think it has something to do with Arnie?"

I shook my head. *Lord, how much can she take? Comfort her, please. She's been through more than enough these last few days.*

While we waited for the police, we went upstairs to see what if any damage had been done there. We found another mess.

In the master bedroom the closet stood open, and dresses and slacks, blouses and blazers littered the floor. The white comforter, strewn with huge pink and scarlet cabbage roses, was thrown back, the bedding jumbled and trailing on the floor, the pillows scattered about the room, but I didn't know whether Jolene never made her bed or if the intruder had tossed it. Dresser drawers were hanging open, some even pulled off their tracks and lying upside down on the floor. Expensive silk scarves, slips, panties, bras, and incredibly feminine and lacy nightgowns—a sharp contrast to the oversized T-shirts I slept in—spilled in a pastel rainbow about the room. It was as if some desperate person had grabbed handfuls of the delicate garments and thrown them.

"Someone's been in my most private stuff!" Jolene shouted, anger now keeping company with her incredulity. "Someone has been running his slimy hands through my underwear!" She shivered with revulsion. "And did you see my coats downstairs? Did you see them? Dumped on the floor and the pockets and sleeves all turned inside out! And up here it's my personal stuff! And my closet!"

She grabbed at some of her underwear like she wanted to put it back in the drawers out of sight, and I grabbed at her. "Don't touch, Jo. Don't touch."

"But I don't want the cops to see all this!"

"Don't worry. They've seen it all before." I dragged her from the bedroom, but not until we'd seen that the medicine chest in the adjoining bath was open and pill bottles and the contents of a tube of toothpaste filled the sink. Towels were pulled off their racks and spread all over the floor.

We waited once again for the police, seated at the kitchen table so we wouldn't disturb the mess—as if it weren't disturbing enough all by itself.

"How did someone get in?" I asked.

"How do I know?" Jolene snapped at me, then recovered enough to throw, "Sorry," in my direction.

"The front door was locked when you last left, wasn't it?" I asked.

"What are you suggesting, Merry? That it was my fault some lowlife broke in and robbed me?"

"Easy," I said, putting my hand up in a pacifying movement. "You've had a very difficult few days. Maybe you forgot to lock up when you last left."

"But I haven't been here since before Arnie was killed, and that was three days ago. All I know is that I usually lock up very carefully. What woman who lives alone doesn't?"

I understood what she meant. I was sort of paranoid about locks too. Still, according to MacDuff's mom . . .

"Did the burglar actually rob you, Jo?"

"How do I know? Look around. How can I tell if something's missing with a mess like this?"

"Point taken," I said.

We sat in glum silence for a few minutes. Then I asked as much out of curiosity as anything, "What did you do for clothes if you weren't here?"

"I've got things at Mom and Dad's. Not much as you can see," she said, indicating her jeans and flannel shirt. She sniffed dramatically. "I couldn't bring myself to come here alone. I just couldn't."

I watched her carefully. "Ever since Arnie's death you've been at your parents'? You haven't been here? You haven't gone anywhere?"

"I haven't been here. I haven't gone anywhere. I've just been crying and holding their hands and picking Mom up off the floor as necessary." She raised shaking hands to her face. "It hasn't been a pretty time."

I stared at her bowed head and thought about the lies. Why did she tell them, especially since they'd be so easy to disprove?

"I can't believe it, Merry." Her distraught voice slid out between her fingers. "Someone's been in my house!"

The doorbell rang and I answered it, delighted to see Sergeant Poole. His craggy face brightened when he saw me.

"Merry," he said as he came in. "What's this? No corpse? A mere robbery? You're losing your magic touch."

"*Mere* robbery nothing," yelled Jolene from the kitchen. "It's my house and there's nothing *mere* about it!"

Jolene stormed into the entry, the fire of righteous indignation blazing in her eyes. She obviously planned to tell him a thing or two. Before she got her mouth open, William held up a hand.

"I'm very sorry," he said with apparent sincerity. "My joke may have seemed inappropriate, though I certainly didn't mean to suggest that your situation wasn't serious. It most certainly is or I wouldn't be here." He held out his clipboard and incident report sheet. "Tell me what you've found in as much detail as you can. Tell me from the time you walked in the front door."

Jolene sniffed, somewhat placated. "Well, we came in and found this mess." She flung her arms wide. "Just look at those coats! Why would someone dump good stuff all over the floor? And upstairs my personal things are scattered all over the bedroom." She shivered. "That's sick; it really is."

She led William from room to room, pointing out the destruction. Finally we stood in the bedroom once again. Jolene sputtered and spit and finally exploded. "Somebody's got to pay for this, and if I find out who ..."

She let the threat trail off, but I was glad I wasn't the culprit. Having Jolene that mad at you seemed a very bad thing, like having the Wicked Witch of the West on your tail, murderous monkeys and all.

William Poole looked at Jolene, his clipboard and pen still in hand. "Look around the room carefully, Mrs. Meister. Are you sure you don't notice anything missing? Nothing's gone from your jewelry box?"

We walked around the bedroom again, and Jolene gave a performance to put any Broadway thespian to shame. She shuddered. She sighed. She wept. She was brave. William and I watched her in amazement.

"I don't see anything missing," she finally said with a weary shake of her head. She poked around in her jewelry box one more time, a great oak affair that looked like a chest of drawers. "I guess he didn't think anything was very valuable in here. It must have been pure vandalism!" She looked at William, her great brown eyes lustrous with unshed tears. "I feel so vulnerable."

"I'm sure you do," William told her. "After you've had time to make a thorough search, please call me if you discover anything missing after all."

Jolene nodded, but somehow I knew she wasn't going to search and so did William. Finally he left with bland and meaningless assurances that the police would do their best to get the bad guys.

"Thank you," she whispered as she gently shut the door behind him. "You're so kind."

As soon as he was gone, she became brisk, picking the plant up off the floor and hanging up the coats.

"You were very impressive," I said as I stuck a navy blue windbreaker back on its hanger. "Have you considered the theater as a career? It'd get you more attention than *The News*, and you'd be A1. Of course you couldn't have dinner with your parents every night if you worked in New York, but you'd soon be rich enough to move them to the city with you. But then you're already rich, aren't you? And you haven't moved them yet."

Jolene stared at me through slitted eyes. Her tongue flicked out and wet her lips. "What are you talking about?"

"I'm not quite sure, Jo." I swallowed my pounding heart, hoping that it would once again take its proper place in my chest. Maybe then I'd be able to hear myself thinking over its tattoo. "I'm trying to imagine a way of thinking and behaving that's totally foreign to me, and I admit it's giving me a lot of trouble. Still, I think I've got you pegged."

"What?" She was livid. "Where do you get the right to 'peg' me?"

I took a deep breath. "Someone really, truly broke in here, didn't he?" I asked. "That's why you're so all-fired mad, right? What did the thief get into, Jo? Your coat closet and your bureau? Is that why you're so angry about those things being tossed about? You set up your little charade, and someone made it the real thing?"

She stared at me, her eyes wide and innocent. "What are you talking about, Merry? You've been hanging out with Mom too much."

"You were really surprised at the locked front door, weren't you? What did you do, go back to the car so I'd be the one to find the door ajar? But it wasn't ajar; it was locked. That must have been a nasty shock."

"Really, Merry." Jolene gave a brisk shake of her ponytail. "I can't believe you're saying such awful things about me. I thought you liked me. I thought we were friends." And she actually worked up a tear in one eye.

"Can it, Jo. I'm not Alvin or Eloise. I know a setup when I see one, and I suspect that Sergeant Poole does too. The questions are, why did you do it and who beat you at your own game?"

"You know, you're not a very nice person sometimes," Jo hissed and stalked to the kitchen.

I had to agree with her; I didn't feel very nice. But certain things had to be said. She couldn't be allowed to set her own rules for life forever. I trailed her to the kitchen and stood leaning against the doorjamb. I watched her clean up the spilled sugar by hand-sweeping it into the sink and washing it down the drain.

"You could always help, you know," she said.

"Not a chance," I said. "You mess it, you clean it."

"You're a hard woman, Merry. I never saw it before, but you are. I pity poor Curt. You're going to make his life miserable."

I didn't even bother to respond to that line. "You messed things up too nicely," I said instead. "If someone had really ransacked the place, things would have been a bit more chaotic. Vandals like to ruin, and nothing's ruined here. The sugar would be ground into the floor along with lots of other kitchen things like oil and syrup and soap—things that damage. The plant in the entry wouldn't have conveniently fallen on a piece of newspaper. The books would have been tossed helter-skelter, their spines broken, their covers damaged. And that toothpaste in the upstairs sink—I bet it's an Arnie leftover and you can't stand the brand."

She went absolutely still for a second and I knew I'd scored.

"Why'd you do it, Jo?" I asked softly. "So the police wouldn't think you had anything to do with Arnie's death?"

"I told you. I haven't been anywhere since Arnie died. How could I do it?"

"I repeat: I'm not Alvin and Eloise. And you could have done it with your lover's help before you left at the crack of dawn this morning. The question is why?"

"My parents will tell you I was at home all night!" she spat. "Just ask!"

I nodded. "I don't doubt they will. I get the feeling that they do pretty much anything you tell them. But Mrs. Forester isn't so docile and easily led. And neither am I." I said it slowly and distinctly. "Though you obviously thought I was when you asked me to bring you here."

Jolene blanched, and her eyes welled with tears once again. "I thought you liked me," she repeated, pain filling her voice. "I thought you cared about me. I thought we could be friends. I wanted us to be friends." Sniff, sniff. "But obviously I read you wrong."

"What?"

"I thought you liked—"

"No," I interrupted. "Not what-please-repeat but what-who-do-you-think-you're-kidding? Hasn't anyone ever told you that friends aren't for manipulating?"

"I know what friends are for," she blazed, pain and sorrow forgotten. "Friends are for supporting and helping. Right?"

When I didn't answer, she repeated, "Right?"

"Right," I said, knowing what was coming.

"Then why aren't you supporting me?" She was ranting full throttle, indignant and self-righteous, as lethal a combination as bleach and ammonia.

"Why aren't you answering me?" I asked my question quietly.

She stared at me for a moment, then spit, "A friend shouldn't have to answer for her actions to a friend. Friends trust each other. They don't accuse."

I was amazed and appalled at her self-deception. I couldn't resist asking, "Didn't you ever hear of right and wrong? Or truth and falsehood?"

"Oh, pul-ease," she said as she picked up what appeared to be never-used dish towels from the floor and threw them angrily into a drawer. "I know you're religious and all, but don't wave the Bible in front of me!"

I had the almost overwhelming urge to scream, sputter, and stammer. If she wanted Bible waving, I could really let her have it. I hadn't gone to Sunday school all those years for nothing. Instead I swallowed my anger and refused to let her lead me away from the real issues.

"Where were you Tuesday afternoon, Jo? After you ran Mac's errands, I mean. Did you go to the house?"

"See what I mean?" She pointed one of her long, perfectly groomed nails at me. "Accusing, accusing. You're conveniently forgetting that I'm in mourning, that my husband's been killed, that I suffered the trauma of finding his body."

I looked at her and shook my head. "I guess that's why you were at Longwood last night, to find relief from the trauma."

She blinked, startled, and it took her a moment to regroup. She hid her distress behind anger. "I told you I haven't gone anywhere since the murder. Whoever told you I was at Longwood was lying."

I shook my head. "No. I know it's the truth because I'm the one who saw you. You can't brazen your way out of this situation."

When she took a deep breath preparatory to more arguing, I turned toward the door. "I'm leaving now, and if you want a ride to your parents, you are too."

I walked out the front door, strode to the car, and climbed in. I sat there for a couple of minutes to give Jo a chance to come out and to give my stomach a chance to cease its heaving and tossing. I had no idea whether she would be willing to get in the car with me or not. I just knew I wasn't willing to be as easily baited as Airy or as easily manipulated as Eloise and Alvin.

When the winter chill began to seep into my feet, I glanced at the house. The lights still blazed upstairs and down. I sighed and reached for the ignition just as the bedroom lights went out. I waited a couple more minutes, and lights blinked off room by room. Finally Jolene appeared on the front porch, pulling the door shut and checking to see that it was locked.

She climbed into the passenger side and sat without talking for the entire trip to Houston Street. I wondered if she thought she was punishing me by withdrawing her presence. If so, she and I weren't close enough friends for that to work. I didn't care enough to be anything more than slightly annoyed at her petty attitude—and greatly relieved at the quiet.

When we pulled up in front of the Lurays, it was 5:30 and I was hungry. What was I going to do about dinner now that Jolene was so mad at me? I tried to remember what was in my freezer.

She turned to me and finally spoke. To listen to her, I'd have thought nothing but sweetness and light had ever passed between us.

"Mom's cooked a ham for you." She smiled warmly. "And she's made her world-famous pineapple casserole and melt-in-your-mouth scalloped potatoes."

I stared. "I'm still coming to dinner?"

"Of course." She laughed a sweet, little I'm-delighted-at-your-wit laugh. "You won't regret it. Nobody beats Eloise Luray in the kitchen. She's even made you a from-scratch apple crumb pie."

I was impressed in spite of my pique. The only apple pies I ever made were Sara Lee's, which, I must say, are the best frozen ones there are.

"Don't hold grudges, Merry," Jolene pled. "Besides, Mom's counting on you. Just don't mention the break-in, okay? I don't want to pick her up off the floor this evening. And don't mention the murder. It's still a sensitive area."

I followed Jo into Wonderland, waving politely at Mrs. Samson, Master Spy, as we went up the steps. Inside Alvin Luray descended on me and snatched my coat, a congenial Mad Hatter.

"I'm not letting you get away this time, Merry," he said. "We've been looking forward to your company all day."

Mrs. Luray came rushing from the kitchen, the flustered White Rabbit. "Hello, June! I'm so glad you came. I've been cooking for you all day. Oh, aren't we glad Jo has a nice friend like June, Daddy?"

The meal was everything Jolene had promised it would be and more, better by far than the food in most restaurants. Jolene herself was sweet and charming and slightly ditzy, all traces of the shrew carefully wiped away. But eating with the Lurays was definitely a down-the-rabbit-hole experience of non sequiturs and nonsense. The third time Eloise Luray asked me if I thought we'd have a white Christmas, I said, "Only if Bing Crosby or Rosemary Clooney comes to sing for us all."

"But Bing's dead, June," Mrs. Luray said seriously. "And Rosemary doesn't live in Amhearst. I don't think anyone famous lives in Amhearst, do you?"

I shook my head, to clear it as much as to indicate a negative, and took another bite of the pineapple.

"That's right, June dear. Eat up. I don't like leftovers. Did I ever tell you about the flowers Arnie brought me the first time he came to take Jolene on a date?" Only about four times. "Daisies and mums. Yellow and white. So pretty. He's such a delightful boy. I'm so glad Jolene married him instead of—"

"Mom!" cut in Jolene quite loudly. I jumped, surprised to hear her voice. She and her father had checked out of the conversation quite some time ago. "Mom, I think Merry wants some of your delicious apple pie."

"Do you, dear?" asked Mrs. Luray, looking pleased.

"We all do, Eloise," said Mr. Luray as he began collecting dirty dishes. "May I help you cut it?"

We were just finishing the wonderful pie when the doorbell rang, and the Red Queen entered.

"Mrs. Samson," fluttered Mrs. Luray. "How nice to see you. Come have a piece of pie with us."

"I can't stay," she said, eyeing Jolene with loathing. *Off with her head!* "But I'll take a piece with me."

"Wonderful," said Mrs. Luray, clapping her hands. "Let me go get it for you."

Mrs. Samson turned to Mr. Luray and smiled. "Alvin, dear," she all but purred, "I need a ride to the grocery store tomorrow. Can you take me?"

Mr. Luray nodded. "Still don't have your car back?"

"No. That deer did me in, let me tell you. Did my car in too. Totaled it."

"Did you hit a deer?" I asked. "Me too!"

"First time," said Mrs. Samson.

"First time for me too," I said. Good grief. I had something in common with the Red Queen. "I was on a back road west of town last night, not too far from the mall."

"At my age I was beginning to hope I would die without hitting one. Then, boom!" She looked at me proudly. "I killed it. I had to be towed."

"Wow," I said, looking properly impressed. "I just needed to get my car repaired."

She turned to Mr. Luray. "This is probably the last time I'll need to bother you, Alvin. I get my new car on Monday."

"Wonderful," he said.

"Reilly went with me this afternoon to buy it. He's such a wonderful boy." And she turned and glared at Jolene.

Ah, I thought as I watched her depart, piece of pie in hand. *The light dawns.*

When I finally left at about 7:30, my stomach was purring with pleasure and my head was about to explode. I rubbed the throbbing vein in my forehead as I walked to the car. Jolene walked with me, her arms wrapped around herself in a vain attempt to keep warm without a coat.

We were halfway down the stairs when Mrs. Samson's door flew open, and Reilly Samson dashed out. "Hey, Jolene."

"Go away, Reilly," she snapped. "Let me alone!"

"You always were a sweetheart," he said sarcastically and disappeared up the street.

"His grandmother thinks you like him," I said.

"His grandmother's an idiot."

I opened the Sable's door and slid in. Jolene stood beside me, looking down. I could feel her hesitation.

"I was trying to protect myself," she said suddenly. "I know they look at the wife first, and I don't want to be looked at. I know they think I did it for the money. It all but screams *motive!* But half of the money's always been mine anyway. But they'll say I wanted it all." She shrugged. "I just wanted to look like a victim too."

"Just tell the police the truth," I said, smiling encouragement. "The truth is always the best course."

She stepped back and smiled sourly. "How did you get to be so naive?" She spun on her heel and ran back into the house.

I clenched my teeth and thought nasty thoughts. Why did I keep expecting consistency from her?

When I braked for the stop sign at the end of the block, I glanced in my rearview mirror. I wasn't all that surprised to see Jo come rushing out of the house, this time with her leather and fur coat on. I turned and watched over my shoulder as she hurried up the street after Reilly Samson. When they met, they clinched and kissed quickly, then climbed in a car and drove off in the general direction of Jolene's condominium.

Did Jolene think the police couldn't deal with her Tuesday afternoon being spent with Reilly? Or was she concerned about Mac finding out what she did on his time? Or maybe she wasn't with Reilly at all.

I asked myself questions, examined what few facts I knew about Arnie and Jolene, and generally set my thoughts whirling all the way home. As I walked past the lilac to my front door, I knew I needed to turn my mind off or I'd never get to sleep. I needed a good movie on TV to lose myself in, a mindless comedy or a John Wayne shoot-'em-up. Whiskers could sit in my lap, quiet and non-demanding. And silent. He might purr his love while I had my Coke and Oreos, but that was all the noise he'd make. I suddenly realized what a wonderful thing lack of vocal cords could be.

I straightened the wreath hanging on my door. Mom had made it for me of the realest looking artificial evergreens, and the red bow kept lurching to the left, causing the fabric angel with the Spanish moss hair to list drunkenly too.

Beautiful but imperfect, I thought, *just like my family. Though since meeting the Lurays, they look a lot more perfect than ever before!*

"I'm mailing you your first Christmas decoration for your new life," Mom had said when she sent me the wreath after I hadn't been able to get home for Thanksgiving. "It's to remind you of us until we see you at Christmas."

My voice had cracked when I said, "I won't be able to get home at Christmas either, Mom. No vacation time yet. And I'm on call."

"Merry!" Mom had wailed. "How can we have Christmas without you?"

She both made my day and broke my heart with that one. "Just send me a piece of Aunt Sissy's pie," I said, trying not to cry.

Oh, dear God, I'm going to miss them! Help me survive, okay?

I pulled my key from my purse and slid it into the lock. I turned the key and prepared to push the door open when it suddenly registered that not only were lights on inside, but through the sheer curtain that covered the glass-paned upper half of the door, I could also see someone moving.

Chapter Eleven

I stood on my porch, frozen, shocked into a numbing paralysis. Someone was in my house!

Go to the car, woman, and fast! Go! Get help!

But before my brain's message was able to cut through my immobility and fear, the person inside rose from my easy chair, up and up and up. Through the sheer curtain, I watched as the giant turned and stalked toward the door. He paused just the other side of the glass panes and stared through the curtain at me. Then he pulled the door open and reached for me.

Suddenly I could move again.

"Jack!" I stepped up and in and he was reduced to his normal size, a mere 5'11". "What are you doing in my house?"

I pushed him out of my way as I strode into the living room. "You've got your nerve, scaring me like that! What do you think you're doing?"

Scowling fiercely and muttering about fear-induced heart attacks, I paced in circles around the living room, my adrenaline surging, rushing. Every time I stopped to tell Jack what I thought of him, I couldn't find the right words. So I kept walking. It was better than shaking. I hugged the dry-cleaning bag to me like it would soothe my racing pulse as I went round and round. Whiskers watched me with great interest from the back of the sofa, and I reached out on one of my circuits to scratch his ears.

After a few minutes I settled down somewhat, and I tossed the dry-cleaning bag and my red coat onto the sofa. Whiskers promptly jumped down to the seat and began circling and kneading. With a sigh he settled into a cozy plastic cocoon and closed his eyes. If you don't understand crazy humans, he seemed to say, go to sleep and ignore them.

Made sense to me.

I turned and saw Jack studying me as if he'd never seen me before. He made me angry all over again. I looked at him as haughtily as I could. "I think it would be a good idea if you went home."

Of course he ignored my suggestion. What else is new?

"Easy, Merry," he said. He reached out for me as I marched past in yet another circuit, but I ducked his embrace.

"Don't you touch me," I snarled.

Jack put his hands up placatingly. I could see him trying to control his anger, though why he was angry was beyond me. I was the one who had been scared out of the few wits I possessed.

"You know, Merry, this move to Amhearst hasn't done much for your disposition." His tone was professorial, like he was commenting on the activities of the mice who ran through his experimental mazes.

That stopped me in my tracks. "What?"

"You used to be this nice, pleasant person who was a joy to be with. You laughed and smiled. Now you're this—this termagant." He hurled the word at me like a pitcher aiming for a brushback.

"I'm what?" I could picture him with his box of a thousand vocabulary flash cards, looking for one that applied to me. He'd found a doozy.

"You're a shrew," he said. "A fury. A harridan. A nasty—"

"I know what termagant means," I said stiffly.

"So what are you going to do about it?" he challenged.

I stared, astonished at his gall. If anyone was being shrewish, it was him, not me.

"You quarrel and pick at me all the time," he said. "You hold me at arm's length. You won't even talk to me on the phone."

"After the way you spoke to me the other night? I should say not."

"Here I am, waiting for you because Friday nights have always been our nights, and you're not even here!" He said the last with such incredulity that I could only stare. How come he couldn't just see things were different? That I was different?

"Of course I'm not here!" I finally shouted. "We never made any plans. You just assumed. In fact, for six years you assumed, and I was stupid enough to meet all your expectations. I was pliable, acquiescent, and stupid. Well, no more, buddy!"

"See what I mean?" he said, pointing an accusatory finger. "See?"

I took a deep, steadying breath. "Jack, there's something you don't understand here," I began. "Over the last four months things have changed."

Did I see a flash of fear race across his face before he grabbed onto his anger again?

"It's not *things* that have changed, Merry," he said, his eyes hot.

I don't know what I would have said, but I was saved by the bell. I stalked to the phone and grabbed the receiver. I took a deep breath and said as calmly as I could, "Hello."

"Hi, it's me."

"Hi, me," I said. There was something about Curt's voice that made my bones turn to water.

"How was your day?" he asked.

"Straight out of Alice in Wonderland," I said. "I'll tell you tomorrow."

"That's what I called about. I'll pick you up at 6:20 and we'll go get Maddie and Doug. Dress up."

"I look forward to it," I said softly.

"Hey, Merry, honey," called Jack loudly. "Isn't dinner ready yet? I'm famished!"

I spun and glared at him. He glared back.

"Who's that?" asked Curt, his voice suddenly taut. "Jack?"

"He's just leaving," I said.

"No, I'm not," Jack said loudly. "The evening's still young. I can't leave my favorite girl yet."

"Want me to come over?" asked Curt, ever the White Knight.

"Why?" I asked, my anger at Jack, at Jolene, at my lack of a Christmas spilling over to scald poor Curt. "To protect me or to see that I behave correctly? I can take care of myself, thank you!"

In the stunned silence that echoed down the phone line, I watched Jack smirk with satisfaction.

I shut my eyes to block him out as I sagged against the wall. My face flamed with mortification. I kept hearing what I'd said and how I'd said it, and it sounded worse with each replay.

I can take care of myself, thank you!

Suddenly I realized I had been yelling that last line directly at Jack, but how could I explain that to Curt? All he knew was that I had screamed at him when he tried to be kind, pouring vituperation—now there was a word to keep termagant company—all over him instead of my usual liquids.

I needed to apologize. I needed to ask forgiveness. I needed to throw myself across my bed and weep at my ineptitude.

But I certainly wasn't going to do any of it in front of Jack.

"Can I call you back in a half hour?" I asked in a small voice. "I think I need some time."

"Please," came the terse answer. "You do."

I hung up and walked into my bedroom, shutting the door behind me. I stood in the darkness and wondered if maybe I had become a termagant. Or maybe it was a matter of Jolene's schizoid tendencies rubbing off on me. Certainly that harpy hadn't been me speaking.

But it had been and my face flamed anew.

I went to the bathroom and turned on the cold water. I stuck my wrists under the flow and let it wash away some of the embarrassed heat. I took my washcloth and soaked it, then bent and pressed it to my face. It was cool and comforting.

Lord, when did I get so nasty?

There was a tentative knock on the bathroom door. My apartment is strange in that the bathroom has two doors, one opening into the bedroom, the door I had come through, and one opening into the living room, the one where the knock sounded. That sort of thing happens when old carriage houses get converted into apartments.

"Merry?" It was Jack.

"Go away," I said wearily.

"Come on, sweetheart. Talk to me."

Now that was exactly what I wanted, more conversation with Jack. I put my washcloth under the cold water again and rubbed it over the back of my neck. I did not answer. Then I sat in the darkness with a wet washcloth in my hand and stared at the bar of light beneath the door.

"Merry!" I should have known he couldn't handle the silence.

"What?"

"Are you all right?"

"I'm fine."

"You don't sound it."

"No?" I was too drained to say more.

After a minute he spoke again, genuine concern in his voice. "I'm sorry, Merry. I didn't mean to upset you."

I snorted, sounding just like Jolene. Just like a termagant.

"I didn't," he insisted. "You know I'd never want to hurt you." But he had, he had, so many times. And he still didn't see it. He only saw his own needs, his own agenda. Poor narrow, insensitive Jack.

He scratched on the door like our collie Andy used to. "Come on out, Merry. Please." He even whined like Andy.

There it was: me being nasty again.

I wanted nothing more than to be alone, to mourn who I had become, but I knew he wasn't going to suddenly become sensitive and go away. Jack was Jack, and I had no one but myself to blame for his thinking he still belonged in my life. I sighed, pulled myself to my feet, and opened the door. The light was so bright that I recoiled and hid my eyes.

Jack came to me immediately, wrapped his arms around me, and kissed my forehead. "It'll be okay," he said gently. I remembered that he could be so kind if he ever got around to thinking about it.

I stood in his embrace and felt all the delight a wooden Indian might. "What'll be okay, Jack?"

"Uh—life, I guess. You and me. Us. Come on. Let me make it all better." He lifted my chin and kissed me.

It didn't make anything all better. It just turned the wooden Indian into a block of ice. Even Jack finally had to acknowledge that I wasn't responding to his kiss. Shoot. I wasn't up to responding to anything. I was barely there.

He dropped his arms and stepped back. He was genuinely confused. "Merry, what have I done? Surely you're not mad because I teased you a bit when what's-his-name called, are you? Come on, sweetheart." He took my limp hands in his. "Tell me. What's really wrong?"

"What's wrong?" I repeated. Tears filled my eyes. How about his being here in Amhearst? Or maybe murder? Theft? Accidents? Snippy coworkers? Collapsing mothers? Pregnant teens? Sharp tongues? And a heart that was so bent on independence that it had just damaged the best thing in my life?

I opened my mouth to explain, then snapped it closed again, overwhelmed. What could I say that he could possibly understand? I stood there mutely, shaking my head.

He led me to the sofa, turned me around, and gently pushed me down. I sat there beside the sleeping Whiskers and stared at the floor. He sat on the edge of the easy chair and stared at me.

Go away, Jack. Lord, could you please help him go away?

After several minutes of heavy, uncomfortable silence, he finally said, "I guess I'd better go, huh?"

I nodded. "Yeah. I think that's the best thing."

He rose and got his coat from the back of a dining-room chair. As he pulled it on, a thought percolated up through my melancholia.

"No. Wait a minute." I stood. "I take that back. Don't go. I need to ask you something."

His face lit up and he threw his coat in the direction of the chair. Neither of us cared that it ended up on the floor. I sank back onto the sofa as he walked over. He stood and waited uncertainly.

"Sit," I said irritably. "I'm not going to stare up at you and give myself a sore neck."

He perched on the edge of the easy chair. He looked very nervous. "Is this about us?"

"Us? No, no." I shook my head. I didn't begin to have the energy needed for a conversation about "us." "It's about Bushay Environmental."

He blinked. "Bushay?" I couldn't have surprised him more.

"Yeah. I keep thinking that there might be some kind of a connection between Bushay and Arnie Meister's murder. What if Arnie knew something sinister about the business or maybe even about Harry Allen himself? What if he knew about or was involved in racketeering or taking kickbacks or something? What if he was dumping illegally?"

He looked at me incredulously. "You've been reading too many girl reporter novels or watching too much TV."

"Come on, Jack. Play along here. Would any indication of illegal dealings show when you did your audit? Could you tell if there had been financial hanky-panky of some kind?"

"Merry, people don't leave evidence like that lying around—if there is such evidence, which I strongly doubt." He reeked skepticism, and I didn't blame him. "I've only been at Bushay for a week, but the company seems exemplary to me. Everyone I've met has been very cooperative and welcoming."

"Do they have a choice?"

He shrugged. "Well, no, but still ..."

"Just do me one favor, Jack. Let me know if you find anything at all odd, okay? Even if you don't know why it's odd, I still want to know. Arnie's money has to come from somewhere."

"But not from Bushay," he said.

"How do we know that? Someone shot him dead, Jack, someone he knew well enough to have in the kitchen of his house. Maybe it was someone from work, maybe even Harry Allen."

"Merry, don't. The police will take care of it." He walked to the sofa and sat beside me, stretching his long arm across my shoulders.

"Don't yourself," I snapped. I stood up and turned to face him. "I want you to take me seriously here, Jack."

He stood too, angry at another rejection. "Take you seriously? Merry, you want to investigate a murder like you're Jessica Fletcher and I'm supposed to take this seriously?" He laughed harshly. "Give me a break."

"Give *me* a break, Jack. I solved a murder once before. I can do it again—if people give me the help I need." I looked at him as steely-eyed as I could. The air between us vibrated with hostility.

"I suppose what's-his-name has bought this fearless girl reporter stuff?" The snarl in his voice made me think once again of Andy, our collie, and we all know how snarl-y and scary collies are.

"You know something?" I said. "He does." At least most of the time.

We glared at each other, and he blinked first.

"I made a mistake coming to Amhearst, didn't I?" he asked with disbelief. "You didn't wait."

I shook my head and looked away. It was that or say something I'd be certain to regret, something about six long years or lack of respect or any of a million things. After an uncomfortable moment he grabbed his coat from the floor, stuffed his arms inside, and stamped out.

He finally knows it's over! Maddie, he knows!

Just before he shut—slammed—the door, he paused. "You'd better get that pane of glass replaced or you're going to have someone besides me in here."

I felt such relief that he was gone. I sagged onto the sofa, pulled Whiskers into my arms, and buried my face in his comforting fur. I still had the problem of Curt to deal with, but Jack was gone, gone!

Then Jack's words penetrated my euphoria. I jumped up, unceremoniously dumping poor Whiskers in the process, and rushed to the door. Replace what pane of glass? What was he talking about? When I left this morning, all the panes were present and accounted for. Not that I'd checked, but surely I'd have noticed, wouldn't I?

I felt the draft even before I pulled the curtain aside. I stared in consternation at the small rectangle in the lower right corner beside the lock. I reached out and thrust my hand through the opening. I took one finger and gingerly felt around the edges.

Whoever had broken the glass out had done a thorough and neat job of it, except for the one small sliver that remained. As I sucked on my cut finger, I bent and studied the floor. I saw no glass fragments. I went to the wastebasket in the living room. Nothing. I found the glass pieces dumped neatly in the kitchen wastebasket, and my dustpan and brush were back in the cabinet, hanging just the opposite of how I normally hang them on the inside of the cabinet door.

So who? Why? I scanned the living room, dining room, and kitchen areas and saw nothing out of place, nothing missing. I went to the bedroom, and this time I turned the light on when I entered.

My top bureau drawers were open, and my slips, scarves, nightgowns, and panties were tumbled all over the floor and the bed. I noted with passing regret how utilitarian my things were compared to Jolene's silky, feminine collection.

On a hunch, I went to my bedroom closet, the only closet in the apartment, another residual effect of carriage house conversion. I wasn't surprised when I found all my jackets, blazers, and coats lying on the floor, their sleeves half inside out, their pockets hanging out like little tongues in need of water. All the detritus on the closet shelf had also been pulled off and scattered, a strange collection of ski caps, gloves, scarves, sweaters, and an Indiana Jones hat my brother Sam had given me for Christmas last year. A collection of used tissues, scraps of paper, loose change, and pen caps cluttered the floor too, residue from countless pockets.

I was staring at the mess, trying to conjure a connection between my break-in and Jolene's when I heard a click in the other room. Then I heard a step and a creak.

Whiskers, I thought, *mad because I dumped him, being noisier than usual.*

At exactly the time that it occurred to me that Whiskers couldn't click, I felt something brush against my ankle. I looked down to see his great eyes staring back. Something had sent him scurrying for protection.

Suddenly I couldn't breathe. I grabbed Whiskers and held him to my chest, a furry shield against any impending attack. I waited without moving, straining to hear. Apparently so did the creaker.

I peeked out of the closet, Whiskers still in my arms. I saw no one, but I hadn't expected to because the noise came from the front of the apartment—which is why I was brave enough to peer out. I was tiptoeing across the bedroom toward the bedside phone when I heard the front door yanked open. Apparently I wasn't the only one tiptoeing around. Before I could move, I heard running, footfalls slapping across the porch and into the yard.

I felt the cold draft from the open door as I ran too, to and through the door. I braked in the front yard and looked right and left. Whiskers let me know very strongly that he didn't like running with me. He squirmed, pushed, made noises deep in his throat. With a great push against me, he leaped to the ground and ran back to the apartment, straight to and under the bed.

My apartment building is down an alley and behind a house. It's pretty dark back here because the landlord believes in forty-watt bulbs and because the streetlights don't reach back here.

Down the alley, almost to the street, ran a figure in black, visible only because of the distant streetlight. The runner veered around the corner onto Oak Lane. I started to run again. I was barely out of the yard when I heard a car start. When I reached Oak Lane, I was just in time to see two taillights disappear around the corner of Oak Lane and Albany Street.

"I have no idea what kind of a car it was," I told William Poole when he came in response to my 911 call. "It was dark, it was too far away, and I don't know makes of cars anyway."

We stood in my bedroom staring at the shambles.

"Could you tell if it was a man or a woman?"

I shook my head. "But it was someone who was slim."

"Is there anything missing?"

"Not that I can tell. I checked while I was waiting for you. Without touching anything," I hastened to add as I saw his face.

We walked back to the living room, and I looked again at the missing pane—or the place where the missing pane should be.

"Do you think this person will be back tonight?" I asked as I imagined a hand, more a green, misshapen claw with long, ugly nails, reaching in to unlock the door. It did not make for expectations of peaceful slumber.

"I don't think he'll be back," William said, his craggy face thoughtful. "Getting trapped in the house was probably more than enough for one night. If you tack some cardboard over the opening until you can get hold of a glazier tomorrow, you should be fine."

Nodding, I looked around my place. It was a very comfortable size for one person, for a couple even, but it had few hiding places. "Where was he all that time?"

We launched a search. I knew he hadn't been lurking in the bedroom because I was there when he ran off. Surely I'd have seen him. And there was that click. Nothing in the bedroom clicked like that.

I tried all the doors in the apartment, listening to the noise they made. Since there were four doors besides the front one, it didn't take long. The back door was still locked on the inside, so I knew it wasn't the one. The bedroom door moved without any noises and shut with a sound more like an *umph* than a click. The bathroom door leading to the bedroom also made no unusual noises. However the bathroom door leading to the living room clicked distinctly when the knob was released.

"That's it," I said. "That's definitely what I heard."

We looked around the little room and were drawn immediately to the most obvious place—behind the shower curtain. Bingo. There in the tub, lying on the blue no-skid mat, was a dusting of dirt, the outside type, not the I-don't-clean-my-tub type, and a couple of dried leaf pieces.

I stared at the debris, then looked at William. "What now?"

He shrugged. "We know someone was here, but that's all we know. Since nothing seems to be missing, there isn't anything much we can do except keep our ears peeled for any information that might lead us to the intruder."

"What's the connection with Jolene's break-in?"

"Good question," he said. "Good question." But he had no answer.

We walked back to the living room. As we left the bathroom, I looked back over my shoulder and shivered. I thought of the fact that I had sat in the dark, a wet cloth to my face, mere inches from the intruder. It was a very spooky feeling, that invasion of my private space.

Before I had time to get too paranoid, William's pager went off. While he borrowed my kitchen phone, I scooped up Whiskers who had finally ventured out from under the bed. Hugging his warm, friendly body helped ease the violation I felt from having someone uninvited in my home, and he seemed to like the closeness as much as I.

"I've got to go, Merry," he said when he hung up. "An unsupervised party over on Trenton Street needs a visit."

After he left, I scrounged around until I found a writing tablet with a sturdy cardboard backing. I pulled the cardboard off, and using the tools Dad had given me when I moved, tacked it over the opening. At least the draft wouldn't be so strong. I knew though, that if the intruder wanted to, he could get back in any time.

Just so it isn't tonight while I'm asleep, Lord. If I ever manage to sleep.

As soon as I'd returned the toolbox to its place in the bathroom closet, I became transfixed by the phone. I had to call Curt, and a much longer period of time had elapsed than the half hour I said I'd call in.

But how can I tell him how sorry I am over the phone? It's so impersonal. I'd rather look him in the face so I can see how he responds.

And I knew I had to go to his house and talk to him in person. I glanced at my watch. It was only ten in spite of all that had happened. A little late maybe, but not prohibitive.

I'd only been to Curt's home once, when I first met him as a reporter doing an interview about his upcoming art show at Amhearst's City Hall. I found his place again with only one false turn. Then I sat in the car at the curb, trying to get up my nerve to go to the door.

What if he doesn't want to talk with me, Lord? What if my snippiness tonight was the final straw? What if he's had all he can take of me and my defensiveness and feistiness? I wouldn't blame him at all if he never wanted to see me again. Everyone has his limits, and I've been so rude and nasty to him. I've even sent half his wardrobe to the cleaners.

I shuddered as I reviewed the past few days.

Dear Lord, I wailed to the One who always understood, *I've fallen in love with him just when he's probably fallen out with me.*

My breath caught in my throat as I listened to what I'd just thought. *I've fallen in love with him.* And I knew it was true. Somehow when I'd been searching for myself, I'd found him.

I laid my head on the steering wheel and thought of the irony of it all.

Oh, Lord, with my usual finesse I've timed everything wrong. You're supposed to fall in love with people when they think everything about you is wonderful, not when they know the truth. Of course, you and I both know that everything about him is wonderful. Mr. Wonderful and Miss Klutz. This isn't what the Bible means when it talks about being unequally yoked, is it?

I pulled myself out of the car and walked sadly to Curt's door. Ending a relationship before it had barely begun was so sad!

When he opened the door, he just stared. "Merry!"

"Hi," I said, waving at him like an idiot. His curly hair was rumpled, his sweatshirt and jeans had paint on them, and he looked tired. In other words, he was gorgeous.

He pushed the storm door open. "Come in," he said, ever the gentleman. "What a surprise!"

I'll bet. I slid past him into the living room, so conscious of him I could barely look at him. I started talking immediately, before I lost my nerve. "I'm sorry! I was so rude. You were being kind and I was abominable."

He opened his mouth, but I kept right on going. "I wasn't mad at you. Never at you. It was Jack. I was furious at *him.* I came home and there he was in my house! And I yelled at *you.* I'm sorry." And I started to blubber.

This time the arms that embraced me were more than welcome, and I responded by breaking down entirely. I sobbed and sobbed, saturating yet another shirt in the whole unlovely process.

"Shh, sweetheart, shh." He ran his hand gently over my head. "It's okay." His fingers caught in my thick curls.

"You're just saying that because you're nice," I sniffled as we struggled to separate my hair from his hand. It didn't pull too much.

"No, I'm not," he insisted.

"Yes, you are." I finally got loose and pulled away to stand on my own power, not because I wanted to but because I felt embarrassed in his arms now that I had discovered how I felt about him, sort of like I was there under false pretenses—or real ones. "But it's okay. Really it is. I like that you're nice."

"Merry, I'm not being nice." His voice was most emphatic.

"Sure you are. Just listen to yourself. You're not criticizing me or anything. Nice. Kind."

"Merry." He took me firmly by the shoulders. "Look at me."

I raised my swollen eyes to his and wished he weren't wearing his glasses. Then he wouldn't be able to see how terrible I must look.

"Stop telling me what I mean," he said. "Do you hear me? It drives me crazy! I'm not being nice. I mean it when I say it's okay."

I stared at him.

"Do you understand me?" His voice sort of kited up at the end.

His nose was practically against mine. All I wanted to do was kiss it so I said, "Can I have a drink of cold water?"

He sighed, straightened, and dropped his hands. He looked at the ceiling and said, "Dear God, why her?" I've rarely heard a more ardent prayer.

He went to the kitchen, and I could hear water running and ice cubes popping. I wanted to follow him because I never wanted to let him out of my sight ever again. I decided to try and be mature instead.

I sat in a rocking chair and looked around. I knew that his studio was in the basement with a wall of windows where the backyard fell away from the house. I knew that down there were large flat worktables and rows of shelves for supplies and racks for finished pictures. I'd been down there when I interviewed him. At that time I'd never really noticed the rest of the house. There had been no reason.

Now there was. I looked around eagerly because you can learn a lot about a person by his house. But as I looked, somehow I knew I wasn't seeing Curt but his mother. This had been his parents' house before their deaths, and at Joan's encouraging, he had quit teaching, moved in here, and given his heart's desire, a career as an artist, a try. I was willing to bet he'd left things just as they were when he got here. He had other, more important things on his mind. Even this rocker, large, pine, with gold decals patterning its back, wasn't him. He would have a sleek cherry or maybe a leather recliner to lie back in and think up new pictures.

I was willing to bet that the empty picture hangers all over the walls were his though.

"What's with the empty hangers?" I asked when he handed me my water.

He glanced at them. "When I have pictures to offer, I hang them up here so people can get a feel for how they would look in a home. The show early this month and Christmas have taken all my reserves. Right now I don't have any extras to hang." He smiled. "It's a wonderful problem to have."

"You know what else you don't have?" I asked. "You don't have a single Christmas anything. No decorations, no tree, no wreath, no candles, no greens. Nothing."

"Yeah, I know." He looked absently around the room. "I'm not much into celebrating Christmas." And he got up and left the room.

Chapter Twelve

I watched Curt's retreating figure thoughtfully. Why did he say he wasn't interested in celebrating Christmas? Everyone was interested, even non-Christians. Everyone liked the music and the lights, the trees and the presents, the angels and, of course, the Babe, even if they only acknowledged his birth and ignored the ramifications of his death and resurrection.

Then it hit me, in a small flash of insight that was as close to an epiphany as I'll probably ever get. This wasn't about celebrating or not celebrating Christmas. It was about being alone. Curt was alone. Was there a more painful time to be alone than Christmas? Maybe if you ignored the holiday, pretended it didn't exist except in its deepest spiritual sense, maybe the aloneness won't hurt so much.

"These days when I think of Christmas, I think of Longwood."

That was what he had said when we were walking toward the conservatory. Not people, not joy, not fun. Longwood. Remembrance with no emotional involvement. And the key words were *these days*. These alone days.

Tears rose as the world suddenly looked gray, not a classy, luminescent pearl gray but a dirty, gritty, grimy gray, the color of exclusion. Sure, I was alone for Christmas too, at least geographically, but I knew there were people back in Pittsburgh who wanted me there as much as I wanted to be there. Curt had no family anywhere waiting to be with him.

And I'd been too dumb, too self-absorbed to see his hurt. I had been waiting, even praying, for him to make my Christmas happy when it should have been the other way around. I should have been trying to make his Christmas joyous, trying to fill up the unfillable gaps.

By the time he returned with his own glass of water, I had reached a decision. I was going to make his Christmas a blessed and happy day whether he liked it or not. I even had a plan, and I set in motion immediately.

"Curt, I want to get a Christmas tree tomorrow. I haven't gotten one so far because I didn't feel tall enough or strong enough to handle getting it inside and into a stand and all that stuff. My father made such a big deal of getting the tree just right that I'm paranoid."

In my memory, I could see Dad lying flat on his stomach under the tree, muttering to himself as he tightened the stand screws while Mom, Sam, and I stood around the tree telling him which way it was leaning.

"A little to the left," Mom would say. "No, no. Too much. Stop, Phil! Stop! Now it's leaning to the right. Why can't you just stop when I say? I swear, every year when you get under that tree, your hearing goes."

"Come on, Barb," Dad would call, his voice wafting up between the boughs. "I'm not asking that much of you. How hard can it be to see straight? I'm the one getting a stiff neck and back down here."

"It'd be a lot easier if we weren't dealing with a Scrooge who felt he had to kill our tree by screwing it to death," Mom would fire back. "Listen to me or I quit!"

It was their annual fight, as strong a Christmas memory as their kissing beneath the mistletoe and their sitting side by side, smiling, as Sam and I opened our gifts.

I looked at Curt. With his broad shoulders and strong arms, lugging a Christmas tree would be nothing. "Will you come with me to help me out?"

"Why not get an artificial one? It'd be so much easier to deal with."

"Did you have an artificial one?" I asked with dread. Could a live tree person and an artificial tree person have an enduring relationship?

He shook his head. "Nope. We'd always go cut our own."

"Really?" I was enchanted. We'd never done that. We just went to the Boy Scouts in the Tasty Freeze parking lot.

"Don't get too starry-eyed about it," he said. "It always managed to rain or sleet or something the Saturday we went. It's cold, messy work getting a tree."

"Take me wherever it is that you go, okay? Please?" I could see us now, walking hand in hand through snowdrifts, cheeks rosy, breath spurting out in little foggy puffs. Curt would have an ax swung over his shoulder, and after we found the perfect tree, he'd fell it with a few well-placed chops. Then we'd drag it down the hill to a house which had the smoke from a cozy fire coming out the chimney. We would sit and sip hot chocolate before the fire while the tree, filled with a myriad little lights and shining balls and scarlet ribbons, gleamed in the background.

Who cared that our last snow had melted and that my apartment wasn't at the bottom of a hill and that it lacked a fireplace? I could at least get some hot chocolate, the Nestle's Instant kind with the little marshmallows that I love. And we could sip it on the sofa while Whiskers purred beside us.

"It's supposed to rain tomorrow," Curt said.

"Please."

"Don't bat your eyes like that at me," he said, but it worked. He sighed in acquiescence. "I'll pick you up at nine. Just be sure you wear your warmest long johns. I'm afraid you're going to need them."

I hugged him in thanks. "After my adventures tonight, I look forward to a sweet Saturday."

"What happened tonight?" Curt asked, concern and what-now? warring for dominance. After I regaled him with a long, lurid, and detailed rendition of the thefts, the Lurays, the break-in, and Jack, Curt followed me home.

"I can't leave you alone for a minute," he muttered as he nailed a piece of board over the cardboard insert I'd put on the window. "I think you have some sort of magnetic field that shimmers about you, attracting the most bizarre occurrences." He studied me over the raised hammer. "You look normal. You talk normally. You act—" Pause. Swallow. "—almost normally. I just don't understand it." He put the hammer back in my toolbox and backed out my door. "Nine," he said from the front porch. "Long johns. Now let me hear the lock click."

I was ready at nine though I wasn't wearing long johns. I didn't own any. I did put a pair of heavy opaque hose on under my jeans, though, and I bundled up with scarves and gloves and my Indiana Jones hat. I also wore my raincoat and my L. L. Bean duck shoes.

When we climbed out of the car at the tree farm, I squinted through the downpour as Curt opened the trunk. He drew out a small bow saw.

"What, no ax?" I said.

"Trust me," he said, looking superior.

We began walking between rows of evergreens, comparing them as if it really mattered whether my tree was five feet tall or six feet tall, whether it was fat or skinny, whether it sat in the corner and could therefore have a larger bald spot.

Finally I peered through the drips falling from the brim of my hat and pronounced, "This is the one."

"You're sure?" Curt asked. "You can't change your mind, you know."

I was sure. It wasn't as fat as some we'd seen or as thick. But it was healthy and it had a straight back and a top spear of branch just right for my angel to sit on. Of course, I didn't have the angel yet, but I would before the day was over.

Curt got down on one knee, lifted the lowest branches, and began to saw. A few healthy swipes and our tree toppled. That was when I realized that we had to drag it uphill to get back to the car.

By the time we reached the crest of the hill, had the tree bound and tied to the roof, and grabbed a couple of free fistfuls of greens, I was shivering. My jeans were soaked from the knees down. I could no longer feel my feet, though I assumed they were still dry. At least no liquid squished out when I walked. My hair was one giant frizz ball, and Curt's glasses needed wipers.

"What fun!" I said as I collapsed into the front seat.

Curt looked at me and shook his head. "I believe you mean that."

But he was smiling softly and I knew he'd had fun too. I sat in the car and gently steamed dry while he ran into Kmart to get a tree stand. By the time I pushed him out the apartment door so I could get ready for my lunch interview with Lonni, the tree sat straight and true in the living room.

"We'll decorate it tonight after dinner," I said. "Maddie and Doug can help too if they want."

"Whiskers will un-help," Curt said, pointing to the animal delicately batting the lower branches. As we watched, he disappeared under the evergreen, which suddenly began shaking and threatened to topple.

"What's wrong? What did we do?" I rushed to steady it.

"We? It's him. Whiskers is climbing the trunk." As he walked to his car, he turned to offer a final word of advice. "Don't buy expensive baubles. They won't live into the New Year."

When I rushed into Ferretti's, I was only ten minutes late. Lonni was waiting for me in a booth against the far wall. As I slid in across from her, I looked at her long blonde hair, combed straight and shining, her wonderful dark eyes, and her slim graceful hands. She was a beautiful girl except for the unhappy set of her mouth and the shadow in her eyes.

The first few minutes were spent placing our orders and getting organized. I set my little tape recorder on the table where she could see it but enough to the side that hopefully she'd forget it.

"So, tell me about yourself, Lonni," I began. "How old are you?" She was one of those girl/women who looked older than they actually are. I only knew she was in high school because she was at His House.

"I'm seventeen and I'm a junior at Amhearst High," she said. "And I can't wait until I'm eighteen!"

"Freedom?" I suggested.

"Freedom," she agreed. "I can finally do whatever I want whenever I want with whoever I want."

Not really, I thought, looking at her protruding belly, but I didn't say anything. Instead I asked, "How about your family?"

She took a deep breath. "I'm an only child. My mother went away when I was four. I see her sometimes in the summer, but she doesn't care much for me and I don't care much for her. She lives on a ranch in the middle of absolutely nowhere. Talk about boring!"

Our sandwiches arrived, a hamburger with everything for her and a BLT on wheat toast for me. She took a huge bite before she continued. I was pleased to note that she chewed with her mouth closed. You never knew what to expect these days.

"But I want to tell you about my father." She practically choked on the last word. "Everyone thinks he's this wonderful guy. They think he's fun and handsome and charming. 'You're so lucky to have him as your dad,' is what people say all the time. If they only knew the truth, they wouldn't think he was so wonderful." She gave "the truth" as ominous a ring as I'd ever heard.

She stuffed a fry in and wiped off the resultant catsup smear.

"He used to coach my softball team," she said. "All the girls thought he was the sweetest thing. 'He never yells at us, Lonni,' they'd say. 'Not even when we make mistakes. And he always takes all of us to McDonald's after every game.' Like that's some big deal. And all my teachers think he's so great." She grunted. "They just don't know what he's like behind closed doors! He's—he's—"

I listened with my blood turning to ice. I feared I'd inadvertently stumbled into the taping of a talk show on Girls Who Were Ravished by Their Fathers, today, twelve noon, live from Ferretti's.

She tried again. "He's strict!"

I almost wilted in relief. Strict I could deal with.

"It's always, 'Where are you going? What are you doing? When are you coming home? Who's going to be there?' It's like he doesn't trust me or something," she wailed, seeing no irony between her pregnancy and his lack of trust.

I made sympathetic noises though I knew that if she were my parents' daughter, they'd have been asking the same questions. They'd certainly asked them of me and Sam and they'd expected answers.

"He keeps giving me curfews," she said, disbelief heavy in her voice. "'Be home by eleven,' he says. Or midnight. Like I'm his to order around."

"Parents do tend to set limits for their kids," I said.

"Sure, if you're thirteen," she agreed. "But not if you're an adult."

I refrained from pointing out that she wasn't yet an adult.

Suddenly she grinned mischievously. "I just ignored him. And I got real good at climbing out my bedroom window onto the limb of the big beech tree. I don't think he ever knew."

"I take it you never fell?"

"Nah. I'm a gymnast. That climb was a piece of cake compared to some of the routines I've done."

"How many years?"

"Since I was five. I used to love it when I was young and dumb. I quit two years ago because I got tired of going to practice every day. 'You'll lose your edge, Lonni,' they said. 'You won't get your scholarship.' Like I cared."

"Did you miss it?"

"Not at all, believe me. I had more important things to do."

"Is that when you started dating your baby's father?"

She shook her head. "I didn't know him yet. But it is when my father started leaning on me. 'Lonni, don't do that.' 'Lonni, stay away from that guy. He's no good.' 'Lonni, you're grounded.' Always picking on me. Always on my back. Like he had the right!"

She grabbed the final french fry, bit it savagely in half, and looked at me seriously. "Don't you agree that the restrictions he set for me were abusive? He even wanted me to clean the house and do the dishes! What does he think Lucinda's for? Like I'm supposed to do her job? I told him I'd set the authorities on him if he didn't leave me alone. I even quoted the Child Abuse Hotline number at him."

"Did he ever hit you?" I asked. "Did he ever try to harm you in a sexual context?"

"He wouldn't dare," she said scathingly.

Her poor father, I thought, my sympathies entirely with him. How in the world could he exert any normal parental control over someone as rebellious as Lonni? And she looked so innocent and angelic.

"And my boyfriend," Lonni said, waving the remains of the fry at me. "You should hear the terrible way he talks about him."

"What's your boyfriend's name?"

She smiled. "I call him Hunk."

Too cute, I thought.

"And he calls me Beautiful." She smiled at the memory. "I wouldn't tell my father who Hunk was."

"You mean even after you knew you were pregnant, you still wouldn't tell your father?"

"Nope. I knew what would happen. My father'd have a fit. I was just waiting until I was eighteen and we could get married."

"You didn't think about running away together?"

Lonni shook her head. "I didn't want to cost him his job. I knew my father would go after him and try to ruin him. He's got a awful lot of power, you know. It just seemed better to wait."

I was struck by the fact that Jolene didn't have a lock on inconsistency. Lonni was no slouch in that department herself. She was mature enough to care about and try to protect her boyfriend's job while she was immature enough to think that eighteen meant freedom in spite of a coming baby.

"But my father learned Hunk's identity about a week ago. I think he hired a private detective. Can you believe that? Where's the trust?"

I quickly filled my mouth with the last bite of my BLT just in case Lonni's question wasn't rhetorical.

"Then my father went nuts." Lonni turned white as she recalled the scene. "He screamed. He shouted. He ranted. He said he'd kill Hunk. He threatened to blow his head off or run a knife through his heart or hang him by the neck until dead."

"I'm sure that was just because he was angry," I said.

"You don't know, believe me. I never saw anyone behave like that. It was scary! He'd have killed Hunk right then and there if he could." She dabbed delicately at her eyes. "It hurts to sit there and hear all sorts of terrible things said about someone you love. Your heart sort of bleeds."

"I'm sure it does," I agreed. "But I still wonder if it wasn't exaggerated speech. We all do that when we're angry. It's like a mom saying to her kid, 'You do that one more time and you're grounded for life!' It's overstatement."

"It was more," she said darkly and with absolute conviction. "Believe me, it was more. I know."

I was appalled at the conviction with which she spoke. Who was her father? A would-be Mafia enforcer out to make his bones on her boyfriend?

She washed the last half of her fry down with a swallow of Coke. She smiled brightly and brittlely. "So what else do you want to know?"

"What doesn't your father like about Hunk?"

"I don't know." She seemed honestly confounded by this. "Maybe that he's older and married?"

I almost lost my mouthful of Coke. "You're dating an older married man?"

"Not an old one. He's just older than me."

"By how much?"

"Only ten years." My mind boggled. "And he hates his wife. She's a shrew. He told me so."

"And you believe him?"

She sat up straight and looked down her nose at me. "Hunk would never lie."

No, just sleep with an underage girl while married to someone else. "Maybe your father thinks that Hunk is robbing the cradle?"

"That's only because he still treats me like a kid. Hunk knows I'm a woman. He tells me so all the time. 'You're mature far beyond your years,' he says." She glowed with pride.

Was that to quiet his own conscience? I wondered if he thought saying she was mature frequently enough would actually make it so.

She must have seen the skepticism in my face. "What's our age difference to you or my father anyway? If Hunk and I are happy, why should either of you care? It's none of your business!"

"You don't think sleeping with married men is wrong?" I asked.

She shook her head. "Not if you love each other. The guys in *People* and on TV do it all the time."

Unfortunately that was true. "But what about the Bible?" I asked.

She looked confused. "What's the Bible got to do with anything?"

"It says sex outside marriage is wrong."

"It does?"

I nodded.

"And you agree?"

I nodded again.

"Are you married?" she asked.

"No."

"Ever been married?"

"No."

She looked at me with prejudgment, waiting for my hypocrisy. "Ever had sex?" she challenged.

"No."

She stared. "Never?" She clearly couldn't imagine such a thing as reaching my advanced age as a virgin.

"Never."

"Is something wrong with you?"

I had to smile. "I'm fine, believe me. I just believe in sex in marriage."

"So you think having this baby is wrong?" She was defensive.

I shook my head. "I think having the baby once it's conceived is fine and good. It's the conceiving it outside marriage that I think was wrong."

Lonni stared at me a minute, her eyes narrowed and hard. "And just who are you to tell me what's right and wrong?" she demanded. As she stared at me with her sneering, unrepentant face, I thought that if she looked this way at her father, no wonder he hated Hunk.

"It's not me who says it's wrong," I said, trying to smile to break the judgmental sound of my position. "It's God."

She reached out and grabbed my tape recorder and slapped it on the table. Several people at nearby tables jumped and looked our way. One man even started to get out of his seat. In the back of my mind I found it interesting that Reilly Samson was having lunch at Feretti's too. Small world. He settled back to finish his coffee when he saw Lonni and I were okay.

"Is this supposed to be my interview," Lonni hissed at me, "or your sermon?"

I looked at her with my eyebrow cocked, but I knew I'd said enough. I changed the topic. "Tell me how you came to be living at His House." It seemed a safe and neutral question. Wrong.

"*He* made me go."

"Your father?"

"Who else? But I'll be eighteen in another month. Then I leave. Hunk's proud of me for doing things legally rather than making my father angrier and risking him getting the police involved."

I bet Hunk preferred it that way. We weren't talking statutory rape, but we were talking public opinion at the very least. An adult getting a high school junior pregnant. Nasty.

"What do you like best about His House?" I asked, hoping this was an okay question. For all I knew, she had a vendetta against her housemates too. I wouldn't have been surprised at all. But I'd finally asked a question that got a positive answer.

She half-smiled, and the seventeen-year-old who might have been was visible. "It's going to sound corny," she said, "but what I like best is that the people there care. I like that a lot. Dawn and Julie are wonderful to us. They're not easy on us, but they like us. They put in long hours and will sit and talk anytime we want. They eat meals with us and they watch TV with us. They play games with us and teach us all kinds of stuff because they want to help us."

I smiled. She was confirming my initial response to His House.

"Of course most of what they say is sh—" She caught herself and looked at me. "It's garbage. I was going to use a more descriptive term, but I won't say it because you and God won't like it. But I don't agree with what they say and I won't believe." She spoke slowly and deliberately, daring me to make an issue. I declined.

"How about the other girls there?" I asked. "Do you like them?"

"The others are nice," she said. "Some of them have terrible stories, poverty and beatings and stuff. And their boyfriends! It's

178

enough to curl your hair. Pam's one like that. She says no one ever loved her before. She says no one ever cared what she thought or felt. She says Dawn just loved her to Jesus." Lonni shrugged. "Whatever that means. I just know she's a lot nicer now than she was when I first came. She was a real toughie then. And that baby Karyn. Have you met her? I feel so bad for her. And her mom. She looks like she's dying a little bit more every day." Lonni shook her head in sympathy.

"Don't you think your dad feels that sad about you?"

A derisive puff of air burst from her lips. "Are you kidding? No way. You know what he said to me? 'Since you've got the morals of an alley cat, let's put you somewhere where you can get religion! That'll teach you.' Hah! Like he's some good guy himself."

I had to agree with Lonni that sending her to His House to get religion wasn't a great idea. Talk about waving a red flag in front of an already enraged individual.

Lonni leaned across the table and said in a low voice, "Do you know that he wanted me to get an abortion?"

"Hunk did?"

"No! He was excited. My father did. Can you imagine that?"

Unfortunately I could. "Why did you refuse? To get back at him?"

She flipped her hand through the air like such an idea wasn't worth the time it took to state. "I didn't want an abortion because I want to have Hunk's baby. I love him and I love the baby."

"When will you be getting married?"

Her face was suddenly full of sorrow. "We won't."

"But I thought you said—?"

"Circumstances have changed." That was all she would say. She was too busy trying to keep herself from breaking down in front of me. She kept swallowing and blinking and making abrupt little shakes of her head. "I've got to go," she managed to whisper. She grabbed her coat and stood up. She stared at me, her eyes alive with pain. "Just make sure you let everyone know what a terrible man my father really is. That's all I ask."

She turned away and started for the door. I noted Reilly Samson leaving his seat at the same time.

"Lonni," I called. "I forgot to ask. What's your full name? And do you want me to use a pseudonym when I write about you?"

"Bushay," she said. "Lonni Allen Bushay. And use my real name. Please."

I watched Lonni stride outside, and I watched through the big front windows as Reilly Samson caught up with her on the sidewalk. He put his arm around her shoulders and she leaned into him. He talked gently with her for a few minutes as she cried. His face was full of concern.

Once he turned and looked at me. Our eyes met briefly before he turned back to her. He pulled a handkerchief out of his pants' pocket and gave it to her. She blew her nose and handed him the soiled cloth. He took it and stuffed it in his coat pocket. They walked out of sight, his arm still around her shoulder.

I stared at my soiled place mat, thinking.

Lonni Allen Bushay! She was Harry Allen's daughter. One of Amhearst's outstanding do-gooders had a daughter who wanted to hang him out to dry. The question was: Had Harry Allen done anything wrong? Trying to keep tabs on a rebellious daughter wasn't wrong. Yelling threats in a fit of anger wasn't necessarily wrong. Acting on those threats would be wrong indeed.

Threats to his daughter and a vicious fight about Communists somehow didn't go with the man-about-town image Harry Allen had cultivated. Which was the real Harry Allen?

And how did Reilly Samson fit into things? I thought he was Jolene's current flame. Was he also Hunk? But then he'd have to be married, and I didn't think he was. Or maybe he just told Lonni he was so she could be kept in her place, wherever he perceived that to be.

My head buzzing with ideas, I walked slowly back to *The News* and sat at my desk, staring at my blank terminal. Mac was the only other person in the newsroom.

"Yo, Kramer!" he bellowed and I jumped.

"You don't have to scare me," I said in mild rebuke. "A polite 'Merry, my dear,' will do."

"I called you politely three times with no response," he said. "So I yelled."

I wandered to his desk. "I just had my interview with Lonni Bushay, one of the girls at His House."

"Harry Allen's kid?"

I nodded.

"And?" he prompted when I stopped.

"And something's not ringing true. She wants to hurt her father because she seems to think he'll hurt her boyfriend. She certainly had the opportunity to tell me any stories she wanted about him. She could have made up anything. But everything she told me seemed typical parent/kid conflicts—except for the tiff over her married boyfriend. And I guess that's typical too, at least as typical as married boyfriends."

"She has a married boyfriend?"

I grinned. "She doesn't know why Harry Allen doesn't like him."

Mac shook his head. "I must be getting old. These kids scare me."

We both laughed at the idea of Mac, the perennial playboy, getting old.

"You'll never guess who I'm meeting for lunch tomorrow," I said, leaving Lonni for the minute.

"You mean you actually want me to guess?" he said with his usual acerbity.

"You're a spoilsport," I told him. "It's Dawn. At Ferretti's. Around 1 P.M."

"Like I care," he said, but I could see him storing the information. I wouldn't be at all surprised if he felt a sudden craving for a Ferretti's spaghetti early tomorrow afternoon.

"They have the Eagles on TV," I said as an added incentive—or more correctly, as an excuse should he feel the need for one.

I checked my voice mail just before I left and found a message.

"This is Sandy Rasmussen, Karyn's mom," said the first. "Dawn said you wanted to talk with me. I think that would be a good idea. Call me whenever you can. Karyn and I are renting a small apartment until all this is over. I have nothing to do but sit and wait. At least your phone call will be something positive to wait for." And she left a number.

I glanced at my watch. 2:30. I dialed the number but there was no answer. Apparently Sandy Rasmussen had something to do after all. I hoped it was Christmas shopping and not rushing Karyn to the hospital.

"Don't worry about missing me," I told the answering machine. "I'll call again."

I hung up, dialed the Amhearst police number, and asked for William Poole.

"Yo, Merry," he said. "What can I do for you?"

"Do you ever go home?" I asked.

He laughed but didn't answer. For the first time I wondered if he was married or had children or liked pizza or went to church. It was easy to forget that there was a private life behind the uniform.

"So what's the latest on the fingerprints? Have you heard back from the FBI?" I asked.

"I assume you mean on Arnie Meister. Nothing. No match. Also no surprise."

"Were the fingerprints on the two iced tea glasses the same or different on each?"

"The same and the deceased's, second and third finger, right hand, pretty clear."

"So what do you do next?"

"More of the same: asking questions, listening, analyzing. By the way, Harry Allen Bushay said I should tell you that he found his briefcase, whatever that means."

I was just glad William couldn't see my red face.

I left shortly after that to go shopping for things to hang on my Christmas tree. I drove my white Sable through the last-minute shopping traffic to Waterloo Gardens in Exton and bought a glorious angel in a white gown with gold trim, gold wings, and a gold halo on his/her head. Undoubtedly the girls at His House would think it bland, but it said "keeper" to me. I also bought two scarlet poinsettias, real ones, one for me and one for Curt. It was the quickest way I could think of to get some Christmas into our places. Then I returned to Kmart to shop where my budget was more comfortable.

I was pushing my shopping cart toward the checkout when I saw a familiar mustache sniffling through small appliances. Sean Bennett was Christmas shopping, and I was afraid he was going to be practical. Poor Airy.

"Oh, Sean," Airy would say Christmas morning. "A blender (can opener, mixer, toaster). How thoughtful." Paste on smile.

What is it with guys that they don't realize that Christmas is for giving things they wouldn't run out and buy next week anyway?

I started to push my cart toward him to suggest something personal like a ring or some lingerie or a new scarf when a woman rushed up to him. She wrapped her arms about his neck and kissed him happily on the cheek.

He hugged her back, though in his defense, with considerably less enthusiasm.

"How wonderful to see you, Sean!" she gushed. "You're looking as handsome as ever. I just love that mustache." She reached out and stroked it.

I'll give him credit. He didn't flinch though he did flush. I'd have bitten her finger.

"What are you buying me?" she asked. "Not a blender, I hope? You can give that to Airy."

Unimportant gift, unimportant person.

It was, of course, Jolene.

Chapter Thirteen

Jolene, why do you do it?" I asked.

She and I were in my car driving toward her mansion.

"Do what?" she asked innocently.

"You know exactly what I mean."

She grinned. "You mean, why do I tease people like Sean? Why do you think?"

I had decided to just push my cart to the checkout back in Kmart and make believe I hadn't seen either Sean or Jolene. I was foiled when Jolene saw me, though how she saw me with her face buried in Sean's neck is a mystery to me.

"Merry!" she'd called, her arms still wrapped around Sean. When she lifted one hand to wave at me, Sean broke free. He almost vaulted the counter he and Jolene were standing beside and stood on the other side breathing deeply. He watched Jolene like a hare might watch the fox from whose clutches he had just escaped.

I pushed my cart until I was next to Sean. The poor man was almost hyperventilating.

"Hi, Sean," I said. "We met over spilled Coke the other night, remember?"

He took a second to glance at me. "Oh, yeah. Hi." He scooted past me as Jolene began to make her way around the counter.

"Don't worry, Sean, my love," Jolene said breezily. "My attention is now transferred to Merry. I was so happy to see you, but I *need* to see her."

"Beat it," I said in an aside to Sean. "I'll take care of her."

But Sean had a few more guts than I thought. He stood straight and tall with me and my shopping cart safely between him and Jolene.

"Jolene, I don't know what your problem is," he began. "But I want to say to you that I love my wife and she loves me. You can make both of us miserable if you want. You're very good at it. You make me squirm like no one I know—and that's not a compliment. I don't know how to handle you, and I admit it."

I glanced at Jolene. She was listening with a very serious expression.

Sean continued. "You know how to make Airy lose her temper and behave in ways that aren't characteristic of her. You've been able to do it for years. I'm not quite sure how you got this power over us, but be certain we know that you have it and that we will try and overcome it. And know that no matter what you do, you won't break us up. You may have killed your own marriage, but we won't let you kill ours, no matter how hard you try."

Sean looked at me. "Be careful, Merry. She's a dangerous friend. We know."

I nodded. The man was right.

He looked back at Jolene. "I'm sorry for you, Jolene. I really am. You're a sick lady."

He turned and walked away.

I looked at Jo to see how she had taken this little lecture. To my surprise, she was smiling, a nice, friendly, uncomplicated smile.

"He's a good guy," she said. "I'm glad for Airy."

I blinked, turned my shopping cart, and walked away. I would never understand this woman. Never. I doubted she understood herself.

"Oh, by the way." I paused. "You left your scarf when you picked up your dry cleaning from the car. It's at my place now."

She shook her head. "No, I didn't." And she waved a scarf at me.

"Well, then we've got an extra." And I turned to go.

"Wait, Merry," she said and hurried after me. "I was serious when I told him I needed you."

I stopped. "And I'm supposed to believe you came here to Kmart to find me?"

"I did," she said. "I called the paper and Mac told me you'd be here. When I saw Sean, I got distracted."

"Well," I said very ungraciously, "you found me. What do you want?"

"I want you to go out to the house with me."

I stared at her, no doubt with my mouth hanging open. "Forget that, Jo. I've gone to two too many empty houses with you as it is."

"But the police have released Arnie's body. We're getting ready for the funeral, and I've got to go to the house and get him a suit and all."

"So go," I said, starting up again.

She took hold of my cart and forced me to stop. She looked me in the eye and said, "I can't go alone. I can't possibly."

"So ask someone else," I said, hating the weakening of resolve I felt in me.

"Who, Merry? Tell me that. Sean's right when he says I'm a terrible friend. I don't have anyone I can ask but you."

"How about your dad?"

"Are you kidding? It'd kill him."

I thought that was overstatement but I didn't really know that for sure.

"Then," and I took the plunge, "how about Reilly?"

"Reilly?" She acted all surprised. "What in the world made you think of him? I hardly know him."

"Cut the lies, Jolene." I made my voice cold and hard. "If you can't tell the truth, I certainly can't help you. Now let go of my cart."

She dropped her hand and I surged ahead. I took my place in line and was soon surrounded by harried last-minute shoppers who had no agendas in which I figured. I'd never realized that being surrounded by strangers could be so comforting. I glanced over my shoulder once to be sure Jolene was gone and saw no sign of her lurking. I breathed a mighty sigh of relief, but unfortunately it was premature. I'd no sooner put my paid-for packages back in the cart and started for the door than Jolene fell in step beside me.

"Don't get mad," she said when she saw my face. "Just stop a minute and listen. Please."

Mom, I thought as I stopped just beyond the door, *you should have taught me to be mean instead of polite.*

"You've got to go to the house with me, Merry. You've got to. I can't go alone. The very thought makes me sick." She wrapped her arms around her middle.

"Jo, it's only an empty house." But I knew that wasn't so.

"Merry, please. You're so good in a crisis."

"What?"

"You are. You know who to call and what to do and how not to touch stuff and everything."

"911 and don't touch are hardly signs of genius," I said.

"But it'll be dark soon," she said.

"So go tomorrow."

"I have to have the clothes at the funeral parlor tonight so they can get ready for the service on Monday. We want the burial done before Christmas."

"It's too late for me to go. I have a date at six."

"We'll be back way before then," she assured me. "We're just going to pick out a suit, shirt, and tie." She started walking toward her car. I didn't follow.

"What's wrong?" she said.

I studied her for a minute before I answered. She had her big hair back today, all curled and full. Her eyes wore their expertly applied paint, and her face was rouged and powdered to perfection. Where I had on corduroy slacks and a sweater, she wore an outfit composed of royal blue slacks with a royal blue tunic with black swirls running from right shoulder to left hip. Even her gloves and scarf were royal blue. The coat was the leather and fur one.

"Jolene, why can't you bear to tell the truth?"

Anger flashed across her face as she backed up a step. I could tell she wanted to stomp off, and I knew that was what she would normally do. It was a sign of her desperation that she stayed.

She tried on the role of the haughty ice princess. "My personal life is none of your concern, Merry."

"Sure it is if you keep pulling me into it, Jo. Life can't be put in categories or compartments where you act one way over here and another way over there. You can't tell me I'm wonderful in a crisis but too untrustworthy to know about Reilly. You can't selectively lie to me and expect me not to resent it. Life doesn't work that way. At least not life that I care to get involved in."

"You're such a Girl Scout," she said in a scathing tone.

"If you mean I have strong Christian principles and I try to live by them, you're right. I make no apologies for that."

We stood staring at each other. I truly felt sorry for Jolene, but I refused to let her gain any power over me. I would not become her next Airy.

She broke first. "Oh, all right. If that's the way you're going to be, I can play that game too."

"Wait a minute," I said. "I'm not playing games. That's what you don't understand about me, Jolene. I don't play roles. I'm me and that's all I want to be. My struggle isn't figuring out how I can play the game to get my way. My struggle is with learning how I can be true to myself and the person God wants me to be. I want to learn how to make choices from strength, not how to manipulate people to do as I want. I want to know how I can be consistent and dependable, not devious and deceitful. If I do go with you—and I'm not saying I will—it will be because I want to help you, because I choose to be kind, not because you trick me."

"Well, then what's your problem?" she said, her hands on her hips. She was all chirrupy and happy. I knew she thought she'd found a way out. "Go ahead and be nice, Merry. Go ahead and help me. It sounds to me like we both want the same thing. Let's put these things in the car and go." She reached into the cart to grab a couple of bags.

I put a hand on her arm. "Not so fast, Jo. I want us to work from level ground here, and we can't unless you tell the truth."

She loosened her grip on my tree balls and clasped her royal blue fingers together as if in prayer. "Okay," she said. "The truth." She took a deep breath and held it like she was building up her courage. The next words came out in a rush. "I'm scared to go to the house alone."

I frowned my disappointment. "I don't blame you," I said. "But we both know that's not what I'm talking about."

She spun on her blue suede heel and strode away. I shrugged and pushed my cart to my car. I was putting the packages in the backseat when she was beside me again.

"You don't understand," she said.

"Excuse me, please. I need to put this package in the car." I waited until she moved aside. "And you're right. I don't understand."

"His family hates me and my family hates him. They always have." Her voice was ragged with emotion.

I turned and gave her my full attention. "Why?"

"They think I'm nasty and mean and no good for him. Mine think he's nasty and mean and no good for me."

Sounded like a match to me.

"We've known each other since we were little kids. Every time he visited his grandmother, we got into a fight. Sometimes he'd win; sometimes I would. I gave him more than one shiner and he gave me more than one bloody nose. Right up to junior high we were still kicking and punching."

I could see how the two families, coming to the defense of their own child, would quickly develop deep feelings against the other child.

"In junior high, things changed. We decided we loved each other, and that scared our families as much as the fights, maybe more. 'You're too young. You don't know what love is.' We were too young and we didn't know what love was, but that didn't make any difference to us. It was always Reilly and Jolene. We went together all through high school and beyond.

"We used to have roaring fights just so we could make up. In fact we'd had one just before I met Arnie again at that New Year's Eve party. Reilly was in the Marines then and he'd been home on leave for Christmas. We had a fight over something so stupid I can't even remember what it was. I probably thought his Christmas present wasn't expensive enough and wanted him to trade up. What I do remember is that he wouldn't give in to me. Before that I could always wheedle and cajole and work on him until he did whatever I wanted. But not that time. He was developing a steel I couldn't bend, and I was absolutely furious at him. So I went after Arnie. I thought it was fun to cut in on Airy and fun to spite Reilly. He erupted in a fury."

"But the fun didn't last," I said.

"I knew I'd made a terrible mistake within a week of the wedding, but I was too proud to say anything to anyone. And there was the money."

"Ah, yes, the money."

"It almost kept us together. We had a lot of fun spending it and planning how to spend it. But then Reilly came home and *she* popped up."

"How long have you been involved with Reilly?"

"Since the first day he came back to Amhearst about a year and a half ago. We've just kept it secret. It was easier."

"And I bet you liked the mystery and danger, didn't you? Let's see how many people we can fool. But Jo, you can't play games like that all your life."

"I can if I want to," she snapped.

"How does Reilly feel about all this cloak-and-dagger stuff?"

Jolene didn't answer.

"He doesn't like it, does he?"

"He wants to get married." She sounded distressed.

"And you don't? Don't you love him?"

"I've always loved him. Always."

"Then what's the trouble?"

"None of your business." Her tone was flat and hard.

"See you later, Jolene." I turned to get in my car.

"If I marry him, I'll have to put his needs first," she mumbled.

"What did you say?" I looked at her in astonishment.

"If I marry him, I'll have to put his needs first."

I hugged her. "Jolene, there's hope for you yet!"

She smiled self-consciously. "But what if I can't do that? What if I do to him what I did to Arnie?"

"What did you do to Arnie?"

"I made him miserable. I did everything I could to make his life a living hell."

"Jolene, it couldn't have been that bad."

"Oh, yes," she said. "It was worse than you can imagine. You're too nice to even think of all the awful things I did. The really ugly thing is that I liked making him angry. I liked manipulating him. I liked getting him to storm out of the house in a fury." She stared at the ground and whispered, "I'm not a very nice person, Merry."

"And you're afraid Reilly will find that out."

She looked at me in surprise. "Yes."

"Jolene, he already knows exactly what you're like. All those bloody noses and the tempestuous fights and dumping him for Arnie and your clandestine affair—he already knows."

"I want to be nice," she whispered. "I want to love Reilly forever. I want him to love me forever. But I don't know how to make it all work."

"God can help you, Jo. You just have to turn to him."

"I'm so miserable that only God can help me?" She seemed utterly despondent.

I laughed gently. "Oh, Jo, we're all that miserable. That's what Christmas and Jesus are all about. Now get in the car," I said, gesturing to the front seat. "Let's get this trip over with."

"Really? You'll help me?"

"I said I would if you told the truth, remember?"

Jolene hugged me and ran around the car. I pushed the cart to the area between my car and the one facing me and climbed behind the wheel. For a few minutes neither of us spoke. I was musing on the fact that now that I knew the truth about Jolene and Reilly, it didn't change any of the circumstances. Whether it would change any attitudes or hearts remained to be seen.

We had gotten off the bypass before I asked my next question.

"Jolene, why do you do it?"

"Do what?"

"Stuff like back in Kmart."

"You mean tease Sean?" She grinned. "It's so much fun."

"I don't understand that," I said. "Why is it fun to make people uncomfortable or unhappy?"

"Sean knew," she said.

I thought back over that conversation. *I'm not quite sure how you got this power over us, but be certain we know what you're trying to do,* he'd said.

"Power?" I guessed.

She nodded. "Power. There's something very satisfying about making people do what you want."

"Especially when they all end up hating you," I said dryly. "Jo, you're crazy. You've got all these people you've known all your life, and you're reduced to asking me to go with you. Don't you see something wrong here?"

She squirmed a little in her seat, but she didn't respond. I wasn't surprised. How much truth could I expect her to face in one evening?

We drove a little bit farther in silence. It was quarter after four now, and the evening was beginning to close in. I would be happy to get in and out of that mansion before it was full dark.

"Oh, no!" yelled Jolene, scaring me half to death. "Look at that! It's the old lady!"

She pointed off to the side of the road. I slowed as we drove past, but all I saw was a car pulled onto the shoulder and an older lady climbing up a bank on her way to the car.

"It's Mrs. Samson!" Jolene said.

"It is?" I looked in my rearview mirror. "I think I need to see her peering out between the curtains to really identify her. Mrs. Samson, Master Spy."

Jolene giggled. "What in the world is she doing?"

"Shall we stop to help her?" I began to pull off the road.

"Don't you dare stop for her," Jolene said. "She'll just tell us to get out. She hates me."

"So you've said before. Maybe if we stop, she'll appreciate it and start to like you. After all, if you and Reilly ever get married, she'll be your grandmother-in-law."

Jolene groaned.

"And she may need us."

Our car had come to a stop, and I looked back over my shoulder. Almost immediately I saw the headlights of Mrs. Samson's car snap on and the car begin to move. She pulled onto the road very carefully and drove past us without a second glance.

"That's Reilly's car she's driving," Jolene said. "I wonder how she talked him into letting her use it. She's not the world's best driver."

Out of curiosity I backed up to the place where Mrs. Samson had been and looked out across the cornfield that bordered the road. "What was she doing out here?"

"I wonder if this is where she hit the deer," Jolene said.

"She was all the way out here when she had the accident?"

Jolene nodded. "Reilly told me all about it. He had to go to the hospital to get her. The police made her get checked out because of her age and because of the extent of the damage to the car."

"Did you ever hit a deer?" I asked.

Jo shook her head. "I've been lucky so far. I keep waiting for it to happen though. First I lived out here which is sort of country and now I live in the country again. Some day one's bound to get me."

"It's scary when it happens," I said as I pulled into the driveway at Arnie's house. I shuddered as I thought of that big body sliding across the hood toward me. "Very scary."

We climbed out and stood staring at the large, unlighted structure looming over us in the gathering gloom. The windows that had shown so brightly and warmly before were now flat and forbidding. The great double doors were a drawbridge raised against us. The perfect shrubbery was hunched shapes waiting to spring.

Now *that*, I thought, taking it all in, is scary.

Jolene grabbed my arm. "I hate this," she said. "IhateitIhateitIhateit! I wish I never, ever had to come here again. Who cares how we bury Arnie? He doesn't. I want to go home!"

"You and me both," I said. "Come on. Sooner in, sooner out."

We walked in tiny baby steps to the house, struggling to stay side by side on the brick walk wide enough for one. Neither of us wanted to be first because we remembered too well what the first person had found last time. And neither of us wanted to be last because we both knew that the boogeyman carted off the last guy in line.

We finally reached the porch and stood looking at each other. I thought my face probably looked every bit as strained as Jolene's.

"The keys?" I whispered.

"Right," Jo whispered back. She reached into her gigantic black bag and began rooting. I reached out a hand and, strictly out of curiosity, depressed the tongue above the graceful sweep of the great brass door latch. It gave under my touch and the door swung silently open.

It was all I could do not to scream. I felt like I was in every Halloween movie I'd ever seen. I almost heard the weird laugh and the rustling of chains. I almost saw the secret passage slide open and the disembodied hand reach out for me.

Then reason returned and I wanted to slap Jolene. I had rarely been so furious, not even the time twelve-year-old Sam hid behind the sofa one evening to spy on Jack and me.

"You set me up again!" I shouted, turning on her, my fists clenched. "I can't believe it! Well, I'm not playing along this time!" I turned to stalk back to the car, now mad at myself as well. "How can I be so gullible over and over?"

Jolene, holding onto the doorjamb, made a slight groan and began sliding to the ground. I watched her go dispassionately. She ended up in a heap in front of the open door.

"Oh, that's great," I said. "Pretend to faint. That's sure to impress me."

"I'm going to throw up," she whispered. "Ooooh." The last was a whimper.

She started heaving, great spasms shaking her body. She struggled up onto her knees and crawled to the edge of the porch, retching the whole time. Suddenly I understood that she wasn't acting. She really was petrified to the point of illness. I dropped to my knees beside her just as her stomach emptied itself into the boxwoods.

"Oh, geez, Jolene, I'm sorry." I was smitten across the heart with guilt, and I do guilt well. "Are you all right?" Another one of those wonderfully inane questions. Sure she's all right. All right people always throw up in their front yards.

"I'll be right back," I said and rushed into the house. I flipped on all the light switches I could find and opened doors until I found the downstairs powder room. I grabbed a towel from the rack, wet it, and rushed back to Jolene.

She was sitting propped up against the house looking utterly spent. I knelt and held out the damp towel.

"Thank you," she whispered and started crying. "You're so good to me. I don't deserve it. Thank you. Thank you. You're so good."

Now I really felt guilty. I had screamed and yelled at her and she was thanking me. "How can you thank me after what I did?"

She looked at me, confusion in her eyes. "What did you do? You mean opening the door?" She shuddered. "I've never been so scared in my life. I thought we were going to die. I *knew* we were going to die."

I realized with intense relief that she hadn't heard a word I'd screamed at her. Fear had made her deaf. It didn't seem right that my horrible accusations would go unpunished, but I recognized a gift when I saw it.

Thank you, Lord. I won't let it happen again. I promise.

"Come on," I said, offering her my hand. "Let's get this over with."

I pulled her to her feet, and after leaning against the house for a couple of minutes, she nodded her head.

"Okay," she whispered. "Let's do it."

We walked into the front hall, and this time I took time to look around. It was obvious the police had been at work here. There was fingerprint dust all over things, and furniture had been moved about as a thorough search for any possible clues had been made. My eyes were drawn to the kitchen door where I knew the disorder would be greatest, but I was not going to go check it out. Not for anything did I want to see that pool of blood and that bullet hole in the cabinet again.

We turned toward the steps and began a slow ascent. The master bedroom was our goal.

"Arnie had a navy pinstripe suit that I always liked," Jolene said. "Let's get that. And a white shirt and his yellow power tie."

"That sounds good," I said. "Do we have to get underwear too? And socks and shoes?"

"I don't know," said Jolene. "I never had to do anything like this before. I'm trying to remember what the funeral guy told me."

"We'd better take them," I said. "If he doesn't need them, no harm done. But if we don't take them and he needs them ..."

"We'll take them," said Jolene. "I'm not coming back here ever again. Not ever."

The master bedroom was as beautifully decorated as the downstairs with a marvelous verdigris iron bedstead with a canopy of what looked like hand-tatted lace. The greens and blues of the bedspread and curtains were soft yet vibrant, and the blue rug was every bit as thick as the one in the living room.

I stood and stared while Jolene went into the closet. I tried to imagine what it was like to sleep in such a fairytale bed and to wake up each morning in such luxury. I began wandering around the room, looking at the pictures, all wonderful impressionistic watercolors, misty and inviting. This was a room carefully designed for relaxing, for forgetting life's troubles.

"Shall I get some underwear and socks?" I called when I reached Arnie's tall bureau. "Or do you want to make a selection?"

"Go ahead. You pick." Jolene's voice echoed eerily from the depths of the walk-in closet.

I opened a drawer and found more pairs of socks than my father had owned in his entire life. I chose a pair of navy ones with little cranberry insignia all over them. In another drawer I found piles of silk underwear. I knew it was silk because I read the label. I didn't know men wore silk underwear. Certainly those in my family didn't. I took a pair of briefs and a T-shirt.

"Should he wear any jewelry?" I asked as I looked at his collection of rings sitting on top of the bureau.

"I don't think so," Jolene called. "He hardly ever wore them. He just bought them when we first got the money and we were spending it on anything. That was before we learned its limits."

"Oh," I said, turning from the bureau toward the bed. "Speaking of the money, where—"

The words caught in my throat as I stared at the table beside the bed. I blinked and looked again.

It was a picture of the two of them. Arnie stood tall and muscular in jeans and a red polo shirt. Snuggled against him, laughing at the camera, was a girl in jeans and a purple T-shirt. She was slim and tanned and wore her long blonde hair caught up in a ponytail.

"The little tramp," hissed Jolene.

I jumped the proverbial mile. She had walked up beside me without my hearing. Thick rugs are great for sneaking around.

"She's Arnie's girl? The one that broke up your marriage?"

Jolene hesitated. "I can't say that she broke up our marriage because there were others before her. But she's the one he finally fixed on. Their affair had been going on for over a year."

I picked up the photo and looked again at the smiling face of Lonni Allen Bushay. I traced a crack in the glass across the lower left corner just above the fluted brass frame.

"I did that," said Jolene, pointing to the crack. "The night I threw it at him."

Throwing things at people was beyond my ken, so I said, "Do you know how old she is?"

Jolene shrugged. "Who cares?"

"She's seventeen."

Jolene shrugged again. "That sounds like Arnie."

"And she's pregnant."

"What?" Jolene had finally heard something that shocked her.

"She's due in a couple of months. They were going to get married as soon as she turned eighteen, about a month before the baby would be born."

Jolene stared at the picture. "I wonder," she said slowly, "what this does to his money. What do you think?"

But I barely heard her. I was lost in memories of my conversation with Lonni.

"Then my father went nuts. He screamed. He shouted. He ranted. He said he'd kill Hunk. He threatened to blow his head off or run a knife through his heart or hang him by the neck until dead."

Had Harry Allen followed through on his threats? Had he come out here and shot Arnie?

And the argument that Elsa, the secretary, overheard in Harry Allen's office. It wasn't Commies that Arnie and Harry Allen were arguing about. It was Lonni.

Did Sergeant Poole know all this? He was certainly questioning Harry Allen. I knew that because of the briefcase comment. But did William understand about Arnie and Lonni?

Jolene studied my face. "What's wrong with you?"

"I may know who murdered Arnie."

She grabbed me by the arm and spun me to face her. "Who?"

"Her father threatened Arnie, and he and Arnie had a terrible fight the day before Arnie was killed."

"The slut's father? But that's Harry Allen Bushay, isn't it?"

I nodded, surprised she knew.

"But everybody in Amhearst knows him. How could he possibly do something as awful as kill Arnie? He's too nice a guy."

"If you think someone has hurt your baby daughter, you can do almost anything," I said just like I knew what I was talking about.

Jolene looked skeptical. "She's hardly a baby. And he was hardly hurting her. This was a full consent romance."

"I know that and you know that. Lonni certainly knows that. But maybe Harry Allen's having trouble with that idea. Daughters are always their fathers' babies, to be protected at all costs. Why do you think your father doesn't like Reilly? Because he thinks he's not nice to his baby girl."

"Maybe," said Jolene. "But right now I need to know what color shoes. Brown or black?"

I followed Jolene around the abrupt corner in her mental road. "With a navy suit? Black definitely. And don't forget a belt." But I still thought Harry Allen was a good suspect.

While Jolene went back to the closet for the shoes, I wandered into the master bath. It was every bit as gorgeous as I'd thought. The Jacuzzi-type tub was big enough for four, though why you'd have four in your bathroom I couldn't imagine, and the vanity counter, miles long, held two sinks. The shower stall was silvered, and I found myself staring at myself. What a depressing sight. I needed to get home and do something with this hair before Curt came.

On impulse—I've got to stop giving in to impulses. They're nothing but trouble—I pulled the door open. I almost dropped my teeth.

Staring at me, a horrified expression on her face, was Airy Bennett.

Chapter Fourteen

Why neither Airy nor I screamed is beyond me. We just stared at each other, equally appalled. It apparently never dawned on either of us to be afraid of the other or to wonder if the other had a weapon. Maybe my lack of fear of her had something to do with the fact that she wore tan jeans and a red and yellow patterned sweater, a blue and red ski jacket, and a blue tam. Who ever heard of a dangerous housebreaker wearing a colorful outfit like that?

When I finally found my voice, I hissed, "What are you doing here?"

She put her finger to her lips in an unspoken plea for my silence. She peered over my shoulder, fear large in her eyes.

"Don't worry," I whispered. "I won't give you away. I don't want to witness what Jolene would do if she knew you were here."

Airy sagged in relief, grabbing the cold water faucet as she did. A spray of water danced out, drenching her head and splashing onto my jacket. I jumped back with a squeak while she fumbled madly to turn the spigot off. I grabbed a towel, brushed it quickly down my front to get the worst of the water, and handed it to her. She pulled her soaked tam off and rubbed the towel across her face. She stuffed the tam in her pocket and passed the towel back to me.

"Hey, Merry," called Jolene from the next room, her voice close at hand. Airy and I both froze, certain she'd heard the shower or my squeak or something. I pushed the shower stall door but didn't click it shut. I stepped to the sink, towel in hand. Just in time. Jolene appeared in the doorway. "I've got Arnie's black shoes. Let's get out of here. The place still gives me the creeps."

"In a minute, Jo," I said as I slid the towel back on the rack. I was pleased to hear that my voice barely shook. "I think maybe I'm going to use the facilities while we're here. You go on down."

She looked at the wet towel. "Most people wash their hands afterwards, you know."

"Yeah, well, you know me." I laughed weakly. "Always doing things differently."

"Just hurry, okay?" she said as she backed out of the room, pulling the door shut behind her. "I need to set the alarm system and make sure the place is properly locked up when we leave. You never know who might wander in if I don't. We're just lucky that we were the only ones who found that unlocked door." And the bathroom door clicked shut.

"You know it," I called. I waited a beat, then pulled the shower door open again. I looked at Airy cringing in the corner. "Was it unlocked when you arrived?" I whispered.

She nodded as she put her finger to her lips again and looked frantically at the bedroom door.

"Sergeant Poole's going to hear about this, believe me," Jolene continued, her voice moving farther and farther away. "Talk about incompetence! Anyone could have come in here and robbed me blind. Look what someone did to my other place." And she giggled.

I moved to the bathroom door and listened for a couple of minutes, but I couldn't tell whether Jolene had gone downstairs yet or not. The rug deadened the sounds too well. I peered cautiously into the room. The closet light was off and so was the overhead light. The only ones remaining on were in the bathroom where Airy and I were and in the upstairs hall. Then I heard the click of Jolene's steps across the parquet floor downstairs.

I turned back to Airy and repeated my question. "What are you doing here?"

She opened her mouth but no words came out.

"Are you here to pay some last respects to Arnie or something strange like that?" I couldn't think of any other reason. Theft never crossed my mind where she was concerned.

She shook her head quite violently. "No, no! Nothing like that, for heaven's sake. That's sick."

I acted like I hadn't seen the movement or heard the words. "What would Sean say if he knew you were here? I know how much he loves you. I really thought you loved him, too."

She flinched and said with desperation, "I love Sean. I do. That's why I sneaked in here. I don't want Sean to know. I'm afraid of what will happen if he knows. He won't understand!" The last was a cry from the heart.

I ran my hand through my hair, totally confused. "He's not the only one who doesn't understand."

"I don't want him to know I was here. But I can't find it." She started to slide down the shower wall in despair. "I can't find it."

I grabbed her none-too-gently by one arm and dragged her out of the stall. "I don't care whether you can find it, whatever it is, or not. You've got to get out of here before Jo finds you or you get locked in."

"But if I don't find it, they'll know I was here. Sean will know I was here."

"When?" I asked, going after a fact I felt I could get my hands on. "When were you here? Do you mean now? Tonight?"

She shook her head. "No."

"Come on, Airy. Talk to me. If you don't, I'll turn you over to the police. Breaking and entering's a serious matter. You'll have to talk to them."

She just looked at me, mouth stubbornly closed.

"Or I can turn you over to Jolene."

Terror leaped to her eyes. She pulled her arm free from my grasp and pushed me with all her might. Her move was so unexpected that I went flying. I fell to the tiled floor, my elbow taking the brunt of my weight. Talk about pain!

She pulled the door open and was out the room and across the bedroom before I struggled painfully to my feet. Holding my elbow, I raced after her into the upstairs hall. She looked back just as I burst through the bedroom door, and my wild countenance scared her enough to throw her footing off slightly. She careened into the wall and bounced off. I launched myself at her legs, thankful for all those years of tackle football I'd played with Sam and Jack.

We tumbled to the floor and slid along the rug. While I was thankful for the cushioning and thankful my elbow didn't take another shot, I was worried about the raspberry effect on my cheek. We lay panting, trying to get our breath.

"Are you okay, Merry?" Jolene's voice floated up the stairs. "What was that noise?"

"I'm fine," I said, trying not to gasp too audibly. "I tripped." Sort of.

"Merry, be nimble; Merry, be neat," she chanted. "Merry tripped over her own two big feet."

"Charming," I called, rolling my eyes.

She giggled again. "I'm taking the suit and shoes out to the car. I'll come back to set the alarm."

"Good idea," I said. I heard the front door open and close.

I sat up and looked at Airy, still lying full out on the hall floor. All the stuffing had been knocked out of her.

"Okay," I said. "We've got a couple of minutes here. Tell me what in the world you've been talking about."

Airy rolled over onto her back. "I don't want to lose Sean," she sobbed.

"That's nice," I said. "I don't want you to lose him either. But what makes you think you will?"

"I came to see Arnie."

That didn't seem like grounds for divorce to me unless— "When?" I asked.

"After Jolene and I had our fight."

"The day he was killed."

She nodded. "See why I don't want anyone to know?"

No, I didn't see. Just because you came to see someone didn't mean you killed him. "Why did you come?"

"I wanted to ask him how I should handle Jolene. He must have handled her well because he ended up with the house and the money when they split."

"Half the money. And I'm not so sure he handled her very well at all."

"Oh. Well, it seemed a good idea at the time," she said defensively.

"I'm sure it did. Was he dead when you got here?"

"She used to make up poems like that about me," Airy said. "You have no idea how I hated it."

"You were a kid. Of course you hated it. But now you're an adult, so you'd better face a few issues. Was Arnie dead when you got here?"

At first she wouldn't look at me.

"Come on, Airy. He must have been or you wouldn't be so scared."

She nodded, her face strained. "I rang the bell but he didn't answer, so I tried the door. It opened, just like tonight, so I came in. I called for Arnie, but still no answer. I thought maybe I'd misunderstood his secretary when I called his office. Maybe she hadn't said he was working at home after all. I thought that I'd just check the kitchen to be sure he wasn't on the phone or something." She stopped and swallowed. "It was awful!"

I nodded. "I know." We were both silent for a couple of seconds, thinking about what we'd seen. Then I asked, "So what happened next?"

"I got out of there as fast as I could. I didn't want anyone to know I'd been anywhere near him, not with our history. Too many people remember the fool I made of myself when he married Jolene, screaming and crying and making all kinds of threats. I didn't realize until later what a favor she'd done me, not until I met Sean. I'm always afraid that people think Sean was my second choice and a poor second at that. But that's not so. Sean is so much more wonderful than Arnie that I can't even explain."

I nodded, thinking of Jack and Curt. "But I'm still missing something here. Why did you come back here tonight? Whatever made you take such a risk?"

"Because I can't find my scarf."

"Your scarf," I repeated. Suddenly I saw Jolene's bedroom and my bedroom and our closets, and things went *click*.

"I thought maybe I left it here," she continued. "When I saw Arnie lying there"—and she shivered—"I put my purse and things down on the kitchen table so my hands would be free. I had to be sure he was dead. I thought he was. I'd never seen anyone dead before, but I was pretty sure. Still, if he was only hurt, I needed to call for help. I felt for his heartbeat and I felt his carotid artery. He was dead."

"And you knew this when we met at McDonald's that night." I thought of her white face and distress when Curt mentioned Arnie's death. "Airy! I was so worried for you, you little actress!" I snarled the last two words like they were obscenities.

"I know. You were so sweet." And she had the nerve to smile at me.

I stared at her as she pulled herself into a seated position and leaned against the hall wall.

"Anyway, when I was sure Arnie was dead, I grabbed my things and ran, but I could never find my scarf again." She put her hands over her face. "I must have dropped it here, and I'm afraid someone will recognize it. But I can't find it, and I don't know where else to look."

"What if the police have it?" I asked, knowing full well they didn't. It was lying at home on my bureau.

"I don't care if they do. They won't know where it came from. It's Jo I worry about. She's the one who gave it to me. It was a gift the Christmas of that infamous New Year's Eve party."

"Ah." And Jo had seen it and not even felt a glimmer of recognition. "So you broke into my house looking for it," I said, giving her a hard-eyed look. "And Jolene's. Don't you see an inappropriate behavior pattern here, Airy?"

Her face turned scarlet. "I'm sorry. I was desperate. I had to be certain neither of you had the scarf. It would be just like Jo to keep it to make my life miserable. Then I thought maybe you'd picked it up by mistake. I thought I'd die when that guy showed up at your place. And then you came into the bathroom!"

I tried to work up some sympathy for her hiding behind my shower curtain, but I couldn't. I was too busy remembering my feelings of apprehension and invasion.

The front door opened and Jolene clicked into the foyer.

"You ready, Merry?"

"Be right down," I called.

"You know those little hooks in cars for hanging clothes?" she called. "Well, the one in your car is terrible. The suit hanger's curved, you know? I thought I'd never get it to stay hooked on that little bracket, but I finally did."

"Good for you," I called. "The last thing you want is a wrinkled suit for Arnie."

I looked at Airy. Did I want to report her to the police? Or more pressing, did I think she was telling the truth about finding Arnie dead? Or did I think she had something to do with his death?

But why would she kill him? With what I knew about the convoluted relationships of these people, I could see no motive. But I could see Airy coming to Arnie for advice. I could see her finding him dead. I could see her panicking. I could see her trying to protect her back rather than risk Sean's lack of understanding.

I decided that when I called William Poole to tell him that Harry Allen had a beaut of a motive, I would tell him about Airy. He could deal with it as he felt best. In the meantime, how were we going to get her out of the house if Jolene set the alarm? Of course it would serve her right to get stuck, breaking and entering like she had. Talk about making choices from weakness rather than strength!

I took Arnie's underwear and socks and put them on the hall table. I turned to Airy and indicated she should be quiet and wait right where she was. I had an idea. She nodded her understanding.

I went down the stairs, turning off the hall light as I went. I found Jolene by the front door pushing a number pad.

"What activates the alarm?" I asked. "Pushing the numbers or closing the door? Or both?" I hope, I hope.

"Both," she said. "Let's go."

We went out the front door and Jolene reached for the latch to pull it tight.

"Wait a minute," I said, putting my foot on the doorsill. "I think I left Arnie's socks and underwear upstairs." I searched my empty pockets.

"Merry!" Jolene wasn't pleased.

"Go on," I said. "Here are the keys. Start the engine and get the heat going. Then turn on the headlights so I can see when I come out. I'll only be a minute."

Sighing and shaking her head, Jolene accepted the keys and started toward the car. I went back inside, flicked on the foyer lights, and pushed the door almost closed. Then I raced upstairs, turning on the upper hall light as I ran. I grabbed the underwear and socks and turned to Airy. I grabbed her too.

"Come on. This is your only chance."

We hurried downstairs and I turned toward the kitchen. Airy froze.

"I can't go in there," she whispered. "I just can't."

"You don't have a choice," I said, dragging her with me. "If I can do it, you can do it."

We crept through the dark kitchen to the back sliding glass door, both taking care not to look toward the spot where Arnie had lain. From the cloying, butcher-shop smell, I was afraid the pool of blood was probably still there. Jolene would have to get a cleaning service in here, the kind that specialized in cleaning up after crimes.

In the light seeping from the front hall, I found and flicked up the lock on the door. I pulled, but the door refused to slide open.

"What in the—" I shoved at the door again.

"Burglar bar," Airy hissed and bent to lift it free.

The door slid open at last and I pushed Airy out.

"Get lost," I hissed. I pulled the door shut, threw the lock in place, and raced back to the front hall. I was flipping off the upstairs hall light just as Jolene walked in the front door.

"I've got to check the alarm again just so I know everything's okay," she said. "It sure is drafty in here, isn't it?"

"A bit," I said as I hit the foyer light switch. "A bit."

We walked outside together and pulled the door firmly shut, engaging the alarm. The dark house loomed behind us, but I no longer felt a threat. It was just a beautiful, sad place where people and marriages had died.

I don't know what Jolene was thinking as we backed out of the drive, but I was wondering where Airy was lurking. I scanned the shrubbery, but I didn't see any sign of her. If she was smart, she was crouching somewhere out back until we were well out of sight.

We drove down the street in silence, passing a parked car some distance from the house. Airy's? As we turned the corner a quarter of a mile away, I glanced back at the mansion.

"Funny, isn't it, how it looks like the front hall light is still on?"

And the house disappeared from sight behind a copse of trees.

I finally got home fifteen minutes before Curt was due. I spent most of the time trying to get control of my hair. Finally, by using a set of combs, I was able to curb my usual finger-in-the-light-socket coiffure. I was pulling up the zipper on my red dress when the front doorbell rang. I went to let Curt in as I pinned my favorite family piece, Grandmom Richards' cut glass Christmas tree, high on my left shoulder.

Curt took one look at me and actually whistled. I don't think anyone had ever whistled at me before, at least no one who counted. Construction workers don't count, at least not unless you're dating one.

"You look beautiful, Merry," he said. "That red is stunning with your hair and eyes, but it's the incandescent smile that I like best."

I glowed and we stood staring at each other. It was a wonderful, ridiculous Hallmark moment. Then he extended a paper bag to me.

"What's this?" I took the bag and reached inside.

"I thought you might like them," Curt said.

One by one I pulled out tree ornaments wrapped in tissue paper. I opened each like it was a priceless treasure because in a sense each was. The first was a clear glass ball with an angel remarkably like my new angel flying inside.

"I don't know where this came from, but it was always my favorite tree decoration as a little boy," Curt said, running his finger softly over the glass. "I just knew this was what angels really looked like."

I smiled. "Me too." I dug out my new angel for him to admire.

"See?" he said. "I was right."

The next treasure from Curt's bag was a cross-stitched sprig of holly with red berries and ribbons on a cream background, the initials JCE in the corner.

"Joan?" I asked, fingering the initials.

Curt nodded. "She made it her last Christmas."

I laid it reverently on the coffee table next to the glass ball.

There were two matte white tree balls with Christmas scenes reminiscent of Currier and Ives painted on them.

"You did these?"

"No. My mother."

"No wonder you're so talented," I said, laying them beside Joan's work.

Next I extracted a felt cardinal, a chickadee, and a partridge without his pear tree, all stuffed and wearing hand-crocheted hanging loops.

"Mom," said Curt. "She liked to make something new for the tree every year."

"Oh, Curt." My eyes were full of tears. "They're all wonderful!"

I pulled out the last bauble and opened it. I gasped as I stared at a small picture in a little gilt frame with a red ribbon hanger.

"It's me," I said, delighted. "How did you do it?"

The picture was a line drawing bordering on caricature. My wild black curls were there, my eyes, my smile, my chin. The marvelous part was the economy of strokes presenting a complete individual.

I went to my tree and hung the little piece of art front and center.

"So everyone will be sure to see it," I said. Then I threw my arms around him and hugged my thanks.

He helped me on with my red coat, and we walked to the car arm in arm. We held hands all the way to Maddie and Doug's. Then I climbed into the backseat with Maddie, and Doug, with his extralong legs, sat in the front with Curt.

I had never been to Dilworthtown Inn before, and it was all I'd heard it would be. The service was excellent and the food delicious. I basked in the rosy glow of Curt's gift and the pleasure of good food and fine company, at least until I told the tale of Airy in the shower stall and our rush to get her outside without Jolene seeing her.

"I just pushed her out the back door and ran for the foyer," I said. "I hope she found her way home."

That's when the curious phenomenon that had occurred the other morning on the way to Mr. Hamish's happened again. Curt withdrew. Oh, he was still there. He still ate and laughed and talked, but he had withdrawn. From me.

Doug and Maddie had laughed at my story.

"How do you get yourself in fixes like that all the time?" Maddie asked.

"I've never known anyone who has such strange things happen to her," Doug said. "Knowing you has added a whole new dimension to our lives."

Curt said nothing. He just pulled away. Doug and Maddie didn't seem to notice anything, but then he talked to them and laughed with them as animatedly as before. It was me he ceased to respond to.

My rosy glow faded, and though I smiled brightly, I felt hurt and confused. What was going on? Why this now hot, now cold attitude? What set it off? What did it mean? Was it proof that what I sometimes feared—that Curt would decide I wasn't what he wanted after all—was coming to pass? Was the idea that I was falling in love with him when he was falling out with me accurate?

At one point when both Doug and Maddie excused themselves for a few minutes, I turned to Curt.

"What's wrong?" I asked, putting my hand on his.

He looked at me in surprise. "What do you mean?"

"You've done it again, just like the other morning. You're here but you're not."

He smiled and lifted his coffee cup for a drink. "You must be mistaken. Everything's fine."

But it wasn't. He'd let his hand sit in his lap like a log rather than turn it palm up and clasp mine. When we left, he put his hand on my back to guide me, and when we had to wait in the parking lot for a car to back out, he rested his hand on my shoulder. But he didn't stand close. He didn't smile at me like I was special. I could have been any woman being treated politely by any man.

I climbed into the backseat beside Maddie. "Do you two want to come back to my place and help us decorate my Christmas tree?" I asked. I didn't know whether I wanted them to say yes or no because I didn't know whether I wanted to be alone with Curt or not.

"That sounds like fun," said Maddie. "We'd love to. It's much too early to go home."

I put all our coats on my bed and watched Whiskers climb up to inspect them. I felt a perverse pleasure when he climbed onto Curt's camel topcoat and circled and circled. I didn't shoo him down. It would serve Curt right to wear cat hair.

Maddie and I let the guys fight with the lights even though the final product was a bit lopsided with more lights on the left side of the tree.

"Don't worry," Maddie whispered. "You can restring them tomorrow."

I pulled a dining-room chair up to the tree and slipped out of my heels. "I'm going to put my angel on the top," I announced.

I climbed onto the wooden chair and reached for the top of the tree. As I did, I felt my feet, slick in their hose, slip.

"Oh, no!" I yelped.

Curt leaped toward me and grabbed me around the waist. I ended up with my arms around his neck and my feet dangling inches from the floor as he pressed me against him. My angel dangled down his back.

He held me for a split second, looking at me with that distant expression in his eyes. Then, almost as if a little switch somewhere had been thrown, a marvelous smile lit his face.

"All I can say," he said as he put me back on the chair, "is that I'm glad you had nothing liquid in your hands." And he held me steady while I put my angel in place.

Just that easily he was back. Just as easily I welcomed him.

Maddie and Doug left shortly before eleven, but Curt stayed a while. We turned out all the lights except the tree and sat on the sofa, me resting against Curt, his arm across my shoulders. Whiskers came out of the bedroom and climbed up beside me. He curled against my side and began to purr. The three of us sat companionably, mesmerized by the tree.

"Isn't it beautiful?" I said.

"Um."

"Aren't you glad we got it?"

"Um."

I turned to face him. "Aren't you glad I got you to celebrate at least a little bit of Christmas?"

He looked at me, his eyes warm. "I am."

"Will you come for dinner Christmas Day? You can help me learn to cook a turkey."

"I will, and with pleasure."

Sighing happily, I turned back to the tree. Curt put his hand on my head and guided it until I was resting on his shoulder.

"And it came to pass in those days," said Curt, "that there went out a decree from Caesar Augustus, that all the world should be taxed."

"And this taxing was first made when Cyrenius was governor of Syria," I said.

"And all went to be taxed, every one to his own city. And Joseph went up from Galilee, out of the city of Nazareth, to the city of David, which is called Bethlehem, to be taxed with Mary, his espoused wife, being great with child."

I continued the story. "And so it was, that, while they were there, the days were accomplished that she should be delivered. And she brought forth her firstborn son, and wrapped him in swaddling clothes, and laid him in a manger; because there was no room for them in the inn."

"And there were in the same country shepherds abiding in the fields, keeping watch over their flocks by night. And, lo, the angel of the Lord came upon them, and the glory of the Lord shown round about them: and they were sore afraid."

Whiskers stirred and rearranged himself, his chin resting on my knee. I laid my hand on his head and said, "And the angel said unto them, Fear not: for, behold, I bring you good tidings of great joy, which shall be to all people. For unto you is born this day in the city of David a Savior, which is Christ the Lord. And this shall be a sign unto you; Ye shall find the babe wrapped in swaddling clothes, lying in a manger."

"And suddenly," said Curt, "there was with the angel a multitude of the heavenly hosts, praising God, and saying, Glory to God in the highest, and on earth peace, good will toward men. And it came to pass, as the angels were gone away from them into heaven, the shepherds said one to another, Let us now go even unto Bethlehem, and see this thing which has come to pass, which the Lord has made known unto us."

"And they came with haste, and found Mary, and Joseph, and the babe lying in a manger."

We looked at each other and grinned.

"Not too bad," I said.

We were quiet a minute. Then Curt said softly, "Amen."

Chapter Fifteen

Dawn and I met for lunch at Ferretti's after church Sunday.

"Your bell choir number was wonderful," Dawn said as soon as we'd given our orders. "That sound always makes me think of angels for some reason."

"I was scared to death this morning," I said. "I made an awful mess of things at our last rehearsal, and I just knew I was going to ruin the whole Christmas service. You have no idea how nerve-wracking playing is for me. I lose sleep over it."

"Then why do you do it?"

"Because I love it."

Dawn laughed at me, then said, "I don't know why I'm laughing. I know exactly what you mean. I regularly lose sleep over the girls at His House, but there's nothing else I'd rather do."

"How's Pam?" I asked. "Is she okay?"

Dawn waved her hands back and forth. "So-so. It's hard for her right now. She's convinced she did the right thing, but she misses David immensely. 'My belly's empty and my arms are empty,' she told me yesterday."

"Poor girl. Will she ever get over it?"

Dawn raised her shoulders and let them drop. "Yes and no. She'll move on with her life. Hopefully she'll go back to school and graduate. Maybe she'll marry some nice man and have more kids. She'll have a full life, especially if she continues to follow the Lord. But there will always be that baby out there growing into a man, and she'll always wonder what he's like, if he's okay, if the people who adopted him have done a good job in raising him."

"Maybe some day she'll search him out," I said as I welcomed my grilled cheese. "Wouldn't that be wonderful?"

"Maybe," Dawn said, studying her tuna salad on wheat toast like she wondered whether she'd made a mistake ordering it. "Sometimes finding children or birthparents is a good thing. Sometimes it's traumatic. We always tell our girls that if they ever decide they want to find their babies, wait until they've grown. There's just too much emotion involved to put a child or a young teen through it. And we encourage them to go through a third party in case the children don't want to be found."

"Not want to be found? Why wouldn't they want to meet their mother?"

"Because they have another mom, one they've known for eighteen or twenty or more years. Some don't want the confusion of a second mother."

I ate a forkful of cole slaw. "Sandy Rasmussen called me."

Dawn nodded. "I thought she might. You'll like her. She's an interesting lady. She and Karyn are renting an apartment at Sweet Meadow."

"She's a single mom?"

"Oh, no." Dawn poured another mound of catsup and continued dunking her french fries. "She has three other older children at home with their father. He's a doctor, a pediatrician. He's a very nice guy. He tries to get down to see Karyn and Sandy at least every other weekend. He usually brings one or more of the older kids with him. I think they're all arriving this afternoon for the holidays. If things go as expected, they might be here for the birth too."

"I wonder if they'd all talk with me?"

Dawn shrugged. "They might. You can always ask."

I looked at my little tape recorder whirring on the table between us. "You know, there's more to this whole issue than the quick story Mac wanted. I need to talk with him about a series."

"You need to talk to me about what?"

I looked up. "Gosh, Mac, what a surprise seeing you here," I said. "I think you know Dawn Trauber?"

"Sure he knows me," said Dawn. "We've met several times before. How are you, Mac? Want to join us?" She smiled at him and slid over, totally unaware that she was making his day.

Mac, grinning like an idiot and uncharacteristically tongue-tied, slid into the booth beside Dawn.

The waitress saved the day by appearing at just that moment. "Can I get you ladies any dessert? How about something for you, Mac?"

"Ah," teased Dawn, looking at me. "She knows Mac's name. I bet all the ladies know Mac."

I watched in amazement as he flushed a brilliant crimson.

"I'll take a spaghetti," Mac said. "No garlic bread."

The waitress looked startled at the last part of the order, but she wisely said nothing.

"We'll wait dessert for Mac," Dawn told the waitress, and I wanted to laugh out loud at Mac's delighted expression.

Dawn looked at me. "Would you like to interview Pam? She's willing."

"Are you serious? Would I ever! But how do you feel about that?"

"I think it would be good for her right now. I think the more she talks about David, the better it is."

"Why'd you change your mind?" I asked.

"Because I can trust you," Dawn said simply.

I was overwhelmed and speechless.

Mac grinned at me sardonically. "Not much shuts her up, Dawn. You've accomplished a great feat here."

Dawn grinned at me. Then she sobered. "Pam's not my greatest concern though, believe it or not. I'm worried sick about Lonni. Something's wrong—besides the pregnancy, I mean. And she won't talk to me about it."

Mac and I looked at each other over his salad.

"What?" asked Dawn. "Do you two know something I don't?"

"Merry knows it all," Mac said.

Little did he know. I hadn't had a chance to tell him about Arnie.

"All what?" Dawn asked.

"Do you know who Hunk is?" I asked her.

"Do you?" asked Mac, startled.

I nodded.

"Wow," he said, impressed. "You're good. So tell us. Who is it and how did you find out?"

"Yes," said Dawn. "Who is it? If I hear that ridiculous name one more time, I'll puke."

Mac blinked and looked at Dawn. "Puke?"

"Yeah, you know," said Dawn. "Barf. Toss. Hurl."

"Please," he said, looking pained. "I'm eating." His dish of spaghetti steamed enticingly before him.

But it wasn't that Mac was unfamiliar with the word. I suspected he knew every synonym Dawn did and more. It was the fact that Dawn said a slang word referring to a bodily function. How high, I wondered, was the pedestal he had her on?

"Okay," said Dawn, returning to the subject we were discussing. "Tell me what you know about Lonni."

"Hunk is Arnie Meister."

"You're kidding!" Mac was incredulous. I got great satisfaction in seeing his disbelieving expression.

Dawn looked hesitant. "I don't think I know him."

"The guy who was murdered a few days ago," said Mac.

Dawn sat back in her seat and stared at us, appalled.

"And she thinks her father might have done it," said Mac.

Dawn looked at me for confirmation. I nodded.

"But Harry Allen's been wonderful to her," Dawn said. "I wish all fathers were as supportive of daughters in trouble as he is."

We were silent a minute, absently watching Mac twirl his spaghetti.

"You don't really think he did it, do you?" Dawn asked him just as he put a forkful in his mouth. "Not Harry Allen!" I found it very interesting that she asked Mac and not me, especially since I was the one who got the information.

Mac chewed manfully until he could speak. "It's hard to imagine."

"I need to learn more about this Arnie," she said.

"Go ahead, Mac. Tell her everything we know." I gathered my gloves and scarf and slid out of my seat. "I've got to call Sandy Rasmussen and set up an interview before her family gets here. By the way, Dawn and I think that His House and its residents need a series, not a single article. Right, Dawn?" And grabbing my tape recorder, I left.

I called Sandy Rasmussen as soon as I got home and we set up an appointment for tomorrow, Monday, at 10 A.M. at my place.

"There's no way we could talk around here," Sandy said. "Karyn's dad and brother and sisters are getting here late this afternoon. They had to be at home this morning to be in the choir for the Christmas service. They left right afterwards and should get here about five."

"How far do they have to drive?" I asked.

"From Massachusetts. Thankfully the weather isn't bad."

"How's Karyn doing?" I asked.

"Better than I am," she answered, laughing. "She could deliver anytime."

"A Christmas baby," I said and gave Sandy directions to my place.

Then I made another phone call and issued another invitation. I smiled at another acceptance.

I worked for a while on the His House article, focusing on Dawn and Julie and their responsibilities. I told the story of Pam's being rushed to the hospital and the excitement and prayers of the rest of the girls. I told of Dawn's job as birth coach and encourager and Julie's as teacher of the facts of living as a single mom.

I was just putting the laptop away when the phone rang.

"Merry, are you coming to the funeral?"

"Jolene?"

"Who else? Are you?"

"When is it?"

"I told you. Monday."

"Right, but Monday when? Morning? Afternoon?"

"The viewing's at noon. The service is at one."

"Sure, I'll be there."

"June?" It was Mrs. Luray on an extension. "Will you come to our house tomorrow evening? We're having a Christmas Eve open house, and I especially want you to come. You're Jolene's nicest friend."

"Well, thank you, Mrs. Luray." How about Jolene's only friend? "I was going to go to the Christmas Eve service tomorrow night with a friend. What time is your open house? Maybe I can come over after the service."

"We'll be here from eight to midnight," she said. "We always do this, you know. Why don't you bring your friend? There's always room for one more." She sighed. "Arnie won't be here this year though. I'm so sad that he and Jolene Marie are getting a divorce."

There was a little silence while I tried to figure out how to respond to that one.

"Okay, Mom," said Jolene, her voice a mix of frustration and sorrow. "That's enough. Say good-bye to Merry. You'll see her tomorrow. Right now I have to talk with her."

"All right, Jolene," Eloise Luray said. "Good-bye, June, dear." And there was a click.

"Sorry," said Jolene. "She gets more impossible all the time."

"Is there an open house tomorrow evening," I asked, "or does she just think there's one?"

"There really is one. We've done it for years. It's a bit awkward this year, coming only hours after the funeral, but what can we do? Mom loves to cook as you know, and she lays out a wonderful spread. She's been looking forward to this for months. Dad says we have to let her do it because she wouldn't understand if we don't. We'd have collapses galore."

"He's probably right," I said.

"Yeah, I know. Please come. I need your support. And bring Curt. Mac will be here too, and I think he's bringing someone, though I'm not certain who."

"Jolene," I said hesitantly. "I know it's none of my business, but have you thought about your parents going to some sort of a retirement facility where your mom would get the appropriate care?"

Jolene sighed. "I've been talking about a setup like that for years, ever since Mom started to fail so dramatically. I want them to go to Tel Hai over in Honey Brook. They'd love it there, I know. I finally got Dad to put their names on the waiting list. He's been called three times about a possible cottage on the grounds, and he's turned them down every time. Arnie almost had him convinced last time, but now that Arnie's gone, we're back to square one. 'All Eloise needs is me,' Dad says. 'I can take care of her fine.' For the moment, maybe, I say. But what if something happens to you? 'We'll deal with that when it happens,' Dad says."

"But then it's too late," I said. "They'll have to take what they can get whether it's what they want or not."

"Tell me something I don't know," Jolene said. "I can't let myself think about it too much. It drives me crazy. Now let's change the subject before I get too depressed. How was your date last night?"

I quickly gave her the short version of my evening.

"He seems like such a nice guy," she said. "I bet your mother and father like him a lot."

"They haven't met him yet, but they've heard enough about him. They even sent him a couple of Christmas gifts since I told them he doesn't have a family."

"That's nice," said Jo and sighed. I knew she was thinking about her family's animosity toward Reilly.

"Jo," I said hesitantly, "would you and Reilly like to go to the Christmas Eve service with Curt and me? Or do you have to be there to help your mother?"

"No, she won't let me help her. Mrs. Samson comes over, and the ladies rule the kitchen. I might as well still be ten years old."

"Well, then, will you come with us? You can see me play in the bell choir."

"You play in a bell choir? I'll tell you, Merry. You never cease to amaze me."

"That's what Curt says, but I'm not sure it's a compliment."

"Let me talk to Reilly and I'll let you know, okay?"

"That sounds good."

"I'll see you at Martin's Funeral Parlor then," Jolene said.

"Wait, Jo. I've got another question for you."

"Sure." In the background Mrs. Luray called, "Jolene Marie, dinner's ready."

"Where did you and Arnie get your money?" I said it in a rush because it was such an impertinent question. I tensed, waiting for Jolene to tell me it was none of my business.

To my surprise she began to laugh. "Are you serious? You don't know? I thought everyone knew." She laughed some more. "Though come to think of it, you hadn't moved here yet, had you? You probably hadn't even heard of Amhearst that long ago."

I was totally confused. "I guess not."

"We won the state lottery," she said. "Can you believe it? Twelve million dollars. Fifty thousand a month for twenty years. Remember that certificate hanging on the refrigerator? I made that for him at work the week we won. We each put down half the money for the winning ticket, so we split the jackpot evenly. I guess I ought to have made him a new one that read $25,000 when I left."

I pulled the phone from my ear and looked at it in amazement. "You're kidding," I said. "You must be. Real people don't win those things."

"I know," she agreed. "But we did. Fortunately Harry Allen Bushay sat Arnie down and talked to him about the realities and limitations of the money. 'You haven't got a family,' Harry Allen said. 'So I'm talking to you like your father would if he were here.' He was great. Otherwise I think we'd be in a terrible financial mess. Lots of these millionaires end up declaring bankruptcy. It's not like you ever have twelve million in your hand, you know."

"You actually won the lottery," I said. It boggled my mind. "Do you get Arnie's half now?"

"I thought I might," she answered. "After all, we're not divorced yet. I even went to our lawyer, Mr. Grassley, to ask him about it."

"And?" I said when she stopped talking.

"And Arnie made a new will a couple of months ago. It seems when the little slut got pregnant, he named her and the baby his beneficiaries. They each get three million—or what's left of it. We've already gotten two years of payments. Only eighteen to go. The little tramp and her kid won't be hurting, you can be sure of that. Not that she ever was. Harry Allen's not exactly poor."

"Geez, Jolene. I still can't believe it. The lottery."

In the background Mrs. Luray called Jolene to the table again. Jo laughed at me and said, "See you. I've got to go before Mom faints."

I wandered around in a daze for a while, trying to believe that someone I knew had actually won money on such a grand scale. I finally settled down enough to watch a TV movie with Whiskers, but I was still reeling from the absurdity of it all when I went to bed. In my dream, the twinkling tree in the yellow carpeted living room in Arnie's mansion no longer had lights. It was decorated in $100 bills that blinked on and off.

"Take one," Arnie told all us guests. "I've got more. Lots more."

I got up with a headache.

I drove home from work in time to meet Sandy Rasmussen at my apartment. I made us some tea and put out some crumb cake. I plugged in the tree to lighten the interview.

Sandy looked incredibly weary and had great circles under her eyes testifying to countless sleepless nights, but the overwhelming sorrow seemed to have abated.

"I feel better," she said when I noted as much as I poured her a cup of Constant Comment. "Just having Dan and the other kids here makes a great difference. I'm not alone."

"If being here by yourself with Karyn is so difficult, why did you bring her here instead of staying at home?" I asked.

"She was thirteen," Sandy said. "Thirteen! She had her whole life ahead of her. We felt we couldn't prejudice everyone against her at this young an age."

"You think people today would treat her badly? Isn't there more compassion and understanding than fifty or a hundred years ago?"

"Sure there is, and philosophically everyone would agree that she shouldn't be penalized for such a tragic mistake. But let's be realistic. Who in middle-class America wants their thirteen-year-old daughter hanging out with another girl that age about to have a baby? In the parents' minds, these girls have barely put their Barbies aside. Do you think they want Karyn at their kids' slumber parties? And the boys! What would they think of her? She'd be labeled as a tramp."

I flinched mentally.

"So Dan and I decided to take her away to save her in the long run."

"How did you ever hear about His House?"

"Dawn came to speak to a women's meeting at our church," Sandy said. "I don't know how the church ever heard of her or His House, and I don't care. We think it was God taking care of us before we even knew we needed that care."

"How did such a thing happen to Karyn? You and Dan obviously care for her. How did a situation that led to this result ever develop?"

Sandy stalled answering by raising her cup of tea and sipping. She fiddled with her napkin, tearing at the edges until they looked like the fringe on a rug. Finally she took a deep breath.

"I struggle every time I talk about this because I feel such seething resentment toward the boy. He knew exactly what he was doing. He was a friend of our sixteen-year-old son. He came over one day when Zach was out and he knew Zach was out. Karyn had a crush on him, and when he asked if he could come in and spend time with her, she was delighted. At first he sweet-talked her, but when she got scared and said no more, all she wanted was a kiss, he forced himself on her."

Sandy's voice was shaking almost as much as her hands. My heart broke for her.

"When I got home, she was in bed, bundled up to her neck, crying, her eyes huge and scared. 'Am I still a virgin?' she asked. 'I want to be. Am I? Can I be again?'" And Sandy began to cry.

I sat there, my throat tight, my eyes filled with tears.

Sandy mopped at her face. "I'm sorry."

"Please, don't apologize," I said. "Cry as much as you want."

"You'd think I'd be cried out, wouldn't you?" she asked. "Nine months of tears, an ocean."

"What do you plan to do about the baby, keep it or give it up?" I asked.

"I don't know," Sandy said hopelessly. "I'm as confused today as I was the day we found out Karyn was pregnant. This is my grandchild. How can I give away my grandchild? But how can I keep her? The whole reason for living in Amhearst for these five months was to protect Karyn. If we suddenly come home with a baby, don't you think people will know where it came from?" Her hands fluttered helplessly in the air. "I don't know what to do. I'm exhausted from going around in mental circles. I keep asking God to show me what's right."

"How does Karyn feel?" I asked.

"On her sunny days, she wants to keep the baby. She thinks it'll be like having a live doll. But the bottom line is that she'll do whatever we think is best because she's as confused as the rest of us."

Sandy laughed without humor. "We've been going to Faith Community, and I decided we should work in the nursery every Sunday so Karyn would get used to babies. She can't easily go to Sunday school with the junior high kids, so we take nursery during the Sunday school hour. Good training for her. A few of the facts of life."

I thought of the nursery at church, full to bulging with often screaming little people. It seemed an imminently suitable place for a little girl to learn about some hard baby realities.

"At first Karyn thought it was a great lark. Then as cold weather set in, so did colds and runny noses and crankiness. Just last Sunday she was holding a crying little guy about fifteen months old when he had a very loose bowel movement. I thought Karyn would die. 'Mom, he got it all over me!' I made her clean him up before she could clean herself up. 'That's babies,' I said. 'They can't help it.' 'Not mine,' she said. 'Mine's going to be cute like her.' And she picked up the cutest little poppet who promptly threw up all over her."

I couldn't help laughing. "Poor Karyn."

"I just started law school," said Sandy urgently. "If we keep the baby, I'll have to drop out. I can't do four teenagers and a baby and law school. I know I don't have the stamina. As it is, I've taken a semester off. Is it horrible of me to want to go to school instead of raise this baby?" Her eyes were tragic. "But she's my grandchild!"

The doorbell rang and I went to let Maddie in.

"Sandy, this is my friend Maddie. She and her husband have been thinking about adopting."

"Merry!" Maddie said, not expecting an introduction like that.

"Maddie, this is Sandy. Her thirteen-year-old daughter is about to have a baby. They haven't yet decided what they plan to do."

The women looked at each other with interest and discomfort. I picked up the teapot.

"Let me get some more hot water for Maddie," I said and left them. In the kitchen I leaned against the counter.

Dear Lord, please don't let me have made a terrible mistake. Please. This is miracle season, isn't it?

Chapter Sixteen

I sat on the end of the fourth row at the Christmas Eve service. All of us in the bell choir sat up front as did the others who had special music responsibilities. Curt sat beside me with Jolene and Reilly beyond him.

"What are you doing?" Jolene had hissed when I led the way up front. "I want to sit in the back!"

"I have to sit up front because of the bells." I pointed to the tables set with our music, gloves, and instruments. "Besides it's more fun up here. The singing comes forward at you and you can sing better."

"Like I know the songs." She scowled as she slid into the pew. "I'm never going anywhere with you again."

Reilly just looked at his beloved and smiled. Her bad temper didn't seem to faze him at all, but then after all the years he'd known her and all the questionable behavior he'd seen from her, I guess he was used to her.

We stood to sing "O Come All Ye Faithful" and "It Came Upon A Midnight Clear," the words flashed up front on a large screen. I heard Jolene whisper in surprise, "I know this!" I have no idea what she thought we sang, but I hoped and prayed she'd relax enough to enjoy herself.

Suddenly someone was in the aisle beside me.

"Move over," whispered Jack.

I stared at him, openmouthed. I hadn't seen him since our confrontation Friday night. What was he doing here?

"Move," he hissed.

I moved. And Curt, Jolene, and Reilly moved too. The Domino Principle. When we sat down, I was scrunched between the two men. I sat, staring straight ahead, mortified. Here I was in the front of the church where everyone could see me, a man on each side.

Dear Lord, why me? Why now?

Out of the corner of my eye, I saw Jolene lean forward and grin.

Okay, Lord, I'll try to be philosophical about my predicament. At least Jo's now enjoying herself.

When it was time for the bell number, Jack stood and stepped into the aisle to make room for me to exit. Just what I needed. More attention.

As I pulled on my white cotton gloves and made certain my four bells were in order, I felt so self-conscious I could have been thirteen again. It took every ounce of concentration I possessed to play correctly. I only forgot to change to C sharp at one place and I didn't let it throw me. Hopefully no one but Ned realized the temporary musical clash was my fault.

It was a great relief to pull the gloves off and return to my seat—until Jack stood again to allow me to get into the row.

We stood again to sing "Hark! The Herald Angels Sing" and Curt looked down at me and smiled. We know about angels, the smile seemed to say. I smiled back and moved closer to him. He took my hand.

When we sat, Jack settled himself comfortably into the pew beside me and slid his arm across my back, resting his hand on my far shoulder. Short of telling him to keep his crumby arms to himself, something that didn't go over well in most church services, there was little I could do. I spent the rest of the meeting with Curt holding my hand and Jack putting his arm around me.

I felt like Hester Prynne in *The Scarlet Letter* or Gomer when she was running around on Hosea. Don't ask me why, especially when a real, modern Hester/Gomer was just a couple of seats from me. I just did, that's all I know. Needless to say, I didn't hear much of Pastor Brinkley's Christmas charge.

After the service we swarmed into the aisles like everyone else. Somehow Jolene elbowed her way to my side in no time flat.

"That was the best Christmas service I ever went to," she said, and I didn't think she was referring to any spiritual blessings she received. "I didn't know church could be such fun. Like I said before, Merry. You do amaze me."

"Shut up," I muttered. "I'm embarrassed enough without any help from you."

She laughed heartily.

Suddenly I was face-to-face with Sandy Rasmussen

"Hey, Sandy. Merry Christmas." I gave her a holiday hug. I felt a little awkward seeing her because I didn't know how she felt about my springing Maddie on her this morning. She had been very polite when she left, but it could have been merely good manners.

"And Karyn." I hugged her too. "How are you doing?"

"I don't think I'm feeling too good. It's hard to sit so long."

"Merry," said Sandy, "I want you to meet Dan and the kids."

We shook hands all the way around, and I was pleased to see Dan standing with his arm around Karyn. Another good dad.

As Dan shook my hand, he said, "Sandy told me about your interview today, especially about meeting Maddie. Thanks for arranging it. I don't know if anything will come of it, but it moved Sandy out of the quagmire of doubt where she's been drowning these last few months."

I looked at Sandy. She nodded. "I was mad at you at first. How presumptuous, I thought. But then as I talked with Maddie, and then as the three of us talked, I realized you were trying to help us."

"I was," I said. "I love Maddie, and I care what happens to this young lady over here." I gave Karyn's hand a squeeze.

Out of the corner of my eye I saw Curt get swept past me in the crowd. "I'll see you outside," he said as he swirled by. Then Jack passed. "I'll see you in the foyer," he called.

I turned back to the Rasmussens to find Karyn watching me in fascination. Suddenly she said, much too loudly, "They both sat with you, didn't they? One on each side. Which one is your boyfriend, Merry? The one who had his arm around you or the curly-haired guy? I think they're both cute."

Blushing, I backed out of the pew where we had taken refuge from the crowds surging up the aisles.

"I've got to go put my music away," I said and made my escape.

I was putting my bells in their velvet case when I felt an arm slide around my waist. I was afraid to look and see whether it belonged to Curt or Jack.

"Thanks, Merry."

With relief I realized it was Maddie. I turned to hug her. "You're not mad at me?"

"I was at first, but the longer I talked to Sandy, the more excited I got. Did you know she asked me back to their apartment where I met Karyn? Just as a friend of her mother's, nothing more. She's adorable. Then I went home, and Doug and I have been talking ever since."

She smiled as Doug came up and put an arm across her shoulders. "I don't know if anything will happen, but thank you for caring."

Thank you, Lord, thank you!

She looked over my shoulder. "Hi. Are you ready?"

I turned. The Rasmussen clan stood there.

"They're coming over for a late supper," Maddie said.

I stood there, suffused with joy as I watched all of them walk up the aisle together.

It is miracle season, isn't it, Lord?

Jack was waiting for me when I walked into the foyer. My heart dropped. I didn't want a confrontation. I wanted to feel toasty and warm about the Reeders and the Rasmussens.

"I'm driving to Pittsburgh, Merry. I'm leaving in about five minutes." Jack grinned his most engaging smile. "If you come along, you can still be home in time for Christmas."

"Oh, Jack, I wish I could, but I can't. You know that. Work and all."

He looked at me for a minute. "Do you even want to go home? I mean, if you could, would you?"

I looked at him in surprise, and not just because he asked those questions, though that itself was astonishing given Jack's usual level of insight. I was surprised by my heart's answer. I didn't want to go home. Not anymore. I glanced over Jack's shoulder and saw Jolene and Reilly standing by the front door waiting for me. I saw Curt spot me and break into a broad smile. I saw Maddie and Sandy talking like old friends as they bundled the kids outside ahead of them.

And I knew. I didn't want to go home because I was home. Amhearst was where I belonged. Sure I'd miss Mom and Dad and Sam. I'd miss the familiar fun of our extended family. But if I went home, I'd miss Amhearst more.

Jack saw the answer in my face. A flash of sadness, so quickly come and gone that I wasn't sure I'd seen it, darted across his eyes. Then his usual carefree smirk returned. He leaned over and kissed my cheek.

"Merry Christmas, Merry girl. I'll see you next year."

He turned and walked toward the door, past Jolene and Reilly, past Curt. At the last possible moment, he paused and stuck out his hand to Curt. The two men eyed each other, nodded, and shook.

Jack left.

The crowd at Jolene's house surprised me both in its size and diversity. I don't know why I expected it to be only the few people I knew in common with Jo, but it wasn't. There were friends of Mr. and Mrs. Luray as well as several relatives of the Lurays and Mrs. Samson. Most of them were a maze of faces that came and went through the evening.

By far the most fascinating relative was Reilly's father. He looked just like a male Mrs. Samson. The biggest difference between them was that he smiled and she didn't. Reilly's mother was present, too, a skinny little thing who fluttered nervously whenever her mother-in-law entered the room, not that I blamed her.

"Reilly," Mrs. Samson called when we entered the living room. She had to call to be heard. Christmas music played at a level that made normal conversation impossible unless you spoke directly into someone's ear—which, in all the best circles, is considered very impolite.

Mrs. Samson, wearing a highly practical, thoroughly unseasonal apron of orange and yellow tied around her ample middle, rushed to Reilly's side. "Where have you been? You're late."

"We went to church, Grandmom, to the Christmas Eve service," he said, bending to plant a kiss on her withered cheek.

"To church?" The disbelief and horror on her face were almost comic. "You didn't!" You'd have thought he told her he'd gone to Sodom or Gomorrah.

"But we're here now," he smiled, "so let the party begin."

Mrs. Samson reached out a hand and caressed his cheek. "You are my most precious possession, Reilly," she said.

"I know, Grandmom, but you have to remember something. I may love you, but I'm not your possession. I make my own choices." Casually he reached out and rested his hand on the nape of Jolene's neck. She looked over her shoulder at him and smiled. He looked at his grandmother. "Do you understand?"

Mrs. Samson looked at Jolene with loathing, then turned her back and marched to the kitchen.

"Thank you, Reilly," Jolene said quietly, sliding her arm around his waist. "Now let's get some food."

I watched Jolene and Reilly with interest. A public declaration was being made, no question about it.

Jolene led us to the dining room where the table was stretched by extra leaves to truly impressive length. A gaudy red and green plaid tablecloth with gold threads running through it covered the table, and candles in a centerpiece of greens shed a soft light over the bounteous and mind-boggling array.

Some of the food I expected. There was a tray of cold cuts and the ubiquitous Jello salads, a tureen of potato salad and a casserole of baked beans. Butter cookies, Russian teaballs, brownies, and chocolate chip cookies filled a doily-covered tray. But there were wonderful unexpected treats. Kielbasa and sauerkraut sat beside cabbage rolls. A baking dish of manicotti bumped against another of macaroni and cheese. Individual tarts with glazed fruit shared a tray with pizzelles and macaroons. And there were rolls: snowflake, kaiser, cloverleaf, homemade, and store bought. The Lurays could open their own bakery.

As I wondered how in the world I could manage to taste it all, Mrs. Luray walked in with a Crock-Pot full of roast beef and gravy and Mrs. Samson came in with a tray of baked ham with pineapple sauce.

Curt and I filled our dishes and carried them to the living room. There wasn't a seat to be found. We wandered into the hallway and found a deacon's bench against one wall. We grabbed it and enjoyed a private dining corner where we could actually hear each other talk.

The doorbell rang as we sat there, and I got up to answer it. Mac came in, Dawn on his arm. He looked at me and smirked as he helped her off with her coat. Dawn saw me and smiled.

"The bells were great again," she said. "Weren't they, Mac?"

"You were at church?" I blurted to Mac.

"Don't drop your dinner over it," he growled as he steadied my plate, which was bending under the weight of too much food. "I just hope it counts for something with my mother and God. Now where's Eloise? I have to give her a Christmas kiss and a poinsettia."

"Here I am, dear Mac," Mrs. Luray said, bustling into the hall and holding her cheek out for his peck. "This is Jolene's boss, June. He thinks he's gruff and tough, but he's not."

I nodded. "He's my boss too. Remember?"

There was a brief struggle in the fuzzy depths of Mrs. Luray's mind, and the saner part won for a change. "Of course," she said with her sweet smile. "How silly of me. If you work with Jolene and Mac is Jolene's boss, he's yours too." She turned to the unsuspecting Curt. "Is he yours?"

"No," Curt said. "I don't work at the paper. I'm self-employed."

"Oh," said Mrs. Luray. She reached out and patted his hand. "Well, I hope you get a job soon."

I grinned at Curt's bemused expression as Mrs. Luray turned her attention to Dawn. "And who's this lovely lady, Mac? Your girlfriend? June brought her boyfriend, you know."

"This is Dawn, Eloise," Mac said.

"No, dear boy," Mrs. Luray said, glancing out the window beside the door. "It's nighttime."

"No, I mean that's her name," Mac said.

"Really? Well, how do you do, dear," Mrs. Luray said. "I'm so glad you've come. Now let's get you two some food."

We'd barely started eating again when the doorbell rang for the second time. Before I could answer it, Harry Allen Bushay let himself in with a rush of cold air, followed by a petulant and unhappy Lonni.

"Just be polite, Lonni. That's all I ask," he muttered, scowling. "We don't need a scene to ruin everyone's Christmas Eve."

Then he saw us and became all smiles as he slid out of his coat.

"Curt and his young reporter friend," he said too heartily. "Merry Christmas." He took my hand. "I must thank you for the food project article and picture. Both were very well done."

Lonni noticed me for the first time and frowned. "What are *you* doing here?"

Had I been feeling especially sensitive, I'd have collapsed like a sand castle at high tide under the venom of her greeting.

"I work with Jolene," I said sweetly. "Remember?"

Mrs. Samson came bustling into the hallway.

"Lonni, my baby," she cried. "How are you?" She threw her arms wide and grabbed the girl in a fierce hug.

"Careful, Grandmom," Lonni said, struggling to break free. "You'll squish the baby."

Grandmom? I stared at Lonni and Mrs. Samson. Grandmom?

"Oh, honey girl," said Mrs. Samson, placing her hand against Lonni's cheek. "You're my prized possession."

"Yeah, I know." Lonni sounded unimpressed. She handed her jacket to Harry Allen and headed for the dining room.

"Hi, Mom," said Harry Allen as he kissed Mrs. Samson on the forehead. "How's my favorite mother-in-law tonight?"

I blinked and shook my head. Never in a million years would I have made that connection.

"I'm fine, fine," she said absently, watching Lonni. "I'm glad you brought her."

"It was a fight. She did not want to come, believe me. She wanted to stay and feel sorry for herself out at His House." His eyes followed his daughter too. "I guess the holidays have her extra upset." He paused, then added, "She's become terribly hostile to me in the last few days, and I don't know what to do about it."

"Don't worry," Mrs. Samson said. "Whatever it is, she'll get over it."

Harry Allen didn't look convinced, as well he shouldn't.

"By the way," said Mrs. Samson. "I got my annual Christmas call from Eileen this afternoon."

"Oh," Harry Allen said, unmoved at the mention of his long-departed wife. "How's she doing?"

Mrs. Samson looked disgusted. "She's still living with that horrible cowboy. She did say they want to get married, finally! So I expect you'll get a letter from some Wyoming lawyer one of these days about a divorce. I tell you, Harry Allen, you're more my son than she ever was my daughter. Now let's get you some food."

With a nod in our direction, Harry Allen followed Mrs. Samson as she almost raced to the dining room.

"He's her son-in-law," I said to Curt.

"Apparently."

"And Lonni's her granddaughter."

"Yep."

"That means Reilly must be Lonni's cousin."

"That sounds about right," Curt said. "Want some more to eat?"

"Talk about a small world," I said. And I began to think furiously.

"Yo, Merry." Curt waved his hand before my eyes. "More food?"

I blinked and looked at my plate. It was still full of food and I wasn't certain I could eat another bite. "Thanks, no. Why don't you go get some more if you want, and I'll get rid of these dirty dishes after I take another nibble or two?"

I took his empty plate and slid it under mine to keep mine from collapsing. It would be a shame to dump lime Jello with pureed pears and cottage cheese all over the floor. Curt walked down the hall to the dining room, braving the level of conversation and the high decibels of the music. I sat in our relatively quiet corner, eating absently and thinking for a few more minutes. Then I got up, ready to take our dirty things to the kitchen.

As I passed the living room door, I heard Jolene say to Reilly's father, "The funeral went very well, thanks, Mr. Samson. Lots of our old friends from high school came."

Mr. Samson nodded. "That's not surprising. Arnie was always well-liked."

I paused to hear any other comments. I had thought the funeral depressing and without hope, and I'd been disconcerted when a minister who had obviously never met Arnie read a sterile and impersonal funeral service from a prayer book of some kind.

"It was a nice service," agreed Harry Allen. "Given all the unusual circumstances surrounding it, I doubt it could have been better."

The people near me fell silent a minute, thinking about murder and young death to a background of "Jingle Bell Rock."

"I wasn't allowed to go," Lonni suddenly announced loudly to the room at large.

"Of course not," said Mr. Luray who was offering everyone some more coffee from an insulated pitcher. "A funeral is no place for a young lady like you, especially when you didn't know him."

"I knew him," she shouted as her face contorted with pain. "I knew him better than any of the rest of you!"

"Easy, Lonni," said Harry Allen, watching her with worried eyes.

"Sure you knew him. He was Jolene's husband," said the unaware Mr. Luray. He was too busy serving his coffee to feel the emotional currents flying around the room. "Just don't mention the funeral in front of Mrs. Luray, okay? She's having a hard time accepting Arnie's death."

"*She's* having a hard time?" Lonni said. "What about me?" And she started to cry. "What about me?"

"You shouldn't have brought her, Uncle Harry," said Reilly, moving toward Lonni. "It's too raw. Come on, Lonni, honey. Let's you and me go somewhere quiet."

But Harry Allen reached the girl first and tried to hug her. She screamed and jumped back. "Don't touch me," she shouted, arms wrapped protectively about her stomach and the baby. "I hate you! You killed him!" And she broke and ran, heading for the hall stairs, Reilly right after her.

Harry Allen stood frozen in the middle of the room. His face was gray, his shoulders stooped. No one looked at him and no one said anything. Nat King Cole began to sing about chestnuts roasting and Jack Frost nipping.

I felt sorry for Harry Allen, especially since just twenty-four hours ago, I was willing to cast him in the role of villain myself. Now with my new information I knew better.

The tense silence was broken by Eloise Luray who had come into the room in the middle of Lonni's tirade. "Harry Allen, you didn't kill anyone, did you?" She didn't wait for an answer. "Of course you didn't. But did you know that someone killed Arnie? Jolene thinks I don't know he's dead, but I do." She smiled sweetly at her daughter who, drawn by the loud voices, had come to stand beside me.

Jolene smiled back. "You're smarter than I thought, Mom." As she talked, she held out her hand so only I could see the "heart medicine" in it.

"Whenever I hear raised voices," Jo whispered, "I never know the effect on Mom."

But Eloise Luray seemed fine. "Now there's lots more food on the table, everyone. Harry Allen, why don't you go get some? It'll help you feel better. Besides, you're too nice to kill anyone. It was someone not very nice who killed Arnie." She took Harry Allen's arm and led him out of the room.

In the silence that followed, the Mormon Tabernacle Choir sang the "Hallelujah Chorus." Suddenly there was lots of shuffling and coughing as people became busy with their food and drink. I was no different. I took a bite of the Jello/pear salad I had no room for.

As I looked down at my plate, I saw on the floor the backpack-pocketbook Lonni had dropped when she dashed from the room. It had dumped itself at my feet. I set my plate on an end table, stooped and scooped up lipsticks and a compact, keys and tissues, pens, a date book and a huge blue wallet, a brush and hair spray and slid them all back into the black leather bag. The last thing I picked up was a framed picture that had fallen facedown.

I turned it over automatically as I rose, and there was Lonni in her purple T-shirt leaning against Arnie in his red polo shirt. Their smiling faces were captured in a fluted brass frame with a crack in the glass in the lower left corner.

I elbowed Jolene. "Look."

Her index finger traced the crack in the corner. "That's from the bedroom at the house." She frowned. "The kid must have been there last night after we left."

"Maybe," I said. "But what if she was there when we got there? That would explain why the door was unlocked." I fished in Lonni's pocketbook and drew out three keys. "Do any look familiar?"

Jolene pointed to a large gold key. "That's the front door, I'll bet anything. And of course, if she had a key, she had the alarm code." She smiled sourly. "I guess I'm glad I didn't get hold of Sergeant Poole after all."

Me too, I thought, as I glanced in Harry Allen's direction.

I put Lonni's purse on the hall table and picked up my dirty dishes. I pushed through the crowd and then through the swinging door into the kitchen. I looked for and quickly found a large trash can lined with a giant plastic bag and full of all kinds of garbage. I dumped our paper plates in with the rest.

It was comparatively quiet out here with the sound muffled by the door, an oasis for splitting eardrums. I relaxed into the quiet, wondering how soon Curt and I could leave. Lots of loud music for a prolonged period always made me jittery. As I turned to reenter the fray and find him, Mrs. Samson pushed through the swinging door, bringing Gene Autry and Rudolph with her.

"Oh," she said. "Jolene's friend." Somehow she made it sound as if I had infected the party with a terrible social disease.

"I have enjoyed the food so much," I said with my most charming smile as I edged toward the door. "You and Mrs. Luray have done a magnificent job."

Mrs. Samson looked surprised. "Thank you," she said and almost smiled. "*Someone* I know never says thank you." There was no doubt who *someone* was. In fact at that exact moment she pushed through the swinging door too, Gene's voice now on foggy Christmas Eves. Soon we could have our own party out here. Not a good idea.

"I need something cold to drink," Jolene announced. "The temperature must be at least eighty in there." She pointed to the rest of the house. She pulled the refrigerator door open. "Want a beer, Merry?"

I shook my head. "But I'd love a Coke."

Soon Jolene and I stood side by side, leaning against the kitchen counter enjoying the cold bubbles sliding down our throats.

"Say, Mrs. Samson, we saw you the other day out near Arnie's," Jolene said, obviously trying to have a conversation with Reilly's grandmother. Too bad this was the first topic that popped into her head.

I bumped her elbow and she almost dropped her beer. "Let's get back to the party," I said brightly.

"Watch it, Merry," she said. "In a minute." She returned her attention to Mrs. Samson. "You were looking for something, weren't you? At least that's what we thought." She pointed to herself and me. "Did you find it? Did you drop it after the accident or something?"

"You must be mistaken," Mrs. Samson said. "I haven't been out that way for a long time."

"No mistake," Jolene said. "You were driving Reilly's car. I'd know it anywhere."

"Let's go join the others, Jo," I said, taking her arm.

She pulled free. "Nah, I want to stay out here a bit longer. It's cooler."

"Then let's go out in the backyard. It's really cool there."

"Oh, I remember now," Mrs. Samson said. "I was looking for the deer I hit."

"I thought you killed it," Jo said.

"There were others with it. I wanted to make certain they were all right."

Jo looked at Mrs. Samson strangely. "You didn't think they'd still be there how many days after the accident? Five?"

"You're right. They weren't." She laughed in a strained manner. "Silly of me, wasn't it?"

Suddenly Jolene got very still and my heart sank. "What day was your accident?" she demanded.

Mrs. Samson said nothing.

"And what time of day? Midafternoon? It was! I remember! Did you know about Arnie and Lonni? Did you hate him as much as you hate me?"

I grabbed Jolene by the arm and began dragging her toward the door. "We'll see you later, Mrs. Samson."

"Merry, she—"

"Shut up, Jo. Shut up," I hissed, pushing her ahead of me. "We'll discuss it later." But I wasn't fast enough.

The feel of the little gun pressed against my spine was chilling.

"Stop," ordered Mrs. Samson, but she didn't need to say it. I had stopped. "You too, Jolene, or I'll hurt your friend."

Jolene looked at me curiously.

"She found what she was looking for when we saw her," I said. "She's got it pressed to my spine. And it isn't a gun that needs cocking. The slightest pressure on the trigger, and I'm gone or paralyzed."

At precisely that moment the door swung open again and Eloise Luray bustled in to "Silver Bells."

"Oh, how nice," she said, smiling happily. "Jolene and June have come out to help us. Aren't you such sweet girls."

"Ah, Mom," said Jolene, looking desperately from her mother to me to Mrs. Samson.

"Eloise," snapped Mrs. Samson with all the crack and snarl of a bullwhip. "Get back in there and check on the coffee. You know that's your job. Everyone needs another cup."

Mrs. Luray's face fell. "Oh. I'm sorry. I thought I was supposed—"

"Go, Eloise. And don't come back out here until I call you. And keep everyone else out too."

Lip trembling at her scolding, Mrs. Luray went back into the dining room.

As I watched the door swing shut, I contemplated my chances if I threw myself to the side or tried to whirl around and disarm Mrs. Samson. Because of the type of gun she had, the gun that had shot Arnie, the gun she had hidden in the field after she killed Arnie and hit the deer but before the police came, the gun she had gone back to retrieve, because of that gun, I had no chance of escaping injury or death. For the moment, she had me.

"Now turn the kitchen lights off, Jolene," ordered Mrs. Samson.

Jolene had her typical response to an order. "No."

I groaned.

Mrs. Samson placed the little gun under my chin so Jolene could see it. "Lights off."

Lips clamped in fury, Jolene flicked the lights off.

"Now slide that cabinet in front of the door. I don't want any unexpected visitors."

Jolene put her shoulder against a white wooden cabinet about four feet tall and pushed. It creaked and protested for a minute, but finally it slid across the door. Jolene straightened and stood glaring, arms crossed.

"Now get over there and open the cellar door."

"I'm not going anywhere," spat Jolene. "And neither's Merry."

"I shot someone before, Jolene," Mrs. Samson said. "I'll do it again."

"No, you won't. You'd get caught. There's people out there who'd hear."

"But you'd be dead," Mrs. Samson said. "And Reilly would be safe. Just like Lonni's safe."

"No wonder Mr. Samson never came back from Korea. He thought dying was preferable to living with you!"

I squeezed my eyes shut and moaned as I felt the gun skitter across my neck. "Jolene, shut up," I pleaded. "Just open the door."

Suddenly Mrs. Samson grabbed hold of my hair and yanked. I had been leaning to one side, trying to get away from the gun, and she pulled in that direction. I overbalanced and knocked into the trash can. Garbage and I sprawled all over the floor, and I had a fleeting sad thought for my new green velvet dress.

Before I could regain my feet, Mrs. Samson lunged at Jolene. Jo screamed and turned to run, but Mrs. Samson's hand flew out and she brought the gun down on Jolene's temple. Jolene fell where she stood as blood gushed from the laceration caused by the blow. Mrs. Samson, careful to stay out of the blood, went down beside her to kneel with the gun at the unconscious woman's throat.

"Don't try anything," she said to me, her voice quiet and even and unflustered. "I would love to shoot her."

Slowly I finished standing upright, but I held my hands in front of me in a placating gesture.

"Now you open the cellar door," she said.

I moved cautiously to the door located on the inside wall between the stove and the entrance to a pantry. Slowly I pulled it open.

"Now take her to the top of the steps."

"Mrs. Samson, you don't want to hurt Jolene. Reilly will hate you for it."

"Reilly bought me this gun. Did you know that? He took me to the target range and taught me to shoot it. He thought it wasn't safe for me to live alone with no protection." She raised the gun and pointed it at me. "I'm very good with it."

I didn't doubt her. There was an aura of comfort about the way she handled the weapon that supported her claims.

"Take her to the top of the steps."

Sighing, I took the still bleeding Jolene under the armpits and pulled her toward the steps.

Head wounds bleed excessively, I kept telling myself. *It's not a sign of the severity of her injury but of surface blood vessels. It's already beginning to coagulate. It is. Dear God, please let it be coagulating!*

"You can't get away with hurting us or killing us," I said. "You can't."

Mrs. Samson smiled. "Getting away is not my goal," she said.

I stood at the top of the cellar steps, Jolene propped against my leg, a dead weight. "What now?"

"Turn around."

"What?"

"Turn around!"

"So you can shoot me in the back? No, ma'am."

"I don't want to shoot you," she said. "I barely know you. I have no reason to shoot you. I had a reason to shoot Arnie. Look what he did to Lonni. And I had a reason to shoot Tony."

I blinked in confusion. "Who's Tony?"

"My husband."

"The one who died in the Korean War?"

"That's what everybody thinks. But he came home, planning to divorce me so he could marry his Korean girlfriend."

Paradigm shift. "So you shot him?"

"I did."

"And nobody noticed?"

"Nobody saw him but me. He made sure of that. He knew everyone would pressure him not to return to her, so he didn't tell anyone he was coming. He only saw me because he needed my signature on the divorce papers."

"But what did you do with his body?" I asked. As I understood murder, the disposal of the body was one of the hardest parts of the whole process. I'd certainly never know how to dispose of someone. Besides, I had to keep her talking. I could feel Jolene stirring slightly as she lay against me. Maybe if she regained consciousness, we could save ourselves somehow.

"I put him where all bodies go," she said.

"In a cemetery?" I was incredulous.

She nodded.

"But who did the funeral director think he was burying?"

"I buried him."

"What?"

"I'd been to a funeral at this little cemetery outside Coatesville near the reservoir. I noticed a huge pile of dirt near the back of the property, loose dirt left from the graves, I guess. There was also old flower arrangements and baskets dumped there. Not that I was looking for a place to bury someone then. But I remembered it when I had Tony lying at my feet."

"So you went out and buried Tony in that dirt pile?"

"I did. As far as I know, he's still there."

I stared at this old woman, trying to imagine her forty-five years ago, young, strong, and scorned, spurned for another woman. "Don't you think there are better ways to handle a disintegrating marriage than murder?" It popped out before I could stop it.

"Don't get smart with me, young lady."

I put my hands up in apology. "Didn't anyone see you? At the cemetery, I mean."

"I went at night. It was summer. All the trees and shrubs were full, and I didn't think the people at the closest house, which wasn't very close, would ever see or hear anything." She shrugged. "I was right."

Jolene chose that moment to groan and slide onto her side. Her eyes flickered.

Mrs. Samson glanced at her briefly, then without warning ran straight at me, gun hand extended.

I flinched, stuck my hands out in front of me to protect myself, and took an automatic step backwards. My left hand struck her gun and knocked it flying. I could never have done such a good job if I'd planned it. The gun hit the floor, fired once, and spun under the refrigerator across the room.

Victory's ours, I thought. We'll get her now!

But that involuntary step backwards did me in. I'd stepped onto air. I lost my balance and fell down the cellar steps. I hit my head on the stair railing and my back on a step. I hit my cheekbone on a railing support.

Everything went black.

Chapter Seventeen

I lay, groggy, trying to remember what had happened to me, but the harder I tried, the murkier things seemed. I turned my head to the right and saw darkness, to the left and saw darkness. Overhead was darkness too.

Maybe I was asleep. It was dark when you shut your eyes. But my eyes blinked and I knew they were open. You don't sleep with your eyes open.

I reached beneath me and felt a smooth, hard, cold surface. I knew that I knew what it was called; I just couldn't remember right this very minute. I reached above and felt only air. Well, I was in a large, open space.

I tried to think where that space might be, but my mind was leaden and dull. I rolled on my side, and leaden and dull instantly metamorphosed into brilliant stabs of pain. My elbow! With a great groan, I rolled onto my back again, but the pain had cleared my mind somewhat. I remembered falling on that elbow in the bathroom at Arnie's house.

But this wasn't Arnie's house.

Now how did I know that? I concentrated, trying to follow logical thought patterns. I knew this wasn't Arnie's because, because— Jolene and I had left there last night!

Yes! I felt as proud as a kid who's just finished his first chapter book by himself. I could reason! I could think! I was going to be all right.

I tried again. I knew this wasn't Arnie's house because, because—I went to church with Curt and Jolene and Reilly—and Jack?—tonight. I knew this wasn't Arnie's house because I went to an open house at the Lurays after church.

I felt positively giddy with success.

And I knew this wasn't Arnie's because I knew who had killed Arnie.

With a shudder I remembered Mrs. Samson and her little gun. I remembered dragging an unconscious, bleeding Jolene across the kitchen. I remembered standing at the top of the cellar stairs. I remembered falling backwards into the cellar.

Well, there was no great problem then. I could get out of the cellar. All I had to do was climb back up the stairs. I rolled onto my side, the one without the sore elbow, and pulled my knees up. I pushed myself into a crawling position. Even that little bit of movement was all it took for my head to explode. I saw red and yellow stars just like in the comic strips. I groaned, nauseous, afraid to move. I swallowed convulsively as saliva poured into my mouth and bile rose in my throat.

Concussion. I had a concussion. I huddled miserably on my knees, waiting for the clamminess, the nausea to pass. I think I may have blacked out for a few minutes, but when I was aware once again, my head was a tad clearer.

I pushed myself up with my good arm until I was upright on my knees. All I felt was a minor case of *mal de mere*. I was making progress. I put one foot flat on the floor, then rested from the enormous effort this move had required. I realized suddenly that I was sore not only in my elbow but all over. The tumble down the steps had beaten me up but good.

I was trying to work up the fortitude to block out the pain and the courage to stand upright when I heard a muffled explosion. I turned toward the sound and saw a narrow band of light flash high in the air.

That's the door, I thought. *I must get up to that door.*

But the staircase, open on both sides, might as well have been Everest. Even if I clung to the wooden railing that marched up one side, the thought of scaling such a steep incline was overwhelming.

As I stared at the door, I realized my concussion was worse than I had thought. I had begun hallucinating. I watched, fascinated, as my mind conjured up liquid fire which rolled under the door and began falling, falling in a molten sheet, tumbling, running, sliding down the steps toward me. I watched from my knee, enchanted as one stair step, then another and another became ledges over which the fiery fluid flowed.

It was the most beautiful thing I had ever seen. I needed to stand so I could see it better. I pushed myself upright and stood weaving, mesmerized by the reds and golds and the flickering blue. Drops of flame plunged off the edges of the steps to splash like raindrops of fire on the concrete and flatten into tiny flickering pools. If I could have clapped my hands in pleasure, I would have, but my right arm hung limp, made useless by the re-injured elbow.

It was now that somewhere in the deepest part of my mind, an alarm began to sound. I became nervous and uncomfortable, fidgety. Something wasn't right. I raised my good hand to my head, trying to think.

At that moment the cellar door ignited, bursting into hungry, devouring, roaring flames. Then the top step came alive, no longer merely a burning sheet of—what? Gasoline? Kerosene? It crackled and burned, its wood feeding the ravenous fire. The second step flared. Black smoke, far blacker than the cellar, began billowing, mushrooming across the ceiling with terrifying speed. And heat. I could feel heat traveling with the smoke, pressing down from above. The third step ignited. The railing. The rafters.

This was no hallucination!

"Help! Help!" I screamed. "Curt! I'm down here! Get me out!" The roaring, rushing of the flames ate my voice.

Oh, God, get me out!

There should be windows somewhere down here. All cellars had windows high on the walls. Crouching low because of the smoke, I searched frantically.

There! Wasn't that a window with the shine of a distant street-light cutting through the dirt and grime and smoke? I lurched toward it as another stair burst into fire. The smoke roiled about my head like an angry serpent, undulating, rippling, convulsing. I knew that it would poison me, devour me if it could.

Oh, dear God, help me!

I ran toward the window. It was small, but I wasn't very big. If I could get up to it, I could get through it. If I could get up to it.

God, how do I ever reach a window that high in the wall? And what can I break the glass with once I get there?

I was concentrating so hard on the window that I wasn't watching where I was going. I tripped and lost my balance, falling forward onto a large flat surface. It was a table and the fact that I could see it so clearly terrified me. The fire had gained so in intensity that the once-dark cellar was awash in light.

I heard a crash and spun to see pieces of a rafter falling, spreading the fire to the old furniture and the bags of newspapers on which it fell. I slipped under the table for protection, and as I did, I spotted a line of paint cans against the outside wall.

I groaned. All I needed was for them to blow.

I felt a curious mental prodding, and I looked at them again.

They'll break glass! Thanks, Lord.

I grabbed the closest can and taking a deep breath close to the ground, stood and put the can on the table. Pushing the table with all my strength, I shoved it under the window. I bent for another deep breath, then climbed awkwardly onto the table, favoring my poor right arm. I grasped the paint can in my left hand and rammed it with all my strength into the window.

The glass shattered with a satisfyingly loud report, and I put my arms up to protect my eyes from the flying shards. Fresh cool air, rich in oxygen, poured in.

"Yes!" I yelled. I was reaching toward the window and my escape when a roaring like a thousand waves crashing on a rocky shore stopped me. I spun to see the fire mushrooming across the ceiling, lunging at me, rushing for me, its greedy tongues hungry. When I broke the window, I had created a chimney, and its draft worked all too well.

I dropped from the table to the floor, devastated as I understood that I could never get out of that window before the flames reached it.

Crying, I crouched and ran away from my window, away from my salvation.

But if there's one window, shouldn't there be two? Three? There had to be!

Dear Lord, there has to be!

The air currents were alive as the fire reached and burst through the broken window and began licking up the outside wall of the house.

Didn't anyone see that? Didn't anyone hear the fire? Smell the fire?

Didn't anyone miss me?

I saw a second window but only because its glass reflected the fire burning its wooden frame. Suddenly the window shattered from the heat and with a great *woosh!* the flames dove to and through it.

I huddled in the farthest corner beyond tears and, certain I was going to die, hugged myself against the chill.

Against the chill? But the room was superheated.

I concentrated fiercely and knew that I wasn't crazy. Cool air hit my back and streamed past me. I spun around and cried out. Stairs! Concrete stairs! They rose to a Bilco door, those slanted cellar doors that open up and out.

Oh, God! Thank you!

I scrambled into the tiny alcove and pressed my face against the cool metal. I sucked in great drafts of fresh air. My head cleared and I began pounding on the doors.

"Help! Help! Curt! God! Somebody!"

Suddenly someone pounded back from the outside.

"Help me!" I shouted. "Help me! Open the doors!"

"Merry! Oh, thank God, it's Merry!"

"Curt! Open the doors!" I glanced back over my shoulder and saw nothing but fire and smoke. "Hurry! Hurry!"

I heard the doors rumble and groan as people struggled to lift them. I felt them heave and shudder, but they didn't open.

"Merry!" It was Curt. "The doors are locked on the inside! *You* have to unlock them!"

I started to cry again. "I can't," I bawled. "I can't."

"Come on, sweetheart," he yelled. "You can! Oh, God, help her do it!"

Hiccupping and sniffing, I ran my hands back and forth across the inside of the door, searching for a handle, a latch, anything. All I felt was a smooth surface. Suddenly I rammed my hand painfully against the latch.

"I found it! I found the latch, but it's stuck!"

I pulled. I pushed. I shoved to the right, then to the left. And I came as close to sheer panic as I ever had. Safety and freedom were so close! So close! And the fire was too. A paint can exploded and the can sailed across the cellar streaming fire behind it.

"Open!" I screamed. "Open!"

"Come on, Merry." It was Mac sounding insufferably calm on the safe side of the door. "You're going to be okay. Dawn's out here holding a prayer meeting for you. They're going to sing 'Amazing Grace' in four-part harmony any minute now."

I giggled and gulped and the panic receded.

"Turn the latch counterclockwise," Curt called to me. "Mr. Luray says to turn it counterclockwise!"

I wrenched at the latch counterclockwise and I felt a movement.

"Yes," I screamed. "It's moving! Tell Dawn to keep praying!"

I twisted harder, making the most of my one good arm. Again and again I felt the latch give ever so slightly. Then there was a terrible, grinding screech of metal and the latch released completely. It was so sudden that I almost fell over, down the stairs, and into the fire.

I righted myself as my heart hammered and gave a mighty heave at the same time Curt gave a mighty pull. The doors exploded into the wonderful, sweet night air. I stumbled up and out into Curt's embrace as the oxygen-rich air surged in a low sweeping arc down the concrete stairs to rise inside the cellar, feeding the flames until they burst through the floor to join the fire already devouring the rest of the house.

I clung to Curt and couldn't stop shaking. His arms locked around me.

Thank you, dear Jesus! Thank you!

Suddenly Curt yelled, "No, Reilly! No!" He let go of me so quickly I almost fell. He grabbed wildly at Reilly who stood on the steps of the Bilco door, his arm over his face as he searched the flames.

"She's not there, Reilly! She's not there!" I called, but I wasn't sure he heard over the noise of the fire.

Curt grabbed him by one arm and Mac by the other, and they pulled him away from the house.

"Reilly, son." It was Mr. Luray, his face haggard and scared. He rested his hand on Reilly's sleeve. "You can't go in there. You can't. We can't lose both of you."

"But she's not in there," I repeated. "I was in the cellar alone."

"Then where is she?" Reilly said, his voice raw with anguish.

Suddenly Mrs. Luray stood beside me, staring with rapt face at the flames eating her house. "Isn't it pretty, June? Isn't it beautiful?"

I slid my arm around her and gave her a squeeze. For once it was a good thing that she didn't understand real life anymore.

I turned to Reilly. "I don't know where she is. The last time I saw her, she was lying semiconscious on the kitchen floor. Then I fell down the stairs."

"Nobody was in the kitchen when we cleared the house," Curt said quickly. "I checked."

I glanced at him. He must have seen the blood, but he didn't mention it.

"How did she get hurt to begin with?" asked Mr. Luray. He looked at me with eyes as full of pain as Reilly's. "What happened to her?"

I closed my eyes and rubbed my forehead. I didn't want to tell him. The answer would just inflict more pain on these already hurting people.

"Please, Merry, we have to know," he said, and of course he was right.

"Mrs. Samson knocked her unconscious."

"*Grandmom* knocked her unconscious?" Reilly was incredulous.

I nodded. "She used the gun she shot Arnie with."

There was a small minute of frozen disbelief when the roar of the fire was the only sound. Then Lonni screamed, a great cry of anguish. "Grandmom? Grandmom shot Arnie? Grandmom?"

"Shush, baby." Harry Allen pulled his daughter into his arms. "Shush, baby."

This time Lonni clung to him. "Daddy," she sobbed, "how could she? How could she?"

Sirens sounded and suddenly the street and then the yard became alive with men shouting and running. We moved back near the alley, clustered for comfort.

My mind was running as quickly as the firefighters, spinning and tumbling with my own mad ideas.

"Reilly, where does your grandmother keep her car?" I asked.

"She got her new car today," he said. "It's in the garage." He pointed to a garage facing on the alley.

"Is it?"

As a group we turned and ran.

"Where are we going, June?" asked Mrs. Luray, holding back as she tried to look over her shoulder at the fire.

Reilly reached the garage first and lifted the great door. The garage was empty.

"Listen. I have an idea." I hesitated. "But it's a crazy idea."

"It's the only one we've got," said Curt. "Go on. Tell us."

I took a deep breath. "Just before I fell downstairs, Mrs. Samson told me the strangest story. She said she killed her husband—"

"She killed Tony?" Mr. Luray interrupted.

"Tony," said Mrs. Luray. "He was a nice man. Very handsome. He died."

Mr. Luray nodded. "In the Korean War."

"He didn't. He came home wanting a divorce so he could marry some Korean woman he'd fallen in love with. Mrs. Samson shot him rather than deal with the embarrassment. Then she buried him in a dirt pile in some little cemetery outside Coatesville by the reservoir."

"It's too bizarre to be true," said Harry Allen skeptically. "People don't do things like that. *She* wouldn't do something like that. She was nasty and critical, but ..."

"But what if it is true?" said Mac. "I've been a newspaperman long enough to know that people will do just about anything given the right circumstances. If William Poole were here, he'd say the same thing."

I could see Mac's newsman's mind turning. He wanted everything I'd said to be true. It was a fantastic story and it was all his! (I didn't count.) It was sure to make the wire services, and he could break it before TV even knew it existed. The editorship might just become his permanently.

"It's true, all right," I said. "Remember, I saw her. I heard her. And I think she took Jolene out to that little cemetery."

"Here, Reilly." Mr. Luray held out a car key. "Find out if Merry's story is true. Find out if Jolene's out there at that little cemetery. That's my garage." And he pointed to the next building on the alley.

Reilly rushed to the Luray garage and threw the door open. A brand-new Jeep Grand Cherokee stood there.

That's from Jolene, I thought. No wonder her dad drives her to work in iffy weather.

Reilly ran to the driver's side.

"You can't go out there alone," yelled Mac. "It's too dangerous." He grabbed Dawn by the hand and jumped in the backseat.

I looked at Curt and found him watching me. He had that distant look again. "I'm going too," I said.

He blinked once, twice, then nodded. "I know." He turned and yelled as Reilly backed out of the garage. "Wait for us!"

We climbed in beside Reilly, and Curt had barely shut the door before we tore down the alley. Reilly screeched around the corner and burst onto Houston Street. He dodged a fire truck and roared away at top speed. A policeman at the fire to help with crowd control saw us career off and took chase. I guess he thought we were speeders at best or criminals leaving the scene of an arson at worst.

I managed to snap my seat belt, but it was Curt's arm around my shoulder that held me steady as we rushed through the night. I turned to him to make certain he was belted in too and saw that he still wore that distant look. What had happened to the desperation and love I'd seen when he pulled me from the cellar?

He felt my glance and looked down at me. He smiled kindly. Kindly!

Reilly hit a pothole, and I groaned and grabbed my arm.

Instantly the distance left Curt. "Are you okay?" he asked, his forehead wrinkled in concern. "I never should have let you come along! You're in no shape to be caught up in this danger. Whatever was I thinking? You need to go to the hospital."

I didn't answer. My mind was much too fragmented and fatigued to deal with his mixed signals. Besides, it took all my energy to hold on as Reilly tore along Business 30, empty at midnight Christmas Eve, and ran every red light he met all the way through Coatesville. He went around the corner at Route 82 North on two wheels, then cut to the left and raced through Rock Run. He barreled along the narrow, twisting macadam road smack in the center. The police were right behind us, lights flashing and sirens blaring.

Oh, Lord, please don't let there be anyone coming toward us!

I glanced back at Dawn and knew she was praying exactly the same thing and just as hard.

Suddenly Reilly wrenched the wheel left and hit the brakes so hard we all would have gone through various windows if it weren't for seat belts. We stopped inches from a heavy chain that blocked our way as it stretched across the access road to the tiny cemetery. Parked beside the chain was a brand-new red Saturn.

"Grandmom's car," Reilly said grimly.

He threw the Cherokee in reverse, backed clear of the chain, and threw the Jeep into drive. We bounced off the road and into the weeds, shrubs, and small trees at the edge of the woods, completely circumventing the chain.

"Three cheers for four-wheel drive," muttered Mac. His eyes were bright with the excitement of the chase.

The Jeep lumbered back onto the access road as the police pulled up beside the Saturn.

A bullhorn cut the night. "Stop! Police!"

Reilly kept going. As he rounded a curve in the road, the headlights limned an unforgettable tableau.

A mound of earth, red and loosely packed, rose about seven feet, a small mountain of soil collected from graves that never needed all their fill after they received their contents. Caught shovel in hand was Mrs. Samson, a freshly turned, much smaller pile of dirt at her feet. The beginnings of a small tunnel in the large dirt pile showed her handiwork.

Lying in a huddle off to the side about ten feet was Jolene, her red Christmas outfit a bloody slash in the dark forest.

Reilly jumped out of the Jeep and raced toward Jolene. The rest of us climbed out more cautiously.

"I don't think she's got her gun anymore," I said. "I think it's under the refrigerator, but I don't *know*. But I do know she won't shoot Reilly. The rest of us maybe, but not Reilly. He can run any-where he wants." I took a shaky breath. "We'd better be careful." In my mind I saw that gun falling on Jolene's skull. I saw Mrs. Samson lunge at me. "We'd better be careful."

Behind us the police crashed through the underbrush yelling, "Stop! Put your hands up!"

Reilly dropped to his knees beside Jolene and felt her throat.

"She's alive!" he cried, his voice thick with tears of relief. He bent to kiss her cheek. He straightened and gently brushed her hair from her face. "It's all right now, Jo," he said softly. "I'm here."

I wanted to cry. Without thinking, the four of us surged forward with relief. When I saw one of Jo's legs move, I did cry.

Blinking at the tears, I turned and limped toward the police.

"We need an ambulance right away," I called. "There's a badly injured woman up here."

A light blazed in my face, and I raised my hands defensively. "I'm not dangerous," I said foolishly. "We need your help."

"Merry?" said a surprised voice. "Is that you? What happened to you? You look awful!"

"William! Oh, William! How wonderful!" I threw my arms around his neck in relief, only to feel my knees buckle as my right elbow protested vociferously at such careless treatment. I clutched it to me and swallowed against the pain.

"Merry!" His concern was comforting, but I waved it away.

"It's Jolene Meister up there. She's been injured. She needs an ambulance."

He turned to run back to his cruiser. "And we have a murderer cornered up there too. You might want some backup."

I hurried to Jolene as fast as my aching body would allow. I lowered myself to the ground so that Dawn and I sat one on each side, each holding one of her hands, our legs stretched along her body to try and offer some warmth. William brought a blanket to cover her with and another to throw around my coatless shoulders. I hadn't been conscious of the cold before, but now I immediately began to shiver.

While we waited for the ambulance, Reilly, flanked by Curt and Mac, tried to reason with his grandmother.

"Grandmom," Reilly said, his hands held out toward her, "the police need to talk to you."

"I don't want to talk to them."

"You have to, Grandmom."

"Don't tell me what I have to do, Reilly Samson. No one tells me what I have to do." With that, she lifted the carving knife she'd been holding and rested its point against her throat. "If the police come near me, I'll use this on myself since I can't use it on her."

Reilly jerked. "Grandmom, put that knife down!"

"I just told you: Don't tell me what to do." Mrs. Samson said it slowly, through clenched teeth. Reilly quickly and wisely changed the subject.

"What happened to Jolene, Grandmom? How did she get hurt?"

"I knocked her out." Mrs. Samson's voice was as calm as if she were talking about going to the store for a loaf of bread.

"But Grandmom, you can't go around hurting people like that!"

"She deserved it. She hurt you!"

"Grandmom!"

"She did! You know she did."

Reilly nodded. "You're right. She hurt me when she married Arnie. Both she and I regret that act deeply. But that doesn't mean you can hurt her back."

"She's no good, Reilly. Like Arnie was no good and Tony was no good."

"Grandmom!"

"Listen to me, Reilly. It's not too late. Get away from her. You don't want to love her!"

"It's too late, Grandmom. I do love her. I've always loved her."

"I love you, Reilly."

"Grandmom!"

"You're my most prized possession."

Reilly's hopeless sigh slid sadly through the night and his shoulders sagged. "You've still got it wrong, Grandmom. I'm not your possession."

Into the small silence that fell Mac spoke. "Hey, Mrs. Samson." His voice was perky and full of interest.

The old woman jumped and the knife wobbled dangerously. It was almost as if she saw him for the first time. "Who are you? What are you doing here? Reilly!"

Mac put out his hand to keep Reilly quiet and kept talking, ignoring her agitation. "How come you didn't kill Jolene before you brought her here? Wouldn't it have been easier?"

Mrs. Samson stiffened. "Just who are you to question me?" she demanded.

I thought he was going to say, "*The News* editor" or "Jolene's boss," and make her furious because he'd be on the wrong team. But Mac could be cagey when he wanted to be.

"I'm Reilly's friend," he said. "I'm just curious. That's all. I don't mean to get you mad at me."

Mrs. Samson stared at him a minute, though I doubted she could see any more than a silhouette backlit by the Jeep's headlights. "I didn't want to get blood on my new car," she finally announced. "Reilly helped me buy it."

"But wasn't she sort of bloody from when you knocked her out?" Mac asked conversationally.

"I cleaned her up," Mrs. Samson said. "I just wiped the blood from her face and made certain she rode in the trunk on some newspapers. They're sort of messy, but the car's okay."

"Good thinking," said Mac.

As he talked, the ambulance pulled quietly up the road past the chain cut by the police. The emergency techs came swiftly to Jolene, and Dawn and I moved aside. At least she did and I tried to. Eventually she had to pull me to my feet and help me out of the way. The cold ground had done an amazing job of stiffening my bruised body. We stood watching as the EMTs stabilized Jo, then lifted her onto a gurney and quickly put her into the ambulance. As the door slammed, I saw one of them was already slipping an IV into her arm.

When the ambulance was gone, William Poole stepped into the circle of light thrown by the Jeep's headlights.

"Mrs. Samson," he called.

Her expression bitter, she had been watching the men work over Jolene. She seemed so focused on her hatred that she didn't know the sergeant was there and spun nervously toward him. She appeared shocked when she saw his uniform.

"Who are you?" she asked.

"I'm Sergeant Poole of the Amhearst police, Mrs. Samson. I'd like to ask you to give me your knife."

"You can't make me," she said.

Suddenly a dozen officers stepped into the circle of light. I hadn't even been aware of their presence.

Mrs. Samson looked totally disconcerted.

"Grandmom," called Reilly. "Please give us your knife." He began walking slowly toward her, one arm extended. "Please don't hurt yourself. I don't want to feel any worse than I already do."

"It's that Jolene that makes you feel bad," Mrs. Samson said, waving the knife for emphasis. "I love you."

"Then give me a hug. Please. I need one." He reached out and gathered his grandmother into his arms. As she hugged him back, the knife hanging over his shoulders, Curt reached out and quietly took it from her unprotesting fingers.

When Reilly stepped back, Sergeant Poole and another officer were there, and each took one of her arms. As they led her away, she called, "Reilly, I love you. You're my most prized possession. Don't ever forget: I did it for Lonni and you."

Curt had to drive us to the hospital to see how Jolene was because Reilly couldn't stop shaking. I don't think he even realized he had tears streaming down his cheeks.

Chapter Eighteen

I wrestled my first-ever-made turkey into the oven at two o'clock Christmas afternoon for dinner at six. It was a small turkey, more the size of a large roasting chicken, but handling it with one arm in a sling was still a challenge. I set the timer carefully even though the bird had one of those little plastic doodads that pop up when everything's done. I didn't want any mistakes here. I knew four hours was way more than enough time according to the directions on the wrapping, but I remembered that Mom always let the bird "rest" before carving. I wanted to make sure I had enough resting time.

This dinner was important to me. It was to be the backdrop for a talk with Curt, a talk he wasn't yet aware we were going to have, a talk I had to have before I went crazy. I was hoping that if dinner went well, so would the talk, sort of like if you smiled for the photographer, the picture had a better chance of being good. The catch was that for either my metaphorical picture or my very real conversation to turn out well, there had to be something worthwhile to photograph, to discuss.

I'd spent a lot of time thinking about Curt during the small hours of the night after I'd finally gotten home. I'd tried to sleep, but every time I rolled over, my elbow woke me. Finally I gave up, plumped my pillows, and sat, stroking a blissfully snoring Whiskers. As I sat, I thought. And thought. When Christmas Day finally dawned, I was weary but determined. Then I surprised myself by falling asleep for a couple of hours.

Now, somewhat rested as I peered into the oven at my turkey, my phone rang. It was probably Mom calling to wish me a merry Christmas.

It was Maddie. "Good news!" she said, excitement spilling down the phone lines. "Karyn had her baby about two hours ago."

"How wonderful! Is everybody okay?"

"Mother and daughter are fine." Suddenly Maddie was crying. "They let me be in the delivery room," she said. "It was Sandy, Karyn, and me. And they let me be the first to hold her."

"Oh, Maddie! Merry Christmas. What's her name?"

"Holly Claire. Karyn wanted Holly because it's Christmas, and Claire has always been my favorite name. Oh, Merry, nothing's for sure yet. There's so much legal stuff that none of us know much about and counseling stuff and all. But pray for us? Please pray!"

When I hung up, I was crying a bit myself.

I went to the hospital to visit Jolene after I was certain the oven wasn't going to incinerate my turkey when I turned my back. I'd had enough incinerations to last a lifetime. I shuddered when I thought of the rubble that was all that was left of the Lurays' home. They had lost everything. Everything, that is, except Jolene.

She was going to be all right. The doctors had finally told us everything they knew last night to get us all to go home. She had a non-displaced fracture of the skull, they said, from the blunt instrument trauma, but there were no further complications like blood clots or anything. She would not need surgery if the CT scan was normal, as they expected it to be. She probably would have amnesia of the event but they thought little if any other effect. She'd have to stay in the hospital for a few days for observation just to be on the safe side, but she should be fine.

When I got to her room, she was lying flat, tubes and wires running to all sorts of machines. Reilly, scruffy and unshaven, sat in the chair beside the bed holding her hand. Mr. and Mrs. Luray sat on two other chairs and watched TV.

"June, look!" Mrs. Luray called to me, pointing to the screen. "It's my favorite movie."

Mr. Luray, face drawn and pale, smiled sadly at me. "She's never seen it before," he said.

I gave both a hug, then turned to Jolene.

"Hey," I said as I leaned over and gave her a light kiss. "Merry Christmas."

She opened her eyes for a few seconds and smiled vaguely at me. Then her eyes dropped shut and she slept.

"She's been asleep most of the time," Reilly said. "But she's doing very well."

"How about you?" I asked. "You've had a pretty brutal time of it."

"I'm okay," he said. "*She'll* be all right"—and he looked at her with such love that tears came to my eyes—"so how can I be anything but fine?"

But I knew—and he knew—it wouldn't always be fine for him. He'd always know that his grandmother had murdered his grandfather as well as the man who might have been his cousin-in-law. She had also tried to kill the woman he loved. But most heartrending and difficult would be his Judas hug that had turned Mrs. Samson over to the police. That there was no choice for him would not do much to alleviate his guilt.

I left almost as soon as I arrived. I had come not for Jolene or Reilly or the Lurays. They didn't need me. I had come for myself, and I felt free now to enjoy my first Amhearst Christmas.

Mr. Luray, his steps dragging, walked me to the elevator. "We're going to Tel Hai Retirement Community as soon as there's a cottage available," he said softly. "In the meantime we're staying with relatives." He sighed. "I've known we should do something like this for a long time, but I was always afraid of what it would do to Eloise. Now there's no choice."

"I think that's a wonderful decision, Mr. Luray." I gave him a quick, one-armed hug and kissed his wrinkled cheek. He smiled faintly. "Do they know how the fire started?"

"Adele Samson did it. The fire officials said she made a crude incendiary device out of a plastic milk jug and kerosene with a dish towel for a fuse. Apparently she filled the jug halfway—if she'd filled it all the way, you wouldn't have stood a chance—lit the kerosene-soaked wick, and fled, taking Jolene with her."

I tried to imagine Mrs. Samson dragging Jolene across the darkened lawn to the rear garage. My mind boggled.

"The bomb exploded a few minutes after they had gone."

I nodded. "I heard the explosion," I said. "And I saw the flash of light under the door. I thought I was hallucinating when the fire came rolling down the stairs." I shuddered at the memory.

Mr. Luray patted my shoulder awkwardly. "Thank God you're all right." And he gave a mighty sniff.

"You are a sweet man to care so much about me," I said and kissed his cheek again. The elevator came and I stepped on. "Merry Christmas."

When I got home, I was relieved that the oven was still behaving and the turkey was smelling ever more wonderful. I opened the oven door just to be sure and admired my nicely browning bird.

I peeled some potatoes and put them on to boil. I got out a box of stuffing, read the directions, and soon had a fragrant casserole dish of the stuff ready for the oven. I cooked some broccoli, mixed cheese, milk, and eggs, and poured them over the broccoli for a cheesy custard effect I hoped would impress Curt. It had sure impressed my father the first time my mother made it. I mashed the potatoes, adding sour cream and cream cheese for extra richness. Then I squeezed everything, including the potatoes, into the oven. I put the can of cranberry sauce, the cardboard canister of dinner rolls, and the packets of gravy mix on the counter for last-minute use.

On the way to the bedroom to change, I checked my table setting. My only tablecloth, a white, wrinkle-free number, looked festive with the red napkins and the poinsettia and red candle centerpiece. My mismatched silver didn't dampen the posh effect too much, and my Kmart goblets looked much better than they were.

As I forced my injured arm through the arm of my prettiest red sweater, I grimaced, but it was worth the pain for the color it brought to my face. Of course, the color was somewhat undercut by the large, rapidly darkening bruise splashed across my left cheek. I pulled on a pair of black corduroy slacks, knowing black was an absurd choice with a black and white cat in the house. But Mom and Dad had sent them to me, and I wanted to feel close to them.

The doorbell rang, and my heart jumped. I put my comb down with shaking hands. Did realizing you loved someone and needed to talk always make people candidates for antacid tablets and cardiac care?

Curt came in on a gust of cold air, tall and handsome, his hair in ringlets, his eyes shining through his glasses. In his hands he held a flat rectangle which could be nothing other than a picture. But when I turned from hanging up his coat, he was no longer holding it. Neither was it under the tree.

I eyed him uncertainly.

"It smells wonderful in here," he said, sniffing the air appreciatively. He was warm, gracious, and distant.

I smiled tentatively and led the way to the kitchen. I looked in the oven.

"The little doodad's up," I said. I reached for my oven mitts and started pulling food from the oven. Finally I got to the turkey, put it on the counter to "rest," and put everything else back to keep cooking.

I looked at Curt and he looked noncommittally, politely back. My heart became a lump in my chest. I knew I'd never be able to eat dinner without clearing the air first.

Oh, Lord, I'm so scared. What if he truly doesn't care anymore? What if he's only here because I'm just marginally better than an empty house?

Don't worry. I care. And I'll always care. Remember the Babe.

I took a deep breath as I let the truth of God's love ease my fear.

"Come with me," I said. "We need to talk."

He looked at me warily but followed me to the living room.

"Sit," I said, pointing to the chair. He sat or rather perched on the edge, a long-legged, bespectacled bird ready to fly away at the slightest provocation. I sat on the sofa facing him.

"We need to talk," I said again.

He gave me no encouragement, just sat waiting.

"You're driving me nuts, Curt!" I blurted, ever the diplomat.

He looked somewhat startled, but his look of polite disinterest didn't change.

"You have become the most frustrating, the most irritating, the most maddening, the most—" I paused, searching for another word. "—the most *aggravating* man I know."

His face became a study in surprise and wounded offense. At least the look of bland boredom was gone. "Me? I'm irritating? I'm aggravating? I'm frustrating? Me?"

"Yes, you," I said, pointing a finger at him. I noted with dismay that the nail and cuticle were still sooty in spite of all the showers, shampoos, and food preparation they'd been through. It would be nice if some day I could be suave and sophisticated when I tried to make a point, waving one of those long, perfect nails that grew only on other women. People might actually pay attention to me then.

"Listen, lady," Curt said through clenched teeth. "I'm not the one who goes around trying to get herself killed all the time. I'm not the one who risks life and limb regardless of other people's feelings and fears. I'm not the one who ties other people's innards into knots on a regular basis." He was on his feet, glaring down at me like I was suddenly the villain. Well, I wasn't. Not in my script.

I got to my feet too and stood, hands on hips, chin raised defiantly. "Don't try and make me the problem! *You're* the one who keeps offering affection and then withdrawing it. Which is a million times worse and more hurtful than anything I might do." I felt tears prick and I blinked furiously. I would not cry. I would not. I would stay strong. I would stay in control. This was, after all, my confrontation. "I don't know anymore whether you love me or not."

There. I'd said it, though it sounded a bit more plaintive than I meant it to. And I also meant to clamp my mouth shut at this point and let him feel like a heel. Instead, I kept going. "I mean, here I am, falling in love with you, and there you are, pulling back. What in the world's going on?"

He started to speak, and I put up my hand. "Not that I blame you for pulling back; I don't. I'm a mess. I know that. But Curt," I looked at him, as open and naked and vulnerable as ever I'd been my entire life, "you can't have it both ways." And I started to cry in spite of myself.

"Oh, Merry!" And Curt wrapped his arms about me and held me so close it would have hurt if it hadn't felt so comforting. I laced my good arm around his waist and held on too.

After a couple of minutes, I stepped back. Or tried to. Curt only let me retreat to arm's length as he kept his hands on my shoulders. Then he reached out and gently traced my bruised cheek.

"I haven't had anyone to love for a long time," he said. "And I do love you. That fact isn't open for question. You make me feel like no one ever has before—which is part of the problem."

"That's good," I said. "That you feel like that about me, I mean."

"It's frightening," he countered with unexpected vehemence. "What if I lose you too?" There was anguish in his voice.

"Is that why you withdraw?" I thought about the times he'd pulled back. It had been when I hit the deer, when I went with Jo to Arnie's at night, when we chased a murderer. In other words, when I had been in potential danger.

"I keep thinking that if I don't get too close, I can't get hurt again." He looked embarrassed.

"Just like if you don't celebrate Christmas, the loneliness won't strike?"

He stared, startled.

"But it hasn't worked, has it? You've still been lonely, right?"

He nodded.

"Pulling back from me won't work either, Curt." I drew him down to the sofa so we faced each other. "Loving isn't that easy to control."

He leaned forward and kissed me softly. "Tell me about it."

My heart soared at the kiss, but I made myself stick to the point. "You've got to decide whether I'm worth the risk that loving entails."

"You don't ask much, do you?" His voice was abrupt, but his eyes loved me. "I know what I'll do. I'll just wrap you up in some bubble wrap and keep you safe on my studio shelf. Then I'll always know where you are and what you're doing."

"And we'll both be bored stiff."

"I just want to take care of you," he said. "To keep you safe."

I bristled a bit. "I can't take care of myself?"

"Don't make more of my comment than was intended. You do that, you know."

I ignored him and said, "You don't need to be my savior. I already have One."

He looked at me, exasperated. "Merry, you don't understand. I don't *need* to be your savior, except maybe for my peace of mind. I want to. I want to take care of you, to protect you. Maybe it's a guy thing; I don't know. Maybe it's just me. All I know is that anything that concerns you, hurts you, or distresses you, I want to fix. Not because you can't fix it and I can, but because I love you."

I reached out and laid a hand on his cheek. "Poor Curt. To have fallen in love with me."

"I've talked to the Lord about this unsought turn of events quite a bit, believe me."

"And what does the Lord say?"

"That you're perfect for me."

He looked so woebegone that I laughed. "If it's any consolation, I love you more every day."

He took my hand and held it. "Just as I am, protectiveness, fears, and all?"

I brushed a dark curl back from his forehead, enjoying the way it wrapped itself around my finger. Our eyes met, and I spoke from my heart. "I'll take you just as you are—" He smiled. "—if you'll take me just as I am."

"Risky," he said.

"Scary," I agreed. "But worth it?"

In answer he got up from the sofa and reached behind it. He pulled out the flat package he'd brought with him.

"So that's where it went," I said.

"I was trying to decide whether to give it to you or not. I was trying to decide where I stood on the risk factor."

"And now you know?"

"And now I know—though I think I've always known deep down." He offered me the gift.

I tore off the wrapping paper, and my breath caught in my throat. I was looking at a painting of two hands entwined, lovers' hands. Curt's hand and mine.

"When did you do this?" I asked, knowing the power of the picture told me much more than his words ever would.

"This morning."

"You did know," I said.

"I guess I did."

I laced my fingers in his to mimic the picture.

"I love you," I said. "Always."

"At any risk," he agreed.

Also check out Book #1 in the Amhearst Mystery Series!

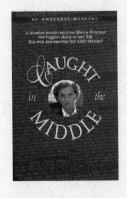

Caught in the Middle
Gayle Roper

A corpse was not what Merry was looking for when she opened the car trunk.

Things like this just don't happen to real people, she thought. But Merry Kramer is new in town—and has yet to discover what hides behind the smiling faces of the residents of Amhearst, Pennsylvania.

As a staff reporter for a local newspaper, Merry finds the job contrasts incredible: as shocking as finding a body one night. .. as routine as writing a human interest story on a local artist the next day. But when another death is discovered, suspicion begins to dawn... and seemingly inconsequential choices forge a link that makes Merry the next target.

Merry realizes she knows something the murderer wants to keep hidden. The question is, what is it... and can she survive long enough to find out?

Softcover 0-310-20995-1

ZondervanPublishingHouse
Grand Rapids, Michigan

A Division of HarperCollinsPublishers

We want to hear from you. Please send your comments about this
book to us in care of the address below. Thank you.

ZondervanPublishingHouse
Grand Rapids, Michigan 49530
http://www.zondervan.com